What the Cat Dragged In

Gilbert Morris

HARVEST HOUSE PUBLISHERS
EUGENE, OREGON

Unless otherwise indicated, all Scripture quotations are taken from the King James Version of the Bible.

Cover by Abris, Veneta, Oregon

Cover illustrations © Simon Spoon / iStockphoto; A-Digit / iStockphoto / Abris

Published in association with the literary agency of WordServe Literary Group, Ltd., 10152 S. Knoll Circle, Highlands Ranch, CO 80130

WHAT THE CAT DRAGGED IN
Copyright © 2007 by Gilbert Morris
Published by Harvest House Publishers
Eugene, Oregon 97402
www.harvesthousepublishers.com

Library of Congress Cataloging-in-Publication Data
  Morris, Gilbert.
  What the cat dragged in / Gilbert Morris.
    p. cm.—(Jacques & Cleo, cat detectives ; bk. 1)
  ISBN-13: 978-0-7369-1964-7 (pbk.)
  ISBN-10: 0-7369-1964-3
  1. Cats—Fiction. 2. Cat owners—Fiction. 3. Single mothers—Fiction. 4. Mothers and sons—Fiction. 5. Inheritance and succession—Fiction. 6. Murder—Investigation—Fiction I. Title.
  PS3563.08742W43 2007
  813'.54—dc22
                                                            2006030641

Printed in the United States of America

  08 09 10 11 12 13 14 15 / LB-SK / 11 10 9 8 7 6 5 4 3 2

Special thanks to the staff at the Thomas B. Norton Public Library in Gulf Shores, Alabama, particularly:

Wendy Congiardo, library director, happily married to Michael, and enthusiastic aunt to Cole and Maddie. She enjoys reading, cooking, scrapbooking, and spends time taking care of her own pets, a black cat, Vandy, and a chocolate lab, Hershey.

Linda Tetrault, assistant director, married, mom to five, and grandmother of seven. She loves to travel, is an artist/painter, and dog lover, who dotes on her two, Sophie and Sadie.

Laura Clark-Moody, reference librarian, ardent photographer and crafter.

Jack Coyle, technical services, married, father of two, and an avid RC airplane hobbyist.

Sherry Hoffman, serials librarian, married to Marty, and mom to three boys. She is a true "GRIT" (Girl Raised in the South) who has been a Mardi Gras Queen, and has a passion for fashion.

Jerri Sartore, children's librarian, married, mother of two, and a new grandmother. She welcomes people to enjoy the beach with her at her B & B, Fernhill by the Sea. She enjoys quilting, and loves two dogs of her own, Buffy and Sam.

Barbara Schild, circulation specialist, married, mother of two, and a devoted grandmother. She loves to read, and is fond of her own cat, Clancy.

Melody Solstad, circulation specialist, originally from Minnesota, and married to Ken. She is a cat collector with three, Daisy, Dixie, and Sunny. New boat owner and novice, but enthusiastic, deep sea fisherperson.

Julie Teague-Maly, head of technical services, musician/artist, and keen reader. She is also a cat fancier with three of her own, Dixie, Pinky, and Davy.

One

"Hey, doll, what's happening?"

She looked up at the six-foot hunk with the mop of tawny hair, one lock artistically arranged to fall over his forehead. He wore skin-tight vintage washed jeans and a Dixie Outfitters shirt with a rebel flag on the chest. He reeked of Brut cologne and sweat. Leaning forward he winked at her. "Hey, I'm Billy Roy Pruitt. You tight with anyone?"

Mary Katherine Forrest noted that he was staring not only at her I.D. badge, which said "Kate," but taking in the rest of her as well. Kate recognized his type, one that never looked above the neck. She said "No," with the absolute certainty that nothing she said would put a damper on Billy Roy Pruitt.

"No kidding? Well shoot, this is your lucky day!"

Picking up a fifty-pound sack of dog food, Billy Roy tossed it on the counter and gave Kate a dazzling smile. Kate was numb from what amounted to an eleven-hour workday. As best as she could remember, Billy Roy was the fifth guy who had hit on her today. She rang up the dog food thinking that anyone with tribal armbands tattooed on his biceps was not the man of her dreams.

"Hey, doll, how about you and me do a little line dancing after you get off?"

Kate leaned forward and whispered seductively, "Are you sure you want to take the chance, Billy Roy?"

"What chance you mean, doll?"

"I have a fatal social disease." Kate smiled sweetly, and leaned forward and whispered confidentially, "My last two boyfriends died of it, in agony, poor guys! But if you're willing to take a chance, hey, let's go for it."

Billy Roy's eyes widened with shock, then he backed away abruptly. Fumbling in the pocket of his jeans, he pulled out a crumpled ten-dollar bill and tossed it on the counter. "I get off at six-thirty." Kate smiled. "Be waiting for me outside." She gave him his change, and as he took the money, she said sweetly, "Oh, Honey, better wash your hands after handling that money. Can't be too careful, you know."

For one moment Billy Roy stared at the change, then jamming it in his pocket, he snatched up the dog food and scurried out of Wal-Mart, pausing only to throw her a fearful glance.

Kate smiled as she watched him go. "Well, shoot, there goes my chance! Guess it's not my lucky day after all. And he had all his tattoos spelled right, too."

It was a ruse that had a fast effect on the jerks who thought she was an easy date. The other successful ploy was the more truthful one—when she told the guys, "I'm a Christian. Would you like to accompany me to my Wednesday night Bible study?" That usually brought an equally swift departure.

Next in line was a tall, gaunt woman with mean-looking eyes the color of dishwater. Her mouth puckered up like the drawstring of a purse as she snapped, "If you're all done with your romancin', I'd like to get waited on."

"Yes, ma'am." Kate picked up the toaster the woman had put on the conveyor belt.

"It's on sale—make sure you get the right price."

Kate shook her head. "There's no sale tag. I'll have to get a price check."

"I can tell you what it costs. It is fourteen dollars and ninety-five cents."

"Yes, ma'am, but I still have to have a price check."

"Why is it every time I come to this place I can't get through the stupid line? I can get better service at K-Mart!"

It took all of Kate's restraint to keep from saying, *Well, get your rear out of here and go to K-Mart, you old witch!* but she said in a moderate tone, "I'll get a check as quick as I can, ma'am."

As she waited for the price check, Kate looked around and for one moment the interior of Wal-Mart seemed to close in on her. It occurred to her, not for the first time, that there were probably a thousand more Wal-Marts all looking exactly like this one and a hundred thousand young women like her battling egocentric idiots like Billy Roy Pruitt and old women with eyes too close together who treated all cashiers like dirt.

She had worked the morning shift at the world's largest fast-food chain, dealing with kids who all demanded their McDonald's burgers and fries to clog their arteries, and now she was ending her shift as a cashier at the world's largest retail corporation, catering to people who seemed to show their worst traits while standing in her line. She had bought a pair of shoes half a size too small because they were cheap, and now her feet felt like they were encased in burning iron. A sudden wild impulse swept through her—simply to turn and walk out of Wal-Mart and never come back, but she knew it was impossible. She listened as the woman whined to the man in line behind her, "I got a curse. Every time I get into line in this place, they gotta have a price check or something. They ort to close this dumb place down!"

Melvin Trask, an assistant manager, came bearing the new price. Kate took it, saying, "With tax that'll be sixteen dollars and eighty-six cents please."

"I *told* you it was fourteen ninety-five!"

Kate rang the purchase up, gave the woman her change, and for one instant she had an almost overwhelming desire to say, "Have a rotten, terrible day!" But she came out with the most meaningless phrase in the English language: "Have a nice day."

For the next fifteen minutes Kate mechanically processed the customers who shuffled by in an apparently unending line. Finally six-fifteen arrived along with her replacement, Mary Ellen Jamison, eyes bright and full of good humor. Mary Ellen was always cheerful, and even the mindless tedium of Wal-Mart could not quench her spirit. She spoke cheerfully as the change-over was made, and when Kate moved to leave, Mary Ellen called out, "Have a nice evening, Kate."

Kate turned and said flatly in a voice drained of emotion, "I'm sorry—I have other plans." She turned, aware that Mary Ellen and the customers were staring at her. She went through the drawer audit at Customer Service, then limping to the back of the store, she prepared to leave, pausing only to clock out and change the new shoes for her old ones. As she left the room, she was cornered by Assistant Manager Trask, the forty-year-old Romeo of Wal-Mart, who managed to brush against her. He grinned and took her arm, turning her around saying, "You know you're going to go out with me sooner or later, Kate. How about tonight?"

Kate jerked her arm back and stared at Trask with distaste. "Sure, Mel.

We'll take your wife and two kids with us." She turned and left the store with a feeling of relief. Crossing the parking lot, she went to her ancient Taurus. Someone had crunched the front door on the driver's side, and she thought sourly, *Why couldn't it have been one of the other three doors?* She grasped the handle and the metal screeched like a wounded hyena as she muscled the door open and collapsed into the seat. As she reached to start the engine, she glanced back at the building. *There's some difference between this store and the penitentiary—but not much.*

The bitterness of the thought shocked Kate—she wasn't normally given to such attitudes. Two years of working double shifts and struggling to pay bills with never enough money had worn her down. She realized that she was not the same woman she'd been before Vic's death. Forced into a succession of dead-end jobs, the daily grind hadn't been hard at first, but facing customers with a cheerful smile for ten to twelve hours a day had eventually sapped her vitality.

Shoving the acid thoughts out of her mind, Kate turned the key and held her breath. The engine turned over reluctantly as if it couldn't make up its mind whether to start or not. Finally it caught with an unhealthy cough, then with an explosive backfire started hitting on five of the six cylinders—which was above average.

As the Taurus limped out of the parking lot in a series of rough jerks, Kate turned northward putting the skyline of Memphis to her back. She lived on the outskirts of the city and wished that she could live even further. The country to the south was Mississippi River Delta all the way to the Gulf Coast, nothing but flat, monotonous cotton fields on each side of the road. A more boring country she couldn't imagine!

As she drove, Kate's mind seemed to be dulled, and for one moment a rebellious thought came to her. *Maybe I should have gone out with Billy Roy. At least it would be a change.* She pushed the thought away immediately, knowing she was simply frustrated and bored. She'd gone out with clones of Billy Roy Pruitt several times in the past two years—and always returned home with the same thought: *I wonder where all the good men are hiding? They can't all be as trashy as Billy Roy!* If they were out there, she sure didn't know how to meet them.

At twenty-nine, Kate still wasn't sure how to act insofar as men were concerned. She wasn't a high-school girl anymore, as she had been when she had married Vic, but now she was a mature woman with a 12-year-old son. But the men in her age group were either shopworn or completely immature. She had given up dating only two months earlier, and as she continued her trek through the grimy streets of Memphis, she realized she was a lonely woman—and likely to be so for a long time.

• • •

Kate pulled up in front of her concrete block apartment house with the impressive and meaningless name, *The Royal Arms*. The building consisted of six apartments on the first floor and six on the second, and had all the warmth and charm of the county morgue. As Kate got out and headed for the stairs, she saw that the eternal basketball game was still going on in the parking lot. The several young men were limber, loose-jointed, and seemingly tireless. She noted that Jeremy was not among them. He had begged to join the game, but Kate had forbidden him. The game got rough, sometimes turning into fist fights, and she was afraid for her son.

At the foot of the stairway that led to her apartment, a fat cat with the majestic name of Cleopatra stirred from one of her many naps, stretched mightily, and yawned, exposing a cavernous red mouth and gleaming white teeth. She was large, weighing almost twenty pounds, and her eyes were startlingly blue. Her longhair coat was a gorgeous silken white with dark markings on her face, legs, and tail. Kate had bought her from a breeder of Ragdolls when she was only a kitten. Kate had always longed for a Ragdoll, and had sacrificed every convenience to buy the kitten.

"Hello, Cleo," Kate said and smiled. The big cat looked up and grinned. As always when Cleo did this, Kate laughed. "You're the only cat in the solar system who smiles—except the Cheshire cat Alice met in Wonderland, of course."

Reaching down, she picked Cleo up and draped her over her right shoulder. Instantly the big cat began purring with content. "You sound like a jet engine, Cleo!"

Kate mounted the stairs and turned right to her apartment, which was on the east side. Cleo had cheered her up a bit, but as always, Kate was awash with guilt for not arriving home until seven in the evening. She was vaguely aware of the smell of cabbage cooking in one of the apartments and of a vitriolic and profane argument going on below. Opening the door was awkward with twenty pounds of furry feline draped over her shoulder, but she managed to get her key out. Unlocking the door, she felt the cool air and was glad that she had managed to scrape together enough money to buy a window air conditioner.

One half of the apartment was composed of a dining area with a kitchen on the end and a "living room," which consisted of a couch, a worn Lazy Boy recliner, two end tables, and a coffee table. The rest of the space consisted of two small bedrooms with a bath between.

"Hey, sweetie," Kate called to Jeremy, who was sitting on the couch engrossed by his Game Boy. He returned her greeting with a brief grunt.

As soon as she put Cleo down, the cat went to the lower cabinet beside the sink, put one paw on the door, and turned to face Kate. Her body language spoke as plainly as words: *How about my treat, Person? I'm starving to death here!* Actually what Cleo said was more like "Wow!" but Kate was totally convinced that both her cats spoke in all but words.

"Wow, my foot!" Kate said, but went to remove a can of tuna packed in spring water from the cabinet. She opened it with an electric can opener and dumped the contents into a heavy pink ceramic dessert bowl. She watched as Cleo ate daintily as always. "You're nothing but a bottomless pit, Cleopatra. There's not enough tuna in Memphis to fill you up."

Kate moved toward Jeremy, but hesitated for a long moment, watching him. A sharp stab of regret came to her as she saw him there alone, and she wondered if she had gone wrong somewhere. Jeremy didn't make friends easily and was as sensitive a boy as Kate had ever seen. He was smart, but this didn't seem to count for much in today's world. She studied his thin face and the auburn hair that came from her. *He doesn't look anything at all like Vic—he's more like me,* she thought. A gust of relief washed through her, and a bitter memory of her marriage ran along her nerves.

Pushing the thought aside, she plunked herself down beside Jeremy. "Hey, good looking, what's up?" The springs of the couch were almost gone, so she was thrown back into a reclining position, but she put her arms around Jeremy, hugged him, and kissed him resoundingly on the cheek. "How about a kiss?" She turned her cheek, took his peck and said, "So, how was your day?"

"It was okay." The standard answer—which meant things were not okay. But she knew that was all she'd get out of him for now.

"Well, mine was okay, too, but I'm pretty tired," she said. "Instead of cooking tonight, let's splurge. What would you like to order?"

"Pizza, I guess," the boy said, finally setting his Game Boy down.

"Now why didn't I guess that? Tell you what, I'll let you order it. I've clipped some coupons. Dominos has a three-for-one sale. You can get three medium pizzas for five dollars each. Order me a pepperoni and you can have two supremes." She tried to get up but without success. "Hey, give me a push," she said.

That brought a chuckle from Jeremy, who pushed her until she came to her feet. She fished her cell phone and the coupons out of her purse and handed them to him. "You call. I'm going to take a shower. I must smell like a septic tank!"

"You smell fine, Mom."

"We'd better have your smeller checked, then," she said with a motherly smirk.

Kate went into her bedroom. The place had been unfurnished, but by the grace of God and the Salvation Army she had managed to buy enough used furniture to get by. She undressed quickly, pulled on a robe from the closet, and padded barefoot to the bathroom. She paused to glance into the small mirror over the sink and for a moment studied herself. What she saw was an oval face framed by long, thick auburn hair—with a widow's peak, which she hated. Her eyes were large and wide-spaced, a gray-green color depending on what she was wearing that day. The mirror was no more than two-by-three so she couldn't see herself completely, but as she slipped off her robe, she reminded herself that she was only twenty-nine and still had a youthful figure. Even though she was short-waisted and her form was fuller than she would have liked, at least she couldn't deny her long shapely legs.

Getting into the shower, she luxuriated as the water flowed over her. She washed her hair, and then stood under the pulsating showerhead for five minutes, enjoying the refreshing coolness.

Reluctantly she got out and dried off with a thick fluffy towel. Towels and washcloths were the one thing she didn't skimp on. She hated worn terry cloth and retired her linens when they started wearing out. Finally she put on her pajamas and robe and joined Jeremy in the living room.

"Pizza not here yet?"

"Not yet, Mom," Jeremy answered, once again engrossed in his Game Boy.

"Well, I'm going to make some chocolate milk. Want some?"

"Sure."

"Pizza and chocolate milk. That's the food pyramid for us—bottom half pizza, top half chocolate milk. A well-balanced diet perfect for a good-looking guy like you."

"I'm not good-looking, Mom," Jeremy answered with a roll of his eyes.

"Sure you are." Kate mixed the chocolate syrup and milk in an oversized glass, put coffee on for herself, and then moving over to the ancient recliner, sat down and closed her eyes. Sleep was only a few moments away, but she felt something touch her bare calf. "That you, Jacques?" she muttered sleepily. She didn't have the affection for her male cat that she had for Cleo, but she had to admit that Jacques was one of a kind and had earned a soft spot in her heart. She hadn't wanted a second pet, but her friend Callie Franklin had begged her to take the kitten with the plea, *I'm gettin' married, and Darin is allergic to cats. He's real expensive. He's a Savannah—half African Serval wildcat and half American domestic. They cost a bundle, but you can have him for nothing!*

Kate had reluctantly agreed, knowing that even as a kitten, Jacques had been a slasher—scratching and even attacking anyone he didn't like, human or animal. But the cat had always been pleasant around her and Jeremy, so they settled him into the apartment, renaming him Jacques the Ripper. Kate hoped Jacques might prove to be some small means of protection for them. Jacques looked for all the world like a miniature black panther, with his ebony pelt, round amber eyes, and impressive size, and was surely intimidating enough to scare off anyone who didn't belong. Kate had installed an oversized cat door, so Jacques came and went as he pleased.

Forcing her eyes open, Kate leaned forward and reached out to stroke Jacques's battle-scarred head. "Have you been a good...?"

Kate never finished her question. With a high-pitched yell, she came out of the chair, shouting, "Jacques—not again!"

"What's wrong, Mom?" Jeremy tossed his Game Boy aside and rushed to Kate's side.

Kate was calming down and kneeled on the floor, holding her hand out to Jacques. "Oh, just another rat. Scared me. I wasn't expecting it."

Jeremy looked down and grinned. Stooping over Jacques, he came up with a tiny mouse. "It's not a rat, Mom—just a mouse."

"Okay, Hon. Will you take the poor little mouse back outside? Thanks."

"But, Mom, it's a present from Jacques. It shows he likes you."

"That's nice, Jeremy, but we don't need a mouse in the house. Now will you get it out of here, *please?*"

As Jeremy moved to take the mouse outside, Kate glared at the huge cat. "Jacques—what am I going to do with you?"

Jacques tossed his head in a way that said, *What an ingrate! I never thought I'd have to put up with this sort of thing when I agreed to make you my Person.* He gave Kate a look of absolute and utter disgust, then turned and stalked out of the apartment as Jeremy returned. "I think you hurt his feelings, Mom."

"He'll have to get over it," Kate said firmly. And indeed, Jacques's gifts were always a bit of a surprise, no matter how often he brought them. He had presented her with an infinite variety of mice, shrews, baby rabbits, small birds, lizards, toads, grasshoppers, and snakes. Worse, she always felt sorry for the small animals, and if they were hurt she took care of them until they were well enough to be on their own. Kate had been forced to raise tiny birds and animals so often that she sometimes felt like a zookeeper.

Jeremy started to speak, but a loud knocking at the door interrupted him. "That must be the pizza," Kate said. She fished the money from her purse, then opened the door to the young man standing there with the pizzas. She took them, paid him, and gave him a dollar tip that didn't seem to thrill him. He shrugged, mumbled, "Thanks," and left.

"Supper time, Jeremy. Let's just eat here on the couch and watch whatever movie you like."

"*The Fellowship of the Ring!*"

"Why did I bother to ask? Okay...put it on."

They sat there eating pizza and Cleo quickly joined them, waiting expectantly for her share. "Pizza is not for cats," Kate said firmly. As she glanced over to Jeremy, she saw his lips moving in time with the movie and laughed. "You could lip-sync this entire movie if you wanted to."

"I want to get parts two and three."

"Well, we can't afford them yet. You'll have to wait until they go on sale."

"Mom, sometimes I wish we could get *one* thing that's not on sale."

The words hurt Kate, though she knew Jeremy had merely uttered them in frustration. In fact, if she were honest with herself, she could've said the same thing. Life would be so much easier with a bit more financial freedom.

As they sat there eating the pizza, Kate admired how Jeremy always threw himself into the movie. He had that ability to become a part of what he was watching on the screen. It was good—and bad. Kate often wished that Jeremy could be as immersed in the real world as he was in the fictional world. His dependence on books and movies seemed to foster his hanging back from friendships and after-school activities.

After the movie was over, she said, "Don't you have homework?"

"Already done it, Mom," he answered. "I got a note from my teacher though."

Kate studied Jeremy's face. "Oh? What does it say?"

"Well, I didn't read it. It's in an envelope, but it probably says I'm not paying attention in class."

"Are you?"

"I get so bored hearing the same old stuff."

Kate well knew that Jeremy was so smart that he did the class work and then had to sit there while the teacher droned on, dragging the minds of less gifted students with her. She opened the note and read it quickly. It confirmed Jeremy's prediction. "I'll have a talk with her. I know you get bored in class. You need to be in an advanced school."

"Aw, I don't mind, Mom."

The two sat there on the couch, and finally Jeremy said, "Guess I'll go to bed. Can I play my Game Boy for a few more minutes?"

"Sure." Kate struggled up off the couch, gave him a kiss, and said, "I'll tell you what. We'll buy part two of The Lord of the Rings tomorrow."

"That's cool, Mom! You're the best!" Jeremy kissed her, and she was glad he wasn't afraid to show affection. In fact, he couldn't seem to get enough of it.

After Jeremy shut the door, as tired as Kate was, she was glad to have a little time to herself. She picked up the book she was reading, the latest mystery by P.D. James, and began reading. Within minutes, she started to fall asleep but was startled awake when a knock came at the door.

She stood up, the book dropping from her lap to the floor. She moved cautiously to the door—then hesitated. It was after ten o'clock, and she wasn't expecting anyone. This was certainly not a part of Memphis where you trusted strangers. The chain was in place and she opened the door a crack. A big man stood there, and she asked curtly, "What is it?"

He was a tall, broad man dressed in a blue suit that seemed too heavy for summer weather. He had on a white shirt and a maroon tie with geometrical figures on it. "You're Mary Katherine Forrest?"

"Yes. What do you want?"

"My name is Leon Bonhoffer. I'm an attorney." Reaching into his pocket, he pulled out a card and slipped it through the crack. "I would've called, but I felt it was important we meet in person."

Kate looked at the card, which seemed official enough. "What do you want, Mr. Bonhoffer? It's late."

"I know it's late, and I apologize. But I finally tracked you down, and I felt this couldn't wait." He held up an envelope that was in his left hand. "I have some good news for you, Mrs. Forrest."

"What do you mean, good news?"

"It appears you're in line to inherit a rather sizable estate."

Kate smiled cynically. "Right. And my son's in line to become King of England."

Bonhoffer grinned. "I understand your skepticism. Could you meet with me tomorrow morning in my office?"

"It sounds like a scam to me."

"Believe me, Mrs. Forrest, it's not. You can call the Memphis police station. Ask Captain Whitaker about me. He'll tell you that I'm on the level. I think—" Bonhoffer looked down and his jaw dropped open. "That's the biggest cat I ever saw!" He leaned over to pet Jacques, and Kate tried to warn him. "He doesn't like to be touched!"

Her warning came too late, for Jacques moved quickly. His claws drew four bloody furrows on the back of Bonhoffer's hand. Bonhoffer jumped back in alarm, cradling his wounded hand.

"I'm so sorry—he doesn't like strangers." For a moment, Kate hesitated, then said, "Come in, Mr. Bonhoffer. I'll put some antiseptic on that, and a bandage."

Bonhoffer had pulled a handkerchief from his pocket, and placing it over the wound, edged into the apartment—keeping a wary eye on Jacques. "Does he do that to everybody?"

"Pretty much. Sit here, and I'll get something for your hand." Moving quickly, Kate assembled the first aid kit she used for Jacques's victims. She wiped the blood away, applied peroxide generously, then expertly applied a large bandage.

"You're pretty good at that," Bonhoffer said. "Are you a nurse?"

"No, but I get lots of practice."

"What kind of a cat is that anyway?"

"He's a Savannah. It's a strange breed—half African wild cat and half domestic breed."

Bonhoffer rose to his feet. "You could get a lawsuit over a cat like that."

"From you?"

"No, not from me. But it's bound to happen." He moved to the door, and she followed him. He turned and allowed his eyes to rove around her apartment. "Be sure to come to my office. This could change your life."

Kate shrugged. "All right—I only work one job tomorrow. I can come in first thing. But what's this all about?"

"We'll talk about it tomorrow. I promise you I'm on the up and up. The address of my office is on the card. Be there anytime after eight. Good night."

Kate closed the door, then scurried to the window and watched as the lawyer got into a big Lincoln. She looked at the card, then shook her head doubtfully. "It's some kind of a scam..."

● ● ●

The next morning Kate took Jeremy to school and then went straight to downtown Memphis. Before leaving the apartment, she had checked on her caller's credentials. Captain Whitaker assured Kate that the attorney was a straight arrow. "He's a high-priced attorney; just about the only lawyer I really trust."

Bonhoffer's office was on the sixth floor of the largest building in the city. She entered the impressive reception area and took in the muted colors, the thick carpeting, and the classical musical softly playing from a hidden speaker somewhere. With apprehension she approached the young woman behind the desk, who seemed to be expecting her. "Mr. Bonhoffer said you might come in, Mrs. Forrest. Let me see if he's free." She pushed the buzzer and said, "Mrs. Forrest is here to see you, sir."

A moment later, the receptionist said, "You can go right in, Mrs. Forrest."

Kate entered the adjoining office and saw Mr. Bonhoffer rising to meet her. He was balding and in his late fifties, but still was a strong-looking individual. "Sit down here, Mrs. Forrest. I'm glad you came by." He waited until she was seated and then said, "I'll try to explain this quickly." He picked up a file from his desk, sat down and pulled a chair opposite her. "Have you ever heard of a woman named Zophia Krizova?"

Kate thought for a moment, then said, "No, I don't think so."

"Well, you may not be aware of it, but this woman was a distant relative of yours from Czechoslovakia."

"I never heard of her," Kate said, "although I think my grandfather came from Czechoslovakia."

"That's correct. Miss Zophia was from a well-to-do family. Her father was a physician. She moved to this country some years ago when she was just a young woman. Her husband was alive then, and they bought some property in White Sands, Alabama, on the beach. Her husband apparently did well in business, but he died in 1942. Miss Zophia never remarried, but she had a brother and sister. They immigrated to this country as well. Her brother was your grandfather."

"I didn't know my grandfather," Kate said suddenly. "I heard my father speak of him though."

"Let me give you the big picture. Zophia Krizova died recently. She was my mother's best friend. As a matter of fact, Miss Zophia took very good care of my mother during her last illness and we became good friends. She appointed me the executor of her estate. The problem is, Mrs. Forrest, she had no immediate family, and had long since lost touch with her brother and sister, so she had no idea if any relatives existed. She instructed me to find any living relatives and see that they inherited her estate. As far as I can tell, you're the only living relative—the inheritor of her estate."

Kate was stunned. She remained silent, trying to understand.

"I have all of the details here," the lawyer continued. "Basically there are two conditions to your inheriting the estate. There's a fine home on the beach in White Sands, Alabama, as I said. The Krizovas bought it many years ago when beach property wasn't so expensive. What it amounts to is seven lots with a fine home right in the middle. A beautiful home, I must say. Have you ever been to White Sands?"

"No. I've never been to any beach."

"You'd like it, I'm sure. The rest of her assets are in blue chip stocks. The principal can't be touched, but whoever inherits the estate will get a fairly large check every month."

"A check? Every month?" Kate could scarcely take it in. "I've had a hard time financially and I have a twelve-year-old son."

"And your husband has passed away. I checked on that. Well, the property in question is very valuable. Developers would like to buy it and put a condo complex there, but Miss Zophia's instructions prohibit that. Still, the income from the property will be considerable, several thousand each month depending on how the stocks go, of course."

"What do I have to do?" Kate asked. Surely there was a catch of some sort.

"There are two conditions. If you don't meet them, the property and all of the assets will go to the SPCA, the Society for the Prevention of Cruelty to Animals."

"What are the conditions?" Kate asked. Maybe it *was* a scam.

"Number one, you must agree to live in the house."

"Well, that shouldn't be too difficult." *So far, so good,* Kate thought.

"I would think not," the lawyer agreed. "People are breaking their necks to move to the Gulf Coast. But there is one other circumstance that must be considered." Bonhoffer leaned back and studied the young woman carefully. "The other requirement is that whoever inherits the estate must care for Miss Zophia's remaining pets."

"That wouldn't be any trouble for me," Kate said. "I love animals."

"Miss Zophia had no children, so she poured her love out on her animals. The will spells out the conditions very carefully. The animals will be checked on a regular basis by a local veterinarian and all deaths must be certified by the same veterinarian. Any mistreatment of the animals will terminate the trust."

"She must have loved her pets very much," Kate said.

"Yes, she did. They were like children to her." The attorney waited a moment, then asked, "Now, do you have any questions, Mrs. Forrest?"

Kate was too confused to ask questions. She dropped her head and thought for a moment, then said, "I'll need a little time to think this over, and to talk with my son. It would mean a big relocation for us, and he'd have to change schools."

"Of course. Why don't you give me a call when you've made up your mind."

They both rose, and Bonhoffer turned his head to one side and looked at her quizzically. "I think it'd be a very wise thing if you were to make this move, Mrs. Forrest. I'll be expecting to hear from you soon."

● ● ●

Jeremy sat very still listening as Kate told him about her visit to the lawyer's office. He didn't say a word until she had finished, then he burst out, "Let's get out of this crummy place, Mom! Wherever we go couldn't be any worse than this."

Kate reached out and ruffled his hair. She smiled with a hope that had begun in her heart and had grown all the way home from Bonhoffer's office. "I think you're right, Jeremy. We'll pray about it until we're sure it's the right thing."

Jeremy nodded. "Maybe it's the answer to prayers we've already prayed. I don't think we need to pray very hard about this, Mom."

"No, I suppose we don't. It *is* an answer, isn't it? Jeremy, let's go for it."

Two

As usual the Chicago Cubs were losing—but Zuriel Tischler was accustomed to minor tragedies. Sitting in a worn cane-bottom chair inside the pawnshop that had been in his family for three generations, he listened as the announcer conveyed the bad news that the Cubs just didn't have it this year.

"As if they had it any other year," Zuriel muttered. He lowered his eyes to the Yiddish newspaper and stroked his nose first, then his luxurious black beard.

A raucous sound brought his head up, and he lowered the paper to stare at the man who had pulled a motorcycle up directly on the sidewalk. His eyes narrowed as the rider unstrapped a large box from the rear of the cycle and carried it in through the front door. With a sigh, Zuriel folded the paper and stood to greet his visitor. He took in the tough-looking face that contradicted its tender years, the short black hair, and the half-hooded hazel eyes. "Novak, what do you want?"

"Tischler, I've decided to let you have first call on this item because you've been so generous to me in the past."

"What is it, kid?" Zuriel asked with a definite lack of interest.

"Just look at this, my friend."

Tischler watched as the big man opened the top of the box and began unloading components of a complex audio system. "There you are," he said. "She's a whizzer, isn't she?"

"Novak, I'm overstocked with stereos."

"This ain't just a stereo, bud. Check it out—top of the line Bose home theater. Plays CDs, DVDs and MP3s. Five-disc changer...separate subwoofer...surround sound...850-watt speakers!" He began running his hands over the exterior of the set, and there was such a longing in his face that Zuriel laughed.

"That's not a girl you're stroking, Novak."

"Better than a girl."

Tischler shrugged his shoulders. "I can let you have three hundred."

"Three hundred! Get serious, Tischler! This set's worth eighteen hundred!"

The haggling began as both Jake Novak and Zuriel Tischler knew it would. The Cubs went down, valiantly losing by a score of twelve to one, and in the end Novak reluctantly agreed to take the four hundred dollars Tischler offered.

Tischler moved over to the counter, reached down to unlock a box, and came up with a small sheaf of bills. He placed them in Novak's hands, who remarked, "You're getting a bargain, Zuriel."

Zuriel watched as Novak paused by the stereo and gave it a sorrowful look. "Get a woman, kid," Zuriel said sourly. "You won't miss her this much when she walks out on you."

Novak stuck the bills in his pocket, gave one more regretful look at the Bose, then left the pawnshop. Mounting his Harley, he kicked it into a start and roared off down the street as if anxious to leave the scene of a crime. He had parted with human friends with less regret than he parted with that system, but he put it behind him as best he could.

Jake Novak had learned to put many things behind him, and as he rode across the streets of Chicago, weaving in and out of the traffic in a suicidal fashion, he promised himself, *I'm going to get that set back as soon as I make my pile.*

He turned down Twenty-third Street and pulled up in front of a small grocery store. Ignoring the parking meter, he walked inside and went to the meat counter. "Hello, Al," he said. "What's good today?"

"We got some cheap bologna over in the freezer area," Al Polinko said with a grin. He was a rotund individual—everything about him was round including his face. He winked and said, "I got some of the prettiest baby backs you ever saw, but they're out of your class. Seven bucks a pound."

"You don't know what you're talking about, Al," Jack said with a wink. "Weigh me out the best looking side you got."

Polinko grunted. "You're the boss." He removed a heavy slab of baby back ribs and threw them on the scale. As he noted the weight, he slapped them down and wrapped them in white paper. "You were right about that Ramirez fight. How'd you know Ramirez would lose?"

"I saw his legs in the last fight. He's out of it. When a fighter loses his legs, he might as well hang up the gloves."

"No charge for the ribs, Jake."

Novak stared at Polinko in disbelief. "I hadn't heard you'd started a charitable institution, Al."

"No problem. I laid a bet down on Biers when you told me he was going to beat Ramirez. The ribs are your cut. You win any money on the fight?" he asked, laying the meat on the counter.

"I never bet on sports."

"What else is there to bet on?"

"Thanks for the ribs, Al. I'll think of you while I'm scarfing them down."

Moving out of the store, Novak jammed the meat into the saddlebags of the Harley, started the engine, and roared down the street. Ten minutes later he pulled up in front of his apartment house. It was an ancient brownstone in what had once been a fashionable area of Chicago. Times had changed and urban cancer had swept across this part of Chicago, turning it into a ghetto. A group of tough-looking young men turned to face him, and one of them said, "Hey, lend me ten bucks, Novak."

"Go to the Goodwill, Dink. They're handing out ten-dollar bills, I hear." The men all laughed, but none of them made a move toward Novak. Jake remembered how they'd tried him out when he had first moved in, and he had administered bodily harm to several of their members. Now they accepted his whiteness as a necessary evil and left him alone.

Entering what had once been the lobby of a palatial home, he met his landlady, a Puerto Rican woman of forty, small and delicate but with the manners of a Marine drill sergeant. "Time's up, Jake. I want the rent money."

"Here you go, Maria." Jake pulled out a thin sheaf of bills and handed her two of them. "Payment in advance for another two weeks."

Taking the money, Maria stared at him. "You get a job?"

"I've already got a job."

"Writing stories is no job! Not for a big, strong boy like you. You ever sell anything you wrote?"

"Not yet, sweetheart, but when my novel wins the National Book Award, you'll eat those words."

She snorted and turned around. Quickly Jake reached out and patted her rear. She whirled and slapped at him, but he blocked the blow and grinned. "You better watch out for us guys, Maria. We're not trustworthy." He laughed and bounded up the stairs taking them three at a time. He moved with an athletic grace that strangely seemed natural, though he was such a big man. His muscles weren't bulky like a weightlifter but lean like those of an acrobat or a swimmer. Turning to the left at the top of the stairs, he went to the last room on the left, opened the door, and stepped inside. He stopped for one moment and looked around the apartment.

"You're all mine," he said, "for at least another two weeks." As was his custom, Jake spoke aloud to whatever inanimate object concerned him. A quirk for sure—but most writers had some sort of oddity, he reasoned. Quickly he glanced across the apartment with a certain fondness, although there was little enough to be proud of—basically one room with a couch against the wall. An end table supported a lamp that had lost its brass finish. It was one of those lamps that was supposed to go on and off by clapping your hands, but the switch was broken, so the only way to control it was by unplugging it from the receptacle and plugging it back in. Novak had come to accept the crippled lamp as a metaphor for his life. Not very old, but worn beyond its years.

A coffee table with several books stacked neatly on it fronted the couch. One more chair, rarely used, sat across the room. Every wall was covered with books in makeshift bookcases formed by boards laid across concrete blocks rising all the way to the ceiling. At the other end of the apartment was a compact kitchen consisting of a few cabinets, an apartment-sized stove, a small refrigerator, and a sink, over which a large window looked out into the street. The view was nothing, merely another grimy apartment house, but Novak hadn't rented the room for a view but because it was the cheapest thing he could find.

The dining area boasted a small dinette table with chrome legs and a sickly green Formica top. Three chairs—one for himself, one for friendship, and the third for society. He grinned to himself as he remembered an old captain saying that. Funny how he'd adopted sayings and tastes similar to guys so much older than him.

Unwrapping the baby backs, he placed them on the table and ran his hands over them. He was hungry, but it would take a while to fix the kind of supper he wanted. Moving quickly, he went to the window over the sink. Reaching out, he pulled in a small barbecue grill perched on a framework he'd built. Carefully he dumped the old hunks of charcoal into the garbage, replenished it, and then soaked it with lighter fluid. Setting it back outside, he touched a match to it and with satisfaction watched it flame up. It was against the law to cook outside an apartment, but that didn't bother Novak. "Don't you worry, little grill, the cops are all out catching murderers. They won't have time to arrest us. You just get nice and hot."

Shutting the window against the smoke that the briquettes sent up, Novak went to the refrigerator. He pulled out bowls and saucers covered with cellophane until the table was covered. He marinated the ribs in a sauce of his own concoction, then began making a salad, taking great pleasure in it. He spoke to the vegetables individually as he chopped and sliced and arranged them. "Radish, my friend, you stay right there. I can see you're going to add a lot to this salad—and you, old stalk of celery, you are one cool dude. How nice of you to sacrifice yourself for poor old Jake, but it's for a noble cause..."

Jake Novak's service in the Army's Delta Force as one of their youngest-ever soldiers, and his more recent stint as a homicide detective here in Chicago, had left him with a cynical view of life. He had left both services unhappy and dissatisfied, his ideals pretty well chopped into small pieces. At 29, he was young enough to be enjoying life, but he found himself in the process of reinventing himself and discovering the simpler pleasures. To his own surprise, he had learned to enjoy both writing and cooking. A salad wasn't simply a few vegetables chopped up but an artistic creation. He worked in lettuce and chives and carrots as Van Gogh worked in oils. He made his own salad dressing with a formula that he guarded jealously. Salad dressing off the shelf was pure poison.

He added iceberg and romaine lettuce together with some purple cabbage, baby-leaf spinach, chopped carrots, radishes, celery, chives, and topped it off with homemade croutons, small cherry red tomatoes, and a little freshly grated Parmesan cheese. After the salad was made, he slipped it back into the refrigerator and went to get cleaned up.

There was no shower, just an old claw-footed tub with the enamel worn thin, but Jake had learned in his military service to make do. He filled the tub with cold water, stripped, sat down, and folded his six-foot-two into it. For twenty minutes he soaked in the peace and quiet of the cool water. Finally he stood up, soaped himself vigorously, dunked back in, came up sputtering, then stepped out and dried off. He put on a pair of shorts and an oversized T-shirt and went into the kitchen. Opening the window, he saw that the briquettes were all a uniform gray. "Just right, my charcoal friends," he said with satisfaction. He put the grill on, laid the slab of ribs on the top and closed the lid. He waited until smoke began to puff through the small slots in the top and then went back and closed the window.

He put a disc in a small CD player and Glenn Miller's "Tuxedo Junction" filled the apartment. The music sounded cheap and tinny after the Bose, but it would have to do. Sitting down at his laptop, he opened the machine and for a few seconds sat there, but then began typing. He'd heard that Stephen King liked to write while listening to loud heavy metal music and he'd tried it, but found he worked better to the big bands of the 1940s or even some classical every now and then. It seemed to relax him and keep him focused.

He typed steadily for twenty minutes. Several times he went to turn the ribs over but then went right back to his writing. He had the ability to shut out everything when he wrote. It was as if he could get into a box and shut the top down. Just he and words were inside.

Finally he got up, shut his laptop down, and went over to look at the meat. Opening the window and lifting the lid of the grill, he saw that the ribs were just as he liked them. Using a sharp knife, he impaled the ribs, lifted them up, and placed them on a platter. He put the platter on the table, removed the salad from the refrigerator, and grabbed a bottle of mineral water, then sat down. He leaned over and inhaled the succulent steaming meat. "Baby backs, I love you—but I'm about to incorporate you, so say goodbye to everything you know." Using a sharp steak knife, he sliced off the first rib, picked it up, and ate it gingerly. It was hot but delicious. From time to time he would take a bite of the salad and the French bread he had toasted in the oven.

After he finished, he got up and did the dishes, such as they were. When he was done, the kitchen was as immaculate as the rest of the apartment. He went to the couch and put another disc into the CD player. This time it was the smooth voice of Nat King Cole singing "Nature Boy." Picking up a tattered paperback, he plugged in the light, punched a pillow to his comfort, lay flat on his back, and began to read *Bleak House* by Charles Dickens—for the sixth time.

● ● ●

The next morning, as always, Novak came instantly out of sleep into full awareness. He had been that way even as a child. His buddies in the army could never understand it nor had he figured it out himself. It was just one of those things that made him what he was. Getting up, he headed to the kitchen, where he made freshly squeezed orange juice, toasted two pieces of French bread, and cooked six slices of turkey bacon. He was amazed at how content he was in this quiet life—cooking, writing, reading, listening to music.

As soon as he had eaten, he put on a pair of shorts, a tan T-shirt with BAD SPELLERS OF THE WORLD—UNTIE! emblazoned on the front, then went out for his morning run.

Running on the streets of Chicago was an adventure. There'd been a time when he had carried a jackknife in the pocket of his shorts, but he'd decided it was just asking for trouble, so he had determined he would simply outrun anybody who tried to shake him down. He ran for five miles, dodging foot traffic while receiving angry comments from several pedestrians he brushed against. He remembered a vacation he had taken once in the Shenandoah Valley of North Carolina. He had run through the Blue Ridge Mountains, and the air there had been, he remembered, like wine. Now the air of Chicago seemed to need a filter rather badly.

Arriving back at his apartment, he moved the furniture around so that he had at least a little space. He popped in one of his favorite high-energy CDs, the Red Hot Chili Peppers, and did push-ups, sit-ups, curls and a series of other exercises for half an hour. When he was out of breath and covered with sweat, he plunged into the tub again, sinking his head under the water and sputtering like a horse as he came to the surface. Coming out of the tub, he dried off with a rough towel and put on a pair of boxer shorts. Sitting down at his laptop, he traded his rock music for a Chopin disc.

For several minutes, he stared at the screen, but for some reason he could not think of anything to write. He read what he'd written the previous day. Idly he typed, "I cannot think of anything to write." Leaning back, he said, "All right, computer, that's all I've got. Give me a little help here?" Thoughts were running through his brain like lightning, but they didn't form a cohesive idea, so he reached forward and typed, "I still can't think of anything to write, but I'm going to write something until something good comes. I can always go back and take out this mess that I'm putting in here now."

That was the beginning of his workday, and he worked steadily, pausing only for half an hour at noon to eat a sandwich and an apple. He was still plugging away when his cell phone went off. It startled him as he got almost no calls since he didn't give his number out to very many people.

Cautiously he picked up the phone and said, "Yes?"

"Mr. Jacob Novak?"

"Who is this? How'd you get this number?"

"My name is Leon Bonhoffer. I'm an attorney in Memphis, Tennessee."

"Answer my question. How'd you get this number?"

"I hired a detective in Chicago to get it for me when I found out you were living there."

"What do you want?"

"I want to talk to you. It will take a few minutes."

"Whatever you're selling, Bonhoffer, I'm not buying."

"I'm not selling anything, Mr. Novak. I understand your doubts. The telemarketers are out of control these days, aren't they? But I'm not one of them. Call the police department in Memphis, Tennessee, downtown precinct. Talk to Captain Whitaker and ask him about me. When you check me out, call me back." He then gave Jake two numbers, and hung up without even saying goodbye.

Novak stared at the phone for a moment then shrugged slightly. "Maybe he represents a publisher who wants to make me rich and famous by publishing my novel." He dialed the number, spoke to the police captain, and after getting a positive recommendation, he called Bonhoffer back.

"Okay, I checked you out," he said with mild curiosity. "What do you want?"

"Mr. Novak, does the name Zophia Krizova mean anything to you?" Bonhoffer asked

Jake paused. The name stirred some faint memory. "Uhh—I've heard it but I can't remember in what context—I've met a lot of people."

"Zophia Krizova was from Czechoslovakia."

"My family came from Czechoslovakia a long time ago."

"Exactly. One of them was a relative of Zophia Krizova. I'll spell this out very clearly. Zophia Krizova moved to America from Czechoslovakia many years ago. She had one brother and one sister. They came here with her parents. Miss Krizova died at an advanced age recently and I'm the executor of her estate. I've been running down her heirs. If you can prove that you are the son of the Thomas Novak who was married to Zophia's niece, then that will be all the evidence I need."

Jake paused, then said, "Well, I remember my dad mentioning someone. His mother, I think. She was connected to somebody named Krizova."

"Yes. The sister and the brother of Zophia Krizova immigrated here, and you're in the sister's line."

"What kind of estate are we talking about?"

"Pretty sizable by any standard, Mr. Novak. However, there are some unusual requirements before you can inherit."

"Tell me how much and what are the requirements."

"The bulk of the estate is in two forms, one an expensive house on the coast in White Sands, Alabama, along with six lots that accompany it. Seven lots total. Very valuable property."

"How valuable?"

"I've had the house itself appraised at around two million, with each of the surrounding lots worth over a mil as well. So we're talking eight to ten million, roughly, in beachfront land. Property's escalating in that area. Anything on the beach is going up like a missile. The rest of the estate is tied up in blue chip stocks. You can't get at the principal, according to the will, but you could take the interest which will amount to a tidy sum. Several thousand dollars a month at present. It will be more as the stocks go up."

"If you're serious about this, I'm serious."

"Wait a minute, Mr. Novak. I said there are two requirements."

"And they are?"

"You have to live in the house to get the inheritance. If you move out, you forfeit. And the property can't be sold. Secondly, the old woman loved her pets. You have to agree to take care of the pets."

"That's all?"

"Those are the requirements in Miss Zophia's will. But there's one more thing."

"What's that? Is there another catch?"

"You might think so. There's another heir. You'll have to share the house and the money fifty-fifty."

"For that kind of money I'd room with Dracula. It's still a good deal. I'll put up with them no matter who it is. What do I do next?"

"You'll need to come to my office in Memphis. I'll have the papers drawn up. It took me a long time to locate you, but everything is ready now."

"I'll be there in two days."

Novak wrote the address and phone number down and hung up. He looked around the apartment and began to smile. "Well, apartment, it's been great, but I'm moving on up. Goodbye, Chicago. Hello, White Sands, Alabama!"

Three

Kate had once been intrigued by a single line from an Emily Dickinson poem: "Hope is the thing with feathers that perches in the soul." Hope had indeed been an endangered species for Kate for two long years. Day by day the demanding and tedious struggle to simply endure had drained her of most of her natural exuberance. The visit to Bonhoffer's office had created in her a rebirth of something very much like joy. She had almost forgotten what it was like to have something to look forward to, but the possibility of leaving behind everything tasteless and grim for a beautiful house on the sands of the Gulf changed that. She imagined she felt much the same as King Arthur's knights had felt when envisioning the Holy Grail.

"Mom, you've been acting totally differently lately," Jeremy said as he got out of the car at school. Before shutting the door, he leaned forward and said, "You're happy, aren't you?"

Kate smiled. "I'm really happy, Jeremy. It's going to be a new life for us." She reached out, took his hand, and when he grasped it, she pulled him forward, hugged him, and rubbed his head. "Go on to school now. I'm going to see Mr. Bonhoffer this morning. I think we'll be leaving for our new home pretty soon."

As soon as Jeremy shut the door, Kate nursed the limping Taurus to downtown Memphis. She found a parking place and got out with the Miss Dickinson's feathered hope singing loudly in her spirit. She felt like running to Bonhoffer's office, but forced herself to walk at a moderate pace. As the elevator rose to the attorney's floor, she had the fanciful thought that it was going to keep rising past Bonhoffer's floor and carry her straight into the celestial realm. *You've got to stop being so foolish, girl,* she chided herself. When the elevator did indeed stop at the correct floor, Kate got out and entered Bonhoffer's office, with at least an outward semblance of serenity.

"Good morning, Mrs. Forrest," the secretary said, smiling. "You can go right in. Mr. Bonhoffer's waiting for you."

Entering the office, Kate found Leon Bonhoffer standing beside his window looking down at the street. As soon as he turned to her, she saw that he was troubled. She didn't know him well, but in their previous meetings there had been an openness about the man. A dark, gloomy weight rose up and enveloped her.

"Something's gone wrong, hasn't it?" Kate asked, her hopes dashed. "It's not going to happen, is it?"

"No, no, Mrs. Forrest, nothing's gone wrong," Bonhoffer assured her. "It's just that we've had another development...but it's not altogether bad."

"Just tell me what it is." Kate sighed. "I want to know the worst."

Bonhoffer pulled his hand over his balding pate and gave her a worried smile. "As I've told you, I was commissioned by Miss Zophia to find all her possible heirs. I thought I had. As I told you, you were the only one I'd found. But since we talked last, I've located another relative who has a claim on the estate. I'd been trying to track him for some time. It was a complicated search and I'd given up, but just two days ago I found him. I had to check out his credentials, and in so doing, I've confirmed that he is a bona fide claimant to the estate just as you are."

Kate took the news with resignation. "Who is he?"

"His name is Jacob Novak. He's on his way over now. That's why I asked you to come in. I wanted you two to meet, because if you both agree to the arrangement you're going to be seeing a great deal of each other."

Even as Bonhoffer spoke, the intercom sounded. "Mr. Novak is here, Sir."

"Send him right in, Eileen."

Kate turned to face the door. For some reason she had put herself completely on the defensive. Her dreams had been crowded with excitement and plans, but they hadn't included a stranger. A sense of possessiveness and jealousy rose in her as she realized that she would have to share the paradise she had created in her mind. When the door opened, she took a deep breath and clamped her lips together. One look at the man brought a hard sense of resentment.

The two men shook hands and then Bonhoffer said, "Mr. Novak, this is Mary Katherine Forrest. Mrs. Forrest, Mr. Jacob Novak."

Kate nodded but did not speak. There was something ominous about the man. Her first startled thought was, *He looks just like Russell Crowe!* Indeed, Novak did have the actor's tapered face, wide mouth, and half-hooded eyes, though his hair was darker. He had a broken nose, a scar on his eyebrow, another beside his mouth, and there was a sense of unleashed power in his body. He was wearing a pair of worn denims and a limp gray T-shirt that had a faded picture of Clint Eastwood complete with sombrero, serape, and cigar. His stubble of black wiry whiskers gave him a disreputable look.

"Hello, Mary Katherine," Jake said firmly.

"It's Kate," was her reluctant answer.

Novak was considering her with his sleepy hazel eyes in a way that troubled Kate. Then, apparently conscious of the way he looked, Jake said, "I drove right through. The air conditioner on the U-Haul went out, so I'm just about cooked. Didn't stop for a shave or a bath, so I'm pretty ripe."

"Well, I'm glad you could make it," Bonhoffer said quickly. "Why don't you two sit down while we go over some things."

As they sat down, Bonhoffer cleared his throat nervously as he took a seat behind his desk. Something about Novak disturbed him, Kate noticed. He drummed his fingers on the desk and appeared to be searching for the right thing to say. "You two are related in a way, a distant way, of course. Both of you are from Zophia Krizova's family..."

As the lawyer spoke, Kate had her full attention on Novak. He sat lazily in the chair, and his nonchalant demeanor suggested something ominous. *He looks just like the gladiator in that movie!* she thought. *He's probably a hit man for the mafia!*

"What are you getting at, Bonhoffer?" Novak interrupted.

"Well, it means you will be equal heirs, of course. And both of you will have to meet the terms of the will in order to inherit."

Kate sat straight up as the implication of the lawyer's words came to her. "You mean we both have to live in the house—together?"

"If you want to inherit, yes."

"I can't live with him!" She spoke of Novak as if he weren't in the room. Then, more calmly, she said, "I can't live in a house with a strange man."

Novak gave Kate a twisted grin. "And I can't live in a house with a strange woman. After all, I've got my reputation to think of. Can't one of us buy the other out?"

Bonhoffer laid a folder down on the desk. "The will prohibits it. I handled the estate myself so the will's unbreakable, I assure you. If you want to inherit, you follow the two conditions I've already set out. You live in the house and you care for the pets." A thought occurred to him. "And you can't sue each other. The will's ironclad. I made it that way." He stood up. "I know this is unexpected...but there you have it. Why don't you two go out for a cup of coffee and talk it over. Come back when you can tell me your decision."

Kate got to her feet and cast a desperate look at Bonhoffer, but his face was adamant. No hope there! She turned and walked out, aware that Novak was right behind her. They left the outer office and when they were standing in front of the elevator, Novak said, "Neither one of us likes this, but we've got to talk about it."

"What is there to say?"

"Well, I honestly don't know. But I'm starved. I haven't had anything to eat for hours. Let's go get something to eat. Maybe we can come up with something."

Kate wanted desperately to simply dismiss the whole thing, but the dream that had been so vivid was rapidly drying out to nothing. She had to resuscitate it and so she nodded briefly. "I don't suppose it'll hurt to talk."

The two went down to the ground floor, and when they left the building, she said, "There's a Wendy's two blocks away."

Novak did not answer. He was looking up and down the street. "There's a better place," he said, nodding toward it.

"That's Manfred's. We can't go there."

"Why not?"

"It's way too expensive and they have all kinds of—limitations." She looked at his disreputable garb adding, "Like a dress code."

Novak grinned. His teeth were white against his tanned skin, and the smile made him look at least slightly less dangerous. "Maybe it'll be good enough for us millionaires. Let's check it out."

He led her across the street jaywalking, and when they reached the entrance of Manfred's, they went inside. They were met by a maitre d', a tall sallow-faced man with a pencil-thin mustache and a cool manner. "I'm sorry, sir, but we require a jacket and a tie."

"No problem. Be right back," Novak said. He turned and nodded toward Kate. "Wait right here, Mary Katherine." Turning quickly, he walked out and the maitre d' stared at Kate. "You would be welcome to come in, miss."

"Ah—no, I'll wait," she said, somewhat confused.

The wait wasn't long. In less than five minutes Novak came through the door. He was wearing exactly the same clothes except he had added a worn denim jacket with a Harley emblem on the left breast. Around his neck was what appeared to be a boot lace tied in a knot. He came to stand before the maitre d' and gave him a challenging look. "Coat and tie. Let's have that table."

For a moment the maitre d' appeared nonplussed, but then a smile turned the corners of his lips upward. "Certainly, sir. This way."

He led the two to a table and seated them. "You will be served presently. Enjoy your meal."

"Thanks, pal," Novak said. He leaned back in his chair and was gazing around the room. "Nice place," he said. "With my luck—the food's probably terrible. Have you ever noticed—sometimes, the fancier the surroundings, the worse the food? Some of the best food I ever got came from truck stops with not a lot of décor. You'd be surprised at the number of talented chefs who hide away in roadside diners."

The server was there almost immediately, and his face was a mask, but his eyes were sparkling with humor. "Welcome to Manfred's, sir, and you, miss."

Kate looked at the menu and noted that there were no prices. She searched desperately for something that might be inexpensive, but there were no cheeseburgers. "I'll just have a salad, please."

"Of course, miss."

"Bring her a Mediterranean salad with marinated chicken. If the chef needs any help, I'll be glad to come back and give him a few pointers." Jake gave the waiter a wink.

"I'll certainly let him know," the waiter replied, attempting to go along with the humor. "What will you have, Sir?"

"I think I'll have a small Caesar salad to start and then the sherry mushroom chicken, twice baked potatoes, and the honey-lime carrots."

"Shall I bring you something to drink while you're waiting?"

"I'll have a glass of the Vino Nobile di Montepulciano, Riserva 1997." He looked at Kate and she said, "Just water, please."

As soon as the server had left, Novak said, "Well, Mary Katherine, what do you think about our future?"

Something about the way he said *our* future grated on Kate's nerves—as well as his use of her formal name despite having already corrected him. It was as if they were somehow joined together in a union she didn't want. "It's exactly as I told Mr. Bonhoffer. I can't live in the same house with you. I don't know anything about you."

"That's easy enough to fix." He leaned back and spoke in an easy tone. "I was born in Detroit, almost thirty years ago. Neither of my parents are living. I joined the army when I was eighteen, and it didn't take long before I was recruited to Delta Force. Was with them for two years." His eyes grew thoughtful and somehow hooded.

"Isn't that an elite part of the military?"

"Yep. Got out with a medical discharge. Later I joined Chicago P.D. and was a cop on the beat for a couple years, then spent some time in the homicide division."

"What do you do now?"

"I'm a writer."

"What kind of a writer?"

"I'm writing the Great American Novel."

Kate was confused. She knew the Special Forces contained some of the toughest human beings on earth—and that the homicide division of Chicago was bound to be almost as rough. She couldn't make sense of him. She tried desperately to think of something to say but nothing came.

"If you want references, I got 'em. You can call my chief in Chicago. Name's Williams. Or you can call my sergeant, who's in the VA hospital all shot to pieces. He knows me better than anybody, I guess." Humor touched the hazel eyes of Novak, and he added, "Or you can call Solly Desalvo. He's on death row where I put him."

Kate stared at the big man lounging across from her. "What did he do?" she asked faintly.

"He tortured and murdered six young women."

"How awful! Will he be put to death?"

"No. He'll sit in jail for a few years then some liberal judge will turn him loose. If I had to do it over again, I'd have saved the state a lot of money and planted one right between his eyes." He shifted as if he were tired of the conversation. "So what's your story?"

"Well, it's certainly not as exciting as yours." Kate tried to look back on her life, but it seemed dull in comparison—drudgery broken only by heartbreak. The overriding bright spot was Jeremy—her lifesaver. She said finally, "You and I are the same age. I was born in Jackson, Mississippi. I graduated from high school when I was 17—the same year I married my husband, Victor. We had our son, Jeremy, right away."

Novak stared across. "So there's a husband in this deal? And a kid?"

"My husband's dead," Kate said flatly. "He was a pilot and his small plane went down in a hurricane. They never found the plane or his body." Then she said quickly, "I've been making a living for me and my son as best I could."

"He didn't leave any insurance?"

"He left me with Jeremy."

"How old's the kid?"

"My *son* is twelve. He's mature for his age."

The meal came, and Kate bowed her head and silently said a quick prayer of thanks. When she opened her eyes, Jake was staring at her.

"What?" she asked, a bit defensive.

"You're *praying?*"

"Just saying grace."

Jake shook his head and began eating. "This might turn out to be a bit tougher than we thought."

Kate started into her meal and was surprised how much she enjoyed the salad. She ate slowly, expecting Novak to scarf his food down, but he ate daintily as a gentleman. He finally finished and set his napkin on the table. "You want coffee or dessert?"

"No."

"Me either." He reached up and ran his hand across his hair. "Well, Mary Katherine Forrest, I'm going to take the old lady's house and the money. What *you* do will be entirely up to you." He looked at her carefully and said, "Look, I know I look like a thug, which I probably am, but I'm telling you now—you and your son will be safe as far as I'm concerned. In fact, you're safer with me than by yourselves."

Kate sat quietly and looked down at her hands. Finally she said, "Mr. Novak, I can't give you an answer now. I'll have to pray about it."

The answer seemed to amuse Novak. He smiled and said, "Fine. When you and God make up your minds, let me know." He reached into his pocket, pulled out a billfold and extracted a card. He wrote a number on it and said,

"There's my cell phone. You can get me anytime." He got up, pulled some bills out of his pocket, and tossed them on the table. He waited until she preceded him out of the building, and as she walked outside in the sunlight, she glanced up at the blue sky. *Lord—I don't know what in the world to do—please help me!*

• • •

For two days Kate wrestled with her decision. She prayed desperately for an answer, and it finally came in the middle of the night.

On Thursday night after tossing restlessly, she gave up on sleep, got out of bed, and picked up her Bible. She sat there trying to pray and finally said, "Lord, I don't believe in using the Bible as a fortune-teller, but I need to know what to do. I would be so grateful if You would just lead me to a scripture. Speak to my heart, Lord." She prayed fervently, and finally in desperation she opened the Bible and began to read. For the past several days, she had been reading through the entire Bible and was starting on the first chapter of Deuteronomy. She read the first few verses and then the sixth verse seemed to strike her with unusual force. She put her finger on it and read it aloud: "The Lord our God spake unto us in Horeb saying, Ye have dwelt long enough in this mount."

Something like a light seemed to go off in Kate's mind, and yet it was not a light produced by the sun or an incandescent bulb. It was more like a slight electrical shock—yet it wasn't quite like that either. She read the last part again. *Ye have dwelt long enough in this mount...*

Kate put her hands over her eyes and prayed, "Lord, is this a command or a promise?" She waited, and the longer she stayed before God, the more the verse echoed in her mind almost vocally. She opened her eyes and the next verse said, "Turn you, and take your journey..."

For over an hour Kate struggled and finally said, "Lord, I don't know how to find Your will perfectly. I'm going to take this as a green light. If I'm doing the wrong thing, please give me at least a yellow light to warn me. I don't want to do anything out of Your will, and if You give me a red light, I will refuse this offer and stay where I am."

She closed the Bible and went to sleep filled with a sense of peace, and even as she drifted off, she found herself whispering, "Thank You, Lord..."

● ● ●

As soon as the knock came on the door, Kate opened it. Novak stood there, looking amazingly neat. He was wearing a pair of loose-fitting cotton chinos and a russet-colored polo shirt and a pair of bitterroot-colored shoes with a whip-stitched design.

"Come in, Mr. Novak."

Novak entered, but stopped abruptly. He stared down at Cleo, who greeted him by rubbing against his leg. "Uh, I hate cats," Novak said shortly, stepping back to avoid contact.

"Why?"

"They're snobbish. Not friendly like dogs."

"Cleo isn't snobbish," Kate said sharply. "She's very loving."

Suddenly Jacques materialized. He had been napping on Jeremy's bed, but now he was creeping toward Novak with obvious intentions.

"What kind of a cat is *that?*" Novak demanded, staring at the animal. "He's a monster!"

"He's a Savannah."

"Never heard of it. Why is he creeping up on me?"

"He doesn't like strangers."

Jeremy had risen from the couch and was watching Jacques, who appeared to be getting into the attack position. "We call him Jacques the Ripper," Jeremy offered. He was obviously enjoying Novak's reaction. "He's a wild cat from Africa."

As if at a signal, Jacques leaped forward and swiped at Novak's leg. His claws caught and Novak yelled and tried to free himself. "Keep him away from me!"

"Take Jacques outside, Jeremy," Kate said, and when the boy picked up the cat, Novak held the door open. He closed it and asked shortly, "Well, have you made up your mind?"

"Jeremy and I are going to accept the offer," Kate said.

Jake grinned. "Glad you and God came up with that."

Ignoring Novak's cynical remark, Kate said, "I wanted you to meet my son." She called Jeremy and when he came back in, she said, "Jeremy, this is Mr. Novak. This is my son, Jeremy."

"Hey, kid," Jake said, putting out his hand. "Why don't both of you just call me Jake."

Novak glanced over the apartment and after a moment, said, "You're not a very good housekeeper. I don't like messy houses. I like things neat."

Kate's temper flared. "In case you didn't notice, I am *not* a housekeeper. I'm a mom and I work two full-time jobs."

"Uhhh...right," Jake said sheepishly. "Guess we'll have something to argue about from the very first day." Jake's look was amused. "I'll bring the U-Haul by tomorrow. We'll load whatever you want to take."

Kate was mollified. "Thank you, Mr. Novak."

"Just Jake. Since we're going to live together and be one happy family, we might as well be on a first name basis." He turned, then with a swift movement he whirled back.

"I'm assuming you'll need to bring your car. I've got a tow package for the U-Haul."

"Thanks. But what about *your* car?"

Jake grinned. "My *car* is a Harley—and it fits nicely in the back of the truck. See ya tomorrow." And he was gone.

Jeremy was staring at the door and he turned to look at his mother. "He looks cool, Mom. But I'm not sure about him."

"Me neither, but he goes with the deal. We have no choice." She went over and put her arm around him. "You'll have to help me keep him in his place."

Four

It's bad news, Cleo. I don't like changes, and it's pretty clear that our People are going to move us to a new place.

Cleo was washing her chest assiduously with strokes of her red tongue, but she paused and watched the Woman and the Boy stuff some items into a box.

It'll be a nice place, Jacques. Probably someplace with green grass and lots of birds to catch.

Jacques glared at Cleo, his amber eyes glowing like live coals. *It's just as likely to be someplace with big dogs and fleas. I like it here, but does she ask us what we'd like?* Jacques switched his tail angrily. *I'm going to be in a bad mood, Cleo.*

You're always in a bad mood, Jacques. Why can't you be nice like me?

Jacques gave Cleo a look of utter disdain, and walked over to the green ceramic food bowl beside the sink. *Look at this—no water in my bowl. Somebody's going to be sorry about this.* He extended his saberlike claws and raked the floor with grim anticipation.

The two cats continued to watch the Woman and the Boy pack, and even Cleo, normally a placid feline, was somewhat disturbed over the activities that had been going on the past few days.

Kate didn't even look up at the cats. The packing and planning had been exhausting, and she'd been too preoccupied to pay much attention to Cleo and Jacques. She'd had to give notice at both of her jobs—or at least she felt that she should. There hadn't been a line of mourners waiting to weep on her shoulder when she had announced she was leaving. She realized how few friends she had made at either of her jobs. Only the people at her church had expressed regret at seeing her leave. It was a very small church, but Kate had loved it. Brother Seth Lowell, the pastor, a green young man making his first attempts at shepherding a small flock, was loaded mostly with inexperience, but he loved God and he worked hard. When she had said goodbye, he had said mournfully, "We'll miss you, Kate. You've been a blessing to me and the whole church." That and saying goodbye to her fellow believers had been more difficult than Kate had expected.

She had scurried to get Jeremy's records from school, and had called ahead to the school district in White Sands to make arrangements for Jeremy to start school immediately upon their arrival. She had called to get the utilities turned off, transferred the mail service, and had spent a great deal of time packing. From Bonhoffer's words she understood that the house on the beach was furnished, but some of her own furniture had come down from her parents. Kate was, admittedly, a certified pack rat and unable to throw anything of possible significance away. She had boxes of her grade school efforts, the crudely drawn crayon pictures on rough paper and souvenirs that she had collected. She had made up her mind to finally throw things away, but in the end she simply packed them up, thinking, *I'll have plenty of room to store them in White Sands.*

It was noon when Jeremy, who was standing at the window, said, "He's here, Mom."

Going to the window, Kate watched as Jake Novak got out of a U-Haul truck and walked toward the stairs. She didn't wait until he knocked but opened the door and stepped back.

"Hello, Mary Katherine." Novak walked into the room, his eyes going over the stack of boxes. He turned to Kate and shook his head. "I hope there's room in the truck—" He spotted Jacques sitting guardedly on a packed box and leaped back, warning, "Keep that monster away from me!"

Kate didn't even try to restrain the smile that turned up the corners of her lips. "I don't think he likes you."

"We've got to haul him all the way to Alabama?" Jake snorted with disgust.

"You'll get used to him," Kate answered. "I've got two carriers. They won't be any trouble."

"Yes, they will," Jake cut the words off shortly. He took a step backward, saying nervously, "Does this one try to claw people, too?"

"No, Cleo loves everyone."

Jake stood still as Cleo nudged his leg, purring loudly. "I hate cats," he reminded Kate. "Get her away from me, will you? And we've got to put that black monster in a carrier right now." He gave a nervous look at Jacques the Ripper, and Kate said, "Don't be afraid of Jacques."

"I'm not afraid," Novak said stiffly. "I just don't want to get clawed by that...*thing*." He then took stock of the stacked boxes and shrugged his shoulders. "Maybe I should have gotten a bigger truck. You're not moving the furniture, are you?"

"Some of it. It belonged to my family."

"My philosophy about moving? Pile most of the stuff on the curb and torch it. Looks like junk to me."

"We're taking it," Kate said flatly, meeting his eyes with determination. "I put a little green sticker on all the furniture that goes."

Novak snorted again and then went over, picked up a recliner as if it weighed nothing, and walked out of the room with it.

"I'll bring some of the lighter things," Kate called after him. Turning, she said, "Jeremy, you can help carry the boxes..."

● ● ●

For the next hour and a half they marched down and up the stairs, until finally the last piece went into the truck.

"I've got to vacuum and clean up," Kate said. "Then we can go."

"Let it go. The next tenant will do that."

"No. It wouldn't be right."

"Well, I'll go down and hook up your car to the back of the truck. Hurry it up, will you?"

"Can we drive all the way to White Sands today, Mr. Novak?" Jeremy asked.

"We could have if we started early, but now we'll have to make it in two jumps. You want to come downstairs with me?"

"No, Sir. I'll stay here."

Novak turned and said, "Jeremy, you don't have to call me Mr. Novak and *sir* me all the time."

Instantly Kate spoke up. "He can call you whatever you please, but I've taught him to say *yes, sir* and *no, ma'am*."

Novak grinned suddenly. "That's some of that Southern background you've got. Makes me feel like I'm in a movie with Rhett Butler and Scarlett O'Hara. Just call me Jake, kid." He turned and walked down the stairs without another word.

Quickly Kate cleaned the house as best she could. At least everything was much cleaner than when she had moved in. Going down the steps, she found Novak playing basketball with a bunch of the black kids. Though he looked very large, he moved smoothly and with grace. He saw her and worked his way out of the game, saying, "You guys are too good for me."

"You pretty good for white bread," one of the guys called after him.

"Let's get on the road," Jake said, and then stopped, looking at Jeremy. He reached out and fingered the collar of Jeremy's red jacket, as if curious. "You're not gonna need that thing where we're going. I hear it's pretty warm there."

Kate interjected, "Leave him alone, Jake. It's his Darth Vader jacket. He's taking it."

Jake shrugged and got behind the wheel.

"Jeremy, you get in the middle," Kate said. She saw him turn and look back at the apartment. There was sorrow in him, and she put her hands on his shoulders. "Are you sad to leave?"

"I guess a little bit."

"I thought you'd be glad to leave here. You never liked it."

Jeremy looked up at her and for that moment he seemed even younger and more vulnerable than usual. "It may be worse where we're going."

"No, it won't. It can't be."

Jeremy got in holding his Game Boy in one hand, but when he slid over he uttered a startled cry. As Kate settled herself, she watched as Jake reached behind Jeremy and pulled out a gun.

"Do you have a permit for that?" Kate asked.

"No." Novak leaned over across Jeremy, opened the glove compartment, put the gun in, and shut it.

Jeremy was intrigued. "Did you ever shoot anyone?"

"Yes."

"Ever kill anyone?"

"I never killed anyone who didn't deserve it." Novak bit the words off, turned the key, and started the engine of the van. He shifted to drive and pulled out into the street.

Kate's ears had perked up at his answer, and it shocked her. Reaching into her purse, she pulled out her sunglasses and put them on. She noted that Novak had pulled a pair of aviator glasses out of the pocket of his shirt and donned them.

"Do you know how to get there?" she asked.

"I've got a map. All we do is take 78 out of Memphis all the way to Birmingham. We'll probably stop there for the night. Then we take 65 South almost all the way to the coast."

Jake reached down beneath the seat and pulled out a small CD player. Steering with one hand, he popped the earplug into his ear and dropped the player between himself and Jeremy. As he drove through the streets of Memphis, his head moved in cadence to the music. Jeremy started in on his Game Boy and was soon lost in his own world. Kate sat there, feeling alone and uneasy. She decided she could identify with how Abraham probably felt when he left Ur of the Chaldees for a place he hadn't even seen. He knew that God had spoken, but God hadn't given very specific instructions. Kate settled down for a long and quiet ride, knowing that there would not be a great deal of conversation between the driver and his passengers.

● ● ●

Novak had driven steadily southward on Highway 78 with absolutely no conversation whatsoever. Finally he said, "Look at that sign." Kate and Jeremy both looked up. A large sign said, *TUPELO, MISSISSIPPI—BIRTH-PLACE OF ELVIS PRESLEY.*

"Keep your eyes open, guys. We may see the ghost of Elvis," Novak said, his mouth twitching in a grin.

"Do you believe in ghosts, Jake?" Jeremy asked.

"Of course I don't." He waited and then turned and winked at the boy. "If you'd seen as many of the scoundrels as I have, you wouldn't believe in them, either."

Kate couldn't help smiling at this. "How much further to Birmingham?"

"Not far."

The *not far* turned out to be a three-hour drive, and by the time Novak pulled up in front of a Comfort Suites Hotel on the outskirts of Birmingham, Kate was exhausted. Whether the fatigue was mental or emotional or physical, she found impossible to say.

"Come on. We'll get us a couple of rooms," Jake said as he led the way inside, where he registered for two rooms, paying cash. When he got the keys, he handed one of them to Kate. He also counted out some money. "Here's five hundred dollars. I got a thousand from Bonhoffer in advance."

Kate took the money and stared at it. She swallowed hard contemplating how long she would have had to work for such a sum punching a cash register for a line of unending, ungrateful customers. "Thank you," she said.

"Don't thank me. It all comes from Miss Zophia." He led the way out to the truck, rolled up the back door, and glared sourly at the two carriers. "You're taking them in?"

"Of course." Kate reached out and struggled to pick up the carrier bearing Cleo. "They can't stay cooped up in the truck all night."

"Probably get us thrown out of here," Novak grumbled. He took the two carriers, saying, "You guys get your luggage. I'll take the illegal stuff inside. The cats will have to stay in your room, Mary Katherine. I don't want Jacques ripping my throat out while I'm asleep."

They fished their bags out of the back of the U-Haul and deposited them in the room. Kate arranged the litter boxes and the cat food she'd brought. She filled two large bowls with water. When she opened the carrier doors, both cats went for the litter boxes, then moved to the food.

Novak said, "Let's get out of here before they attack me. I saw a Chinese place down the way. Let's go eat."

"What if I don't like Chinese?"

Novak turned and stared at Kate. "Everybody likes Chinese." Then he shrugged and said, "We can go somewhere else."

"No," she said and managed a smile. "I really like Chinese. I just like to be asked."

Novak snorted and shook his head as if he couldn't fathom her words.

"You're not in the army now, Novak—I don't take orders," Kate said.

Novak grinned. "Well, partner, if Chinese suits you, let's go." He glanced back toward the room. "I hope Jacques the Ripper doesn't get out and eat the manager."

● ● ●

The meal had been interesting. The buffet had almost an infinite number of dishes, but Jake ordered duck off the menu. When he tasted it, Jeremy asked, "Is it good?"

"It's okay. I could cook it better."

"Do you cook a lot?"

"Yes." Novak noticed Jeremy looking puzzled. "You got a problem with that?"

"I just didn't think men cooked."

"The best cooks in the world are men. Go into any fine restaurant and the chef will be a man." He turned to Kate and lifted one heavy black brow. "How come you don't teach the kid things like that?"

"It never came up," Kate snapped. "Besides, I think he's right. Real men should build bridges and put out fires."

Her remark amused Novak. He grinned and winked at her. "The biggest wimp I ever met was a guy who designed bridges. And I knew a fireman once who was afraid of spiders. Gotta be careful with those stereotypes, Little Missy."

They finished their meal and he said, "They've got a nice indoor pool back at the hotel. Let's go for a swim."

"We don't have swimming suits." Kate replied.

"We'll get some. I saw a Wal-Mart down the way."

"I'm not sure I want to go swimming. It's kinda late."

"Sounds fun, Mom," Jeremy said. "Let's go!"

Kate looked at him. "All right. I suppose we'll need swimsuits when we get to the beach anyway."

● ● ●

Back at the room, Kate slipped into the one-piece black suit she had bought at Wal-Mart. She had tried on a bikini and had embarrassed herself. She had an innate modesty, and the black suit was the most appropriate she could find. She stepped out of the room to find Jeremy and Novak waiting for her.

Jake took one look at her bathing suit and grinned broadly. "Hey, Mary Katherine, your bathing suit's got a hole in the knee."

She knew he was making fun of the modest suit and ignored him. "Come on, Jeremy, let's see if you can remember the swimming lessons I gave you."

They found the indoor pool, and the two plunged in while Jake headed to the Jacuzzi. While Kate swam with Jeremy, keeping pace with him, she noticed a bottle-blonde wearing what looked like a pair of Band-Aids for a swimsuit sitting in the hot tub with Jake. She was laughing at something he said and leaning flirtatiously toward him. Kate looked the other way, a curious disappointment coming over her. *So he's a womanizer. I knew that the first time I saw him.*

For half an hour she swam with Jeremy, encouraging him. He had been afraid of the water when he was younger, but Kate had instilled in him some of her delight in swimming. Finally she came out and saw Novak sitting on the edge of the hot tub, still talking to the bikini bimbo. A sense of mischief stirred within her.

"How about a race, Jake?"

The young woman wearing the Band-Aids gave Jake a sharp look. "This your wife?"

"No, she's my sister."

"You don't look alike."

"Well, actually she's adopted. I'm the true blood."

Kate found this amusing. "So, how about it?"

Novak stared at her. "I don't want to embarrass you, Sister. I've told you a hundred times men are better swimmers than women."

"Suit yourself. I knew you'd chicken out."

Jake came to his feet, a smile creasing his lips. "All right. How much of a handicap you want?"

"Just watch yourself, that's all. I don't want to run over you when I lap you."

The two went to the end of the large pool. "Five laps?" she queried.

"Make it easy on yourself, Sister."

They both assumed the racing dive position, and Jake curled his toes over the edge of the concrete. "On three," he said. Then he counted, "One, two—" and then lunged out in a flat dive.

Kate was caught off guard, but she hit the water immediately after him. She caught up with him by the time they reached the end of the pool, and when she made a racing turn she was already ahead of him. She lapped him easily, and although he was a good swimmer he wasn't great. Kate had been on her high school swimming team and hadn't lost much of her speed in the dozen years since. She came out of the water in one smooth motion and was waiting for him when he finally reached the end of the pool. "You've got another lap to go," she taunted.

Jake emerged from the pool and stood for a moment toweling off. "I did that on purpose," he finally said.

"I'll give you a chance to beat me at something else—if we can find anything."

"How about we shoot a game of pool?"

"You can beat me at that, I'm sure. You probably spent your childhood hanging around pool halls while I was reading great books and listening to classical music." She looked over and said, "Better get back to your bimbo. I'm going to take a shower and watch TV. What time do you want to leave in the morning?"

"When you hear my knock on the door, you'll know it's time to go."

She laughed. "A control freak. I should have known. Your feelings are hurt, aren't they? You hate to get beat by a woman."

Jeremy came over, grinning at Jake. "Mom really beat you, didn't she, Jake?"

Novak was cavalier. "I let her win. Wouldn't want her to be embarrassed."

Kate laughed. "How gallant of you. I always forget what a gentleman you are, dear *brother*." She turned. "Come on, Jeremy. We'd better leave Jake to his lady friend."

● ● ●

The sun was just lighting the eastern skies when Kate opened the door at the sound of the knock. Novak stood there obviously expecting her to still be in bed, and she found his disappointment amusing. "We've been waiting for you," she said with a slight smirk. "Where have you been?"

"Been looking for a good place to eat," he said. "Come on. I've already checked us out."

"Aren't we going to eat in the restaurant here?"

"Nah, these motel breakfasts are no good. I'm sure we can find a truck stop with some decent grub."

The three loaded their bags and the cat carriers, got into the van, and drove down the highway. After a short time, Jake pulled up in front of a monstrous truck stop. The big eighteen-wheelers seemed to fill the world, and when they went inside, Novak nodded. "Food here should be pretty good."

"How do you know?" Kate asked. "You've never eaten here."

"Look. They've got three calendars on the wall."

Kate stared at the calendars that featured voluptuous young women in skimpy bathing suits.

"What's with all the calendars?" Jeremy asked. "Can't they remember the date with just one calendar?"

"Don't they teach you anything in school?" Jake asked and grinned. "You judge a truck stop by the number of calendars on the wall. If they don't have any calendars, forget it. You'll get ptomaine poisoning. Two calendars, you can keep the food down, but three or more calendars—that's first rate!"

The restaurant was crowded mostly with husky-looking men wearing jeans and T-shirts. One of the booths was empty, and they grabbed it. A waitress walked up, asking "Ya'll want coffee?" She was a buxom woman in her mid-twenties. She had a smear of ketchup over her right pocket next to a name tag that said "Jenni," and her fingernails were chewed down to the quick, but she was cheerful enough. "Ya'll wanna' order now?"

"Decaf for me," Kate said. "And do you have any hot chocolate?"

"Sure, Honey, we got it. What about you, Hon?" She smiled at Jake.

"Coffee."

"You want sugar or cream?"

"Real men don't use that stuff. And I'll have an omelet." He gave explicit instructions on how the omelet was to be prepared, and the waitress grinned at him. "Sounds like maybe you'd better come back and cook it, Hon."

"I'll do that if the first one doesn't suit me. Tell the cook there's a discerning customer out here, Jenni."

Jeremy ordered pancakes and Kate requested bacon and eggs. She asked for turkey bacon, which was not available so she changed her order to ham. "Bring me some grits, too," she added.

After the waitress left, Jake said, "Maybe I ought to try a grit. Get used to this Southern cooking."

"Try a grit? You can't have a single grit!"

"Why can't I?"

"Because it doesn't come like that. It would be like having one oatmeal or a bean."

He laughed and said, "Sounds like I may have to have some good Yankee food flown in once in awhile. I've heard about this Southern cooking—stuff like pig innards."

After Jenni left, Jeremy said, "Tell me about being in the army, Jake. What's it like?"

"You wouldn't like it, Slick."

"Slick?"

"Just a name. You look slick. It's a compliment. My granddad told me it's what Whitey Ford called Mickey Mantle."

Jeremy looked disconcerted at this. "Who's Whitey Ford?"

Jake winked and said, "Better bone up on your baseball history, Kid. But I think Slick suits you."

Suddenly Jeremy smiled. "Okay. You can call me Slick. I never had a nickname before. Do you have one, Jake?"

"Sure. Everyone calls me Good Lookin'."

Kate rolled her eyes.

Thirty minutes later, the three were just finishing their meal when two big bikers entered. They were both loud and had redneck written all over them. They sat down in the booth next to where the three were sitting, and one of them looked around and whispered to Kate, "Hey, Sweetheart, why don't you dump this guy and come out with a real man?"

Kate ignored him. She had learned to disregard such things a long time ago. She glanced at Novak, who seemed to be paying no attention. At that moment the waitress came, and Jake said, "I'm still hungry. I think I'll have a bowl of cornflakes with two percent milk."

"Sure, Hon." The waitress scurried off, and one of the bikers laughed roughly. "You sure you can stand the excitement of all them cornflakes, Junior?"

At that moment the other biker made a raw comment about Kate. Something seemed to change in Novak's face. It was not that his features changed but his hazel eyes glowed with some sort of incandescent light. He turned around in his seat and studied the two and then said mildly, "I would appreciate it if you two would watch your language."

"You gonna slap my wrists?" the bigger of the two asked.

"No. I'm not going to slap your wrists. I'm going to hurt you severely."

The waitress came up hurriedly, saying, "Mike, you and Pete behave yourselves." She turned to Kate and said, "I'm sorry, Hon. Just don't pay them no attention. They got no manners."

"Aw, Jenni, don't say that." The bigger of the two men was angry. "It's a free country. I can say anything I want."

Jenni looked at Novak. He had gotten out of his seat and something she saw in his face made her back away. "Don't pay 'em no attention," she repeated nervously.

Novak moved to stand over the two. His voice was low and calm. "I think you two had better go find another place to eat."

The pair stared at Novak, and then looked at each other and laughed. They both outweighed Novak by at least twenty pounds, and they had big bellies and battered faces that spoke of lives spent fighting and rough-housing. The one called Pete turned to Kate and started to say, "Well, look at that body on that filly. I especially like—"

He never finished his words because Jake hit him in the throat with the edge of his hand in a movement almost too quick to be seen. Pete grabbed his throat, gagging for breath, his eyes bugging out. The other guy flew out of his seat, throwing a roundhouse right that Novak blocked with his left hand and then hit the bigger man a fierce blow far below the belt. It made a thudding sound, and the biker doubled up and immediately fell to the floor in the fetal position.

Jake glanced at Kate and Jeremy. "Finished eating?" he inquired in a mild tone, smiling slightly.

Kate couldn't speak. The violence had exploded as suddenly as a bomb going off. She got up without a word and watched as Jake took some bills out and tossed them on the table. He looked down at the man on the floor who was still making odd noises and at the one who was trying to breathe. "Have a nice day, guys," he said pleasantly.

When they were in the truck, Jake said, "The food wasn't as good as some truck stops, but it wasn't bad. Maybe tonight we can find some good sea-food. There ought to be at least one good restaurant there on the coast."

Neither Kate nor Jeremy said a word. Finally Jeremy spoke. "Uh, Jake, were you scared?"

"Scared of what, Slick?"

"Of those two men."

"Them? No."

Novak began whistling a tune under his breath and started the truck.

"Have you ever been scared of anyone?" Jeremy asked.

"Well, I was scared of my mom when I was about your age, but she was tougher than those two guys." He turned and smiled. "Those weren't really bad guys. They were all talk. No need to be scared of people like that."

Kate had wondered from the time she had seen Jake Novak what kind of man he was. Now she knew. A violence lay in him that needed only a spark to set it off. She had seen it in the way he moved and in his hazel eyes. Violence had flared out with all the suddenness of a land mine. She stared out the window as the scenery flew by and wondered how she could possibly put her life and Jeremy's together with such a man.

Five

Jake drove steadily after taking Interstate 65 south out of Birmingham. When they reached Montgomery, they saw a sign that said: *First Home of the Confederacy*.

"Do you want to stop and see how the losers celebrate?" Jake asked, grinning.

"No, I don't," Kate said. "I'm anxious to get there."

"All right." He passed the exit and pushed on the accelerator, speeding up to 70. "Not really much to see on these interstates," he said. "Anything interesting is on the old Blue Highways, as they used to be called."

Ten minutes later he said, "We don't go to Mobile. We turn off here on 59." He made a turn, and they got on a four-lane highway. They passed through a small town called Bay Minette. Fifteen minutes later they went under Interstate 10 and began going through a series of small towns: Loxley, Robertsdale, Summerdale, Foley.

"White Sands next stop," Jake finally announced.

They came to an arching bridge, and as soon as they crossed it, they saw a sign that said: *Beaches This Way*.

Jake drove straight down through the middle of town until finally Highway 59 dead-ended in the Gulf of Mexico. Jake made a left turn and said, "This is Highway 182, the Beach Highway."

The Beach Highway, for the most part, was lined with condominiums that crowded the Gulf area. It was difficult to see the Gulf itself, but finally they got clear of downtown White Sands and Jake said, "There's only three towns on the Alabama Gulf. White Sands is one. Orange Beach and Gulf

Shores are the others. They're about five miles apart, I guess. Our place is just about halfway between them."

"How will you know it?"

"Bonhoffer gave us a picture. It's in the folder."

Kate opened the glove compartment, saw the gun, and ignored it. She pulled out an envelope and extracted an eight by ten picture. It showed a two-story aqua-colored house with white trim sitting all by itself. Behind it the Gulf spread out, and the picture apparently had been taken late in the afternoon because the sun was setting.

"Where are the rest of the houses?" Jeremy asked.

"Miss Zophia's family bought seven lots decades ago when they were cheap. They built the house right in the middle of them so there'd be room on each side. Pretty smart. The lots are worth a lot of money now."

Suddenly Kate said, "Look! That's it, isn't it?"

All three of them looked and there it was. The house was the most brilliant aqua possible, with gleaming white shutters and trim.

"It's beautiful!" she whispered.

"First thing we do is paint that sucker," Novak said, disgust in his voice. "Looks like a New Orleans cathouse."

"I like it," Kate said stubbornly. "We're *not* going to paint it."

Jake turned into the long driveway and nodded toward a man working in the yard. "Looks like the handyman is here."

Jake pulled up in front of the house alongside a four-wheel drive Ram pickup with a Confederate flag emblem on the bumper and a .30-.30 Winchester across the back window. The rig also had a bumper sticker that said, *Welcome, Yankees—Now Go Home!*

"Makes you feel kind of warm and welcome, doesn't it, Mary Katherine?"

The yardman turned and walked slowly toward them, holding a pair of clippers in his hands. "You must be the folks goin' be livin' here."

"I guess so. I'm Jake Novak. This is Mary Katherine Forrest and her son, Jeremy."

The gardener was tall and angular with a lantern jaw and a pair of light-blue eyes. His hair was orange-red and his lower lip was packed with what appeared to be snuff. It showed itself in the corners of his mouth. He stared at Jake and said, "You ain't from 'round here, are you?"

"Chicago."

"Ya'll won't like it here none."

Jake stared at the man and laughed. "What makes you think so?"

"This ain't Yankee country."

"Well, I'll do my best to acclimate myself."

"I'm Orsino Gates. Folks just call me Pearly. I'll be glad to be shut of this job."

"You're quitting? You don't want to take care of the place?"

"I'll take keer of the outside, but I don't want inside with them varmints."

"Oh, Miss Zophia's pets?" Kate asked.

"You kin call 'em pets if you've got a mind to. Pests, more like it. They're goin' ta kill somebody one of these days."

"Oh, come on, Gates. They can't be that bad."

Pearly sniffed and studied Jake with disdain. "Ya'll go on in. You'll see. I'll take keer of the outside work if you want, but I ain't fiddling with them animals no more—especially that dawg."

"Uh, I think we'd better leave Jacques and Cleo in the truck until we've had a look inside," Kate said. She looked at the house with trepidation and shrugged. "Well, let's have a look."

The three went up the steps, and Jake opened the door. He stepped back and Kate started in, but the way was blocked by a stubborn-looking white dog with black markings. He was growling deep in his throat, and Jake warned, "Look out, Mary Katherine. That's a pit bull!"

Kate stood absolutely still for a moment. She'd always loved dogs and had worked during her high school days as a groomer at the local vet's office. Now she took a step forward. Holding out her hand, she was absolutely still. The big pit bull stared at her and the growl rumbled low in his throat. When she didn't move, he came forward and sniffed at her hand. Kate remained motionless until finally he licked her hand. She laughed and stroked his broad forehead. "You're just a bluff. What's your name?"

"His name's Trouble!" Pearly Gates yelled. He had come to the lower steps to stare at them, warning, "He'll take yer hand off at the wrist!"

Trouble looked up into Kate's face, then moved closer—and sat down on her feet.

"I've never seen a dog who loves to sit on feet." Kate laughed. "Come and pet him, Jeremy."

Jeremy cautiously advanced and gingerly touched the dog's head. Kate looked over at Novak.

"You'd better make friends with him, Jake," Kate said.

"You kiddin'? I'm not making friends with a killer dog."

"Don't be foolish. He won't hurt you." But Jake shook his head and finally Kate said, "Well, let's go in." She led the way and noticed that the walls were lined with fish tanks filled with tropical fish. Along one wall were two enormous bird cages filled with brilliantly colored birds.

A sudden flash of color fluttered down from the vaulted ceiling and a raucous voice shouted an obscene phrase.

"That's Bad Louie," Pearly said from the doorway. "You'll wish parrots couldn't talk 'fore long. He cusses like a sailor."

"Why does he use such terrible words?" Kate asked.

"He was raised by a buncha construction workers. You know how they talk! Bad Louie jist says whut he heard."

Jake grinned. "Sounds like my kinda bird." He looked down and exclaimed, "What's wrong with that rabbit?"

"Oh, that's Miss Boo." Pearly shrugged. "Dunno whut's wrong with her ears. They just kind of flop down. Reckon she was born that way."

Kate bent over and stroked the silky fur of the rabbit, which did indeed have floppy ears. "I've seen this breed in pet stores. I think she's cute."

"She ain't long for this world," Pearly said. "She loves to chew on lamp cords. Been knocked silly more than once."

Jake was moving around the room and stopped to stare at a very large glass cage. "What's this? There aren't any animals—" He broke off and scrambled backward. "That's a snake!" he yelped.

Pearly giggled, a strange high-pitched sound. "That there is Big Bertha. Ain't she a doozy?"

"I hate snakes," Jake muttered.

"I think she's beautiful," Kate said. She moved closer and read the brass plate. "She's an albino Burmese python."

"She's part of the breed that got us kicked out of the Garden of Eden!" Jake said stiffly. "I'm not feeding that thing!"

Jake edged away from the snake and Jeremy said, "Look at that, Mom!" Kate and Jake saw what Jeremy was pointing at—a full-grown raccoon. He came through a door and stood there looking up at them.

"That there's Bandit." Pearly grinned. He had stepped just inside the front door and was evidently enjoying their reactions. "He'll git into everything you let him into. He got in the kitchen once and opened every jar and everything else he could find. Biggest mess you ever see!"

"He's so adorable!" Kate exclaimed. "They look like burglars wearing masks."

"I heard they carry hydrophobia," Novak said sourly, but on Jeremy's questioning look, he clarified, "Rabies." The coon watched them and then scurried out. There was a swinging door cut low in the wall that apparently gave the animals freedom to enter and leave the house.

"There's a weasel, too. Her name's Abigail," Pearly said. "Why anybody'd want to keep a weasel, I don't know."

"A weasel? You must mean a ferret," Kate said. "They're so cute."

Pearly grinned, exposing several missing teeth. "A coupla birds over there in the smaller cage," he said and pointed. "Romeo and Julio, or some such thing."

Kate looked at the tag on the birds' cage. "Romeo and Juliet!" she exclaimed. "They're love birds! How precious!"

Pearly snorted. "I ain't comin' in here no more. You can take keer of these. It's a dad-blasted zoo, thet's whut it is."

After Pearly left, they explored the house. Downstairs they found an enormous room that opened on to a spacious dining area and airy kitchen. There were two large bedrooms, each with its own luxurious bath.

The kitchen interested Jake. It had obviously been recently renovated and was state of the art, with granite countertops, stainless steel Viking appliances, and a sizeable center island. He nodded. "Sweet. This is gonna do just fine."

"Let's see what's on the second floor."

The upper level was a pleasant surprise. It had a roomy living area and a single bedroom that faced out on the Gulf, with an attached bathroom and whirlpool. There was also a balcony with beach furniture and a glass-top table. Jake announced, "This'll be mine."

"That will work fine," Kate said. "You'll have the upstairs, and we'll take the downstairs."

"We'll have to share the kitchen though."

"Yes, and we'll all have to take care of the animals."

"Fine. I'll help with Zophia's animals, but I'm not having anything to do with your stupid Jacques! Or the snake." Then, as a peace offering, Jake added, "Tell you what I will do, though. I'll fix us up a nice supper."

"Oh, let's don't do that tonight. We don't have any food anyway. Let's go out for some fresh seafood," Kate said.

"Sounds good to me," Jake said. "I guess I can cook tomorrow."

"Before we go out, I think I'd better introduce Jacques and Cleo to their new home."

"Ha! Jacques will probably put most of these pets in the animal hospital," Jake remarked, but he helped by carrying Jacques's carrier into the house. Kate brought Cleo's carrier in and set it down. Jake backed off.

"You can let them out, Mary Katherine," he said. "Can't wait to see Jacques and that pit bull have at it."

Pearly was still hanging around the front door, and his eyes widened as Kate opened the door of the carrier and Jacques came out. "That a baby tiger?" he whispered. "I never seed such a cat!" He slowly backed away and finally wheeled and scooted off, slamming the door behind him.

Jacques immediately spotted Trouble and began to stalk him. Trouble growled deep in his throat, but didn't move. "Be nice to the doggie, Jacques," Kate said apprehensively. Jacques continued to advance, and Trouble got up and went behind Kate. He looked around her legs, and when Jacques stopped a few inches away, he poked his nose forward, and the two animals touched noses.

"Well, dang!" Jake exclaimed, shock evident on his features. "Will you look at that? What a wimp!"

"They like each other," Kate said firmly. "Pit bulls have a bad reputation, but Trouble is sweet."

Novak was disgusted. "You're a *wuss,* Trouble!" he snorted. "I'm going to report you to the Cowardly Dog Association."

"He's like most males," Kate said, smiling triumphantly. "Tough on the outside but soft on the inside. Now, let's unload Cleo."

Cleo came out, looked around, and immediately started cleaning herself. She was as calm as she could be.

"Well, that's that," Kate announced. "Let's unpack."

Kate drafted Pearly to help unload the furniture, and when the job was done, she gave him a twenty-dollar tip. "Thanks for helping us, Pearly," she said.

"Wal, now, Miz Forrest, I figure you won't be stayin' long, so I want to be hospitable." He turned to go, then stopped and turned. "If you ain't left by Sunday, Ya'll might like to visit our church. I'm one of the elders, don't you see."

"What kind of church is it?" Kate asked.

"It's over on 98, just north of Lillian. Name of it is Fire Baptized Two-Seed-in-the-Spirit Deliverance Church. Had a time gettin' all that on the sign!"

"Is it a large church?" Kate asked.

"Used to be, but we had some splits, so it ain't too big now. Ya'll come, you hear?" He started to leave, but then faced Novak. "You can't wear no necktie," he said firmly. "Them neck rags is the sign of the Antichrist. If you wear one, me and the other elders will have to deliver you of it. Ya'll come, you hear?"

As soon as Pearly Gates roared off in his pickup, Novak turned to Kate, saying, "Well, dang! We can't go there. I promised my mother I'd always wear a necktie in church. Come on, I'm starved!"

They piled into the van and drove down the Beach Highway until Novak pulled up in front of a restaurant called Zeke's. He led them inside, and they all had delicious deep-fried catfish with the customary Southern trimmings. Novak wanted to give the cook a few tips on how to prepare the fish, but Kate talked him out of it.

On the way back they stopped for groceries, a comedy in itself as Jake and Kate each loaded their own carts and smirked at each other's choices. After they returned to the house and put the groceries away, Kate was delighted to find Abigail, the ferret, who came out to make friends. Her little face and bright eyes portrayed an unexpected intelligence. Jeremy took to her right away. "She can sleep with me, Mom," he said.

"If she wants to, I guess," Kate said.

"And you can sleep with Jacques the Ripper, Kate," Jake said.

"And how about you sleeping with Cleo?"

"I'm not sleeping with any animals. I'll feed the fish and take care of some of the birds—tomorrow. Good night."

At that, Jake turned and went upstairs without another word.

"Sheesh, he's sure grouchy sometimes," Jeremy said. He was holding Abigail in his hands and discovered he could almost tie her in a knot. "Look how flexible she is!" he whispered with delight. He put her on his shoulder, and she started sniffing him. "Her whiskers tickle!"

● ● ●

As soon as he got upstairs, Jake stripped his clothes off, got into the whirlpool, and soaked. He loved whirlpools, but he believed they did make a man weak. Finally he crawled out, dried off, and put on a pair of shorts and a T-shirt. He went out on the balcony to look at the ocean. He admired the line of light the moon reflected. Jake remembered this was what the Vikings had called the Whale's Way. He stood there for a long time and took a deep breath with satisfaction. "This isn't going to be bad. Not bad at all."

Going to the bed, Jake pulled the covers off except for one sheet, got in, and relaxed. He was tired and content and drifted peacefully. But just as he was about to fall into a deep sleep, he felt something touch his leg.

"What the—" He turned on the light, and what he saw brought a hoarse yell of terror. He fell out of the bed and stumbled into the side table with the glass top. It went over with a tremendous crash. Jake scrambled to his feet and moved to press his back against the wall, calling, "Uhh...Mary Katherine!" He stood there hearing footsteps on the stairs, and when Kate and Jeremy burst through the door, he pointed. "There's a snake in my bed!"

Kate stared at the snake that was coiled there and said, "It's just Big Bertha. She won't hurt anybody."

"Get...that...thing...out!"

Kate turned to Jeremy. "Run downstairs and get me one of the packing boxes." Jeremy took off, and Kate turned to Jake. "There must be an opening in Big Bertha's cage that I didn't notice. You know they're nocturnal, so it's not unusual for them to wander at night. She obviously found a nice warm place to sleep!"

Kate was grinning at Jake, but he just looked at her in disbelief. Jeremy returned with a box, and she gently lifted Big Bertha and laid her inside.

"I'll go make sure her cage is secure. Jeremy, will you carry Big Bertha for me?" Kate turned back to Jake. "She's just a baby, Jake," she said. She couldn't restrain a smile. "I think she likes you."

But Jake's face was pale as paste, and his lips were trembling. "I can't stand snakes! Get him out of here, Mary Katherine!"

Kate started to speak but saw that it would be useless. She left, but Jeremy paused, staring at Jake as he picked up the box. "I didn't think you were scared of anything." There was a trace of disappointment in his voice.

Jake Novak, who had once gone into a dead-end alley after a drug-crazed kid armed with a .45, and who had rescued a downed Blackhawk pilot from Islamic terrorists, was trembling. He looked at his hands and clasped them together to stop the shaking. Finally he looked up and through lips that seemed frozen, he whispered, "Ophidiophobia. Had it all my life."

At Jeremy's questioning look, Jake just shook his head. "We're all scared of something, Slick."

Six

The first gray light of dawn filtered through the large windows at the end of the house, striking Jacques, who had found his place for the night on top of the Bose stereo that Jake had managed to retrieve from the pawnshop before leaving Chicago. As soon as the murky light touched him, Jacques's eyes flew open. They were large, golden, and round as saucers. For a brief moment he lay there stretching his body, then reached out all four legs, unsheathing his impressive claws. He got to his feet, yawned mightily, and leaped lightly down to the floor. He was, for all his impressive bulk, as agile and quick-moving as any smaller cat. Although the house was new to him, he was stirred by faint memories of the apartment that had been his home for so long. He had a brief flash of a bowl of food and padded across the tile floor past the island, before stopping abruptly. His lips drew back, and he uttered a warning hiss.

Bandit, the coon, lifted his head from the bowl and stared with alarm at the black cat, every bit as large as himself. The Science Diet he was gorging on was not his usual fare, but it was good and he wasn't about to give it up. Looking for all the world like his namesake—a miniature bandit with a perfectly shaped black mask highlighting his black eyes—he glared at Jacques. Cautiously Bandit moved forward and picked up a nugget of the Science Diet and was about to put it into his mouth.

Jacques the Ripper was merely a flash as he leaped forward and swiped at Bandit. The tip of his saber-like claws caught Bandit on the nose, and the startled coon gave a frightened grunt, whirled, and scrambled across the tile floor to the animal door. He hit it full-speed and disappeared, leaving the door swinging and making a creaky sound.

Jacques looked at the door with satisfaction. *That'll teach that overgrown squirrel to eat out of my dish!* He turned to the bowl and found it empty save for five small fragments. His tail switched back and forth disgusted. He moved smoothly out of the kitchen and toward one of the bedroom doors. Shoving it open, he moved inside and, with one smooth, fluid motion, leaped up on the bed. He had heard his Person say many times that it was amazing no matter how far a cat leaped, it always leaped to exactly the right height and not one centimeter over. If he could have answered, Jacques would have said, *Of course we do. Why leap higher than necessary?*

The cover was drawn back and for a moment Jacques stared at his sleeping Person. He was not a particularly affectionate animal—obviously—but if there was anything he did have a fondness for, it was the woman who lay there on her back, her lips slightly open, breathing evenly. It was not so much that she fed him the glorious tuna packed in spring water—he could have foraged for himself and had often done so. But somehow from the very murky memories of his kittenhood, Jacques remembered this woman taking him in when his previous Person no longer wanted him. At times Jacques felt rather ashamed of this feeling of attachment, or whatever it was, but now he moved forward and without preamble put his front paws on her chest and began rhythmically kneading her in the familiar manner cats have.

Instantly his Person's eyes flew open, and she cried out, "Jacques, you always scare me to death when you do that!"

Indeed, why should you be scared? I do it every morning.

Jacques began to purr as he continued to knead. The material of Kate's upper garment was thin, and his claws dug through it so that she cried out, "That hurts!" Jacques paid not the least attention while she fussed at him except to retract his claws so that he was mainly pushing against her with his soft pads. Jacques could not have said why he performed this ceremony. It was just something he did and that people had to put up with. His eyes were half closed with the pleasure of the act, and for a time Kate simply lay there rubbing the big cat's head.

Suddenly her eyes went to the clock and she whispered in alarm, "Oh, murder!" She shoved Jacques to one side, filling him with indignation, and jumped out of bed. Without pausing to grab a robe she left the bedroom. She was wearing a pair of worn shorts and an oversized Fruit of the Loom

T-shirt—a sleeping outfit not found in any Neiman Marcus catalog, but it was comfortable.

Without pausing she sailed into Jeremy's room and began shaking him. "Jeremy, wake up! We're late!"

"What?" Jeremy muttered. He came to a sitting position and shoved her away, confused. He was a hard sleeper and even harder to come out of sleep.

"Wake up, Honey. You need to go take your shower while I fix breakfast."

Understanding dawned on Jeremy, and his lips turned downward in a scowl. "Aw, Mom, there's only a few weeks left of school. Nobody would even miss me if I didn't go."

"You're going to school, Jeremy. You'll meet some friends. Now get out of that bed and get ready."

Kate flew out of the bedroom and went to the kitchen. She began pulling things together for a quick breakfast by buttering bread and throwing it into the Munsey toaster. Neither she nor Jeremy could stand using pop-up toasters, but they loved hot buttered toast cooked in the Munsey oven. She jerked the door of the double refrigerator open, pulled out a carton of orange juice, and had the usual struggle opening it. Finally she poured two glasses full and drank half of hers. She searched for the oatmeal that she'd put away so well she couldn't find it.

As she scurried around frantically, trying to organize her day, she felt a touch of uneasiness. Jeremy wasn't good with people, and she was apprehensive about throwing him into a new school. But it had to be done.

● ● ●

Jake had slept fitfully, but he awoke abruptly when something soft touched his lips.

Snake!

The first thought was that the python was back in bed with him. He stiffened with fear. His eyes flew open and relief washed through him when he saw Cleo sitting beside him. He closed his eyes and felt the soft touch again. Moving his head, he stared at the big cat who was reaching forward.

"What are you doing?" he muttered irritably. "Trying to claw my eyeballs out?" He moved his head slightly, then surprise ran through him. The blasted cat actually seemed to smile at him! The corners of her lips turned up and her white, razor-sharp teeth were exposed in a grin.

Despite himself Jake had to smile, and then he laughed aloud. He reached out and stroked the thick, silky fur. "Well, I'll be dipped in gravy," he said. "Can't believe it. The only cat with a smile I ever heard of was the Cheshire cat." As a writer he would always file strange, unusual things in his mind for later inclusion in books. He knew that sooner or later a smiling cat would appear in something he wrote.

He lay there for a moment and was caught by the light that was coming in through the large windows. Getting out of bed, he pulled on his new swim trunks and a T-shirt with the sleeves cut off. He moved to the window and studied the Gulf, feeling a sense of possession. He had a place now. This house—despite the woman and the boy and the menagerie—this house was his place.

Then he had a desire for a glorious breakfast. Padding barefoot, he left his apartment, walked down the stairs, and entered the kitchen door. As soon as he stepped inside, he heard a shriek, and he looked over to see Kate looking in the refrigerator.

"I'm not dressed! Get out of here!"

Jake stared at her thoughtfully. "Something is burning," he said.

Kate's face was crimson. "You can't come in before I get dressed."

"That toast is going to set the house on fire," he said. He walked over and pulled the tray out of the toaster and stared at the blackened remnants. "What were you planning on, a burnt offering for breakfast?"

Kate turned and stalked past him to her bedroom. Apparently she wasn't accustomed to men walking in on her when she wasn't properly dressed. She called out over her shoulder, "You can either feed the animals or fix breakfast, Novak."

"I'll fix breakfast," he said as he looked down at the toast. "You're not doing such a great job of it."

He looked around and saw that Trouble had materialized and was watching him thoughtfully. "Hello, Trouble," he said. "You want some burnt toast?" He offered the dog one of the blackened pieces of bread. Trouble said, "Woof!" and turned his head away.

"Don't blame you. That woman obviously doesn't know how to cook."

Jake immediately rearranged Kate's plan. He took one look at the store-bought carton of orange juice, poured it down the sink, and removed a sack of oranges he had purchased the previous day. He squeezed the juice into a glass pitcher and began creating one of his favorite breakfasts—omelets a la fiesta. As he chopped ripe tomatoes, bell peppers, and just a touch of jalapeno peppers, a look of peace touched his rough face. In between steps of making the omelets, he looked for some coffee but all he could find was instant. He stared at it with utter disdain, threw it in the garbage can, and said, "That's one thing that'll have to change around here."

By the time he had the omelets ready, the rolls warmed, and real butter on the table, Kate and Jeremy came scurrying in.

"Did you make coffee?" she said.

"There isn't any."

"Yes, there is. It was right there in the shelf."

"I threw it away."

Kate stared at him. "What do you mean you threw it away? That was my coffee."

"We're not having any instant around here. It's not even coffee."

"I like it."

"Well, you can fish it out of the garbage if you want. But I recommend you leave it. The only way to have coffee is to get the beans, grind them up, and brew it fresh. I'll pick up a machine and some beans today. Sit down and eat."

Kate stared at him, about to reply, but was distracted when Jeremy said, "Mom, I don't want to go to school."

"Stop whining, Jeremy. You're *going* to school."

"I think I said that every day of my life until I was eighteen." Jake grinned. "It'll be all right, Slick. You'll have a good time." He moved over to the stove, removed the cover from the skillet, and came over and put three omelets on the plates.

Jeremy stared at it. "What's *this*? It looks like cow flop."

A sudden flash of color appeared in the form of Bad Louie, the parrot. He had flown in and lit on the kitchen cabinet and began screaming, "Cow flop! Cow flop!"

Kate giggled. "I guess we'd better watch what we say around here. Bad Louie seems to catch on pretty quick." Indeed, the parrot with gorgeous hues seemed to have a diabolical gift for language, especially anything slang or crude.

Jeremy was picking at his omelet. "I won't eat this stuff."

Jake reached over, picked up the plate, and slid the omelet onto his own plate. "More for me then."

"Jake, you can't eat his breakfast!" Kate protested.

"Sure I can. He doesn't want it."

Kate stared at Jake with something that looked like disbelief. "What kind of a man are you to eat a boy's breakfast on his first day of school?"

"A hungry one. You missed your chance, Jeremy Forrest." He leaned over and began to eat. Kate stared at him, and then turned to Jeremy. "Here, have some of these rolls and strawberry jam."

Jeremy sullenly ate the rolls, and Jake noticed that Kate wolfed down her omelet. She kept glancing at Jake, and it seemed to him she might be irritated that he was a good cook.

"I've got to take Jeremy and get him registered for school," she said as she finished. She got up and said, "You'll have to take care of the litter boxes—of which I noticed there are several. Come on, Jeremy."

The two left, Jeremy protesting vehemently that he didn't want to go to school. Jake sat back putting fig preserves on a roll. "I've got to get some real figs," he muttered. "This store-bought stuff is no good." He got up, cleaned up the kitchen, put everything back in place, and then went looking for the litter boxes. He paused to stare at Miss Boo, the brown rabbit with floppy ears. "No self-respecting rabbit has ears like that," he commented sourly. "And don't let me catch you eating the insulation off lamp cords!"

Jake studied the litter boxes carefully and looked at both Jacques and Cleo, who were watching him intently. "We've got the world's biggest litter box out there and you've got a cat door. From now on you guys go outside to do your business." He took the litter boxes outside and threw them into the plastic trash container, satisfied that he'd settled the litter box problem forever. Then he walked down toward the beach.

The sandy strip was empty. Novak was aware, with regret, that there was no way he could keep people off his part of the beach. It was public property and this was America, so anyone could walk back and forth. However, the only person he saw was an elderly man sitting in a plastic chair with a fishing rod stuck into a holder.

Jake studied him for a moment then, eager for a swim, he ran into the surf. He hit it full-speed then fell headlong and was pleased that the water seemed just the right bracing temperature. He was a powerful swimmer, if not a fast one, and had always thought of swimming as the best exercise known to man. For the next ten minutes he flung himself into it, and when he came in he was puffing and gasping for breath. He came up onto the sand enjoying the feel of the beach and then wished he had brought a towel.

For a moment he stood there thinking what a glorious thing this was. He wasn't going to miss Chicago in the least. This beach and this house were better than anything he had ever dreamed. For a few moments he stood there, and then he walked over to where the old man was sitting. "Catch anything?" he asked.

For a long moment the man didn't answer, and Jake had the startling thought, *Maybe he's dead!* because the man hadn't moved. But then the fisherman swiveled his head around and studied him. He had a pair of icy gray eyes with a wrinkled face topped by a Boston Red Sox baseball cap. "Caught two."

"Two what?" Jake asked.

"Sharks."

Jake blinked. "Sharks, eh? You don't eat them, do you?"

"Nope. I kill 'em. What's your name?"

"Jake Novak."

"I'm Sid Valentino."

"Valentino like the movie star?"

"Right. That's me." The man turned his head back toward the surf.

Apparently the conversation was over. Jake padded back up toward the house, washed up under the outside shower, then went inside. He walked back upstairs, leaving footprints marking his trail, and dried off with a huge, fluffy towel a disgusting shade of pink. "*That's* got to change," he muttered. He went over to the laptop on his desk.

He had arranged his writing space so that he could look out at the Gulf, and now he sat down, opened the laptop, and for a moment sat there filled with peace and contentment. He looked out the window and saw a flight of pelicans in the familiar V-shaped formation. The sight always pleased him. He wondered, "How do they decide who gets to be the lead guy?" He watched the pelicans until they were gone and then put his hands on the keyboard. "Anybody," he said to Cleo, who had followed him upstairs and was now watching him with her large bluish eyes, "anybody can write the Great American Novel with a set-up like this, right Cleo?"

• • •

Hope Barclay was a pleasant surprise. Kate had gone through the drill at the office of White Sands Middle School and had been directed to Miss Barclay's classroom. She would be Jeremy's homeroom teacher and his counselor. They had found Miss Barclay between classes, and the woman proved to be very welcoming. She had chestnut hair with golden glints in it, large expressive brown eyes, and a fantastic figure. She listened while Kate explained their arrival from Memphis.

"This will be quite a cultural shock for you, Jeremy." Miss Barclay smiled. She had a warm smile and was very quick indeed. She could see that Jeremy was unhappy and added quickly, "Always hard to change schools. I came here from the West Coast, and it was hard for me. But you'll do fine, Jeremy."

"They don't like Yankees here, do they?"

"Well, they do call this place the Redneck Riviera, and I guess there's some truth to that. Where are you living?"

Kate spoke up. "We've got a house on the beach. It's down there...well, it's near some other houses but kind of sits by itself."

"It's blue," Jeremy chimed in. "Bright blue."

"Oh, you bought Zophia's place!"

"Well, we inherited it. Distant relatives."

"I knew Zophia. She was a fine lady. Loved animals better than anybody I ever saw. I met her at the vet, actually."

"You have dogs?"

"One dog, one cat."

"Well, we've got a house full of animals now, so we'll probably be seeing you at the vet's office."

Kate and the teacher sat talking for a few more minutes, and then Hope managed to draw Jeremy into the conversation. Kate was surprised to see how easily her son was taken with Hope.

"If you're church-goers," Hope said, "let me be the first to invite you to mine. It's called Seaside Chapel. It's right on the beach." She gave directions, and Kate said, "Thanks. We'd like to come and visit."

"Actually you could be a big help. We're trying to start something up for the teens and twenty-somethings, a beach ministry with maybe a coffee-house. Kids around here desperately need a place to hang out. A safe place," she added. "If you live on the beach, maybe you could host us...if I'm not being too presumptuous."

"No, I'd like to help," Kate said quickly.

A bell rang, and Hope said, "Time for English class." She turned and winked at Jeremy. "I know you're anxious to get started diagramming complex sentences."

"No way—I can't do that!"

"I can't either. I think it's foolishness. Come on. We're going to see a film today about Charles Dickens. You'll like it. Dickens was an interesting man." She turned and put her hand out to Kate. "I hope I see you at church. Jeremy will get along just fine. I'll keep an eye on him."

"Thank you, Miss Barclay," Kate said, relieved that Jeremy's transfer might not prove so traumatic after all.

If the other teachers were anything like Hope, Jeremy would have a good chance to become a part of things. She got into the Taurus and spent the rest of the morning driving around, familiarizing herself with White Sands and its sister town, Orange Beach.

The lifeline of the Gulf Coast, she had already discovered, was the narrow strip of white sand that composed the beach. Highway 182, called The Beach Road by locals, followed the coastline as closely as possible. On the south side condos and beach houses faced the sparkling aqua-green waters of the Gulf. Hugging the highway on the north side were the oyster bars, fish houses, taverns, shops, and liquor stores—along with cheaply built condos to handle visitors. This narrow strip dominated by tourist attractions seemed cheap and gaudy to Kate, but north of the Beach Road was a real town, with houses, schools, a supermarket, and a few family-owned restaurants. But even here, developers found ways to connect the houses to the Gulf. A complex system of canals linked the housing properties to the Gulf, and a familiar line in the real estate ads was *CAN SEE THE GULF FROM THE LIVING ROOM or BE ON THE BEACH IN FIVE MINUTES.*

As Kate moved off the cluttered highway, she seemed to sense a faint odor of sin, a whiff of brimstone, much as she had sensed in some of the more depraved sections of Memphis. She was discovering that most visitors didn't come to White Sands for Bible study. They came to immerse themselves in the hedonistic lifestyle of the coast.

As she pulled into her new houses's driveway composed of white crushed oyster shells, a sense of being *home* washed over her. This was her place, her little island, and after years spent in run-down apartments, she felt disbelief along with deep gratitude. *Thank You, God, for giving us a place!*

The hot sun enveloped her as she got out of the Taurus. She entered the house and went to the kitchen for a cold drink. Looking around, she wondered where Cleo and Jacques had gotten off to, and hoped they were enjoying their new surroundings. A frown creased her forehead when she noticed the litter boxes were gone. "What can Jake have done with the litter boxes?" she muttered. She walked over to the door that led to the stairs going up to Jake's apartment and didn't know exactly how to announce herself. She opened the door and called out tentatively, "Jake, are you there?"

The voice that came did not sound like Jake Novak's at all. There was a quiet, defeated sound to it. "Yeah, come on up."

Puzzled, Kate walked up the stairs. When she stepped into the large room, she was struck by its brightness and the panoramic view of the water. But Jake sat at the computer desk, staring out moodily. "I just got back," she said. "Hey, what happened to the litter boxes?"

Jake shrugged and said dully, "Take a look outside. Don't need litter boxes."

Kate gazed out at the sand. She wasn't sure she agreed with him, but didn't feel like arguing about it now. Instead she broke her good news.

"I got Jeremy enrolled at school. I think he's going to be fine." Then she began telling him about Hope Barclay, but she quickly realized Novak wasn't listening to her. "What's the matter?" she asked. "You're not listening."

"I've got a disease."

For a moment Kate didn't understand what he meant. "Have you been to a doctor?"

"Don't need a doctor."

"When did you start feeling bad?"

Novak turned to face her, and there was misery in his dark eyes. "I've got writer's block."

Suddenly Kate laughed. "Is that all! I thought you had leprosy or something."

"It's not funny! I've always maintained there isn't such a thing as writer's block. I never heard of plumber's block, have you? Did you ever hear a plumber say, 'I just can't clean this drain. I just don't feel it!' Did you ever hear of fireman's block? Teacher's block? I've always laughed at writers who said they just couldn't write because they didn't *feel* it. But look at this. I've sat at this blasted computer all morning long and can't get a word to come. I could do better back in Chicago with a one-dollar composition book and a stub of a pencil."

Kate didn't know how to respond. She was still trying to get used to the contrasts in this man's personality. One minute he exuded a blatant roughness, the next he revealed patches of surprising vulnerability. Despite herself a sudden compassion welled up. She came over and stood beside him, putting her hand on his shoulder.

"Jake, you know, we've both been through a big change. It'll take us some time to adjust. But I'm sure before you know it, you'll be writing like Faulkner."

Novak glanced up, but quickly returned his gaze to the Gulf. He appeared surprised by her gentleness. This was the first time she'd exposed her tender side.

It was a rather shocking moment for Kate as she realized they'd each revealed a little more of themselves than they had intended. But then she shivered as another thought occurred to her. She didn't want to like Jake Novak. She needed to keep her distance. He was everything she detested in a man, and now she was angry with herself for feeling—feeling *what?* She couldn't identify it, but she knew she had to end the moment. "You'll be all right," she said abruptly. "Come on. We'll go take care of the animals. I'll teach you how to do it. You don't know a thing about animals, do you?"

Jake Novak rose and followed her down the stairs. He didn't say a word, but as she moved from one station to another explaining how to feed birds and mammals and fish, she sensed a subtle change in his demeanor. *Good,* she thought. *Maybe he won't be quite so insufferable from now on.*

Seven

The surf was coming in chest high, and Jake found great pleasure in running to meet it. Like every day for the past week, it repeatedly knocked him backward, and for a moment he felt foolish. *What am I going to do, pound the Gulf back all the way down to South America?* The thought amused him. Finally he swam out almost half a mile and turned over on his back and stared up at the azure sky arching above him like a huge bow. Far to the south, fleecy clouds drifted along, and Jake watched them leisurely before rolling over and swimming as hard as he could to shore.

As he came in, he stood on the beach huffing and puffing. *When I was eighteen I could have done this without even drawing an extra breath. And I'm not even thirty yet!* He trudged across the sand, noticing the blue heron that was watching a fisherman carefully. The fisherman pulled in a small catch. Jake watched as the man took it off the hook, turned, and tossed it to the heron who caught it easily and tossed it up in the air so the head would go down its gullet in one swift action. Jake grinned. He had noticed this same heron came for his dinner each day.

Pausing at the outdoor shower, he rinsed himself off and then, drying himself off on a towel that had already been faded by the sun, he stepped onto the patio, opened the sliding door, and moved into the kitchen area. For a moment he stood there, a frown disturbing the tranquility of his face. His jaw clenched tightly, and he moved toward where Kate was curled up on the couch reading.

"I thought you were going to clean up the kitchen, Mary Katherine."

Startled, Kate looked up and removed the large black-framed reading glasses that gave her an owlish look. "Oh, I forgot! I'm sorry. I'll do it now."

Jake shook his head. "That book you're reading says that cleanliness is next to godliness."

Kate got to her feet and smiled knowingly. She held the Bible up. "That's a myth, Jake. It doesn't say that anywhere in here."

"Well, it ought to."

It had already become an old argument in the brief time they had been in the house. Jake was an immaculate housekeeper, and although Kate tried, she just didn't have it in her to keep house as well as he did.

They moved into the kitchen, and Jake started to throw dishes around. Kate stepped up. "I'll do it," she insisted, and laid the Bible down on the glass-top coffee table.

"No, you won't. I'll do it myself, but let me tell you this—Ow!"

Jake leaped sideways and looked down at Jacques the Ripper, who had taken a swipe at his calf and furrowed it. Blood was running down over his ankle. "I ought to strangle you!" Jake yelped.

"Sorry, Jake," Kate sympathized. "But I don't think Jacques liked your tone of voice. You ought to know by now that he's very protective of me."

Jake glared at the huge black feline, whose golden eyes were studying him with a ferocity he'd only seen in big cats at the zoo. Kate walked over and examined Jake's leg. "Jacques has always been that way. He thinks he's a watchdog." She straightened up and shook her head. "We're going to have to clean that up."

"No, I'll do it myself."

"Don't be silly. You sit down while I get the antiseptic."

Kate gave Jake a little push and he sat down in one of the tall chairs in front of the island. Moving quickly, Kate got the antiseptic and cotton pads and some Band-Aids. She stopped the flow of blood from Jake's scratches and poured a liberal anointing of the antiseptic onto a large pad and applied it to the wounded area.

He grunted and flinched. She glanced up at him with a grin. "Thought you were a tough guy."

"So sue me. It stings."

"Of course it does. Now be still."

Jake stared down at Kate. He tried to think of something cutting to say. "I hate that cat," he finally announced. "He's a menace to society."

"No, he's not. You've just got to learn to make friends with him."

"I'd just as soon make friends with that blasted snake."

At that instant the doorbell rang and Kate said, "Here. You finish putting these Band-Aids on."

"I don't want to wear Band-Aids all over my legs."

"Just until it stops bleeding." Getting up, she walked to the door. When she opened it, she found a man waiting with a smile on his face.

"Hello," he said. "I'm the Welcome Wagon. We usually send a lady around to greet our newcomers, but to tell you the truth, I wanted to meet you personally." He put his hand out. "I'm your mayor, Devoe Palmer."

Kate smiled and took his hand. He was a small man, no more than five-six, but a glance at his shoes revealed that he was probably wearing lifts. He had thick, brown hair with a definite curl, and deep-set hazel eyes. She knew a little about men's fashion, and her quick appraisal identified him as being a real clotheshorse.

"Come in, Mayor. We're just dealing with a little accident."

Palmer stepped inside, looked around, and was met by Jacques. "Wow!" he exclaimed, taking a step back. "Is that thing a cat?"

"Yes, his name is Jacques. We call him Jacques the Ripper."

"If you want any evidence," Jake called out, "come in and look at the wound."

Palmer had his eyes fixed on Jacques. "That's the biggest cat I've ever seen in my life."

"He's part African wildcat, Mayor," Kate explained.

"Should've stayed in Africa, from the looks of things. And everyone calls me Palmer." He looked Kate up and down. "You are, from all reports, Mary Katherine Forrest?"

"That's right."

"Then you must be Mr. Forrest."

Jake grinned. "No, I'm Jake Novak."

Palmer's eyes went from Jake to Kate, and both of them could see his mind running rapidly. She awkwardly began to explain. Devoe Palmer listened as she laid out the reason they were sharing the house, and when she had finished, he turned and gazed out their window at the water. "Well, you got a nice one. This is valuable property. I dabble in real estate—so let me be the first to make you an offer." Palmer winked at her with a smile.

"We can't sell," Kate said quickly. "It's all in the will."

Palmer seemed kind and charming, but Kate had been around the block enough times to know that outwardly he was probably all charisma but in reality, no doubt a skunk. She immediately put up her guard against his obvious attractiveness.

"We're living in sin here, you know," Jake interjected.

Kate shook her head. "Jake, don't be ridiculous. You have your own apartment."

"Hey, you're the holy roller, not me. We live in the same house together with just a single door separating us. Isn't that sinful?" Jake grinned at Palmer. "Actually, I guess you could call us *business associates.*" He gave the words an exaggerated emphasis, and then turned to leave. "Watch out for snakes, Mayor. There's a twenty-foot python loose somewhere in this house."

He left the room, and Palmer watched him go. "You two, as I understand it, have to take care of the animals."

"Yes, it's quite a job. And by the way, the python's only six feet, and she's safely confined. She can't get out."

"I knew Miss Zophia quite well. She was a fine lady. A little bit dotty over her animals, but we're all crazy in some area."

"May I offer you some coffee or lemonade?"

"Lemonade would be nice." He sat down in one of the chairs, and as Kate fixed the lemonade, he turned on the charm. Kate played along, amused. She glanced down at his left hand and didn't see a wedding ring. He caught her glance and said, "I came to invite you to a party."

Kate put the glass down in front of him and met his eyes. "Do you have a wife, Mayor?"

"Not at the moment."

Kate blinked with surprise, and he laughed at her. "I'm divorced, but you'll be safe with me, Mary."

"Oh—actually, I go by Kate."

"Kate, then. Sorry." Palmer sipped the lemonade and said, "The leaders of White Sands are going to get together and talk about how we can improve life on the coast. We'll make a little party of it. But, as I say, you'll be safe. Ray O'Dell will be there. He's the chief of police. Will you come?"

"I'd like to very much. I'd like to start meeting people."

"Good. I'll pick you up a six o'clock tomorrow. It'll be at the Perdido Beach Resort. The food's good there." He got up and put his hand out. When she took it, he pressed it with more pressure than ordinary. "I'm glad you moved in. We need more attractive ladies on the beach." He paused for effect. "Well, I'll see you tomorrow night," he finally said as he turned to leave, running straight into Jake talking to Pearly.

Jake turned to Palmer. "Hey there. Finished sweet-talking the little missus?" He laughed and gave Palmer a knowing look. But Palmer barely registered it, and instead turned to the handyman.

"Hello, Pearly."

"Hello, Mayor. You didn't get snake bit or nothing in there, did you?"

Palmer laughed. "Nah, but it's only a matter of time."

"You got that right," Jake said. "And by the way," he turned to Pearly, "can you get me some mouse traps?"

Pearly laughed out loud. "Mouse traps? What you need them for?"

"Well, for mice obviously. Haven't you seen them?"

"You can't get rid of them mice." Pearly was chewing tobacco and spat an amber stream, baptizing one of the tropical plants that apparently had been hit before as it was slightly droopy. "Ya'll will jist have to put up with 'em."

"What do you mean? I can get rid of mice."

"Not them mice, you can't. Them's the Alabama beach mouse. Touch one of them varmints, and you'll go right to jail."

"That's right, Novak," Palmer said. "There's a big fight over those pests. I agree with you—they're a pain—but the tree huggers have gotten a bill through the legislature, and the pesky things are protected by law." He chewed his lower lip thoughtfully and an angry light touched his eyes. "Some of the property owners are hopping mad. Me for one. You buy beach property to build on, and now we can't build because of the stupid rats."

Jake grinned suddenly. "Well, I guess it's tough when the vermin have all the political power, isn't it, Mayor?"

Palmer laughed. "You're probably right. Listen, I've invited your *business associate* to dinner with some of the town's mucky-mucks. Since you're now one of our prime property owners, I'd like to have you come, too."

"Thanks, but I'm not much for meetings," Jake said. "I'll let Mary Katherine cover for me."

"All right then. Welcome to the coast." He put his hand out, and when Jake took it, the mayor clamped down. For a small man he had a ferocious grip, and the bones in Jake's hands felt like they'd collapsed. He recovered and applied the power right back.

Palmer relented first. "Well, gotta go. Good to meet you, Novak."

The mayor got into his black Porsche, and Jake turned to Pearly. "Seems like a nice enough guy—for a politician, that is."

Pearly baptized the flower again with a large glob of tobacco juice. "He's okay. Just don't turn your back on him."

"I try not to turn my back on anybody, Pearly."

"Good idea. You hang on to that."

● ● ●

The sun had put its afternoon rays on the Gulf, and Jake slumped at his computer while staring outside as a flock of white birds dove again and again after fish. He didn't know what kind of birds they were or what they were catching exactly. They had joined a group of pelicans, and Jake had discovered that one of the pleasures of living on the beach was watching the pelicans as they dove full-speed into the water. They folded their wings and hit with all their might and then disappeared for a moment. Usually they came up with a fish, some of them too big to swallow.

Jake leaned back in the chair, locked his fingers behind his head, and closed his eyes. *There's too much to see here. That's the reason I can't write. I'll have to put up blinds or something.* He mused on the idea that writers ought to be locked in a room with no windows and have food shoved under the door until they produce at least ten fairly readable manuscript pages. But he knew that in this room, he didn't have the willpower to refuse to look at the beauty of the view. After the grimy streets of Chicago, he was just too tempted by the clean aqua water, the azure sky, the fleecy cotton-candy clouds, and the sugar-white sand beaches.

His thoughts were interrupted as he heard Kate drive up. He got up and padded down the stairs in bare feet. Kate was just entering with a small bag of groceries. Jake had stopped to look at Romeo and Juliet in their cage as they pecked and made angry noises at each other.

"I thought these were love birds," he said.

Kate continued on to the kitchen and answered, "They are."

"Why do they fight all the time?"

She smiled. "Hmm. Maybe one's a thug from Chicago and the other's a nice girl from Memphis," she said, a twinkle in her eyes.

"Or maybe one's a smart guy who can cook and the other's a lazy girl who can't keep a house?" he retorted.

"Lazy?" She shook her head, but she wasn't taking him seriously.

Jake turned back to watch the birds and grinned as Romeo backed Juliet into a corner and pecked viciously at her head. "I have a feeling Juliet's days are numbered. I expect a little romance out of love birds, but it looks like I'm not going to get any."

"You interested in romance, Jake?" Kate asked as she put three boxes of cereal into a cabinet. She turned to face him.

"Dream on, Sister. Romance is for stories. Doesn't happen in real life."

"Are you sure about that, Jake?"

Jake moved across the room, keeping his eye on Jacques who was watching him steadily. He sat down and Cleo jumped up into his lap. He stared at her and she grinned.

"That's the only cat I ever saw that smiled. What's she got to be so happy about?"

"She likes you, Jake."

"Well, that makes her a party of one, I guess. So what's with your ideas of romance? You've been married—was it romantic?"

Jake saw Kate's eyes change. It was as if a curtain had been pulled down over them, and her lips tightened into a line. "Mind your own business."

At that instant Bad Louie left his perch and flew around the room yelling obscenities.

"You stop that awful talk, Bad Louie! You hear me?" Kate called out. She waved her arms, chasing him out of the room, and he came up with some curse words that she'd rarely heard. "I'm going to tape your bill shut!"

Jake was amused. "You can't do that. You'd have the Society for the Prevention of Cruelty to Parrots down on you. You go on, Bad Louie. You got your rights. Cuss all you want."

"Don't encourage him!"

Jeremy had been in his room, and now he came out with a slight smile on his face. "I'm learning lots of cool new words from Bad Louie."

"You need to send that parrot off to charm school," Jake said. He got up and stretched and said, "Guess I should think about dinner."

"I'll do it," Kate offered.

"I don't think I need a burnt offering tonight. I'll take care of it." Jake turned and then said, "But it's still early—and I've got a present for Jeremy. You interested, Slick?"

Jeremy's eyes blinked, and he said, "A present for me? What is it?"

"Come on and I'll show you. We men need to get away from cussing parrots that offend our delicate sensibilities." He winked at Kate, who watched them go. There was something pleasing in the sight of her son spending time with the big man who had entered their lives so abruptly. She went over and rubbed Jacques's head. "You be nice to Jake, you hear me, Jacques?"

Jacques half closed his eyes and the purring reminded Kate of some of the deep-throttling motorcraft that passed in the Gulf.

Jake stopped outside the house and went into the storage shed. He came out with two new surf-casting rods. "Take your choice, Slick. Only difference is the color."

Jeremy took a rod and held it gingerly. "This is mine?"

"Sure is. Fine enough to haul in Moby Dick. Come on. How 'bout we try them out before dinner?"

"I don't know how to use these things."

"Neither do I, but we'll just practice a little bit without bait."

The two walked down to where the surf was rolling in, and for the next half hour they moved up and down the beach. At one point they encountered Valentino, who was fishing for shark again.

"Hey, Sid," Jake said, "this is my friend Jeremy Forrest. Sid Valentino, Jeremy."

Valentino turned and stared at Jeremy. "You ever catch a shark?" he demanded.

"No, Sir. Never caught anything."

"You be careful when you land one. They can bite your arm right off." He turned back.

Jake grinned. "End of conversation. Sid doesn't carry on extended dialogue."

The two walked down the beach a bit and came to a halt in front of the house closest to theirs—an impressive two-story set back off the beach. Jeremy asked, "I wonder who lives here?"

"Don't know. They've got money, though."

"I'm gonna try casting again."

The two continued to practice, and after a few minutes Jeremy looked over his shoulder and saw a guy his age walking toward them. "Hey, I know him. I think he's a grade ahead of me. We're in math class together."

The boy who came down to greet them was overweight. He was wearing a Tommy Hilfiger shirt and a pair of blue shorts. "Hey, Jeremy."

"Hey, Derek."

"What you fishing for?"

"Nothing," Jeremy said. "We got new fishing poles. We're just learning how to use them."

"This your dad?"

"No," Jeremy said quickly. "This is Jake Novak. Jake, this is Derek Maddux. We're in math class together."

"How you doing, Derek?" Jake asked. "You know how to use one of these things?"

"Sure."

"Wanna join us?"

"Don't you have any bait?"

"No, thought we'd learn how to use them before we baited up."

As it turned out, Derek was quite the expert. He gave them a quick lesson and then he looked over his shoulder. "Here comes my mom," he said, and waited until she reached them. "Mom, this is Jeremy. He's in my math class. And this is uh...Jake, right?"

Jake reached out his hand to the woman. "Jake Novak."

"Glad to meet you, Mr. Novak. I'm Arlene Maddux."

"Pleasure. Derek here is giving us a few lessons in surf casting."

"Oh yeah, he's good at it. Derek's good at almost everything."

"Except math." Derek grinned. "But Jeremy is going to give me some pointers. Hey, Jeremy, wanna see my new PlayStation?"

Jeremy looked at Jake. "Is it all right?"

"Sure. Go ahead."

Jake took Jeremy's rod and stood there as the kids ran off. He smiled at Arlene. "Have you lived on the beach long?"

"Oh, we don't live here full-time. Mostly in the winter. We have another home in New York. And you? You must be new to the area."

"Just moved in a week ago. Right down the beach from you." He pointed.

"You have other children?"

"Jeremy's not mine. He belongs to Mary Katherine. We share the house."

As Jake had expected, there was a moment in which the woman put things together. It amused him that everybody was eager to assume the relationship between him and Kate was something other than proper.

As they talked, Jake studied the blonde woman. Her eyes were violet, but he suspected contact lenses took care of that. She was slightly over-weight but had a good figure she apparently was not averse to showing off. The outfit she wore was designed just for that purpose.

As the two stood there talking, Jake looked up to see a man approaching. He was one of those ex-athletes who had allowed himself to go to seed. He had reddish, receding hair and freckles scattered across his face. He was sunburned badly, and his nose was peeling in a rather ugly fashion.

When he approached, Arlene said, "Earl, this is Jake Novak. They've taken the animal lady's place."

"Glad to know you." Earl Maddux put his hand out, squeezed too hard, and made eye contact as he had no doubt been taught years earlier in prep school. "Been meaning to get by, but I've been pretty busy."

"We come down to the coast to try and relax," Arlene said rather bitterly, "and all he does is work."

"Well, got to make ends meet."

The two stood there talking, and Jake quickly found out that Maddux had played center for Alabama during his younger days, though Jake could tell the older man had lost most of the power necessary for that position.

"How 'bout you bring your wife on over, and I'll throw some steaks on."

"Oh, I'm not married."

"You're not? Well, who's the woman I've seen coming and going?"

"That's my business associate, Mary Katherine Forrest. Jeremy's mom."

Earl Maddux laughed. "Business associate, huh? Well, that's one way of putting it."

Abruptly Arlene chimed in. "Earl, don't you think Jake looks just a little bit like Tommy?"

"Tommy who?" Earl asked.

"Tommy Selleck. You know, he's got the same kind of eyes that crinkle."

Jake was curious. "You know Tom Selleck?"

"Oh, yes. We were really good friends. I've always liked Tommy."

"How did you meet him?"

"Arlene was in the movies." Earl spoke with an undisguised note of mockery. "A *movie star*."

"Well, not really a *star,* but I like to think I could have been," Arlene said demurely. "But I gave up my career to marry Earl."

"Yeah, if my business turns belly up, she can always go back and be in a movie with *Tommy.*" There was an edge to Earl's tone that Jake didn't miss. He stood there looking back and forth between the two, and finally he said, "Well, I'd better get back. I'm cooking tonight."

"You bring your *business associate* over sometime. I grill a pretty mean steak myself," Earl said. He looked over and said, "Arlene can tell you all about Brad Pitt."

"I didn't know him," Arlene said frostily. But she turned on her charm to Jake. "We'll get together. It's nice the boys are in school together. With our bouncing back and forth between New York and White Sands, it doesn't give Derek much opportunity to make friends."

Jake agreed and soon disengaged himself from the conversation and headed back to the house...and his dinner duties.

● ● ●

An hour later, Jake, Kate, and Jeremy sat down to a lavish meal. Jake had fixed a crisp green salad with toasted pecans, dried cranberries, and mandarin oranges on top, coconut fried shrimp that was crispy on the outside and tender on the inside, a tangy mango dipping sauce, baked potatoes with sour cream, chives, and crumbled bacon, and garlic biscuits. The three diners were soon stuffed, and as they cleared the table, Jeremy asked, "Can I go back over to Derek's? He needs help with his math."

"I suppose so, but don't stay too late," Kate replied as she set a stack of dishes in the sink.

Jeremy scrambled out, dodging Trouble, who took off after him. The big pit bull had become devoted to Jeremy and Kate commented on it. "It's good for Jeremy to have a pet of his own. He never really liked the cats much."

"Trouble's not so bad, I guess," Jake said. "He's scared to death of Jacques—but then, so am I."

As Jake loaded the dishwasher he told Kate about the Alabama beach mice. "I think if Jacques nails one of them varmints, he'll go to jail for it."

When Jake turned the dial for the wash cycle to start, Kate said, "Hey, let's go down and sit on the beach for a while."

Jake's brow wrinkled. "You're asking *me* to sit on the beach with you?"

She playfully whacked him with a dish towel. "No, I'm asking Bad Louie. Of course I'm talking to you! Who else is there?"

"I wasn't sure you'd actually want to...you know...hang out with me."

Kate offered a wry smile. "Don't make a big deal of it, Jake. I'm going to sit by the water. Come with me or not, it's up to you." With that, she went out the door and over the sand.

Jake stood in the kitchen for a moment. *Just like a woman. Always wanting to be chased.* Nevertheless, he went after her and soon caught up. She glanced sideways at him, saying nothing, and continuing toward the water. Finally she chose a spot to sit down as close as possible to the surf without getting wet. He followed suit, and the two were silent for a few moments.

"So, tell me about the Madduxes," Kate asked.

Jake leaned back on his elbows. "Well, Earl Maddux is obviously a rich guy, a businessman of some sort. And apparently Arlene was in the movies. A few bit parts, I think. She talks about a comeback."

Cleo had followed them out, and she pushed her head against Jake's arm.

"Cleo sure loves you, Jake," Kate said.

"That's her mistake," Jake said. "I don't need any clinging females."

Kate glanced at him, and something in his tone affected her. "Do I detect a bit of past history?"

Jake didn't answer. He was staring out over the water and rubbing Cleo's head absentmindedly.

"So now you're gonna clam up."

He waited a moment, then said, "I had one once."

"A clinging female?"

"It's not a very good story, Mary Katherine." He turned to her and said, "I got blindsided by somebody."

Kate was quiet for a time. "I'm sorry," she said quietly.

The two sat there until finally Jake turned and laughed. "Look at that."

Kate turned and saw that Jacques the Ripper had struck again. He was walking toward them with a small creature in his jaws.

"You're under arrest, Jacques, for assaulting an Alabama beach mouse," Jake said. "You better get that thing away from him, Mary Katherine. It's against the law to touch them."

Kate gently removed the mouse, who looked up at her with black eyes and then scurried off. Jacques started after him, but she grabbed his tail. "No!" she said, "Leave the mouse alone."

"He broke the law." Jake grinned. "I'm going to turn him in."

"Oooh, kitty police are going to come and get you, Jacques," Kate said. Jacques looked at her and seemed to scowl. "Oh, don't worry," she said, roughing his fur. "You couldn't help it."

Jake stretched out his legs and laid back in the sand, looking up at the darkening sky. He was quiet for a time and then he murmured, "The penitentiaries are full of people who couldn't help it."

It was an odd remark, and Kate turned toward Jake, but he looked away. The two sat there listening to the sibilant waves as they came ashore, and Kate sensed a strange comradeship that she had never expected to feel with Jake Novak.

Eight

Derek's room was the coolest thing Jeremy had ever seen. Every sort of electronic gimmick ever sold littered the shelves and floor, and rows of DVDs, CDs, and games filled the cases that lined the room's perimeter. A plasma television hung on one wall and a double-size loft bed dominated one side of the room, under which a Dell computer sat on a desk. Jeremy hadn't believed his eyes earlier in the afternoon when he'd first seen Derek's Xbox, PlayStation, *and* Nintendo systems. A large table against one wall was strewn with various electronic knickknacks including two MP3 players, several sets of ear buds, and a cell phone. The walls were lined with posters of rappers like Dr. Dre and 50 Cent and a couple Jeremy didn't recognize.

But for all his possessions, Derek wasn't easy for Jeremy to figure out. For some time Jeremy had been trying to get Derek to work on the math problems that had been giving him such trouble. Jeremy was sitting at the table, having pushed back the junk, while Derek was lying flat on his back on the floor wearing a set of headphones. His right hand tapped the floor rhythmically.

"Derek, I've got to go home pretty soon. You'd better get up here and let me show you how to do these problems."

Derek's eyes moved slowly over to Jeremy, who motioned for him to take off the headset. Derek reluctantly pulled the earphones forward with a great show of impatience. "Can't hear you, Dude. These are totally noise-blocking. State of the art."

"Derek, I thought you wanted help with your math."

"I hate math. Who needs it anyway?"

"Um, you'll need it when you go into business with your dad."

"No, I won't need it," Derek said with a smirk. "I'll just hire some weenie with an accounting degree to do it."

"But you won't know whether he's cheating you or not."

Derek sat up, thought for a second, then said, "Then I'll hire another weenie to watch him. There are plenty of weenies in this world."

To Jeremy, Derek was like a creature from another planet. Jeremy had never been around people with money, and he began to wonder if being rich changed people completely. He and his mother were so used to scraping bottom financially that to see the way Derek regarded wealth was almost frightening.

With a sigh, Jeremy shook his head. "I don't think that'll work. You better come over here and let me show you how to do these problems."

"I got something better than that." Derek rose, walked over to one of the three chests that held his clothes, and opened the bottom drawer. He pulled out a magazine and flopped it down in front of Jeremy. "Take a gander at this, Buddy," he said. "I bet you ain't seen nothing like that lately."

Jeremy glanced down at the magazine and was shocked. He knew about pornographic magazines but had never seen one. Now he swallowed hard and felt his face turn warm.

"I can't believe it, Dude! You're blushing!" Derek laughed. He reached over and hit Jeremy's shoulder with his fist. "Didn't know there was a twelve-year-old kid in America who could blush. What's the matter? You never seen nothing like that?"

"Uh...well, not really."

"Wow, you've led a sheltered life." Derek flipped the pages over carelessly, and Jeremy stared down at the textbook to avoid looking at it. "My old man knows I've got these but he don't care. He looks at them himself. What about your old man?"

Jeremy swallowed hard. It was always difficult for him to speak of his father, and he cut the words off sharply. "He's dead."

"No kidding? How'd he die?"

"He was killed in a plane crash when I was only six. I still remember him though. He used to do things with me. He took me fishing once."

"Did you catch anything?"

"I don't remember that. I just remember being with him."

"My old man's going to take me out deep sea fishing. I'm going to catch a big marlin, maybe break the world's record." Derek got up and grabbed the magazine and then went to shove it back under the drawer. He glanced over at Jeremy and said, "You're too serious, Bro."

"I guess so."

Derek came over and plopped himself down in the chair beside Jeremy. "What about that guy who lives with you. Novak."

"What about him?"

"He's a pretty tough-looking guy."

"He was in the Delta Force a long time ago. And he was a cop, too."

"I saw them scars. He ever tell you how he got them?"

"He doesn't like to talk about it."

"What about him and your mom?"

"What do you mean?"

"Are they sleeping together?"

"No," Jeremy sputtered in confusion. "Of course not! He's got his own apartment. My mom has her own room."

"Yeah, right." Derek laughed. "You're all in the same house together! I bet they got a thing going."

Jeremy paled and said in a low and steady voice, "Don't talk that way about my mom."

Derek stared at the younger boy and shook his head sadly. "You're really something, Jeremy. I never met anyone like you."

"What do you mean—like me?"

"You're so...out of it. You're all, like, optimistic. You actually think people are good."

"Well...aren't they? Mostly, I mean?"

"Not really," Derek said with authority. "Most people cheat and then lie about it. Like everyone at our school. You should see how they cheat on tests and change grades in the computer. And my mom and dad? I'm pretty sure they both, you know, get some on the side. So what?"

Jeremy stared at Derek for a moment, speechless, then asked, "Doesn't that bother you?"

"Why should it? What difference does it make?" Derek laughed harshly, adding, "You'll find out that people are out for number one. You'd better open your eyes, Jeremy. The world's a pretty rotten place. You'll find that out soon enough."

There was something about Derek that drew Jeremy but that also repulsed him. He had heard Jake talking once to his mother, and he had said something about the fact that evil attracts. "That's why people like the *Godfather* movie and all," Jake had said. "They all talk about what a horrible person the godfather was, but they love to watch the movie." Jeremy found the same type of train-wreck morbid fascination with Derek Maddux. Jeremy was mesmerized by the total lack of moral values in his friend, who was only fourteen but who seemed to carry the weight of the world.

Finally Jeremy repeated his offer, "Come on, Derek, I'll show you this problem."

Again Derek wasn't interested. "Hey, we don't have to worry about that."

"Look, Derek, you're gonna have to learn it sometime," Jeremy said. "I can't take the test for you."

Derek leaned toward Jeremy and said, "Sure you can."

"What do you mean? Nobody can take the test for somebody else."

"I got something to show you. You're gonna like it." Springing to his feet, Derek scrambled over and opened a drawer in the desk beneath the loft bed. He came out with a cardboard box, opened it, and said, "What do you think about this?"

"It looks like a calculator."

"Well, that's what it is, but it's more than that. I had this made special. It's got a transmitter in it."

"A transmitter. You mean like a radio?"

"That's right." Derek grinned. "Look, you poke in numbers and then you push this button right here and the little transmitter sends it out."

"Sends it out where?"

"To this one." Derek pulled out another one. "This is mine. You know, Coach Clements doesn't mind if we use calculators to do the problems. He won't know the difference."

Jeremy stared at the two devices. He immediately saw that this was all Derek would need to pass the test.

"You get it, don't you? You do the problem, and then you put the stuff in the calculator and transmit it to me."

"But that wouldn't show you how to do the problems."

"Clements doesn't care," Derek said. "He never looks at the process. All he does is look at the answers. I think even the teacher's aide does that. As long as the answers are right, we're okay."

"That's—" Jeremy started to say something but glanced up quickly and saw that Derek was watching him carefully.

"I know what you're going to say," Derek said. "You're going to say it's cheating. It wouldn't be right."

"Well, it wouldn't."

"Jeremy, listen up. The idea is to pass the test. If you pass the test, you pass the class. You pass enough classes, you get out of school. That's all I'm shooting for. My dad never got past the tenth grade, and he made it big. I'm going to do the same thing."

Jeremy tried desperately to think of an answer that would satisfy Derek, but nothing came. Derek began talking excitedly about how the transmitter worked, and reluctantly Jeremy picked up the calculator. He punched a number in and then touched the button that Derek showed him. He saw the number appear instantly on the display of Derek's calculator. Despite himself he was impressed. "But why not just learn to do the math?" he protested.

"Are you going to be a buddy and help me or not?" Derek asked impatiently.

"I don't know, Derek."

"I'll tell you what. You do this for me—I'm going to do something for you. That's the way life works, Bud. I'll give you the surprise of your life if you get me through this test."

Jeremy felt something cave inside. "Okay, Derek," he muttered. "I guess it doesn't really matter."

The two experimented with the device until they both had it down. Something outside the window caught Derek's attention. "Hey, you've got company." He waited until Jeremy came over and joined him at the window and pointed down the beach to the aqua-blue house. "That's the Barclay broad—the English teacher."

"Yeah. That's Miss Barclay."

"She's hot."

Jeremy swiveled his head. "What are you talking about?"

"You're just about a year or two away from being able to spot stuff like that, but I tell you she's a hot number."

"Don't talk about her like that. She's nice."

"So what? I'm telling you that she's a babe."

"I don't even know what you mean by that. Besides, she's a—she goes to church."

"Church! That's a good one." Derek was watching his friend carefully. He took a perverse pleasure in destroying Jeremy's illusions. "Hey, don't worry about it. She's a good-looking woman. She deserves a good time." Derek switched gears, obviously bored of that topic. "Come on. Let's go out on the jet skis."

The two boys left the room and made for the boat dock. Minutes later, as they roared away, Jeremy was troubled. He knew that the infallible test of right and wrong was whether his mother would approve—and if she knew the truth about Derek, she wouldn't want him within a mile of the kid. He pushed the matter out of his mind, and the two zoomed out into the deep-blue Gulf of Mexico, throwing up fantails of sparkling spray behind them.

● ● ●

"This cake is delicious, Kate." Hope Barclay looked up from across the table at Kate and smiled. "I wish I could cook like you."

"Oh, I didn't make the cake. Jake did."

"Jake? The guy with the great build and the adorable face? He can *cook*, too?"

The question embarrassed Kate. "Well, to tell the truth, he's a great cook and I'm just terrible. Poor Jeremy, he's had to live on microwave meals for so long it's a wonder he's not skinnier than he is."

"Well, it's wonderful to have a good cook...*and* a great looking guy." Hope looked knowingly at Kate and took another bite. "This is really good."

"And he made it from scratch," Kate said. "I asked him how he did it. He said he got tired of store-bought food and learned to cook just for himself. He's a great housekeeper, too." She sighed and shook her head. "We have some big fights over that."

"Fights about housekeeping?" Hope asked.

"Well, I'm not very neat. Jake is." Kate laughed. "We're the odd couple. Felix and Oscar. I'm Oscar. He's Felix. I keep house with a rake, more or less, and it drives him crazy."

"A couple, huh? So you *are* a couple."

"Hope, that's not what I meant. I've told you—"

"I know, I know. I guess I should be glad that he's available. I think he's *gorgeous.* And I think it's wonderful he's going to write that novel. How's it coming?"

"I don't know. He won't talk about it. Won't tell me what it's about or anything. He told me he has writer's block, but he seems to spend an awfully lot of time up there in his room."

"Hmm, a mystery man."

The two women were sitting out on the balcony eating cake and drinking coffee made with freshly ground beans. The Gulf was calm, almost like a mirror, and the breeze was fresh.

"Your beach ministry idea sounds great, Hope," Kate said abruptly, trying to change the subject. "There are so many young people out on the beach, and most of them here for the wrong reasons."

"You're right about that," Hope agreed. "They don't come down to hear sermons, that's for sure. They come to have fun. And having fun doesn't mean what it did when I was younger."

"I know. These kids talk about things and half the time I don't even know what they're saying." Kate said. "I'm afraid for Jeremy. For all of them."

"Jeremy's a good boy. He's doing so well in school. I love having him in my English class. You know what he does? He tries to dumb down."

"He's always done that," Kate said. "Kids made fun of him. They called him brainiac and all these horrible names. So he does all the work but he messes it up so he won't get straight A's."

"I sure didn't have that trouble when I was in school," Hope said dryly.

"Neither did I."

The two talked again about the proposed beach ministry. The pastor of Hope's church—and now Kate's—had enlisted the two women in starting an outreach, and they were working on plans for some way to minister during the upcoming Shrimp Festival. The beaches would be crowded with young people from all over the Southeast, and to catch their attention with the gospel would be difficult indeed.

Finally Hope leaned back and sighed. "This is better than grading themes. I wish I were a math teacher."

"Why?"

"All they have to do is look at the answers. I have to look at the words and read the things, and kids hate to write them."

"It's not a writing generation, is it?"

"Not a reading generation either. Just ask one of them a literary question sometime." She giggled. "Sometimes I like to ask them the name of the whale in *Moby Dick*. You know what they answer?"

"Shamu?"

"Yes!" The two women sighed.

"Jeremy's not like that." Kate couldn't keep a note of motherly pride from creeping into her voice. "He loves the classics."

"Yes, he does, but he's an endangered species."

There was a momentary silence, then Kate decided to confide in Hope about something else. "Hope, Devoe Palmer asked me out again."

"Yeah, the mayor does that," Hope said without surprise. "You're his new target."

"You sound like the voice of experience," Kate commented.

"He's a player, all right. Since his divorce, he's going through every woman under thirty alphabetically."

"He seems to have a lot of money; he drives that fancy Porsche. Lives in a penthouse. I didn't know being mayor paid that much."

"Don't be naive. It doesn't. He's got his hand in everything unsavory in White Sands. I hate to break it to you, but Devoe takes bribes."

"Brides? You're kidding. Who would bribe the mayor?"

"Somebody who wants to build a condo on a spot where it's zoned for single family residences, for example. They just go to Devoe Palmer and somehow magically the City Council votes to change the zoning. Suddenly it's okay to build a twenty-story condo there."

"That's awful."

"Have you driven down the Beach Road?"

"Yes, it's pretty bad."

"You can't even see the beach anymore from the road. Nothing but condos." Hope shook her head. "And you be careful of Palmer. He's out for all he can get."

Kate felt a twinge of curiosity. "So have you gone out with him?"

"Oh, he tried. But teachers have to be like Caesar's wife."

"Caesar's wife?"

"Caesar's wife had to be above reproach." She paused and looked down at her plate. "People come to White Sands to sin. No other way to look at it. They call it the Redneck Riviera, but whether the Riviera's here or in France, people go there to drink, to gamble, to find sexual partners. It's that simple."

"It doesn't sound like a good place for me to be raising my son."

"Pretty much the same everywhere." Hope asked the question that had been on her mind for some time. "But what about you and Jake? I know what you've told me, but you're living together. You can't tell me there's nothing going on."

"Sure I can. There's nothing going on. He has his own apartment."

"Come on. There's one door separating the two of you. Everybody thinks you're living together—you know—*living together*."

"We live under the same roof because we have to. I've explained that it's all in Miss Zophia's will. And what's with everyone talking about there being just one door separating us? It's ridiculous!"

"Yes, I know, but you're never going to convince other people. Besides, it'll never work."

"What are you talking about?"

"He's an attractive man. You're an attractive woman. You're going to have a weak moment one of these days—or he is."

"That'll never happen," Kate replied, but there was a slight tremor in her voice.

● ● ●

Jake watched the blue heron as it moved in slow motion through the shallow waters. The birds were beautiful to Jake, and he admired how nature had designed them to do one thing. Simply to walk along the shallows on their spindly legs, catch sight of a fish, and plunge down to spear their prey with their sharp beaks. He watched as this took place. The heron came up with a small fish, tossed it into the air, caught it with its head down, and swallowed it.

"He got him that time," Jake said. "What a way to make a living."

Jake turned, sensing a presence. One of the bullet scars in his back came from not turning around in time. Ever since, he had developed a sense of someone approaching from behind.

His eyes narrowed and then he grinned. "Hello, Arlene," he said.

"Hello, Jake." Arlene looked out to the Gulf, then slipped off a terry cloth robe to reveal a very skimpy bathing suit. "I thought I'd take a swim."

"Don't you have a pool?" Jake asked, trying not to stare.

"Yes, but who needs a pool?" Arlene towered over him offering him the most revealing look at her figure. "I can swim in a pool in New York. People come down here to swim in the Gulf."

"No, they don't." Jake grinned. "They come down to live in condos and look at the Gulf. Swimming in the Gulf is uncomfortable. Haven't you noticed?"

"It is a little bit sticky, isn't it?"

"Yes, and if you ever get tangled up in one of those jellyfish, you'll wish you'd never been born."

The two were silent for a few moments, then Arlene asked, "Are you settled in?"

"Pretty well, I guess," Jake answered.

"How's your book coming?"

"Not very well."

"What's wrong?" Arlene asked.

"Don't know. I guess my muse died."

Suddenly a voice called out, "Hey, what's coming down?"

Jake and Arlene turned to see Earl Maddux approaching, wearing a pair of baggy shorts and a Hawaiian shirt. His nose was clearly sunburned and his freckles had been heightened by the hot sun. He looked at Arlene and said, "You're not going to swim in the Gulf, are you?"

"I thought I might," she answered.

"Well, not me." He shot a glance at Jake and said, "Hey, you got a minute to talk business? If you've got any money to invest, I'd like to offer you some good stock in my company. Make you a real deal."

"No thanks. I'm not the investor type."

He saw the disdain in Earl's face. A man without a nose for business was like a man without a soul to Earl Maddux. "Yeah, well, I guess that's one way to live. You're more the artistic type, huh? Not that you look it. You could be a prize fighter or something."

"Could be."

The conversation seemed over. Then Earl piped up again, "Hey, how about the party over at Tommy Hart's? You'll be there, of course."

"Wasn't invited," Jake answered.

"Well then, I'm inviting you. You know who Tommy Hart is, don't you?"

"Girly magazines, right?"

"Hey, don't put him down like that. He'll be bigger than Hefner and the Playboy empire one of these days."

Jake knew that Tommy Hart had modeled his business on Hugh Hefner's Playboy Enterprises. He put out a magazine called *Sweetharts* and operated a nightclub in New York called The Sweethart Club. The young "hostesses" there were dressed, more or less, but instead of bunny outfits they wore minimal costumes with red hearts in strategic locations. As a result, Hart had made a "sweetheart" of a fortune.

Maddux winked at him. "You'll get an eyeful at the party. You don't care if I go, do you, Arlene?"

"No, but I'll go along just to be sure none of those bimbos makes a move."

Earl laughed. "Jake, you want me to pick you up? You can bring your business associate. That what you still call her?"

"Actually, Earl, that's what she is."

Arlene frowned. "Bring her along. She needs to find out what the real world's like."

"All right, maybe I'll do that." Jake thought what it would be like to take Mary Katherine to Tommy Hart's Sweethart mansion. The more he thought about it, the more he liked it. "Yeah, I'll see what I can do."

● ● ●

Jacques the Ripper was watching Kate get ready. She had agreed to go to a party with Jake, although he had been rather vague about where it was and who would be there. She had bought a new dress for the occasion, a simple outfit, purchased at the outlet mall in Foley. It fit her well, and now she turned and said, "Do I look all right, Jacques?"

Jacques was watching her intently. He stretched and yawned and then plopped down and went to sleep abruptly.

"Well, I hope Jake appreciates this new dress better than you do." She grabbed her purse and then stopped, looking back at Jacques. "Now why did I say that? Why should I care what Jake thinks?"

She took a final glance in the mirror, then left the room to find Jake waiting for her by the fireplace. This was the first time he had asked her to go anywhere and despite herself, she wanted to make a good appearance.

"Well, you look nice," he said. "If you drop dead, we won't have to do anything to the body."

"What a horrible thing to say!"

"Yeah, I've been told I'm not too good with compliments."

"Well, you clean up pretty nice yourself," Kate said with a grin, and it was true—he was undeniably handsome in his black-on-black ensemble.

"What about Jeremy?" Jake asked. "He'll be okay?"

"He's not here. He's spending the night with Derek."

The two walked outside and got into the car. As she started the old Taurus, Kate said, "This thing's going to die one day. I'm going to buy a new car as soon as I can."

"We're all gonna die. Your Taurus has some miles left on it."

"You say the awfulest things. Now, where is this place we're going?"

"It's on Ono Island."

"Must be rich people then."

"So I hear."

Ono Island was a gated community boundaried not by the Gulf but by a river. It was, indeed, a dwelling place for wealthy people.

When they pulled up to the gate, the guard leaned over and said, "Yes, ma'am?"

Jake said, "Tommy Hart's place. My name's Novak."

The guard looked at him and said, "You're on the list all right. You know how to get there?"

"Nope."

The guard gave directions and when they pulled away, she said, "Harts, that's the people giving the party?"

"That's the one. Tommy Hart. You ever heard of him?"

"Sounds familiar. What does he do?"

"Oh, he's a publisher."

"Might he publish your book when you finish it?"

"I don't think he publishes my kind of book."

They found the Hart residence without difficulty. A young Brad Pitt look-alike was serving as valet. He glanced with disdain at the old Taurus and then grinned. "Do you think it'll last until the party's over, Ma'am?"

"Just park the car," Jake said, "and be respectful."

Brad Pitt started to give a smart rejoinder, but something in Novak's eyes changed his mind. "Yes, Sir."

The two walked up to the front door and Kate examined the house. "It's enormous," she said. "There's no telling how many rooms are in this thing. It must have cost a million dollars."

"Probably more."

"For one house! That's obscene."

"Don't knock it, Sister. You're a millionaire yourself."

Kate was about to respond when the door opened. She gasped at the young woman who stood before her wearing what appeared to be a bustier made out of black lace. The top was composed of two red hearts. She had on extremely high heels and fishnet hose.

Jake grinned as he watched Kate's reaction. "The latest fashion for parlor maids," he said.

Kate couldn't answer. She was embarrassed to even look at the girl, who was obviously well-endowed and covered so scantily. Kate's eyes scanned the room, and she saw several more girls similarly attired.

"What *is* this place, Jake?"

"I told you, it's Tommy Hart's house. He's trying to put Hugh Hefner out of business."

"You mean the *Playboy* man?"

"That's the one."

"That explains it. This is terrible. It looks like a Roman orgy."

"Well, it's close. Come on, let's mingle."

The next thirty minutes were a torment for Kate. The nearly naked girls moved about, smiling at men and serving drinks. The liquor flowed like Niagara Falls, and a six-piece jazz ensemble kept the music going. Arlene and Earl found them and chatted for a few minutes before moving on to mingle with other guests.

After a while Kate and Jake were approached by a small man in his mid-thirties dressed in the latest Italian fashion. "I'm Tommy Hart," he said. "I don't believe I've met you."

"We're gate crashers," Jake said jovially. "I'm Jake Novak and this is Mary Katherine Forrest."

"Glad to see you both. You live here on the coast?"

"Just moved in next to Earl Maddux."

"Ah, Earl. He mentioned he'd invited some new neighbors. Thanks for coming." His eyes were wide and innocent-looking, but there was nothing innocent about him. He was known throughout the industry as a financial genius for taking the *Playboy* concept and stepping it up a notch, resulting in great success.

"Good to be here, Tommy. I like the view," Jake said as his eyes roved among the girls, who were called Sweet Harts. Just then a small brunette with enormous eyes sidled up to Tommy.

Hart put his arm around her. "This is Diane. Isn't she something?"

Jake was looking straight into Diane's eyes. "Yep. She's something, Tommy."

"Well, Jake, why don't you and Diane get better acquainted? I'll look out for Mary Katherine here."

Just then a large man dressed in a black silk suit appeared and spoke to Jake. "What are you doing here, Novak?"

Jake wheeled to face the man and a flash of recognition crossed his face.

"Well, if it isn't the infamous Vince Canelli."

Canelli turned to Hart. "Why'd you invite this guy, Tommy?"

"Another one of my guests invited him," Tommy answered. "That a problem, Vince?"

Jake cut in. "Mary Katherine, let me introduce you to Vince Canelli. Big-time *businessman* from my hometown, Chicago. Import-export, right Vince? And a little skin trade on the side?"

"You don't know what you're talkin' about, Novak."

"Don't I, Vince? Just because you haven't been convicted yet doesn't mean you never will be."

"Dream on, Novak. Nobody's got nothin' on me."

"Well, then let's talk about your brother Gino. I nailed him, didn't I?" Right then someone else joined the group. His face had a hard look, but he remained silent. "Well, speak of the devil," Jake said. "Still up to the same old tricks, Gino?"

Just then, another man walked up—a very unusual-looking man with pale skin, white hair, and a nearly albino look. He wore an oyster-gray suit and had the lightest eyes Kate had ever seen—eyes that were fixed on Jake with an intensity that was frightening.

The pale man spoke in a voice so low it was almost inaudible. "You want me to take him out, Vince?"

Jake wasn't fazed. "Looks like the gang's all here. Whats up, Lazlo?"

The man nodded. "Novak."

"Mary Katherine, meet Dante Lazlo. Another business associate of Vince's." Jake leaned over and whispered in Kate's ear, "He's a heroin addict—and Vince's hired gun."

Lazlo glared at Jake. "Speak up, Novak."

Jake addressed Lazlo. "I was just telling Mary Katherine about your bum heart. How's that goin' anyway?"

"Could kick off at any minute," Dante Lazlo said, "so you and your law enforcement cronies don't scare me, Novak."

"Not law enforcement anymore, Lazlo. Just enjoying life here on the coast." Jake flashed a casual smile.

A cool silence surrounded the small group. Tommy Hart broke the quiet with a jovial, "Well, I'd better mingle. You boys be good." He disappeared into the crowd.

Jake turned toward Vince Canelli, who seemed protected by Gino Canelli and Dante Lazlo on either side of him. "I figured you'd put out a contract on me before now, Vince," Jake said. "You running short of cash?"

"Go on, make jokes," Vince Canelli said evenly. "If I wanted you gone, you'd be gone."

"Well, you'd better tell Lazlo here not to miss because if he does, you won't live to enjoy your ill-gotten gains."

Vince glared at Jake then turned and said, "Come on." Gino turned to walk with his brother, but Dante Lazlo wasn't finished. "I'm surprised you quit the cops."

"I got tired of putting guys like you in jail. Boring."

"You'll never put me in jail, Novak. But I just might put you under."

"Promises, promises! Go on. Your master is waiting for you. He likes his dog to stay close to his heels."

Lazlo gave Jake a measured glance and then turned and walked away.

That pretty much did it for Kate. "Let's go, Jake," she said, turning to leave.

Jake placed his hand lightly on Kate's elbow and steered her through the crowd. They stopped when they came across Tommy Hart again.

"Tommy, it's been fun. Come and see us. We're on the beach down there next to Madduxes. Mary Katherine will read the Bible to you. She's good at that."

Tommy Hart ignored Jake's comments and said in a low tone, "Who do you think you are, talking to Vince Canelli like that?"

"Vince Canelli is an animal," Jake answered. "That's the way I talk to animals. Come on, Mary Katherine."

As the two walked out the door, Kate could feel several pairs of eyes on their backs. They waited for their car to be brought, then got in. Without a word Kate started the car and headed down the road. They were halfway home before Kate said, "That place was creepy, Jake."

"No wonder. They're pretty scary folks." He hesitated then continued. "Never thought I'd run into them in Alabama of all places. But now that they know I'm here..." His voice trailed off.

"What?" Kate asked.

"It might be better if I moved on."

"You mean leave White Sands? Why would you do that?"

"Well, Vince Canelli isn't known for forgiving his enemies. I put his brother Gino in jail and almost got Vince. He's a notorious drug lord and runs several prostitution rings. I shut down a big part of his operation, and gathered quite a bit of intel on his businesses. He's not going to forget that."

"But what can he do?"

"Anything he wants, Mary Katherine. Anything he wants."

Kate took her eyes off the road for a moment. "No," she said, "you have to stay."

Jake studied the night sky. "That's Venus over there—that big bright one."

"You will stay, won't you?"

"We'll see, Mary Katherine. We'll just have to see."

Nine

As Kate bent over to add feed to Abigail's favorite plate, Bad Louie flared his wings and fluttered down beside the dish. He uttered an obscenity and pecked at the food. Brushing him back disgustedly, Kate muttered, "Can't you ever say anything positive, Bad Louie?" The parrot cocked his head to one side and stared at her glassily, then rising up with a flutter of wings, he flew around the room and came to rest on the large chandelier that hung overhead.

As Kate continued to pour the food out, Abigail came scurrying across the room with her curious sideways gait. Her bright eyes gleamed and she made a pass at Kate's hand. She loved to play and to be chased, but Kate was not in a playful mood. She shook her head and said, "Go play with Bandit, Abigail."

Coming to her feet, she went to the freezer, took out a frozen rat she'd bought from the vet, and went over to the large glass case that housed Big Bertha. She hesitated for a moment since feeding the python was not her favorite thing and, lifting the top, dropped the rat in. Big Bertha stirred and lifted her head. A film seemed to glaze her eyes and her tongue ran rapidly. Kate turned away, not liking this part of keeping a python, but there was no getting out of it. She knew it would be useless to suggest that Jake might feed the big snake. He would merely have stared at her in disbelief and stalked off.

Going to the kitchen, Kate opened the refrigerator door, took out some bottled water, and sat down at the island counter. Removing the bottle cap, she sipped the water and gazed out the bank of plateglass windows at the end. She took great pleasure in the Gulf. She hadn't known how she would like living this close to the water, but she enjoyed it right from the start—there was always something to see. Sometimes the Gulf was as still and glassy as a sheet of blue ice. At other times the dark clouds swept across the horizon and forked tongues of lightning descended like fiery fingers that stirred the sea into a choppy frenzy.

She couldn't help but think of the fickle Gulf as a metaphor for her own disposition lately. The initial transition into this new home had been so exciting, yet the last few days she'd been in a pensive mood. It had started after the party, she knew. She'd begun to question the rightness of her and Jeremy being here. If Hart's party was an accurate indication, this Gulf Coast region was even more of a moral danger than their old home in the sprawl of Memphis. And those thugs that Jake was talking to? *Talk about dangerous.* It sent a shiver up her spine.

She sighed. She'd been so certain that this had been God's will for her and Jeremy. Why was it always so difficult to know for sure?

As she sat watching a boat with white sails glide lazily across the horizon, memory like a searchlight moved over her mind, falling on certain scenes. Some of them were pleasant, but memories of her marriage flickered, and she tried to focus on something else. Her marriage had been far from happy. *Just another mistake in a long line of mistakes,* she thought glumly.

But this line of thinking was getting her nowhere. She reminded herself to look around and be grateful for God's luxurious and totally unexpected provision. *Just let me know what to do next, okay, God? Send me signs if we're supposed to leave.*

Even as Kate sat there, she shrugged her shoulders and started to rise. As she did, a movement caught her eye, and she turned quickly. Miss Boo, the flop-eared rabbit, was in the corner and to Kate's horror she saw the rabbit reach out and bite the lamp cord.

"No—Miss Boo, don't!"

Kate's warning cry came too late. As had already happened once, Miss Boo bit into the cord and the current immediately kicked in. The rabbit stiffened and kicked wildly even as Kate raced across the room. Yanking the cord out of the socket, she cried out, "Miss Boo, I told you not to do that!" Miss Boo lay stiffly with her eyes rolled up.

Kate looked up to see that Jake had come down the stairs and stepped into the living area.

"What's the matter?" he asked.

"It's Miss Boo. I think this time was fatal. I think she's dead."

Jake moved quickly. He leaned over and took the situation in at a glance. Without a pause, he picked the rabbit up and said, "I never gave CPR to a rabbit, but it's worth a try."

Kate watched as Jake pushed powerfully at the rabbit's chest, holding his hand behind as a brace. He moved rhythmically and after a few hard pumps Kate cried out, "Look, her eyes! She's not dead!"

Miss Boo gave a few powerful kicks with her hind feet and began to struggle. Her nose twitched violently, and Jake passed the furry animal to Kate. "She's all right, Mary Katherine." He grinned. He watched curiously as Kate cuddled Miss Boo, stroking the silky fur and muttering meaningless phrases. "You really love that flop-eared rabbit, don't you?" he asked

"Yeah, I can't help it," Kate replied.

Jake was silent for a moment, then said, "You'd think you could find something better than a rabbit to love. A guy maybe."

Kate put her cheek on Miss Boo's smooth fur. She found the rabbit's heart, which had been beating rapidly, and listened as it slowed down. "It's possible to love several things at the same time."

Jake grinned, humor gleaming in his deep-set eyes and his wide mouth turning up with an amused smile. "You think a man can love two women at the same time? That'd break your rule, wouldn't it?"

"What rule are you talking about?"

"The Bible rule—one man, one woman as long as they live."

Miss Boo began to kick and, leaning over, Kate deposited her on the floor. "Now, don't bite any more cords, Miss Boo." She straightened up and met Jake's glance evenly. "A man and a woman are united for life when they're married, yes. But a man can love his wife with one kind of love, and his mother and sister with another kind. Don't you think?"

"I never think about things like that. It tires me out. Instead of jabbering, why don't we go out for a swim?"

Kate laughed. "You have a mind like a crazy grasshopper, jumping from discussions of love to going for a swim."

"It's just my charming way of changing the subject," Jake said as he smirked. "Now get that audacious bathing suit of yours on, and I'll go slip into my new lavender thong."

"Don't you dare!"

Ten minutes later the two were walking out of the house. The sun was bright in the sky, and its beams basked on the waters of the Gulf. The sand was warm beneath Kate's feet. She could feel her gloominess from earlier lifting, but she didn't know if it was the sun, the fresh air, or having someone to talk to. She said, "Come on. I'll race you."

Jake broke into a run, but she was faster. They hit the water running at full speed, and Kate threw herself forward and began swimming as hard as she could. The water was deliciously warm, and the salty taste had become a delight to her. She pumped hard and, as usual, quickly drew ahead of Jake. There was a pleasure for her in the expenditure of energy, and finally, when they had covered about half a mile, Jake called out to her, "We'd better turn back!"

"No, let's go until we hit Central America."

"You go for it, Mary Katherine. I'll see you back at the house."

"Okay then." Reluctantly Kate stopped. She was very buoyant, and she floated, barely treading water, and watched as Jake came up to her huffing. When he stopped swimming, he immediately transitioned into a powerful motion of his legs and arms to keep himself afloat. "It irritates me," he gasped, "that women float better than men."

"That's because we're so sweet," Kate said, "like marshmallows floating on hot chocolate."

"No, it's because you babes have a higher percentage of body fat that makes you more buoyant."

Kate reached out to splash water in Jake's face, and he tried to respond by ducking her head under the water, but she laughed and easily moved away. "Come on. I'll race you back to shore."

The two started back and when Kate was twenty feet from the shore, she reached down and found the bottom. She started to stand up when a sudden, terrible stinging pain raked right across the top of her chest and her neck. She stood up gasping and brushing at her chest.

"What's the matter?" Jake had come up beside her.

"I don't know. There's something wrong. My chest is on fire."

Jake turned her around. "Jellyfish sting. A bad one," he said. "Come on."

Kate could barely breathe, the pain was so severe. Jake got her to the shore and half carried, half dragged her across the beach to the house. He burst through the door, pulling her over to the couch and said, "Lie down." She obeyed, wanting to cry. "It's like fire ants eating at me, Jake!"

"Just hang on. I'll fix it." He headed off toward the kitchen.

Kate touched her bare flesh above the top of her suit and found a filmy substance there. She'd never encountered anything like this before and in addition to being in pain, she was repulsed. It was so slimy! She heard noises of Jake rattling around in the kitchen, water running, then the sound of a utensil on a dish. *What in the world?*

Suddenly Jake was back. He had a bowl in his hand that was filled with some kind of paste. He took a spoon and started spreading the paste on her chest and neck.

Instantly Kate closed her eyes with relief. "Oh, that's better."

She lay there while he rubbed more of the paste into her stinging flesh.

"That get the whole area?" he asked.

"Yes, it stopped right away. What kind of medicine is that?"

"Adolf's meat tenderizer," he said.

Kate gasped. "You're putting meat tenderizer on me?"

"That's right. It works better than any medicine. I don't know why."

"How'd you know that?"

"Brandy told me."

"Who's Brandy?"

"One of the Sweet Harts we met at the party the other night. We talked about quite a few interesting things."

"You're kidding me, right? Those girls—"

The doorbell interrupted, and Jake said, "You stay there. I'll come back and give you another treatment."

"Never mind. Give me that stuff." She snatched the bowl from Jake and he laughed, then turned to go get the door. He passed Bandit, the coon, who had come in through the pet door and was now sitting up watching him carefully. Despite himself Jake grinned. The coon looked like nothing so much as a fat, short thief with his mask and his bright black eyes.

Opening the door, Jake found himself face-to-face with a tall, lanky man who had light-blue eyes and straw-colored hair. He was wearing a pair of wrinkled khaki shorts and a T-shirt with Daffy Duck on the chest. "Hey," Jake said.

The man grinned and stuck out his hand. "Hi, there. Elvis Bates. You must be Jake."

Jake couldn't speak for a moment. "*The* Elvis Bates?" he finally stammered as he took the hand that was offered him. "I saw you pitch a no-hitter once against the Cubs."

"That was me."

"I'm still mad at you for quitting baseball while you were at the top of your game."

"You and a lot of others I've heard from," Bates said.

Indeed, Elvis Bates had been the hottest power pitcher to come along since Nolan Ryan. He only pitched for four years with the Rangers, but by all predictions, he was destined for the Hall of Fame. Then amid howls of dismay he had announced he was quitting, and he had stuck with his resolve. Jake remembered reading he had gone to some sort of religious school with the intention of becoming a minister.

"I never did forgive you for beating the Cubs," Jake said.

"Well, I've done worse things," Bates said. "And now I'm the pastor of Seaside Chapel, the church out on the beach down the road."

Jake grinned. "Well, thanks. I'm not a church-going kinda guy, but come on in. Might as well meet the lady of the house."

"Oh, I know Kate. She's visited our church."

Jake led the way, grinning to himself at the thought of a pastor coming in when Kate wasn't properly dressed. "We've got company, Mary Katherine. The pastor's come by to pray for sinners. I told him he could start on you."

Kate came off the couch like a shot. She was still holding the meat tenderizer in one hand and felt like an utter fool dressed in nothing but a bathing suit—with white goo smeared all over her, no less. "Good to see you, Pastor," she said inanely. "You caught us at a bad time."

"I'm sorry—I can come back later if you like."

"Nah, it's fine, Pastor," Jake said. "Mary Katherine just got involved with a jellyfish out there."

"That meat tenderizer?" Bates asked. Kate nodded and he continued, "That's the best thing. It happens all the time along the beach here."

"Yeah, that's what I heard," Jake said.

"Excuse me," said Kate, and quickly left the room. Without warning Jacques the Ripper appeared. He had been perched on the stereo and had come down with that lazy leap cats have, landing as lightly as a feather. Jake grinned. The big black cat was headed straight for the preacher. "Watch out," he said. "Cat's gonna do you some damage."

But Jacques did no such thing. To Jake's amazement he went right up to the minister and when Elvis Bates leaned over and scratched his head, he purred like a miniature outboard motor.

"Well, I'll be dipped!" Jake exclaimed. "That cat's normally a killer. He hates me and just about everybody else."

Pastor Bates ruffled Jacques's fur then stood up. "He probably had a bad experience as a kitten. You know how it is these days. Jacques's a victim like everybody else. Nobody's ever to blame for anything."

Kate reappeared, covered by a light robe, on the heels of Bates's statement, and despite herself, she smiled. She and Elvis Bates shared many opinions. "I've enjoyed your sermons, Pastor."

Bates smiled crookedly. "Right out of a book called *Snappy Sermon Starters.*"

"I know better than that!"

"Well, anyway, I came by to see if Jeremy'd like to join the softball team we're forming. I thought it would be good for him."

"He's not here right now," Kate said. "But I can talk to him about it. I'm afraid he's not much into sports though."

"Sounds like just what we need. We don't win many games, but we have a lot of fun. Maybe you'd like to come out and help us coach, Mr. Forrest."

"It's not Forrest," Jake said firmly. "Jake *Novak.*"

Kate began to clumsily explain the situation, but Bates waved his hand. "Oh, yes, I know about the will. I was a good friend of Miss Zophia's. She didn't come to church, but I came by here and helped her with the animals sometimes."

"Jake has an apartment upstairs," Kate said, the words tumbling out of her mouth. She inexplicably felt the need to apologize and explain, even though she knew she wasn't doing anything wrong. But Bates was casual and accepting and helped her to feel more at ease.

"Well, I'm sorry you got messed up with the jellyfish. That sure hurts. Be glad to have you at the service Sunday, Kate—and you, too, Jake."

"Oh, I'll be there," Kate said.

"Don't look for me, Preacher. I'm still trying to figure God out."

Bates laughed. "Well, let me know if you do."

"Some of the things I've read about in the Bible—well, they just don't sit right with me."

"Like what?"

"Well, like that guy Noah."

"What about him?"

"Well, it seems to me he could have done something about that flood."

Elvis Bates laughed. "I don't know what he could have done except build that ark and save his family like God told him."

"Well, he could have argued with God," Jake said, "That's what Moses did, isn't it? Moses went up into the mountains and while he was gone, the people made a golden calf. It made God mad, and He said He was going to kill them all and just start over again like He did with Noah."

"That's the way it happened."

"But you remember, Preacher, that Moses argued with God. As a matter of fact, he downright talked Him out of killing all the Israelites, didn't he?"

"Yes, he did."

"Well, why couldn't Noah have done that? Talked God out of bringing that flood and killing everybody?"

Bates was studying Jake carefully, a slight smile on his face. "Someone said about me once that I had just enough theology to be dangerous, so I can't answer your question—at least not right now. I don't think anybody could, but I promise you I'll think about it. You all come to church, you hear." He nodded to them and left with a strange shambling gait.

"That's a funny sort of preacher," Jake muttered. "He could have been the greatest pitcher baseball ever had."

"Was he really that good?"

"He was going to be the best, and he quit it all for some silly little church on the beach." Jake shook his head. "That sure was a waste of a good left-hander!"

● ● ●

"Come on, Mom! Let me go over to Derek's house. They've always got something to eat over there."

"No, you're going to stay here and eat supper. Jake's cooking."

"Shoot, I never get to do anything!"

"You get to do a lot of things. Now, I'm going to change clothes. You stay here with Jake."

Kate left the room and Jeremy plopped himself down into one of the tall chairs that faced the island. "Why does she have to be like that?" he groaned. "It wouldn't hurt her to let me go over to Derek's house."

Silence had come from Jake's part of the kitchen, and Jeremy looked up to see the big man was giving him a hard look. He blinked with surprise and said, "What's the matter?"

"You ought to be nicer to your mother, Jeremy." Jake said no more but somehow the words went home to Jeremy. He ducked his head, unable to meet the man's gaze, and finally changed the subject.

"What are you cooking?"

"Venetian pork schnitzel. Why don't you watch how I do it? I could teach you to be a chef."

"I'm not interested in cooking," Jeremy mumbled.

Jake had put the ingredients for supper out on the granite top of the cabinet. He turned to see that both Cleo and Jacques had appeared and were watching him. He cut a bit of meat off of the slabs in front of him and reached out and gave it to Cleo. "There you are, Cleo," he said. "What do you think about that, Jacques the Ripper?" he taunted.

Jacques's golden eyes were round as the moon. His response was to glare at Jake, and Jake turned and said, "You know I can read that cat's mind. He's thinking, 'You just wait, Jake Novak. You can be nice to Cleo all you want, but I'll nail you sooner or later.'"

"Shoot, Jake, cats don't think."

"You're wrong about that. They think all the time." He turned quickly to see Jacques advancing toward him making a hissing noise.

Jake snatched up a utensil used for pounding meat and held it high. "Come on, Jacques, make my day!"

"Clint Eastwood," Jeremy said and grinned. "Would you really hit him?"

"You bet your bird I would!"

Jake waited until Jacques turned and padded away and then said, "All right. Now we can get down to business. You watch this now."

Jeremy was fascinated that Jake Novak, who had been a homicide detective, would waste his time cooking. He watched as Jake trimmed the six-ounce pork chops and flattened the cutlets out between two sheets of plastic wrap until they were practically doubled in size. Jake seasoned them with garlic salt and freshly ground pepper. He then mixed up bread crumbs, dried oregano, and dried basil in a separate bowl. He dipped the cutlets into beaten eggs and dragged them through the bread crumbs. With economical movements he sautéed them in olive oil and then, as a final touch, he heated tomato sauce, poured it into a plate, and arranged the cutlets on top of the sauce. He finished off by topping the cutlets with shaved Parmesan and anchovy filets.

The smell was delicious, but Jeremy wasn't about to admire Jake's handiwork. "Derek says that men who cook are pansies."

"Yeah, he would say that."

Jeremy blinked his eyes with surprise. "Don't you like him?"

"Let's just say I like you better, Slick."

Jeremy was stunned. He couldn't imagine Jake liking him better than Derek.

Jake studied the boy before him carefully and then said, "Derek's always gotten everything he wanted. That's about the most dangerous thing I can think of."

"What do you mean 'dangerous'? What's wrong with that?"

"Sooner or later," Jake said thoughtfully, "he's going to want something he can't have—and that's when he'll step over a line."

Jeremy hesitated. He had seen something of this in Derek but hadn't wanted to admit it. "I don't know what you're talking about."

Jake put the full force of his gaze on the boy. "Yes, you do, Slick. Now, go get your mom. It's time to eat."

Ten

The public beach of White Sands was packed as Jeremy pushed his way through the crowd, heading for the refreshment stand. It was the annual Shrimp Festival, and his mom had encouraged him to go, hoping he'd meet up with some friends. The kids at school had been talking about the event for the past few weeks, but he hadn't seen any of his classmates yet—not that they were really his friends. Jeremy swiveled his head to watch some of the women strolling by in bathing suits that revealed enough to shock him. He'd seen girls like this in the movies, but the real thing, up close and personal, was different. He felt a brief prickle of shame at his reaction, but pushed it away. He hadn't asked for the view—he was just minding his own business, after all!

The air echoed with voices—talking, laughing, and shouting. Music floated from one of the stands where a reggae band was playing upbeat Calypso music. He made his way to the vendors who sold various kinds of food and perused the choices, trying to make up his mind. *Since it's the Shrimp Festival I may as well try some of this.* The woman in the food stand was flush with heat and mopped the sweat from her steaming brow. "What'll it be, Darlin'?"

"Shrimp, please."

"Shrimp it is." He watched as she piled a paper plate full of fried shrimp and motioned toward the condiments. "Help yourself to the sauce," she said.

Jeremy moved back through the crowd looking for a place to sit down, but he hadn't gone far when he heard a loud voice calling his name.

"Hey, Jeremy, wait up!"

Turning, Jeremy saw Derek headed toward him, a big grin on his face. He was wearing an American Eagle T-shirt, khaki shorts, and flip-flops. "Look what I found, gang," he said. "Free lunch."

Before Jeremy could move he was surrounded by the group that was with Derek. Doyle Davis was fifteen, a stocky, muscular boy with red hair and green eyes. He had the fair skin that didn't take the sun well as evidenced by his peeling nose. "Hey, thanks a lot, Jerry buddy." Reaching over, Davis scooped up a handful of fried shrimp and turned around. "Here, Loni, Jerry's feeling generous today."

Loni Walker was a tall, well-developed, fair-skinned girl the same age as Doyle. Her streaked blonde hair was tied up in a pony-tail and her china-blue eyes sparkled like rhinestones. She was wearing a lime green bikini. She winked at Jeremy. "How you doing?"

"Fine."

"Hey, you guys, back off and let me have some of that stuff." Ossie Littlefield was a skinny young black boy of fourteen with bony fingers and ultra-flexible limbs. He was the drummer in a hip-hop group and even now he was beating out time by moving his head back and forth. "Here you go, girl." He scooped up what remained of Jeremy's shrimp and handed it to the girl next to him. Formica Jones was attractive enough with her ebony skin, high cheekbones, and cornrows in her hair, but Jeremy had heard she was always in trouble.

Formica popped a shrimp into her mouth and said, "What's going down, Jeremy?"

"Nothing, Formica." Jeremy thought it was hilarious that a girl would be named for a synthetic countertop material. "I can go get some more shrimp," he offered. This particular group fascinated him. They were known in school as the Wild Bunch, and they stayed on the razor's edge of trouble most of the time. There was something about their daring that drew Jeremy. He never got into trouble himself, but he was attracted nevertheless to others who had a wild streak. He'd once asked his mother, "Why are people always so interested in bad stuff?"

"What do you mean?" she asked.

"Well, they like to slow down and look at car wrecks. And everyone listens to the news about robbers and shootings and stuff. And, like, that movie *Silence of the Lambs*. Hannibal Lecter was a bad guy, but everybody likes it."

"I don't know, Jeremy," his mother had replied. "Maybe it's because there's something not very good in each of us."

Jeremy hadn't pursued the subject, but now he thought of it again as he wondered why he bothered sucking up to this crowd. "Let me go get some more shrimp," he said. "I've got money."

"Skip it. I've got something better than that," Derek said.

"Good call, Bro." Ossie grinned.

Derek led the group away from the throng and out toward the end of the road. They evidently had been there before. It was more or less isolated, and as soon as they were behind a dumpster and out of sight of the people on the beach, Derek opened the messenger bag he wore over his shoulder. "Check it out. I scored some good stuff."

Jeremy stared at the small, funny-looking cigarettes, which he knew were marijuana. In Memphis, pot had been as common as Camels, but he had managed to keep clear of it. Now the pressure was on—they were all looking at him and grinning. "What's the matter? You afraid your mama will paddle you?" Loni taunted. She lit up a joint, inhaled deeply, and passed it on to Ossie. "There ain't nothing like roasting a dube." Her eyes danced and she said, "Get with the program, Jeremy."

Ossie was inhaling, his head bobbing and weaving to a tune he heard inside his head. "Yeah," he said, trying not to exhale while he spoke, "good stuff, Dude."

Ossie passed the joint over to Jeremy, who didn't say anything but gave his head a slight shake. Derek was watching Jeremy carefully. "Come on, it's no big deal. One toke won't hurt you."

"You ain't never smoked a doobie?" Davis asked, as he took the joint from Ossie. "I thought you was from the big city. Ain't this stuff sold in liquor stores and—"

A voice interrupted him. "Hold it right there, all of you."

They all whirled quickly to see a short, wide woman wearing a deputy's uniform. She looked hard as a rock and her dark hair was cut as short as a man's. Her green eyes were taking them all in, and she put her hand on the butt of the gun at her hip. "Well, looks like I made my quota for the day."

"Oh, come on, Officer Prather," Davis said. "Let's don't go through this again."

"Yeah, go out and catch some real criminals, Oralee."

"Officer Prather to you, Derek."

Jeremy had heard about Oralee Prather. He watched as she drew the nightstick from her belt and slapped it into the palm of her hand that seemed no less hard than the wood of the stick itself. Oralee Prather, he had been told, was a dead shot with any kind of firearm and a black belt on top of that. "She's ambitious as the devil," Derek had told him. "She wants to be chief when the old man retires. She thinks she has to be twice as tough as any man."

"Hand over the stash, Derek."

Derek turned the full force of his smile on her. "Oh, come on, Officer. If you arrest everybody on this beach for smoking stuff, your jail won't hold them all."

"It'll hold you. Y'all follow me."

Jeremy's heart sank. He wanted to protest his innocence, but somehow he knew it wouldn't be the best move. He joined the others as Officer Prather led them back toward the crowd. Just then Devoe Palmer caught sight of them. He motioned to the group he was with and came over.

"Hey, Officer. Whatcha got?"

"Smoking pot. What else, Mayor?"

"Well, why don't you let me handle this?"

Deputy Prather glared at him. "What do you mean *handle it?*"

"Well, I mean, after all, it's the festival and look around you. We can't arrest them all. Better if I just deal with this problem right here and now."

Jeremy swiveled his head and caught a smirk on Derek's face. He was fascinated as Palmer spoke and finally felt relief as he realized what was happening. "You're the mayor," she said. "You won't always be."

"Now, that's no way to be, Oralee. You're going to be in line for a bigger job one of these days, and I want to be your friend."

Oralee laughed. "You're everybody's friend, Mayor. You're the kind of politician who'd chop down a redwood and then stand on the stump and make a speech in favor of saving the trees."

"That's the definition of a politician, all right, Oralee. Now just take their stuff, and I'll have a serious talk with them."

"You do that, *Mister* Mayor. I'm sure they'll all go straight down to join the church and give their money to the poor." She held out her hand to Derek, who placed a marijuana cigarette in her hand but made no move to collect the rest from his bag. Oralee turned and stalked off.

"Hey, thanks, Mayor," Derek said. "I'll tell my dad how you helped us out. I mean, after all, we wasn't robbing a bank or nothing."

"Of course you weren't. But look. Be smart, Derek. If I hadn't been here, Officer Prather would have had you in jail and that would be embarrassing for your dad." He turned and said, "Hello, Jeremy."

"Hello, Mr. Palmer."

"Not keeping the best company, I see."

Jeremy didn't know how to answer that.

Derek put his arm around Jeremy. "Don't worry about a thing. We'll look out for him."

"That's exactly what I was afraid of. Jeremy, it's none of my business, but you might wanna find a better crowd. Just a thought." He turned. "See y'all in church." He walked away, greeting people right and left with his politician's smile.

Jeremy finally let out a breath he hadn't realized he was holding. The others laughed.

"I thought we'd had it, Derek," Jeremy admitted.

"Oh, that was nothing. It's happened before. Come on. I got the munchies."

Derek led the group back to the food pavilion where they all stocked up on shrimp, fried red snapper, and crab claws.

"Let's go catch the music," Ossie said. He eagerly led the group down to where they could hear the deep bass and the Caribbean rhythms of the band.

"Hey, Jeremy, there's your mom," Derek said.

For some reason Jeremy didn't want his mother to see him with this crowd so he avoided looking and hoped she wouldn't notice him. The group went right up to the pavilion where they watched the band for a few minutes before Derek started getting antsy.

"Hey, guys, let's blow this taco stand."

"Jeremy—there you are." Jeremy turned and frowned at his mom. "Come here for a moment."

"Aw, Mom, not now."

"There's some people from church I want you to meet."

"We'll catch you later," Derek said. "Good to see you, Mrs. Forrest."

The group left as Jeremy started to follow his mom, but he heard Doyle Davis's cutting question, "Why do you put up with that wimp?"

Derek's response floated clearly on the ocean breeze. "Don't ever do anything without a reason, Davis. That kid's my ticket out of middle school. He's a genius."

● ● ●

Monday morning dawned bright, but Jeremy's mood didn't match. He was trudging dispiritedly to math class when Derek stopped him.

"Hey, here's your calculator." He slapped it into Jeremy's hand. "Don't forget; you agreed to help me."

"I don't know, Derek," Jeremy said. "There are better ways to do this. We're risking a lot."

"Look, it's only a stupid test," Derek said. "We're buds, right? I'd do it for you."

Jeremy went inside the classroom and took his seat in the front row. He glanced back at Derek, who shook his head almost imperceptibly while pointing his eyes toward the teacher.

Mr. Clements began to pass out the tests. "You'll have the whole period," he said. "You can use your calculators. Keep your eyes on your own paper or I'll fall on you and crush you to powder."

Jeremy put his paper down flat and glanced at the first problem. He ran his eyes down and shook his head. *Why doesn't Derek get this? It's so easy. Kid stuff.* But he knew there was no way he could get out of his agreement. He worked the first problem and reached out to his calculator when he looked up and saw Coach Clements standing right over him.

"I've never seen you use a calculator before, Jeremy. You always do things in your head."

"Just—just want to check and be sure." His heart lurched when Clements leaned over and picked up the calculator. "What kind of machine is this? Pretty heavy duty." His eyes came to rest on Jeremy, and Jeremy forced himself to meet them.

"It's brand new," he said. "My mom gave it to me."

Coach Clements opened his lips to say something, but snapped them shut. He put the calculator down without saying another word—but instead of moving around the room as he usually did, he stood right over Jeremy.

He stood within a few feet of Jeremy's desk for the whole period. His eyes darted among the students, but then always came to rest on Jeremy.

Jeremy worked the problems as slowly as he could, forcing himself to use the calculator, but he never had the nerve to look back at Derek, and he never once sent an answer over the transmitter.

Despite working as slowly as he could, he finished, and Clements noticed.

"All through, Jeremy?"

"Yes, Sir."

"Okay, take off." He took the paper but his eyes were still on the calculator. Jeremy quickly scooped it up and left the room. His knees were unsteady, and he realized the worst wasn't over. He dreaded seeing Derek again.

But it wasn't my fault, he reasoned. Might as well face it head-on. Wasn't that what Jake would have told him? Jeremy felt better thinking of Jake's toughness. *I can do this.*

Jeremy waited until the bell rang and watched as the students rushed out of math class. Most of them were complaining about how hard the test was. He gulped when he saw Derek exit and felt the weight of the older boy's eyes on him. He went forward but Derek said, "Get away from me, Worm."

"I couldn't help it," Jeremy answered quickly. "He was standing right over me, didn't you see?"

"Get away from me."

Jeremy reached out and grabbed Derek's sleeve to stop him, but Derek whirled and struck him in the chest. Jeremy wheeled backward, crashing into a locker, and the inevitable cry went up: "Fight! Fight!"

Derek was cursing Jeremy and jabbing at him with his fists, and Jeremy put his hands up to protect his face.

"What's going on here?"

Cecil Grubmeyer, the principal, stood over them. He had a way of materializing out of nowhere, and now he shoved himself between the two boys. He was a short man, stocky, and everyone called him Little Napoleon behind his back.

"What's going on here?" he repeated.

"Nothing," Jeremy said quickly. "We just had a little argument."

"A little argument," Derek sneered. "I'll bust your head!"

"That's enough out of you, Derek. If I hear any more of this, you'll be in detention. Now get on your way."

Derek glared at Jeremy but moved off down the hall and disappeared in the crowd.

"You're new here, Jeremy," the principal said. "I want to warn you...I don't like trouble in my school."

"I'm sorry, Mr. Grubmeyer."

"Just remember, I've got my eye on you."

Suddenly Derek reappeared and patted Jeremy on the back.

"It was all my fault, Mr. Grubmeyer," he said, to Jeremy's surprise. "Just a misunderstanding. We're buddies, see?"

Grubmeyer stared at Derek. "All right. That's the way to act like a man."

As Grubmeyer walked off, Derek glared at Jeremy, saying, "Some friend you are."

"I'll help you with the math, Derek. I'll do all your homework and whatever it takes. I'll get you through this math class."

Something changed in Derek's face. "Sure you will. Don't worry about it." He smiled but the smile didn't quite reach his eyes. "Come on. Let's get this day over with."

Eleven

"Miss Boo—leave that cord alone!"

Kate swooped down on the flop-eared rabbit who had just begun to chew on the lamp cord again. She scooped her up and held her tightly in the crook of her arm. She looked Miss Boo directly in the face and tried to be stern.

"Don't you know you can be electrocuted? You've already used up more lives than a cat." Walking across the room, she went to her bedroom, put the rabbit inside, and shut the door. With a sigh of exasperation, she looked down at Trouble, who had followed her and now sat down on her feet.

"No, Trouble," she said impatiently. She shoved the big dog to one side and started across the room toward one of the aquariums, but she stopped when she saw Jeremy seated on the couch with his feet drawn up cross-legged and staring at the floor morosely.

"Jeremy, you've been sitting on that couch for an hour doing nothing. It's Saturday. Why don't you get out and do something? Have some fun."

"What kind of fun is there around here?" Jeremy asked. He looked up with a rebellious cast in his eyes.

"You're kidding, right?" Kate asked "Did you not notice that we live on the beach?"

"I wish we lived back in Memphis."

"You don't wish any such thing," Kate said. "You were totally miserable there."

"No, I wasn't."

An angry reply rose to Kate's lips but she managed to bite it off. For the past few days Jeremy had been impossible. Everything she had suggested he had rejected angrily. She was reaching the end of her rope.

"Look, there are people who spend every dime they can rake together to come to this beach. There's a regular parade down here from the northern states. You can go fishing or swimming. You could even go rent a jet ski. I'll give you the money."

Jeremy sat there sullenly watching her as she listed the activities available on the coast. He knew everything she said was true, but something black and foreboding rose up and filled his soul with a dark cloud.

As the two argued, Cleo and Jacques sat at one side taking it all in. Cleo was perched up on a leather hassock that Kate had pushed beside the large aquarium while vacuuming the floor. Cleo had been watching the fish longingly and more than once had tried to get up high enough to dabble a paw with razor-sharp talons down into the water. This had proved to be beyond her, and now she glanced over at Jacques, who had eaten the last of the tuna fish Kate had put out for both of them. He began cleaning his fur, but he glanced over at the two who were still arguing.

Look at my Person, will you? What she needs to do is give that kid a swat.

She's not your Person, Jacques, she's ours. And Persons just can't help themselves, you know that. They do the best they can. How would you like it if you had to walk around on two legs all the time instead of being perfectly balanced on four?

Cleo's large round eyes followed the argument as she licked her forepaw.

Cleo, you always think you have the answers.

Just think about it, Jacques. A Person has so many disadvantages. They can't smell anything unless it's stuck right in their faces. Not like us felines, who can smell a fish sandwich a mile away.

I guess you're right about that, Cleo. They're lucky they have us around. If they didn't, they'd be in sorry shape. The place would be overrun with rodents. A lot of appreciation I get. I brought in half a dozen of those silly mice. She calls them Alabama beach mice and acts like they're sacred or something. What's up with that? It's my destiny to kill those vermin.

Cleo rose to her feet and looked toward Kate and every line of her body spoke, *Please, don't fight anymore. It's just not worth it.*

Jacques yawned hugely. *Let them fight. They deserve it.*

Kate looked at Cleo, reached over, and picked her up, draping her over her shoulder. The big Ragdoll loved to be held in this position and would have stayed there all day if Kate permitted it.

"Just go out and do something, Jeremy," Kate stated.

"Do what?"

"I don't care. Just get out of the way. I've got to clean house. You can either help or go outside and pout."

"All right, I will!" Jeremy leaped to his feet and stormed out the door, slamming it behind him.

I'll go with him, Cleo. Jacques made a smooth motion as he headed for the cat door. He paused long enough to reach out and swipe Trouble, who was sitting innocently with his back to the wall. The needle-sharp claws raked across Trouble's chest, and he yelped piteously.

You useless creature! I bet you never caught a rat in your life, and you certainly can't keep yourself clean. With that, Jacques moved out of the cat door and loped across the sand. The many scents of the beach came to him *(aromas that my Person would be blissfully unaware of),* and he dodged through the sea oats reveling in the warmth beneath his feet.

When he caught up with Jeremy, he was rebuked.

"Go on home, Jacques."

Jacques paid no attention at all—his usual response to any two-legged creature's command. From time to time he obeyed Kate, but it was simply because she told him to do something he already wanted to do. Now his black fur gleamed under the midday sun, and his large golden eyes turned to slits as he filtered out the brilliant sunlight.

When the big cat didn't leave, Jeremy kept going down the beach. He walked on that narrow margin of the world where the Gulf waters met the white sand. He encountered a sandpiper that scurried in front of him with its ridiculous tiny steps, running from the incoming wave and chasing it out, pausing to dabble at invisible sea life with his sharp little beak.

Mad at the world, Jeremy picked up a shell and tossed it at the sandpiper. The frightened bird ran away, prompting Jacques to throw himself into motion and attempt to run the sandpiper down. But when the tiny bird simply flew off, Jacques stopped and nonchalantly sat and waited for Jeremy to catch up with him. *I meant to do that. Those birds are so small—not even worth a snack, let alone a meal.* Jacques watched the bird fly away. He'd never caught a sandpiper, which he hated to admit. But, after all, they'd only been here a few weeks.

Jeremy walked on past the Maddux house and glanced to see if Derek was out but saw no one. Ever since his altercation with Derek, he'd felt miserable. Derek was a *somebody* in school. Jeremy had enough wisdom to know that Derek wasn't really his friend, but that didn't mean he wanted Derek as an enemy.

Trudging along the sand, he ignored the beauty of the blue sky and the green water. His head filled with the noise of the crashing surf that ended with a sibilant sound as it curled around his feet.

"Might as well be back in Memphis," Jeremy muttered. He looked down and saw a starfish as big as his hand that had been washed in. He nudged it with his toe and the creature didn't move so he continued to walk along. Most of the houses he passed as he headed west were expensive, ornate affairs set well back from the beach itself. They were painted pastel colors—turquoise, peach, pale yellow. But Jeremy paid little attention to them.

I should have just cheated on that test. Coach Clements never would have known. All I had to do was push a button. Teachers are dumb anyway.

But he knew he was kidding himself. He admired the lanky coach and coveted his approval. He had already gained it by making straight A's in all of his work, and now he was woefully aware that Clements was suspicious of him. *But what difference does it make? It's just an old, stupid math test.* The thought embittered him, and he broke into a jog. He was aware of Jacques loping along beside him and for one moment admired the smooth, easy grace of the big cat's movement. He tried to outrun him, but Jacques simply eased himself into a dead run. Finally they both slowed down, and Jeremy stood still for a moment, catching his breath.

Jeremy kept his head down, staring at the wet sand beneath his feet, his mind dwelling on his failure to help Derek on the test. And what was with Derek's sudden about-face in front of the principal? Jeremy didn't know why, but Derek's strange reaction seemed ominous.

He looked up and suddenly realized he had never walked this far down the beach. He sloshed forward through the ripples of surf and looked around him, curious. To his right was a house of sorts that certainly didn't belong among the massive, expensive homes that lined the coast. This was more of a shack, reminding him of the rundown hovels he'd sometimes seen in the worst sections of Memphis. He slowed down and studied it thoughtfully. It was made of some sort of unpainted wood that had faded to a pale silver. The roof was ancient wooden shakes that rippled in the slight breeze, and the rest of the house seemed just as insubstantial. He wondered how it had withstood the hurricanes that touched the Alabama coast from time to time. It stuck out among the exclusive multimillion-dollar houses in the area, and he couldn't help but wonder how it happened to be there.

A movement caught his eye, and ahead of him he saw a young girl sitting in an aluminum folding chair right at the water line. A large white bucket sat beside her, and she held onto an antique-looking surf casting rod that looked as if it belonged in a museum. As he came closer, he saw that she was younger than himself, but he couldn't really guess her age. Her black curly hair, cut very short, escaped from beneath a dirty white cap with a long bill. The bill threw a shadow over her face, but she turned to watch him as he approached, and he saw that she had strange-colored eyes, almost violet. She was wearing a pair of denim shorts faded almost to a whitewash tint and her arms stuck out from an oversized shirt that had once had something written on the front but was now faded out by long wear and many washings. Just behind her a tall blue heron was pacing, his eyes turned to face Jeremy and especially Jacques the Ripper, who had just spotted him.

Now this is more like it, Jacques said. *This one's a little bit bigger than most—might make a good lunch.*

Jeremy came to a stop as a rather small dog appeared from where it had been lying on a quilt on the far side of the young girl. He had only one eye, a scarred ear, and limped visibly as he came to put himself between Jeremy and the girl. He barked fiercely in that annoying, high-pitched way that small dogs have, and he stared at Jacques, his lips drawn back from his teeth. He was about to leap for Jacques, but the girl quickly snapped, "Lucky! Leave that cat alone."

"Lucky! He doesn't look lucky to me!" Jeremy exclaimed. "That's one of the ugliest dogs I've ever seen."

"Get off this property," the girl said. She got to her feet and set the rod in a piece of hollow PVC pipe driven into the sand. She turned to face him defiantly. "Nobody invited you!"

Her attitude both amused and irritated Jeremy. Here was someone he wouldn't want to lose an argument with. She was scrawny as a bean pole, the shirt hanging loosely on her, and her legs were just as thin. She was tanned a lovely golden color, and it irritated Jeremy. How come everyone else could tan but him?

"This is a public beach," he said. "I've got as much right here as anybody."

His words seemed to irritate Lucky, who moved forward. "That's not much of a dog!" Jeremy snapped. "My cat could eat him for lunch."

"My dog's smarter than you are, I'll bet!"

"You're crazy! I'm smarter than any dog."

"Get on away from here. I'm trying to catch fish."

"You're not going to catch anything with that old stick. Where'd you get it, anyhow?"

The girl glared at him then reached forward and took the lid off the white bucket. She reached in and hauled out a huge red fish. "I caught *him*," she said. "What have *you* caught?"

Jeremy leaned forward. "Hey, that's a red snapper." It was one of the few fish that he knew, and this was a nice one.

"Wow, a genius."

He tried to think of a smart remark, but the girl had turned and snatched the pole up. She began reeling in the line, and Jeremy said, "That's no way to haul in a fish."

"Mind your own beeswax!"

She dragged the line in and there was a small silvery fish on the end. With a snort of disgust, the girl snapped the butt of the pole back into the pipe, removed the fish and held it up so that she was eye-to-eye with it. She said to it exactly as if she were talking to a person, "You didn't have any business biting that, so it's goodbye to you." She turned and tossed the fish back toward the blue heron, who caught it expertly in the middle. Jeremy watched as the bird tossed the fish up in the air, caught it head first, and let it slide down his slender gullet.

"He's a dead fish now. Serves him right for eating my bait!" the girl snapped.

"What's your name?" Jeremy asked.

"What do you want to know for?"

"It must be a dumb name if you're ashamed to tell me."

"I don't tell strangers my name."

"It's probably *Hortense* or *Mayonnaise* or something lame like that."

The girl swiveled her head, her black curls blown by the stiff breeze. "My name is Rye-ANN-on."

"That's not a name."

"That's my name and it's pretty."

"How do you spell it?"

"R-h-i-a-n-n-o-n." She spelled the name out very carefully, as if he were dimwitted.

"Where'd you get a name like that?

"It's Welsh, and Rhiannon was a famous, beautiful woman in Celtic mythology."

"I don't know what you're talking about. I've never heard of that."

"I expect there's a lot of things you've never heard of."

"What's your last name?" he queried, amused at her impudence.

"What do you want to know for?"

Jeremy turned to watch Jacques, who was stalking the heron. "That bird better get out of here."

"That your cat?"

"Yeah."

"If he bothers that heron, I might have to hurt him."

"You couldn't hurt him. He's unhurtable."

"You don't know what you're talking about. You don't even know me."

"How come you're so mean? You got a problem with making new friends?"

The girl studied him, her amazing violet eyes taking in every inch of his height. Jeremy felt as if were being weighed in the balance and found wanting. Finally she shook her head.

"We won't be friends."

What was the matter with this girl? Could she possibly be any more of a brat? "So, I'm not good enough for you?"

"No, I just prefer smart people as friends."

"What makes you think I'm not smart?"

"I just know."

Jeremy didn't know whether to be insulted or laugh out loud. The conversation was ridiculous and the girl was equally bizarre. Meanwhile, she was looking at him as if *he* were the freak. He turned his attention to her crazy-looking canine.

"Where'd you get the sorry looking dog?"

"I saved him."

"Saved him from what?"

"There were two boys who were going to put turpentine on him. I told them I'd shoot them if they didn't leave him alone."

"Shoot them? With what?"

"With a gun, stupid!"

"You don't have a gun!"

With a swift movement the girl turned, threw the edge of the quilt back, and was standing there with a strange-looking gun in her hand. Jeremy had never seen one like it. "This is my grandpa's shotgun. It's a four-ten, but he sawed the barrel off to make it easier for me to handle."

Jeremy stared.

Jacques then made a run at the heron, who easily lifted himself off and left Jacques once again acting blasé.

Didn't want that dang bird anyway. Jacques turned to see Lucky, who was digging at the sand, throwing it behind him and barking furiously.

Rhiannon laughed. "Lucky thinks he's protecting me. He gets a little weird sometimes."

Jeremy was still staring at the gun. *This girl is holding a sawed-off shotgun.* She wasn't pointing it at him, but still there was something ominous about it.

"Did you ever shoot anything with that?"

"Sharks."

"How do you shoot a shark with a shotgun?"

"Well, I catch them first. Don't you know anything at all?"

"How old are you?"

"Old enough to shoot sharks."

"What grade are you in school?"

"I don't go to school."

"Everybody goes to school. It's the law."

"My grandpa teaches me. We have school at home."

As if the girl's conversation had reached the house, a man appeared at the door. He was tall and lean, Jeremy saw, and as he hobbled toward them, he saw that there was an unhealthy pallor in the old man's face. His silvery hair caught the sun, and he jammed a cap on his head as he approached. He moved slowly and carefully as if he were afraid of any sudden move. When he came closer, Jeremy saw that his face was lined and his dark eyes deeply set in his head. Somehow he looked like the young girl except for his age.

"Who's your guest, Rhiannon?" the old man asked.

"I don't know...and I don't care."

"Well, I taught you better manners than that." The man turned to Jeremy and said, "I'm Morgan Brice, young man."

"My name's Jeremy Forrest. I live down the beach."

"Here, Grandpa, sit down," Rhiannon said. "Take the chair."

"I believe I will." The old man moved even more slowly as he eased himself down, but his eyes returned to the boy. "As you can see, I'm not in good health, young man, but I have a fine nurse here." He reached out and his hands touched the girl's black, curly hair. "She takes good care of me." He stroked the girl's hair and smiled, then he said, "*Verus amor nulum novit habere modum.*"

"What kind of language is that?" Jeremy asked, fascinated.

"It's Latin. It was spoken by a Roman named Sextus Propertius about fifty B.C."

Rhiannon said, "It means true love knows no bounds."

Jeremy stared at her. "You know Latin?"

"Yes," Mr. Brice said proudly. "She knows a lot of Latin plus French and a little German. If I last long enough, I'm going to teach her Chinese. Now *there's* an interesting language." He turned and stared at Jacques. "That is a fascinating and beautiful animal. I've never seen a cat like that."

"He's a Savannah." Jeremy felt the need to show he wasn't as stupid as the girl seemed to think he was.

"A Savannah? I don't believe I know that breed."

"They're very rare. They're bred from an African wild cat called a serval and a domestic American cat. He's worth about four or five thousand dollars. Female Savannahs go for twice as much."

"Why, he's worth more than some people!" The old man smiled as if a private joke had occurred to him. "He looks like a killer."

"I guess he could be. We call him Jacques the Ripper."

Morgan Brice laughed. "That's a great name for him. He's a beautiful animal."

Rhiannon reached down into the bucket and pulled out the huge fish. "I caught our supper, Grandpa. A red snapper."

"Why, that's enough for three," Brice said. "You'd be welcome to stay for supper, young man."

"No, thank you, Sir. I've got to go."

"You live here on the beach?"

"Yes, the bright blue house down there, the one all by itself."

"Where the animal lady lived?"

"Yes, Sir. She died and my mother was a relative so we live there now."

"Well, you must come back again," Morgan Brice said. "Say something sweet to our guest, Rhiannon."

Rhiannon stared at him obviously reluctant. Finally a smile touched her lips. "Marshmallows," she said.

Despite himself Jeremy laughed. He found the young girl irritating but at the same time intriguing. "Maybe I'll see you later," he said. He turned and retraced his steps down the beach followed by Jacques.

When he was out of hearing distance, Morgan said quietly, "That's a lonely boy, I think."

"I didn't like him."

"Why not?"

"I don't know."

"You're too quick to judge, Rhiannon." He pulled his hat down over his eyes and leaned backward in the chair. "Now, you can read to me while you're catching another fish."

Rhiannon took the book her grandfather held out to her and sat down at his feet. She opened it where the marker was and began to read aloud in Latin.

Morgan Brice listened as the girl's voice drifted over him. His eyes were almost closed, but he kept them slanted enough to watch the white birds that had gathered for a convocation out over the Gulf. They would dive rapidly, skim the face of the waters, catch some sort of prey, then rise again in the air.

The pair sat there, the girl's voice floating on the wind, and once a grimace of pain caught the man's face, twisting it to one side. He turned his head quickly so the girl couldn't see, but Rhiannon had felt his movement.

"Does it hurt bad today?"

"No, not at all. Read some more."

Rhiannon studied him with concern showing in her violet eyes, and then continued to read the Latin in a clear, treble voice.

● ● ●

"Hey, Jeremy, hold up!"

Jeremy had just passed the Maddux house on his way back down the beach. His stomach gave a little lurch as he saw Derek running out on to the sand. As Derek approached, Jacques ran to meet him, his golden eyes slitted. He uttered a loud, sinister, hissing sound.

"Hey, call this monster off!" Derek yelled.

"Come here, Jacques." Jeremy moved forward, grabbed Jacques's fur on the back of his neck, and jerked him back. With indignation Jacques pulled away and stared longingly at Derek as if he would like to sample a piece of his leg.

"Where you been?"

Jeremy was shocked that Derek was speaking to him. "Just walking down the beach. You know there's a shack down there? It looks like it's about to fall apart."

"Oh, that's that crazy Brice and his granddaughter. You met them?"

"That shack they're living in doesn't look like it would last through a light breeze."

"It won't last much longer. The next storm will probably blow it away."

"They seem kinda strange."

"Yeah, the old man's real sick. Dying, so I hear, and the kid won't go to school."

"I thought they had to. It's the law, isn't it?"

"I heard her grandfather was a teacher at some kind of fancy university. He convinced them he could homeschool her. She's real weird though. You know she nearly shot a couple of guys for messing with some mutt of a dog."

"Yeah, I saw the dog, and I saw the shotgun, too."

"Ought to be locked up, both of them." Derek laughed. "Hey, the fish are running. Let's go catch some."

Jeremy swallowed hard. "Sure...but...well, sorry about that math test."

"Hey, it's all good. No worries. You can make it up to me." His eyes slanted and he turned to face Jeremy. "You can still help me out, right?"

Relief gushed through Jeremy. "Sure. What difference does it make?"

"That's what I say. It's only a stupid math class. Now c'mon, forget about it. Let's go get some fish."

"I'll go tell my mom."

"Tell her we may be out late. And bring a jacket—it gets a little breezy out on the water at night."

"I'll be right back." Jeremy ran toward the house, and the day was bright again. He pushed away the niggling unease about Derek. At least he had someone to hang out with.

● ● ●

The Sunday-morning service had been boring as far as Jeremy was concerned, but at least his mom was happy that he'd gone to church with her. As Kate and Jeremy entered the house, they were almost stopped in their tracks by a delicious smell.

"Come on in. Lunch is almost ready." Jake poked his head out of the kitchen.

"That smells good," Jeremy said. "What is it?"

"Well, I figured if we're going to live on the coast, we might as well learn how to cook some Cajun food. I tried my hand at seafood gumbo."

Kate stepped into the kitchen, avoiding Trouble, who reared up on her. She accidentally stepped on his toes, and he yelped and moved out of the way. He went over to the corner, flopped down, and stared sullenly at the wall.

"You're not hurt, Trouble. You're just aggravated." She turned to Jake. "That does smell good."

"Sit down. It's all ready. Maybe tonight I'll try something different, but for now we'll see how I did with this gumbo."

The three sat down, and Jake ladled them out deep bowls full of the succulent-smelling dish. He waited until Kate asked the blessing, and then watched as the two of them dipped in. It was so hot they had to blow on it, but Jeremy's eyes grew wide after he took his first bite.

"This is the best stuff I've ever had!" Jeremy said.

"Well, I'll take that as a compliment."

"You've never made gumbo before, Jake?" Kate asked.

"Never have, but I got a good recipe from Kandi. She's from New Orleans, you know."

Kate vaguely remembered Kandi Kane as one of Tommy Hart's semi-dressed girls.

"I didn't know you were acquainted with her." She'd noticed that Jake had gone out in the evening a few times and returned very late, but had no idea who he was spending his time with.

"Her real name's not Kandi Kane."

"Why am I not surprised?"

Jake swallowed a bite of the gumbo and said, "Hmm, not bad if I do say so myself. Kandi was right—good recipe. Yeah, we've been out a couple of times."

"How do you make this stuff?" Jeremy asked.

"Well, it's pretty complicated. Look, she wrote it all out for me. This is what it takes."

"It takes all this?" Jeremy stared at the long list of twenty or more ingredients. "It's got leaves in it?"

"That's just a spice. The first thing you have to do," Jake said, "is to make a roux with flour and butter and then you add the garlic, onion, bell peppers, and celery, and you cook all that until it's transparent. Then you start adding water and tomato sauce and okra..."

"I didn't know cooking was so complicated." He glanced at Kate, who smiled knowingly.

"Jeremy's used to me popping things into the microwave."

"All good things take some effort," Jake said.

The three sat there filling themselves up. When they had almost finished, the doorbell rang.

"You expecting company, Mary Katherine?"

"No, I wasn't. I'll get it, though."

Jake got up and said, "Now, to clean up the mess. I don't mind cooking, but I sure hate to wash dishes. Looky there. I think I used every dish in the house just to make a little gumbo."

Kate returned looking drawn, with two police officers following her.

"Jeremy, Jake—this is Police Chief Ray O'Dell and Officer Prather." She nodded toward the officers. "This is my son, Jeremy, and our housemate, Jake Novak."

"I think we've already met," Oralee Prather said, her green eyes fixed on Jeremy. Both officers ignored Jake, who returned the favor.

"I understand you went fishing with Derek Maddux yesterday," O'Dell said. His bright-blue eyes were fixed on Jeremy in a rather demanding fashion. "Is that right, Son?"

"Yes, Sir."

"What time did you get back?"

The two officers frightened Jeremy. "We didn't get back until late. The fish didn't start running until nearly dark. By the time we got back, it was ten o'clock."

"Where did you last see Derek Maddux?" O'Dell asked.

"Over at his boat dock."

"What's this all about, Officer?" Jake asked, moving to where they had to face him. They both eyed him, and O'Dell cleared his throat.

"Derek Maddux is missing. His dad called me early this morning. Apparently Derek never came home last night."

"Yes, Sir, he did," Jeremy said. "Like I said, we got in around ten o'clock."

"The boat's not there," Oralee Prather said. Her voice was gritty and her eyes were hard. "Looks like you were the last one to see him."

"He probably went out again," Jeremy said.

"Is that what he told you he'd do?"

Jeremy swallowed. "No, Sir, he didn't tell me that, but he had to if the boat's not there."

The two officers grilled Jeremy for ten minutes with a dizzying array of questions. Finally O'Dell said, "We've got the marine police out looking for the boat. Maybe he went to stay with one of his friends. We're checking on that."

"I'm sure that's what happened," Kate said nervously. "You know teenagers."

O'Dell nodded and the two turned to leave, but he stopped at the door and said, "Keep yourselves available, Mrs. Forrest, especially Jeremy."

As soon as the two were out the door, Kate began to question Jeremy, but he had nothing more to say except, "It's just like I told them, Mom. We got back. We caught a lot of fish. He gave me some of them, and we cleaned them. I put them in the freezer."

For some reason Kate was frightened. The police had that effect on most people. Jake saw it and said quickly, "Aw, he's probably with a bunch of his friends."

Jeremy found it hard to fathom. "It must be that," he said. "Derek didn't tell me he was going to see somebody else, but I guess he did." His face was ashen.

Kate said, "Well, I'm sure they'll find him. Don't worry about it, Jeremy."

But she was paler than usual, Jake saw, and he knew she was worried. He knew just what to say. "Hey, my Uncle Seedy used to say we spend so much time worrying about things that never happen, we don't have time to take care of the stuff that does. Now, I made a cherry pie. See if you can keep it down, will you?"

Twelve

"Wow!"

Jake looked up from his MacBook to notice that Cleo had come into his study. He frowned at her.

"Don't tell me *wow*." His voice was rough and irritable, and he hadn't shaved in three days, so the stubble darkened his face.

Cleo sat on the floor for a moment, the late afternoon sun highlighting the smoothness of her fur and the azure in her eyes. In a smooth, almost magical, movement, she leaped up on Jake's desk, purring like a small engine, and came over and pushed her head against him.

Jake shook his head and said with irritation threading his tone, "You don't really care anything about me. You just like that boiled chicken I give you." He held up his fist and Cleo thrust her broad head against it, shoving and rubbing and purring even louder.

"You know what you're like, Cleo? You're like Maxine Blackman. You didn't know her, but I did back in Chicago. She was just like you, a beautiful female always throwing herself against me and purring and telling me what a wonderful guy I was. You know what she did then?"

"Wow!"

"Yes, *wow*. The wench ran off with a bookkeeper who was bald and wore Harry Potter glasses. Well, he was a CPA with a big company and made big bucks, end of story. Imagine me, Jake Novak, being dumped for a bookkeeper with no hair."

"Wow!"

"You're just like her. You always want something from me but never give anything back." Jake got to his feet, crossed the room, and opened the door of the small refrigerator. It had been made to fit in a travel trailer and was only big enough to store a few sodas, but Jake managed to keep some treats for Cleo there as well. Taking out a small saucer, he removed some chicken, recovered the saucer with Saran wrap, and shoved it back in. Going back to the desk, he plunked himself down and separated the chunks of chicken into bite-size portions, bite-size for a Ragdoll cat, that is.

He watched as she devoured it and wondered how a cat could eat and purr at the same time. As she ate, he continued his one-sided conversation with her. Although he didn't like anyone else to know, Jake had become convinced that Cleo was smarter than he had thought a cat could be. When he had first become acquainted with Cleo and Jacques, he'd told Kate in disgust, "Cats don't have any brains. They've got a cavity where their brains ought to be." But after a few weeks studying the behavior of the two felines, he'd changed his mind.

Forcing thoughts of cats from his mind, he returned to his desk and the laptop that awaited him.

"Look, Cleo, I'm writing the Great American Novel. Bye-bye, writer's block, you hear what I'm sayin'? Don't know what happened, but the words are coming again. Not necessarily good words, but that'll get better, right? You stick with me, cat, you'll be having king salmon three times a day." He went back to writing, and Cleo finished her chicken. Then she began to delicately wash one of her front paws while watching him intently.

Once Jake gave her a look and said, "I know what you'd say if you could talk. Don't even think it." As it turned out, Jake was pretty close.

He's making a fool of himself. Why can't you be smart like me, Person? I don't do anything but take naps and bathe four times a day and eat chicken. Why do two-legged beings work so hard when they have us cats as perfect role models?

Jake finally gave up and punched the save button, muttering, "I don't know why I'm saving this mess. The words might be coming, but none of them are worth anything." He gave Cleo a brisk ruffle.

"You're right, Cleo. I'm wasting my time." He got to his feet, moved to the stairway followed by Cleo, and walked downstairs. When he entered the kitchen the first thing he saw was Abigail, the ferret, on the island. He walked over and sat down on one of the chairs as she came toward him, sniffing around. He gave her a poke, and she dodged away. She ran to the far end and then came charging back at Jake in her odd, sideways gait. She jumped on his hand, and he let her gnaw on it but finally shook his head.

"You're another worthless mouth to feed. There's too many useless females around this place." He got up, found her food, and scattered a little on the table. He saw her grab a morsel and then dive off the island onto the chair, and then to the floor. She scurried off to find a hiding place for the food. "You'd think we've been starving you, the way you stash food away," Jake muttered.

For a time he sat there trying to make his mind a blank. He didn't want to think about what he'd written today and how inferior it probably was. He needed a break from his thoughts, but it was difficult since his mind ran like an Intel Pentium 4 processor most of the time. When someone asked him once, "How do you think of all those things that go into a novel?" he'd stared at them with astonishment and answered, "Well, how do you *not* think of them?"

Finally in despair Jake got up, walked to the refrigerator, opened it, and stared in. It wasn't as well organized as he'd left it. Neither Jeremy nor Kate seemed to have any ability to keep things in order. Jake had aligned all of the juices, the vegetables in their drawer, the meat in another drawer, all of the sauces, and had the salad dressing lined up carefully in the door. Now all was a ruin. With a sigh and a sad shake of his head Jake closed the door. He could reorganize it now, but didn't feel like it. Why go to the effort when they'd just destroy his work the moment they got home?

A thought struck him, and he walked over to Kate's bedroom. He wanted to go in. He hated to admit it, but he had a curiosity about her. He always felt there must be more to her than she presented on the outside. "Nobody's really that good all the time," he decided. If he did it, he'd have to have just a quick look—she was due home after Jeremy got out of school, and that wasn't very far away.

He stood at the door for a moment, then laughed at himself for his hesitation. "I feel like Raskolnikov wondering whether to kill the old woman or not. Not that anyone in this household would even know who Raskolnikov is. Dostoevsky fans—*not*." He turned to see Trouble and Jacques watching him. In fact, they seemed to be studying him carefully.

"I don't want to hear anything from either one of you. I'm going into Mary Katherine's room to do a little research, you hear? She might be doing something inappropriate, and I need to know about it." When neither of them spoke he added, "She might be hiding copies of *Cosmopolitan,* and I can't let a perversion like that go on in my house. Is that okay with you guys?"

Both of them just stared at him, of course. He'd almost felt like he was waiting for a response.

"All right. If I get caught, you're accessories after the fact. We all go to the slammer together."

Stepping inside the door, he stopped abruptly. Just one glance revealed that Kate's room was an unmitigated mess—and he realized he should have known. Wasn't this the one irritating thing he already knew about her? The floor was covered with jeans, shorts, tops, and shoes. The nightstand was adorned with a half-eaten Snickers bar, a coffee cup that had been there a while, and a book by Billy Graham, which Jake opened to a turned-down page and found to be stained with coffee and smudged with what looked like peanut butter. The sight of the smudges and dog-eared page irritated him.

Desecrating books—definitely one of the seven deadly sins. The Bible says that—or it ought to.

He stepped over the clothes and went to the bathroom, which was even a greater disaster if that were possible. It was a beautiful bath, overly large with a Jacuzzi, a shower, a double sink, and a separate commode stall. Clothes lay on the floor here, too, and every available surface was covered with all sorts of girl stuff—cosmetics, hair brushes, earrings and necklaces, vitamins, and a myriad assortment of bottles. Lotions, hair gels, mouthwash, who knew what all it was. A ceramic toothbrush holder held three toothbrushes of various colors. *Who needs three toothbrushes?* The towel bars were stuffed with thick, plush towels and washcloths that dangled haphazardly. The medicine cabinet, when he opened it, turned out to be stuffed with a collection of perfumes and ointments and other items that Jake couldn't even identify, plus two more Snickers bars.

"How can a woman look so good—and be so disgustingly careless about the room she lives in?"

With a sigh Novak turned and went back to the kitchen, careful to close the door behind him. He opened the refrigerator, pulled the meat drawer open, and checked the T-bone steaks that were marinating in a Ziploc bag. He prodded the bag to stir the marinade, nodded with satisfaction at the nice look of the meat, remembering his negotiations with the butcher at Winn-Dixie. He pulled out the vegetables and started making a salad. He had just started when he heard the car, and a moment later Kate and Jeremy came through the door. He looked up and saw Jeremy disappear into his room as Kate tossed her purse at the couch. It missed and hit the floor, but she paid no attention. He rolled his eyes and went back to chopping vegetables.

She came over to the kitchen and plopped down at the island. She was weary from a long day of helping down at Seaside Chapel, and she was about to mention it to Jake, but she sensed he wasn't in a good mood. She watched him a moment.

"How'd the writing go today?"

"Fine."

"What's the matter, Jake?"

"Nothing."

"Yes, there's something wrong. Why can't you tell me?" She looked at him piercingly.

"I told you nothing's wrong. I wrote twenty pages of the finest prose since Leo Tolstoy."

"Twenty pages—really? The last time we talked about it, you had writer's block. See, I told you it would be fine!"

"It's not *fine*. I'm writing garbage. I was crazy to think I could write in the first place."

Kate paused for a moment, measuring her words. She hated platitudes and knew Jake would resent them even more.

"So you think you can't write."

Jake was whacking away at a bell pepper with a razor-sharp knife and using unnecessary force.

"I can't write because I'm not suffering." He looked directly at her. "Everybody knows geniuses have to suffer to produce their masterpiece."

"You're going to cut your fingers off with that knife. Will that be enough suffering for you?"

"It's a writer's thing," Jake said. "You wouldn't understand."

When Jake was in one of these moods there was no arguing with him. She decided to let it go.

"You want me to help you with supper?"

"No. The board of health might hear about it and close us down."

She smiled in spite of herself. "Well, all right, if you're going to be that way. What are we having?"

"Steaks on the grill."

"It's early yet. Why don't we go out for a quick swim?"

Jake glared at her. "No."

"Why not?"

"That scanty bathing suit of yours would inflame my basic animal instincts." The sarcasm dripped from his words, and Kate shook her head. Well, two could play that game.

"Really. You don't seem to be bothered by Kandi Kane's *scanty* attire."

Jake shoved the dismembered bell peppers to one side and began chopping up celery. He sliced each stalk several times end wise and then whacked them into smaller chunks. He worked smoothly and surely with unnecessary violence.

"Kandi's a good kid. She's had a tough time."

"I'm sure."

"Listen, Miss High and Mighty. You don't know anything about it. She was abused by her father when she was only twelve, and he kicked her out of the house. She ran away when she was fourteen."

Kate instantly felt a pang of remorse. "I'm sorry. You're right. I don't know anything about things like that."

"Of course you don't. I wouldn't expect you to."

Kate sat silent for a moment.

"Well, if you won't go swimming, let's play some badminton."

"No."

She laughed. "You hate it, Jake, because I can play better than you."

"Do not!"

"Yes, you do. You're a terrible loser."

He slashed at the celery without looking at her. "I let you win because I feel sorry for you. I'm going out to start the fire." Without another word he got up and left the kitchen. Kate stared after him and went toward her room but before she entered, she stopped at Jeremy's bedroom, poked her head in the doorway, and said, "We're going to have steak tonight. Don't be eating any junk before dinner."

"Okay, Mom," Jeremy replied.

Going into her room, she stripped off her dress and pulled on a pair of modest shorts and a pale-green shirt that hung loose on her. It wasn't very stylish, she thought with a grimace, but it was comfortable.

Going back outside, she watched Jake as he built a fire in the old-fashioned grill—the kind she remembered her parents using when she was a child. Off to the left was a magnificent gas cooker made of stainless steel with all the possible bells and whistles. She knew it must have cost nearly two thousand dollars since she'd seen one like it at a Sears store in Memphis.

Jake had bought the cooker on sale at Wal-Mart for twenty-five dollars. It was designed to burn charcoal, but store-bought charcoal was beneath Jake. He always used only hickory wood mixed in with a few pieces of fruit wood, apple or pear or peach, claiming it gave the meat extra flavor.

"Why don't you use the gas grill?" Kate asked.

"Because it's worthless," Jake said with a sneer.

"Well, at least you could use charcoal instead of going to all the trouble of building a fire with wood."

She waited for him to defend himself, but he merely gave her his trademark look of disdain and struck a match. He had found what he called "pine rich" wood pieces that burned like a torch. He used them as a starter. She knew there were electric starters and little gas starters on which you just pulled the trigger, but Jake refused to have anything to do with them.

"That's so much trouble," she observed.

"If something's no trouble, it's no good. That's what's wrong with this country today. It's a fast-food, MTV culture. Nobody knows how to take their time with anything."

She listened as he went over the downfall of America due to gas grills and other demonic inventions such as microwave ovens.

"Jake, you're a child of the MTV culture. Gas grills and microwave ovens were around a long time before you were born. You don't know anything about life when things were different—when people took longer doing things. If you're so hung up on taking your time and doing things the old-fashioned way, how come you don't write your book on an old manual typewriter? Or better yet, with a fountain pen and paper?"

Jake glanced over, his eyebrows raised. "You finished?"

"No, as a matter of fact. Are you going to complain about washing machines, too? Why don't you do the laundry like my grandmother did? Go outside and build a fire, put a big black pot over it to heat the water, scrub all the clothes multiple times, and then rinse in cold water and hang everything on the line to dry. Look how easy it is now. You just throw the clothes in the washer and thirty minutes later they're clean."

Jake smirked. "Really, Kate? How would you know? I never see you use the washer. Probably because your clothes live on your bedroom floor."

Kate stared at him. "What are you talking about? Have you been in my room?"

"Not on purpose," he lied.

"What does that mean?"

"Bandit got into your room, and I had to get him out. You know how he gets into everything. I didn't want him messing with your stuff. I couldn't help seeing the mess. Clothes all over the floor—and that bathroom. The only thing that'd help that is a stick of dynamite."

"You were in my bathroom?"

"Just saving you from the coon, Sister. Chill out."

"You stay out of my bedroom!" Kate demanded shrilly. "You hear me? That's my room. I'll do with it what I please. You stay out!"

"I'll be glad to. I'm afraid the fungus on the wet towels will give me an infection."

"You think you're so—" Kate's words were cut off when the doorbell rang. She said, "We'll talk about this later. I may have to get a padlock for the door."

Furious, she walked through the living area, avoiding Miss Boo who hopped in front of her. "Get out of the way, Miss Boo," she said. She opened the door and was surprised to see Chief O'Dell and Deputy Oralee Prather.

"I'm afraid we need to talk to Jeremy again, Mrs. Forrest."

"Well. Come in."

The two entered and Ray O'Dell said, "I've got some bad news. The marine police found the body of Derek Maddux this afternoon."

Kate turned pale. "How terrible!"

"We need to talk to your boy. He was the last one to see him alive, apparently."

"The circumstances are suspicious," Deputy Prather said, her eyes hard as marbles. "Is the boy here?"

"Yes, I'll get him." She excused herself and knocked on Jeremy's door. "Jeremy, come out here, please."

Jeremy stepped out and asked, "What's up, Mom?"

"Chief O'Dell and Deputy Prather are here. They want to ask you some more questions."

"What's wrong?"

Kate hesitated. "It's bad news, Jeremy…Derek is dead, I'm afraid."

Jeremy's face twisted and he cried out, "But—he can't be!"

Kate put her arm around Jeremy's shoulders. Jake entered through the sliding doors. He came over and nodded to the chief and to Prather. "Hello, Oralee," he said.

"It's Deputy."

"Sorry about that. Deputy Oralee."

O'Dell interrupted by clearing his throat and turning his attention on Jeremy.

"At first we thought it was a drowning. The marine police found his boat floating a short distance away from the body, but the medical examiner found that he was killed by a blow to the back of the head."

Jeremy's face was pale so that the freckles seemed to stand out. "You mean somebody killed him?"

"It looks that way. Now, we're going to have to ask you to come down to the station."

"You can question him right here, can't you, Chief?" Jake came over and stood beside Jeremy and put his hand on the boy's shoulders.

"I think you'd better stay out of this, Novak," O'Dell said. His pale eyes were steady and there was something threatening about the man. "You may have been a big-time homicide detective in Chicago, but you're not anything now."

Jake started to answer, but Kate spoke up quickly. "I'm sure Jeremy will answer any questions you ask. But I'd hate for him to have to go down to the station."

"Well, that's up to you, ma'am. Can we sit down somewhere?"

The next thirty minutes were difficult for Kate and even worse for Jeremy. Both O'Dell and Prather fired questions at Jeremy so quickly he became confused. They had obviously done their homework.

"You had a fight with Derek in school last week, didn't you?" O'Dell's voice was flat.

"No, Sir."

"I have witnesses that say that you did."

"It—wasn't a fight," Jeremy said. "It was just a disagreement. It was just we didn't agree."

"That's not the way the witnesses tell it. Mr. Grubmeyer, the principal, was one of the witnesses. He says that it was a fight."

"It wasn't a fight. We were just—"

"You were the last person to see him alive," Oralee Prather said, interrupting Jeremy's protest. "Tell us about that again."

"There's nothing to tell."

Jeremy sounded weak, and Kate had had enough. "You've already asked him all these questions. I think that's enough for tonight."

"We can arrest him, if that's what you want," O'Dell snapped.

"I don't think you want to do that," Jake said. "You don't have any evidence. You're just looking for a perp. The new kid in town's always an easy target, right Ray?"

"I told you to keep out of this, Novak."

"Sure, as long as you show a little respect for people's rights."

There was an aura of almost violence that infiltrated the room. O'Dell straightened up and said, "We'll be back. I don't want the boy leaving town or you either, Mrs. Forrest."

"We're not going anywhere, Chief."

O'Dell turned and left without a word. Oralee Prather gave the boy a quick glance and followed.

Kate put her arms around Jeremy and said, "It'll be all right, Jeremy."

"I'm scared, Mom."

Kate hugged him and turned to Jake. "What will happen next?"

"They'll try to find the killer."

"But I didn't kill Derek," Jeremy whispered. "They can't arrest me if I didn't do it, can they, Jake?"

Novak hesitated, knowing that they could indeed arrest him. It would be a juvenile arrest, but an arrest nonetheless. Jeremy was waiting for his answer, and when Jake didn't respond he whispered, "I saw a story on the news about a man who spent eighteen years in prison for a crime he didn't commit. That could happen to me, couldn't it?"

Jake said heartily, "You may need some help, Slick, but we all do sometimes. I'll be here and your mom's here. They don't have any real evidence. I don't want you worrying about this."

Jake's words didn't seem to comfort Jeremy. Kate said, "We'll pray that the real killer will be found, Jeremy. We'll put our trust in God."

Jake watched the two carefully, turning the situation over in his mind. *They can trust God if they want to, but what they really need is a hotshot lawyer who doesn't know how to lose.*

Thirteen

Usually the soothing sound of the tide put Kate to sleep like an anesthetic, but she had lain awake for hours unable to drift off into sleep. Finally, after what seemed like an eternity, she saw through her window the first faint light that broke the eastern horizon. A glance at the clock showed her that it was almost six o'clock. Throwing the sheet back, she got out of bed and dressed quickly, making as little noise as possible. Her eyes felt grainy. She rubbed them and then picked up her Bible that lay on her bedside table. She slipped through the sliding glass door that opened to the deck. As soon as she stepped outside, the smell of the Gulf came to her, salty, fresh, and invigorating. Quietly she closed the door and walked down the deck that stretched the entire width of the house. When she reached the bottom, She sat down on the last step.

For a long time she simply sat there watching the flickering of the first light on the whitecaps as they broke gently on the shore. The Gulf was calm, the waves rolling in with undulant swells but always breaking up as they arrived at their destination. She remembered what she had read about waves, that they start hundreds of miles away and travel underwater in some mysterious way. Only when they reached their destination did they rise up and come ashore with white foam and hissing.

The warming breeze rippling her hair was almost like fingers running through it, but a sense of loneliness haunted her. The setting was pleasant, and earlier in her life, she would have reveled in the peaceful surroundings, but now the fear that had kept her awake all night in her bed grew within her. Memories swept through her mind, bringing with them morbid doubts and even stronger fears. She shook her shoulders as if to rid herself of unpleasant hands that touched her.

The Mercury lamp that Jake had installed glowed, spreading its feeble beam over the deck as Kate opened her Bible to the Psalms, where she had been reading. She started where she had left off, but the words seemed to have little meaning. Usually she found comfort in reading the Word of God, but the weakness that sapped her body seemed to have also drained her spirit.

Then, as she read on, one verse leaped out at her as if the psalmist had known her very heart. It was the thirteenth Psalm, and Kate whispered the verses aloud as she sat there on the step:

> How long wilt thou forget me, O LORD? for ever? how long wilt thou hide thy face from me?
> How long shall I take counsel in my soul, having sorrow in my heart daily? how long shall mine enemy be exalted over me?
> Consider and hear me, O LORD my God: lighten mine eyes, lest I sleep the sleep of death.

Kate had followed the words with the tip of her right forefinger, and as she whispered them softly, she had a sudden vision of the writer of the Psalm. She identified the Psalms with David, although she knew Moses, Asaph, and others had had a part. She thought of a bearded man wearing a robe, writing on parchment, his face clouded with a tortuous doubt. The vision encouraged Kate as she realized that she wasn't the only one who felt that God was far away at times.

She dropped her head and began to pray. Tears came to her eyes as she whispered, "I'm scared, Lord! I know I should trust You, but I'm just scared to death for Jeremy's sake. Please speak to me, help me to know that things will be all right."

● ● ●

Both Jacques and Cleo had been aware of Kate's leaving the house. Their hearing, like their sense of smell, was so far above that of human beings that it was past expressing. They had been prowling the house, as they often did during the early cobwebby hours of the morning. Jacques had gone over to the dish full of Science Diet Cat Food and was crunching with his eyes half closed with pleasure.

Cleo watched with disgust in her round eyes.

How can you eat, Jacques, when our Person is having such a hard time?

Two-legged creatures always have a hard time, Cleo.

You're terrible. As long as you get food enough to fill your stomach, you don't care about anything else. Our Person takes good care of us. You ought to be more concerned.

What can I do? Jacques lifted his head and glared at Cleo.

You can show a little affection to her.

The muscles on Jacques back rippled and he licked one paw as he studied her.

You go show her some affection. I'll do something useful to make her feel better.

Like what? Cleo was afraid she knew.

I'll go find her a present. I bet if I can catch a baby rabbit or a bird and give it to her, it'll cheer her up.

You are so thick-headed, Jacques, seriously! Cleo rose and moved in that smooth gliding gait that cats have. *Haven't you figured out yet that's not the way to make her feel better? I'm going to comfort her.*

Jacques stared at her. *Females have no practical sense. What our Person needs is a real present.*

He was satisfied with this concept, the difference between male and female, and the chief essence of his thought as he left the house was, *It takes a male to figure things like this out!*

Kate was startled when something touched her arm. She turned quickly and then uttered a sigh of relief. "Cleo, you scared me."

Cleo struggled to get up into Kate's lap. Since she was large and Kate was small, lap space was limited, but that never troubled Cleo.

Kate put her Bible down on the steps and helped Cleo arrange herself on her lap. "You're getting fat, Cleo." She leaned forward, hugged the big cat, and Cleo began to purr and to nudge Kate with her head. It was her way, Kate had long ago figured out, of saying, *I love you.*

The thick, furry body of Cleo brought some comfort to Kate. She continued to stroke the cat's silky fur as she tried to pray, but as the morning light grew stronger, her faith seemed to grow duller, which troubled her exceedingly. She had read all the stories in the Bible about men and women of faith, and at one time had memorized the eleventh chapter of Hebrews, that marvelous list of individuals who had triumphant faith in their God. Memory stirred again within her, and she began quoting the chapter: "Now faith is the substance of things hoped for, the evidence of things not seen. For by it the elders obtained a good report..." She reached the sixth verse and hesitated. When she stopped rubbing Cleo's head, the big cat protested by saying "Wow!" and looking up at her.

"But without faith," Kate whispered, picking up at verse 6: "it is impossible to please him: for he that cometh to God must believe that he is, and that he is a rewarder of them that diligently seek him."

The words struck Kate, and she bowed her head and began to ask God to give her more faith. She felt Cleo's claws clench and she whispered, "Don't put your claws in me. They hurt." Then she looked up and saw that Jacques had arrived—and in his mouth he had a present for her.

Jacque stood there with his golden eyes gleaming, but Kate was almost afraid to look. "Let me see what you have." She held out her hand and saw that it was a sandpiper. Compassion for the little bird crowded out her frustration at her cat's need to hunt innocent creatures.

"Let me have it, Jacques!"

Jacques opened his jaws, and Kate cuddled the small morsel of feathered flesh in her hand. "Are you all right, baby?" she crooned. The bird seemed to be unharmed, much to Kate's surprise.

As Kate handled the bird, speaking softly to it, Jacques looked over at Cleo, his golden eyes gleaming with pride.

You see? That's the way to make our Person feel better.

At that instant Kate opened her hands and tossed the bird upward. The tiny wings beat in the air and with a faint cry the sandpiper flew away into the morning light.

Jacques stared at Kate in disbelief. *No gratitude! I just don't understand females!*

● ● ●

Jake was a heavy sleeper, but when he rolled over and encountered something in the bed with him, he woke up instantly. His first thought was that Big Bertha had gotten into his bed, which had taken the form of a nightmare several times. He pulled away quickly and saw, by the morning light that gleamed through the windows in a long slanted column of luminescence, that Trouble was resting peacefully in the bed beside him.

Jake felt a great gust of relief. "You ornery souphound! Your name is right. Trouble is what you are."

Trouble whined and pulled himself closer.

"Get away from me! You make me feel like that producer in *The Godfather* who woke up with the head of his prize racehorse in the bed with him. Now, get out of my bed, you fleabag!"

Jake shoved Trouble, who thumped off onto the floor, gave Jake a pitiful glance, and then walked over to the corner where two walls met. He threw himself down facing the corner, his body language saying, *Now see what you've done? You've hurt my feelings.*

"I don't care if your feelings are hurt, Trouble. My feelings get hurt, too, but you don't see me pouting like that." The sight of the powerful dog acting like a spoiled child amused Jake. He had gotten fond of the dog, although he would never admit it, even to himself. As a boy, he had always longed for a dog, but his parents would never let him have one. He surmised that as a defensive reaction, he'd developed a dislike of animals.

Getting out of bed, Jake walked over to the window and looked down. He saw Kate and the two cats sitting on the last step. Something about her posture told him she wasn't happy.

Irresolutely he stood there struggling with the impulse to go down and cheer her up. He wondered why he was even thinking about it.

"I didn't sign on to be her shrink, did I, Trouble?" He glanced over at the dog, who pointedly ignored him. Jake turned back to the window. *We don't even like each other. Let her call that preacher. It's his business, not mine.*

Jake didn't want to acknowledge it outright, but he was troubled by Kate's anguish. She was a strong woman in many ways, but he knew that she felt a weakness where her son was concerned. She had once inadvertently let slip that she felt guilty about the way Jeremy wasn't facing adolescence as well as she would like. Jake had tried to explain that adolescents are a breed apart—like aliens from outer space—that there was no right way or wrong way that was always successful.

Finally, with a grunt of displeasure he muttered, "I'll fix her a good breakfast. That'll make her feel better." This resolution of the problem settled him, and he went downstairs. It was only a matter of minutes before he had the coffee brewed. He filled two large mugs, both bearing pictures of cats, and stepped out on the deck.

● ● ●

Kate was startled when Jake appeared. He had made no sound at all as he came down the steps, but Jacques drew himself up and put an arch in his back. His eyes gleamed and he hissed loudly.

"Get away from me, cat," Jake warned. "I'll kick you halfway across the Gulf."

"Jake, don't be mean." Kate reached out and pulled Jacques closer, which was difficult since her lap was full of Cleo.

"That cat has no appreciation for the finer things in life—namely me," Jake said. "Here, fresh, hot coffee. Now I'm gonna go fix you the best breakfast you ever had."

"I'm not hungry."

"You have to eat," Jake said as Kate reluctantly took the coffee cup. Jake stood there, then sat down, keeping a wary eye on Jacques, who was poised to spring if he could catch Jake in an unguarded moment. Jake took a sip of the coffee.

"You can always trust a man who makes a good cup of coffee," he said. "There's some kind of relationship between coffee-making ability and moral values. I read somewhere that Hitler made the worst coffee in the world."

Jake waited for her to respond and saw her put her cup down and turn her face away from him. Before she did, the early morning light revealed the silvery track of a tear on her cheek. He battled warring instincts—to flee or to try and comfort her. He remained where he was but could think of nothing to say. He studied the water along the white beach, noting that it was colored differently from that which was further out. It made a greenish strip about ten yards wide, while the rest of the Gulf was a gray-blue, the same color as the sky would be, only darker. As the waves reached the beach, the water wrinkled slightly like a huge sheet of cellophane.

Jake shook himself and tried to come back to the situation at hand. Ordinarily the beauty of the beach and the Gulf intrigued him, but now he was uneasy because of the obvious sadness of the woman beside him.

"Hey, it's not all that bad, Mary Katherine."

"Yes, it is." She turned to face him, and tears made their tracks down her cheeks. "He's so—so vulnerable, Jake. He was only six when Vic died. But when he lost his father, he seemed to lose part of himself. And in some ways, he's never recovered."

Words poured out of her, and her eyes were filled with a distress that Jake hadn't seen before. "He tries to act like things don't matter. His dad was just like that. But he's more like me. He hurts on the inside." Her voice trembled, and she shook her head. "He's going to pieces over Derek. He had a nightmare last night...just like he did for months after Vic died. I'm afraid for him, and I don't know what to do."

Jake had never known how to respond to situations like this. He'd never been known for his empathy, and everything he could think to say was a platitude. He had an impulse to put his arm around her, but he resisted it. *I can't let myself get emotionally involved with this woman.*

"Look, I'll go see the chief," he finally said. "They don't have any real evidence against Jeremy—nothing that would stand up in court." He tried to make his voice as confident as he could. "This thing won't last forever. We'll get Jeremy cleared. You'll see."

Jake saw that his words had little effect. Kate looked small and defensive as she rose and said, "I'm going to get dressed."

"I'll talk to O'Dell. I can't bring back Derek, but I can help make sure Jeremy's name is cleared."

"Thank you, Jake."

Kate picked up her coffee cup and Bible and moved up the steps. Jake rose, but kept his eyes fixed on Jacques, who was edging closer to him with a malevolent look on his face.

"You remind me of some guys I put behind bars, Jacques."

Jacques, hearing his name, hissed, and made a half-hearted slap at Jake.

Jake laughed. "Get out of here, you mangy cat! I'm just looking for an excuse to take you down." He turned and moved up the steps, taking them two at a time. The two cats watched him go. Cleo moved over to stand beside Jacques.

He's a nice person, Jacques. Why don't you make friends with him? You two are a lot alike, you know. Just be nice.

He's not nice, Cleo. He's an Intruder. Things have gone downhill ever since he set foot into our lives. I'll never make friends with him, Cleo. Come on.

Come on where?

The people in that house across the highway put tuna out for their cat. He's a scrawny, ugly, yellow thing. I'll whip him, and we'll eat the tuna.

That's mean, Jacques. You ought to be kind to a fellow cat.

Survival of the fittest, Cleo—survival of the fittest!

Fourteen

Jeremy pulled a grape off the cluster he had brought outside with him and then turned his eyes on Bandit. The coon had propped himself up in a sitting position and was making little swimming motions with his paws. The mask across his face gave him a rather sinister appearance, but his eyes were bright black and Jeremy figured Bandit was probably the best-natured of any of the animals except Cleo.

Jeremy slowly extended the purple grape, holding it between his thumb and forefinger, and the coon quivered with ecstasy as he took it deftly and stuck it into his mouth. His paws were clever, able to do almost anything that a human's hands could do. Jeremy watched as the coon turned his head upward, his eyes half closed with delight, as he chewed the grape and let the juices run down his throat.

"I don't think there's anything you wouldn't eat, Bandit," Jeremy said. Pulling another grape off, he extended it and Bandit took it daintily and repeated the process.

One by one Jeremy pulled off the grapes. He liked Bandit a great deal, but he was so troubled he couldn't even laugh at the antics of the masked animal. The sun was rising quickly, and he knew it would be a hot day. He looked down the beach to his right and saw Jake approaching at a dead run. Jake did everything at full-speed. Whatever he did, it needed to be done *now*.

Jake ran, legs pumping, arms thrusting back and forth close to his sides. His body was tanned almost like mahogany, and even at a distance Jeremy could see the scars. Jake would never talk about them, but Jeremy was filled with intense curiosity.

Jake finally slowed his pace and trotted up to the house. Sweat glistened on his sleek muscles, and Jeremy noticed that Jake's stomach was as flat as a washboard, his muscles looking like squares. He had never seen abdominal muscles like that except on professional body builders.

"He get here yet?" Jake plopped himself down, breathing heavily.

"Did who get here?"

"The heron. Oh, there he is now."

Jeremy looked up to see a blue heron light on the beach. The bird turned and headed toward where the two sat.

"That bird's punctual enough. He comes about this time every morning. You know," Jake said, "it's funny how beautiful they are when they're flying. He looks like a clipper ship in full sail, an argosy. But when he gets on land he morphs into an awkward, clowning figure. Look at him." Jake motioned toward the heron. "He reminds me of an old vaudeville comedian with a ragged suit and a silly face."

Jeremy watched as the heron moved forward on his long, stick-like legs with three claws pointed forward and one straight behind. The bird moved in slow motion until finally he stood no more than six or seven feet away.

"I know what he's come for." Jake leaned over, reached under the step, and pulled out a plastic bag filled with something. "I brought this out this morning. Here, throw him a bite or two."

Jeremy took the bag and noted that Bandit was watching the bird intently. He was also watching the food with that greedy look he always had.

"What kind of meat is this, Jake?" Jeremy asked.

"Just cheap lunch meat. That old boy's not very picky. Try it."

Jeremy took a morsel of the meat out, tossed it, and the blue heron caught it on the fly. He kept his head cocked with one eye fixed on Jeremy.

"You know, Slick, birds of prey have their eyes in front. Eagles and vultures, carnivores like that. Animals that *are* the prey, they have their eyes on the sides of their heads so they can see a full hundred and eighty degrees. They want to know if a hawk is sneaking up on them. But look, that bird has both."

Jeremy looked closely. Sure enough, the glassy gray eyes of the heron were set on the side of the head, but they were looking at him straight on.

"You know, I think that was very thoughtful of God," Jake remarked.

Jeremy turned to study Jake. The man seemed to have no religion whatsoever and sometimes even mocked it. Was he joking about God again?

"What do you mean, Jake?"

"Well, if the blue heron couldn't see forward, he couldn't see how to spear fish. You've seen him do that."

"Sure I have."

"So, God did just right with the heron's eyes." Jake studied the heron as Jeremy tossed fragments of the lunch meat. "You know, come to think of it, that bird is pretty well made. Everything has a purpose. Those beady eyes spot the fish. And look at those spindly legs, how long they are. They can carry him through the mud and shallow water. I expect the fish think they're some kind of reed. And then that beak. Look at it. Just right for snapping up fish."

Jake watched the bird intently. "He's not a bad flyer, either. Those wings can slip the surly bonds of earth." Jake grinned and slapped Jeremy on the back. "That's a line of poetry. You like it?"

"I'm not much for poems, Jake. Seems kinda girlish."

"Oh? Well, do you think a World War Two fighter pilot was girlish?"

"'Course not. What're you talking about?"

"The poem is called *High Flight,* and it was written by a pilot who died in the war. It's about flying."

Jake laughed at Jeremy's puzzled expression.

"Yep, I'll have to give God an A-plus on making blue herons just exactly right."

Jeremy fed the contents of the bag to the heron, tossing an occasional bite to Bandit, who wolfed it down. Finally the meat was gone.

"Well, that's all, Buddy. You can go now. Shoo!" Jake waved his arm.

The heron lifted himself up, took several steps, and then he was airborne.

"I saw an original painting once by a famous artist named Audubon," Jake said. "He sure could paint birds."

"Jake, will you do me a favor?" Jeremy asked, changing the subject.

"Like what?"

"Ask Mom if I can stay home from school today."

Jake thought for a moment, then said, "I can't do that, Slick. In the first place, it would be wrong for me to try to butt in on this. She's your mom. Second, you need to go."

"Why? School's almost out anyway, and everybody's going to be looking at me funny. Everybody knows I'm a suspect in the murder case." The words were bitter just like the taste in Jeremy's mouth. "I don't want to go."

Jake picked up some sand, held it, and let it sift between his fingers.

"You know, when I first went on duty as a cop in Chicago, I had an older man as my trainer. His name was Simpkins, Bradley Simpkins. He'd been on the force forever. On the third day we got a call, and when we got there, a crime was being committed. A young guy ran down the alley, but he stopped long enough to throw a shot at us. The alley was narrow, and there was no way out. Simpkins said, 'Okay, Novak, go get him.'" Jake laughed. "I said, 'Simpkins, I don't want to go get him.'"

"Simpkins said, 'Well, you don't have to. Just take off your badge and gun and go get a job selling furniture.' It made me pretty mad."

"What'd you do?"

"Well, I knew it was either go in or go sell furniture. Maybe I'd end up as a greeter at Wal-Mart. I'd wanted to be a policeman all my life, so even if I didn't want to go in, I knew I had to. And that's kind of the way it is with this school business. It'll be tough, maybe, for the first day. The toughest time will be on your way when you think about how bad it will be. But you can do it, Slick." Jeremy felt Jake's large hand on the back of his neck, squeezing. "You can do it, Slick. I know you can."

● ● ●

Jake's words stayed with Jeremy all the way to school. His mother said little, but cast glances at him while waiting for him to speak. Finally he turned to her when she pulled up in front of the school.

"Don't worry about me, Mom. I'll be all right."

"Jeremy—" Words failed her, and he saw the concern in her face. It hurt him.

"What is it, Mom?"

"You don't have to go to school if you don't want to."

"But you said—"

"I know what I said, but it must be hard on you. It would be hard on anybody."

Jeremy felt a sudden warmth. He reached over and took her hand and squeezed it. "Don't you worry about me. I'll be all right."

A look of relief came over her, but there was still tension in her voice. "Are you sure?"

"I'm sure. I'll see you when school's out."

Jeremy stepped out and watched as the car pulled away. Other cars were emptying their loads of students, and Jeremy felt as if he had stepped onto a large stage. Everyone, it seemed, was staring at him—which probably was not true, but he felt that way. He started toward the building, and he had gotten only halfway there when he was surrounded by the Wild Bunch. Doyle Davis was scowling as he grabbed Jeremy by the arm. "So you dusted Derek off?"

There was such a threat in Davis's green eyes that fear rose in Jeremy. "No, I didn't kill anybody."

"That ain't what the police say," Ossie Littlefield said. Animosity was playing on his face as he said, "I hope they fry you, Man."

"I told you I didn't do anything," Jeremy repeated. "I don't know anything about it. Derek was my friend."

Formica Jones seemed to be more intrigued than surprised. Jeremy guessed that the idea of criminal activity wasn't anything new to her. "How'd you do it?" she asked.

"Yeah," Loni Walker said, her blue eyes wide. "And why? What'd Derek ever do to you?"

A crowd had gathered around to take in the little drama. The Wild Bunch began to get rougher, and Davis said, "You don't think you're going to get away with it, do you? If the cops don't get you, I'm going to bust your head." He reached out and shoved Jeremy, who stumbled and nearly fell.

Ossie Littlefield knocked Jeremy's books to the ground, his face twisted in anger. "You ain't much," he said. "But you're going to be less when we get through with you."

Suddenly a voice said, "That's enough. Break it up."

Jeremy looked up to see Mr. Clements pushing his way through the crowd. The tall man looked mean and lean, and Jeremy gave a quick sigh of relief, although he knew the Wild Bunch would get to him sooner or later.

"We ain't doing nothing, Mr. Clements," Doyle said.

"Get on inside, Doyle. The rest of you, too. If you don't have anything better to do maybe you can go to the principal's office and get you some detention."

The four turned sullen and faded away.

"You okay, Jeremy?"

"Yes, Sir. Thanks for helping me out."

"Don't pay any attention to that bunch," Clements said. "You know what they're like. Going inside?"

"Yes, Sir."

Jeremy felt a bit better. *At least someone's trying to be nice to me.*

He moved inside and got through his first couple of classes without any outward trouble. He could feel the school had a different atmosphere today, and it wasn't all about him. One of their own had died, and it put a distinct pall over everything. People whispered to each other, and everyone was quieter than usual. A couple of girls even had tears in their eyes. Principal Grubmeyer got on the P.A. system and called a moment of silence for Derek during first period. Jeremy looked down at his desk, as did most of the kids in the class, but he could feel some sideways glances at him.

This has got to be the worst day of my life, he decided.

● ● ●

English was his last class before lunch, and when he got up to leave, Miss Barclay said, "Jeremy, would you wait a minute, please?"

Jeremy walked up to her desk, and when the last student left, she said quietly, "Been a hard day, hasn't it?"

"Um, it hasn't been too good."

"Well, it'll be all right." Hope smiled warmly. She put her hand on his shoulder. "It's very sad about Derek. It's hard on everyone, and I know you were trying to be his friend."

"Yeah, I really was. I would never—"

"I know, Jeremy. Don't pay any attention to the kids. They just want somebody to blame."

"But I haven't done anything to them. And I didn't have anything to do with Derek's death."

"I'm sure you didn't, Jeremy. You just need to stick close to your real friends. You remember what Polonius said about friends to his son Laertes?"

Jeremy couldn't help a nervous smile. "It was on the test."

"What did he say?"

"He said: 'Those friends thou hast, and their adoption tried, grapple them to thy soul with hoops of steel.' But I'm not sure what that means, Miss Barclay."

"It means when you have good friends you hang onto them as tight as you can." She squeezed his shoulder and said, "Shakespeare was right about that."

"I don't have any friends."

"Yes, you do," Hope said earnestly. "You've got me. You've got your mom and Jake Novak. This is a rough time, and it's not easy to deal with someone's death, but you're going to be fine. Just remember that."

"Thanks, Miss Barclay."

As Jeremy left the room, he felt like Hope Barclay had built some sort of hope into him. He would make it through the rest of the day, and though the sadness would remain, the fear would fade. Later, three of his fellow students came to him and said in one way or another, "It's going to be all right, Jeremy," and that helped. The Wild Bunch said nothing more, but Jeremy tried to keep an eye on them out of the corner of his eye.

● ● ●

The funeral of Derek Maddux was surprisingly well attended. Jeremy had done all he could to persuade his mother to let him stay home, but she had said, "You've got to face up to it, Jeremy. If you don't go, it will look as if you're guilty. You and Derek were friends. No matter how hard this is, you've got to show your respect."

Jeremy was glad the chapel was so full that he had to take a back seat with his mother. The silence of the room was so heavy he could almost feel it. Glancing around, he saw some of his classmates staring at him, but most simply looked stricken. They didn't know how to deal with someone their own age having been killed. Some of them were whispering, but most just seemed frozen in their seats. He saw traces of fear in several faces, and a couple students glanced at him with pure hatred. Jeremy saw Mr. and Mrs. Maddux sitting up front, huddled together with their heads hanging low. He couldn't see their faces, but he was gripped with a surprising pain for what they must feel. He couldn't imagine his own mother having to deal with losing *him*.

Just before the service began, Hope Barclay slipped in and sat on the other side of Jeremy. She squeezed his arm.

"I'm glad you came, Jeremy."

"I didn't want to, but Mom said I should."

"She's right. You didn't do anything. You've got to keep your head high. I've had to learn that myself."

Jeremy turned to her with surprise. "You? What did you ever do?"

"It's in the past, and we don't need to talk about it." She smiled. "The point is that I understand how you feel. You did the right thing to come."

Jeremy sat through the service, and the organ music was slow and heavy. The sadness covered him like a thick blanket, only he felt cold, not warm. Unlike many of the students, this wasn't the first funeral he had ever attended, and he flashed back to a hazy memory of standing by his father's grave when he was only six. He tried to shake it off and he looked around him, conscious that just like before, he was the center of attention for some of the mourners. He had a wild impulse to run out of the chapel, but he knew fleeing would be no real escape. Only finding the real killer would make things right again.

The minister spoke briefly, then the coffin was wheeled out by men in dark suits. Jeremy rose. His legs were trembling and at the same time he felt numb. As the people filed out, some looked at him a little strangely while others pointedly ignored him. Doyle Davis glared at him fiercely.

After the service, Jeremy and his mother got into their car, and Jeremy rested his head on the window, sighing.

"I feel real bad, Mom."

"I do too, Hon."

"Derek had his faults, but now nothing good will ever happen to him. He's lost it all."

"I guess that's the reason we need to do all the good we can while we're here, Jeremy."

The two drove home without saying another word, and Jeremy went straight to his room. He lay on his bed listening to music and came out only when his mother called him for supper.

Jake had grilled hamburgers and, as usual, they were delicious. The three sat around the table on the deck, eating the burgers along with homemade fries cooked in a deep-fat fryer. Jake looked back and forth between Jeremy and Kate, who'd both been silent.

"You can always trust a man who makes good hamburgers."

Kate laughed at Jake's familiar adage. "That's not so. I'll bet there have been lots of wicked men who could make good hamburgers. Besides, I thought we were supposed to trust you because you make good coffee."

Jake took a huge bite out of his hamburger and chewed thoughtfully. "The thing is," he thought for another moment. "The thing is, the only guys you can trust are the ones who can make good coffee *and* a good hamburger. From scratch, that is."

The tension from the funeral was starting to drain out of Jeremy, and he started to grin. But then he looked up and he tensed again.

"Look," he said, "there comes Mr. Maddux."

Jake and Kate turned to see Earl Maddux headed straight for their house.

"Looks like trouble," Jake said.

"He looks mad," Kate murmured.

Without hesitation Earl Maddux came up the steps. His face was red, and he ignored Jake and Kate. He spoke directly to Jeremy.

"You killed my son. I'm going to see that you pay for it."

"He didn't kill anybody, Mr. Maddux," Kate said. She stood up to get closer to Jeremy, but before she could say anything else, Earl Maddux lost it. His florid face twisted and he reached out to grab Jeremy as if to shake him.

But Jake was on him, pulling him away from Jeremy.

"That's enough, Earl. You don't want to do this."

"Let go of me, Novak!"

"Sure. You behave yourself, though."

Jake released Maddux but stood balanced on the balls of his feet, ready to move at a moment's notice. Earl's eyes were red, and it appeared he'd been drinking.

"I'm going to see you pay for it, kid. You just see if I don't." He cursed a few times then turned and left, weaving unsteadily on his way down the steps. Jake sat down and leaned toward Jeremy.

"Don't pay any attention to him. People say crazy things when they're under strain."

"That's right, Jeremy." Kate patted Jeremy's back.

"He hates me—and I didn't do anything." Jeremy pushed his plate away. "I'm not very hungry."

Jake and Kate exchanged glances as Jeremy left for his room. "It's hit him pretty hard," Jake said. "He didn't need that from Maddux."

"I guess I can understand it," Kate said. "If I thought somebody had hurt Jeremy, I'd be just as mad."

"No, you wouldn't. Maddux is used to having his own way. Now he's had something handed to him that money won't fix. He'll have to learn how to live with it this time, just like the rest of us."

Kate looked at the hamburger dispiritedly. "I can't eat this."

"I guess I'm not very hungry myself," Jake said, pushing his plate away.

The two began to clean up, feeding the hamburgers to Trouble and Bandit, who were always ready to chow down. Jake took a morsel of the hamburger meat and held it up. "If you'll be nice, Jacques, I'll give you a bite of this."

Jacques merely glared at Jake and when Jake gave a bit to Cleo, he promptly took it away from her.

"That cat's a natural born thug," Jake observed. "He'll never make it to heaven."

"I'm not sure there'll be cats in heaven."

"Why not? What has God got against cats?"

"Nothing. I'm just not sure what it's like in heaven."

"I've heard a preacher or two. They said the streets are made of gold, there's gates of pearl, and pie in the sky for you and I."

"Well, I still don't get it. The book of Revelation mentions some of that, but it's a highly symbolic book." She scraped the dishes and put them in the dishwasher. "Jake, I was reading the Bible last night and I was so scared that I asked God to give me a verse that would help...and something happened."

"Something happened? Like what?"

"Well, I try to memorize verses of Scripture, but I always took the familiar ones like John 3:16. But something came into my mind and it wasn't a verse I had memorized. I didn't even remember reading it. So I went to the concordance and started looking for it. I found it. It's in the sixteenth chapter of Second Chronicles, the ninth verse. It says, 'For the eyes of the LORD run to and fro throughout the whole earth, to show himself strong in the behalf of them whose heart is perfect toward him.'"

She looked up at Jake, and her eyes were wide with wonder. "That was what came to me, and I spent a long time thinking about it. I think it means that God wants to be strong in my life."

"So you're saying your heart is perfect toward God?"

"Well, not perfect, exactly. But I do think He knows that I want to please Him." Kate paused for a moment. "You don't believe the Bible, do you, Jake?"

"Just seems unlikely, you know? Kind of like...hocus pocus. You really believe God spoke that verse to you?"

"How else could I know it? I never memorized it. Anyway, when God puts something in my heart like that, I take it as a promise. I go over it every day. And it seems to really help."

Jake stared at Kate for a moment. *I'd rather trust a top-notch lawyer who knows his way around the legal system than some kind of vision.* But he saw the hope on her face and knew he couldn't say what he really felt. "Well, I hope you're right, Mary Katherine. Times like this a person needs God on his side."

Fifteen

Jeremy kept his eyes on the sand in front of him as he walked, and when the waves came in from time to time he moved to his right to avoid getting his shoes and socks wet. Just ahead of him a small group of sandpipers, seven in all, made exactly the same movements. Jeremy watched as they followed the surf as it went out, their little stem-like legs moving stiffly, very rapidly, and their bodies perfectly still. They were, Jeremy thought, like cartoon characters. They were the busiest creatures on the beach. No handouts for them!

As he hurried past the Maddux house hoping that no one would see him, the birds kept pace staying in front, always by ten feet. When he was past the house, he lifted his eyes to the Gulf and saw in the distance a large ship plowing its way across the waters. For an instant he wished he was on it, but then he remembered that escaping wouldn't solve anything.

He watched as the natty little birds, with never a feather out of place, dashed along the edge of the receding waves. They seemed to be eating some kind of invisible food, moving back just as the tide came in. They were always just one step from being inundated. Jeremy said aloud, "You're just like me. You nearly get caught all the time. I wish I had your reflexes."

Finally he broke into a run and the birds all turned as one unit and dashed inland until he was past. Glancing back, he saw them turn to their feeding station, which was the entire Gulf. They were not colorful like cardinals or woodpeckers, just a plain gray. *You never turn your heads. Just dash along eating whatever it is that comes in on the waves, minding your own business.*

Jeremy was so lost in thought he found himself in front of the house where he had met the little girl and the sick old man. He glanced up at the house curiously. It didn't come within light-years of the other houses stretched along the beach. The tin roofing panels slapped noisily against each other even in the light breeze that was blowing off the Gulf. As he watched, one of the shingles lifted itself and took a short flight to the ground, leaving a vacant space.

The yard was closed in with a picket fence, and he tried to remember the name of the girl. What was it again? Something strange.

Jeremy would have hurried on past, but a voice called to him. "Hey, young fellow, come up here." He saw the old man waving, and reluctantly moved toward them. He passed through the gate and saw that the girl and her grandfather were seated at a table covered with books and paper, rocks strewn about to keep them from blowing away.

"Rhiannon and I are having school, Jeremy. Sit down and join us." *Rhiannon.* That was it. He knew it was a weird name.

"I guess I've had enough school for one week," Jeremy said.

"Well, go on then and walk on the dumb beach!" Rhiannon snapped.

Jeremy stared at her. "What are you mad about?"

"Nothing. I'm having school. I'm learning things."

Jeremy said, "Duh. Isn't that what school is for?"

"Pull up a chair," Morgan Brice said with a grin. He winked at his grand-daughter. "Maybe he can help you with some of these lessons I've been pouring on you."

"No, he can't."

Jeremy was irritated by the girl. Her short curly hair, dark as the blackest thing in nature, was blowing in the breeze and her green eyes looked at him with what he thought was contempt.

"Go get us all some juice, Rhiannon," her grandfatehr said. "I'm thirsty."

The girl got up and went into the house. When she was gone, the old man said, "You'll have to excuse Rhiannon. She's a little bit blunt at times."

"She acts like she's mad at me every time I see her," Jeremy said. "She doesn't like me."

"Don't be too sure about that. She acts mad at me a lot of times, and I know she likes me."

Jeremy looked out at the line that was filled with clothes flapping in the wind. "We've never dried clothes like that," Jeremy said. "We always lived in the city. There was no place to hang them."

Rhiannon was back bearing a pitcher and three glasses. She plunked them down and said, "Clothes smell better if they dry in the air. Don't you know that?"

Jeremy tried to think of an answer but in all truth he had never thought of such a thing. He watched as the girl poured the juice. When he tasted it, he asked, "What kind of juice is this?"

"It's my secret formula. I don't tell anybody what's in it."

"I think I know," Morgan Brice said, sipping from the glass. "She just takes the leftovers in all the juice bottles and mixes it all up. Different every time."

"Well, it worked pretty well this time," said Jeremy.

"Let's get on with our lesson, Grandpa," Rhiannon said, ignoring Jeremy's presence.

"Well, did you find a poem you liked that we could talk about?" He glanced over and said, "I like to throw a bunch of stuff at Rhiannon and let her pick out something she likes. What poem did you find?"

Rhiannon held her head up and quoted rapidly, "I like the one that says:

> *There's music in a hammer*
> *There's music in a nail*
> *There's music in a pussycat*
> *When you step upon his tail.*"

Morgan laughed. He was frail in body but his voice was rich and full. "That's a nice poem. Did you write it yourself?"

"No, I found it in a book."

"Well, I like that one. Tell me of a poem you found that you didn't like."

"I didn't find a poem, but I found something in that book by that Englishman, the preacher, John Donne."

"What does it say?"

Rhiannon kept her eyes fixed on her grandfather. "It says, 'No man is an island entire of itself. Any man's death diminishes me because I am involved in mankind and, therefore, never send to know who for the bell tolls. It tolls for thee.'"

"You know what that means, Rhiannon?" the man asked.

"I don't understand about the bell tolling. What does that mean, Grandpa?"

"Well, in England and even in Wales where we spring from, when somebody died they rang the church bell. They rang it the number of years that the person had lived."

"The best I can understand it, Grandpa, it means that when somebody dies, no matter who they are, somehow I lose something." She looked up and her green eyes were intent. "I don't think that's so."

"Why not?"

"Well, it doesn't make any sense. How could it matter to me if someone in China dies, someone I don't even know? It doesn't have anything to do with me."

Morgan Brice sipped at his juice and sat there meditatively. The wind lifted his silver hair, and he reached up to brush it back. He had the look of one perennially sick, but still there was life in his eyes.

"Donne felt like we were all a family in one sense. That we owe each other something no matter who we meet."

"I'm only interested in some people." She glanced over at Jeremy and said bluntly, "I heard you killed that boy that lives up the beach."

Jeremy was taken aback by the intensity in the young girl's gaze. She was, he had found out, only ten years old, but there was something direct like an adult in her manner. She was more like a policeman interrogating a suspect than a ten-year-old girl drinking juice with her grandfather.

"I didn't," he said.

Morgan Brice said gently, "You shouldn't be so direct, Rhiannon."

"Well, I wanted to know. You always said if I wanted to know something, I should ask."

"Well, now you know!" Jeremy snapped. "You shouldn't pry in things that aren't your business."

"You *are* my business. That's what this man John Donne says, and that's what Grandpa says. He believes we're all connected with everybody."

"Let's get on with the lesson," Morgan said. "Speaking of how much we owe to other people...you know the story of the Good Samaritan, either of you?"

"Of course I know it," Jeremy said. "I read the Bible all the time."

"That's good, Jeremy."

"I know it, too," Rhiannon spoke up.

"Let Jeremy tell it."

Jeremy nodded and repeated the story of the Good Samaritan in a loose translation. "This man got beat up by robbers and two men went by and didn't pay any attention to him, but the third was a Samaritan. He patched him up and took him to a hospital."

"That's the story Jesus told all right," the old man said. "But what does it mean?"

Rhiannon interjected, "It means those first two guys that went by weren't very nice."

"So, you would have stopped and helped this poor guy, would you?" Jeremy demanded.

"Would you?"

"I asked you first."

"I asked you second."

"You two calm down," Mr. Brice said. "Let me tell you a story and then I'll ask you to make a choice. This is your final exam on this subject."

Jeremy cast a glance at Rhiannon, and she stared back at him without expression.

"I read once about a man years ago who was in charge of changing the railroad systems in England. When a train came, he had to throw a switch that would put the train on a new track. If he didn't throw the switch, the train would plunge off into a river and kill all the passengers."

"Why didn't they fix it so it didn't work like that?"

"I think they did later on, but railroads have always been dangerous things. Anyway, this man had one son and he took the boy to work with him pretty often. One day he looked at the clock and heard the whistle of the oncoming train. He reached out to throw the switch, but before he did he looked down and saw that his son, who was only seven or eight years old, had gone down to where the machinery moved the tracks. The man knew that if he threw the switch he would kill his son." Morgan leaned forward. "If he didn't throw the switch, maybe hundreds of people would be killed. But if he did throw the switch, he would kill his own son." He leaned back and studied the two without saying anything else.

Rhiannon said, "I think it's dumb. They should have built a different system."

"That's not an option," the grandfather said. "Which would you choose, Rhiannon, if you had a little boy and he was there, and you had to choose between him and maybe a hundred or more other lives?"

"I'd save my son. That's what I'd do," Rhiannon said, her eyes snapping.

"What about the other people on the train?"

"I'd be sorry for them."

"But that's all?"

"I couldn't kill my own family—not for anybody."

Morgan shifted his gaze. "What about you, Jeremy? What would you do?"

Jeremy blinked with surprise. "I—" He broke off and realized that it was a harder problem than he had thought at first.

"I know what you'd do," Rhiannon said. "You'd do just like I would."

Jeremy nodded slowly. "I don't think I could kill my own son."

"Well, I'd probably do the same thing," Mr. Brice agreed. "But God didn't do that."

Both Rhiannon and Jeremy stared at the old man. "What do you mean, Grandpa?"

"You know John 3:16, don't you?"

Rhiannon leaned forward eagerly. "It says, 'For God so loved the world that he gave his only begotten Son, that whosoever believeth in him, should not perish, but have everlasting life.'"

"That's right. God chose to allow His own son to die so that the rest of us could live. That's the difference between God and us."

Jeremy sat in his chair listening with amazement as the two talked. The girl Rhiannon was small, but there was something grownup about her, too.

Finally Morgan said, "Well, that's the end of the lesson, kids. I'm going to lie down now. Good to see you, Jeremy. Come back anytime."

"Yes, Sir, I will. I enjoyed the lesson."

Jeremy waited until Mr. Brice had disappeared, and then he turned and said, "Are all the lessons like this?"

"They're never the same," Rhiannon said. "Sometimes we just do arithmetic or algebra. I'm starting geometry now. Sometimes he tells me things about history."

"You like school like this?"

"Of course. Grandpa knows more than all the teachers at the school you go to put together."

"I'm not sure about that."

"Well, *I* am," Rhiannon said firmly. She glanced toward the house and her voice softened. "Grandpa wants me to be a good person like he is."

"Well, that ought to be easy for you. You don't have the problems that I do."

Rhiannon stood up and snatched the glass out of Jeremy's hand. "I think you should leave," she said. "You don't know anything."

"What are you mad about?"

"You've got a family. I don't have anybody but Grandpa, and he's dying. Go away and don't come back anymore. I don't like you."

Jeremy got to his feet and found himself shaken by Rhiannon's ferocious gaze.

"I'm sorry, Rhiannon. I didn't mean to..."

"Go! I'm not in a good mood today."

Jeremy watched as the girl went into the house. He felt he'd been scolded. *It's like she thinks she's better than me.* He didn't know how the conversation had taken such a turn, but he felt shame in the way it had ended. Turning, he walked back slowly along the sand, wishing he didn't always mess everything up.

Sixteen

Kate's mother had possessed the strange gift of being able to remember every detail of her dreams. Almost every day at some point, when Kate was still living at home, her mother would begin speaking of the dreams she'd had the night before. Kate had listened entranced at the brilliant detail and the infinite color and sounds that accompanied her mother's dreams.

Kate always felt a little put out because most of her dreams came fleetingly through the night or early morning, and when she woke up she could remember only vague and diaphanous scenes. Nothing solid.

"My dreams are like cotton candy you buy at a carnival," she had proclaimed once to her mother. "You know how that stuff is. You try to bite into it and there's nothing there. It just melts in your mouth. I wish I could remember my dreams the way you do, Mama."

But when Kate awoke on Tuesday morning she lay very still, for the dream she'd been having was as clear and sharp and focused as anything she had seen with her physical eyes. She lay there letting the scene play itself out, almost as if she were watching a movie on a silver screen. She thought of her mother and marveled that this must have been her experience every day.

Finally she got out of bed slowly and began to dress. By the time she was slipping her feet into her shoes, she knew for a certainty that this dream hadn't been an ordinary one. *Maybe I'm having a dream like Joseph in the Bible did.* The thought intrigued her. As she left her room and entered the spacious living area on her way to the kitchen, she tried to think what the dream could mean. It was so strange, however, that she couldn't make any connection with what went on in the dream and any known factor in her own life. Moving into the kitchen, she found Jake sitting at the island on one of the tall stools, a large mug of steaming coffee in front of him. He lifted it to his lips and, not for the first time, Kate was shocked at how he could drink such blistering hot coffee.

"You're going to burn out your sense of taste drinking scalding coffee like that."

Jake turned his head slightly to glare at her. He hadn't shaved and apparently hadn't slept very well either, if the circles under his eyes and his slumped shoulders were any evidence. Ordinarily he was bright and cheerful early in the morning, much more so than Kate herself.

"There's no such thing as coffee too hot," he remarked sourly. With a look of defiance he put the cup to his lips, drank the coffee down, and then slammed the cup on the counter with more force than necessary.

"You're going to break the cup slamming dishes around that way." Kate walked over, poured herself a cup of coffee, and sat on another of the stools. As she glanced outside she saw that rain was sweeping across the Gulf. Although the sun was shining on this particular part of the coast, far off the rain was falling in long, slanting sheets. It always delighted her how the scene changed out on the Gulf no matter how many times you looked.

"I hope you slept well," she said, hoping to turn the conversation on a positive note.

"I didn't sleep a wink," Jake growled.

Kate took a sip of her coffee and said, "My, you're in a bad mood this morning."

"If I am, it's not my fault."

"What do you mean it's not your fault? It certainly is. You can control your moodiness if you really want to."

"No, I can't," Jake said. "Just shows how much you know."

"What are you talking about?"

Jake sighed as if talking to a child. "Don't you know that men lose brain tissue at almost three times the rate of women? And when they do, it curbs their memory, their concentration, and their reasoning."

"You're making that up," Kate said with a laugh. "You always make up arguments when you don't know what you're talking about."

"I do not!"

"Do too!"

"You didn't read *Parade* magazine last Sunday, I can see."

"Ah, *Parade*," Kate said. "The last word on every topic known to man. I should have known."

Jake ignored that. "There's a professor of psychology who's done a scientific study about shrinking brains. He said shrinking brains may make some men grumpier as they age. So you see? I can't help it. He says it's not a man's fault when he's grumpy. Old men have a biological problem."

"That's the silliest thing I ever heard of! In the first place, I don't believe a word of it, and in the second place, even if you read such a thing, you're so far from being an old man it's not even funny."

"I'm old enough to be grumpy."

"Well, you sit there and be grumpy. I'll fix breakfast this morning."

"And take my life in my hands with your cooking?" Jake commented sourly.

"I can scramble eggs. It's impossible to mess up eggs."

"You'll find a way."

Kate got up and began to cook breakfast. She turned on the radio under the cabinet and her selection of stations didn't satisfy Jake either.

"I don't like that music," he said.

"What do you mean you don't like it? It's great music."

"It's Mozart. I don't listen to that miserable man's heavy stuff. Find me some Glenn Miller or Tommy Dorsey, some good old big-band music. Those old guys knew how to play."

Kate gave him a disgusted look. "You think Glenn Miller was greater than Mozart?"

"He was taller."

Kate looked sideways at Jake. "You're impossible. Now, just sit there. How many eggs do you want?"

"I suppose four will hold me for a while."

"*Four* eggs? You'll have cholesterol stuffed in all of your arteries."

"Doesn't matter. I'm over the hill anyway."

Kate fixed the breakfast without speaking again. She had watched him cook eggs before, and she mixed up some jalapenos and bell peppers along with just a trace of garlic. She fixed his in a separate pan. She couldn't bear the taste of his serving so early in the morning.

Finally she made toast in the Munsey oven, nicely buttered, and cooked turkey bacon in the microwave. She set it down before him.

"You go ahead and start."

"I can't start," he said. "It's not been blessed." He had the tiniest trace of a crooked grin as he glanced sideways at her.

Kate smiled. "Well, you can bless it."

"No, that's your job."

Kate sighed dramatically, got her breakfast, and bowed her head. "Lord, I thank You for this food, and I thank You for Jake as gruffy as he is. In Jesus' name. Amen."

"That's the worst prayer I ever heard in my life! Mussolini could have prayed a better prayer than that. Hitler could have prayed better."

"Eat your breakfast."

"I don't know if I can keep it down." He did, however, manage to put away all four eggs and had her make two more slices of toast, which he spread with fresh blackberry jam. The food made him feel better.

"Well, that wasn't bad. If you'd let me give you some lessons, I'd make quite a cook out of you."

"My cooking's good enough for me and Jeremy."

Jake passed a quick glance at her and saw that she hadn't eaten half of her breakfast. "What's the matter?" he said. "Aren't you hungry?"

"I just have a lot on my mind this morning."

"Still worried about Jeremy?"

"Of course I am. He's a suspect in a murder. I know you're used to things like this. But I'm not. Nothing like this has ever happened to me."

"I'm telling you it'll be all right." Jake spoke as forcibly as he could, knowing that Kate was sick with fear. He'd seen several cases turn out badly for suspects who were innocent, but there was nothing to be gained by letting her know how unpredictable these things could be.

"They have nothing but circumstantial evidence. The district attorney knows that. He'll never let it get to trial. All we have to do is let this thing roll along. They'll find the real killer, whoever he is." He glanced at her and saw that his assurance hadn't helped much, but it was all he could offer.

Kate glanced out the window. "I know I shouldn't be worried. I need to trust God in this. He knows Jeremy's innocent. But I can't help it. I'm a mother. And God knows that, too."

Jake got up and began to collect the dishes. He was bothered, although he couldn't put his finger on the exact cause. It had something to do with Kate and the fear he saw in her eyes. Finally he turned to Kate and said,

"I heard a preacher say once that we spend so much time worrying about things that might happen that we don't have time to think about the real problems we have."

"But shouldn't we *do* something, Jake?"

"Yes. You keep the ship afloat and do all you can to support Jeremy. Just be his mom. I've got a few ideas I want to work on." Jake neatly folded the dish towel and hung it up. He headed toward the door. "In fact, I think I'm going to start right now."

"When will you be back?"

"I'll be back when you see me coming."

"Jake, I don't think—" But she didn't finish her sentence. Jake had moved quickly out the back door, and a few seconds later she heard the Harley break into a roar. She went over to the window as he pulled out of the garage and revved the bike until it hit the road. Soon he was out of sight. She turned and took a deep breath, ready for the next part of her morning.

I wish Jeremy didn't have to go to school.

She walked to Jeremy's bedroom door and knocked.

"Jeremy, get up. I'll have breakfast ready in a minute."

● ● ●

Vince Canelli's home was on Ono Island. Jake pulled up to the guard-house, where two uniformed security men checked everyone who went through.

"I'm here to see Mr. Canelli," Jake said. "Jake Novak."

The guard was a short man with the chunky muscles of a weight lifter and a pair of eyes the color of oatmeal. He looked as if he'd had a bad morning already. "Your name's not on the list," he said.

"I'm delivering a package for him," Jake said firmly. "I think he'd be upset if you didn't let me in."

The guard seemed about to argue, but the look on Jake's face stopped him.

"Go ahead then," he said, "but next time call ahead."

"Sure thing," Jake said with a grin.

"You know the house, right? The big one at the end of the road—looks like a castle?"

Jake nodded, and the guard continued. "It's got big iron gates all around it. Just punch the button and wait. People complain about his guards—they get a kick outa shaking people down—but I'm sure you won't have any trouble."

"Well, I'll be on my best behavior," Jake said. He winked at the chunky guard and roared off. He found the Canelli place without any difficulty and, indeed, it was a monstrous house protected by an eight-foot iron fence. He stopped the Harley in front of the front gate, shut the engine off, stepped to the ground, and fastened his helmet to the handle bars. He rang the bell, and it seemed like an inordinately long time before a man appeared who moved with the power of a professional thug. He had a pencil-thin mustache and the muscles of his arms were revealed in the white shirt that he wore.

"Yeah? What do you want?" The thug asked through the bars of the gate.

"I need to see Mr. Canelli," Jake said.

"You got an appointment?"

"No."

"Then you ain't gonna see him."

"Well, I'll have to tell you a secret." Jake stepped forward and started whispering.

"I can't hear what you're saying."

"I don't want the world to know it. Come here."

The guard stepped closer to the gate, and as soon as he was within arm's length, Jake reached through, grabbed his arm and jerked the man against the bars. With his free hand he reached in and circled the guard's head keeping it pressed. He fastened the head firmly under the bend of his elbow and reaching down he pulled the gun out from where it rested on the man's hip. He released him, pointed the nine millimeter straight at the man's belly. "Now you know my secret. Open the gate."

"You won't shoot," the guard sneered. His face was rubbed almost raw where it had been pressed against the gate.

Jake slowly raised the gun and said, "Don't bet on it, Gonzo. I'll plant one right between your eyes, sweetheart."

The man's complexion had changed to a sickly pale. "Wait a minute—don't shoot that thing!"

He unlocked the gate, and as Jake stepped in, he looked as if he might try for the gun. Jake said, "Step outside, Gonzo."

The guard stared at him, and Jake reached out and gave him a shove that sent him sprawling. He pulled the gate shut and it locked with finality. "If you try to come in, I'll scramble your grits," he warned.

Jake moved quickly away, sticking the gun behind his back and inside his belt. Voices were coming from around the back, so he circled the house and saw Gino sunning himself out on the deck.

"Good morning, Gino."

Gino came out of his chair like a scalded cat and stared wildly. "What are you doing here?"

"Came to invite you to go out and have a drink somewhere."

"How'd you get past the guard?"

"Very easily. He doesn't like guns pointed at his forehead. My messages are direct sometimes, Gino. You must remember that." He reached and got the gun from behind his back. "Gino, I'll ask you one question. If you give me the right answer, you win the prize. I know you Canelli brothers have...shall we say, 'dealings' with Earl Maddux. Did something go wrong with one of these 'deals'?"

Gino just stared at him. Jake raised the gun a little higher. "Where were you on the night Derek Maddux was killed?"

Gino seemed to have trouble finding words. "I—I was right here."

"You got a witness for that?"

"Vince knows I was here."

"Well, isn't that neat. Your brother vouches for you."

Suddenly there were voices approaching. Jake turned to see Vince Canelli striding powerfully from the house, flanked by Dante Lazlo and a tall, slender man in a white suit. The man in the white suit looked familiar, but Jake didn't pay any attention to him. His eyes were on Lazlo, who was the first one to speak.

"What are *you* doing here?"

"Just a friendly visit." Jake's tone was calm.

"He's askin' questions about the night the kid was killed," Gino said.

"You can't come busting into my home here," Vince's voice was low and smooth. He looked around to his sidekicks. "Where's the guard?"

Jake cut in. "You call that guy at the gate a guard? Silly me! I thought he was trespassing—so I locked him out. You can thank me later."

"You think you're funny, but you won't think so when you're planted six feet under."

Dante Lazlo's eyes were cold as polar ice. He murmured under his breath, "He's got a gun, Vince."

"I just borrowed it." Jake laid the gun on the table and stepped aside. "Now, you wouldn't shoot an unarmed man, would you, Lazlo?"

"Are you kiddin'?"

"I bet you would at that," Jake said and laughed.

"Put your gun on him, Lazlo," Vince ordered.

Lazlo didn't take his eyes off Jake as the Sig Sauer appeared in his hand magically. "You want me to burn his kite, Vince?"

"No." Vince turned around and hollered to someone Jake couldn't see, "You guys get down here."

Two strong-looking men came running. Both looked as if they spent their days doing nothing but pumping iron. They stopped behind Vince and stood waiting like Dobermans for their orders.

Vince nodded toward Jake. The two men caught the subtle communication and stepped forward.

"Wait a minute, Vincent."

The speaker was the tall man in the white suit who seemed familiar to Jake. He gave Jake a look and then shook his head. "Call them off."

Vince eyed the two big men and gave his head an almost imperceptible shake. The men stopped where they were, but stood staring ominously at Jake.

"You'd be taking too much of a chance," said the white-suited man.

"What chance? I'm going to have him busted up some. That's all."

"The law's getting closer, Vince, remember? You're supposed to be lying low right now. That's why you're stuck down here at the beach. We don't need any trouble. I advise you not to lay a hand on him."

"I'm not putting a hand on him," Vince objected. "That's what I keep these guys for."

Suddenly Jake recognized the man. "How are you, Counselor?" he asked.

"You know me?"

"Oh, I'm a great fan of yours. You're the guy with a hyphen."

"That's one way to identify me."

"Lord Beverly Devon-Hunt. You're the limey that gets scum like Canelli here off."

Devon-Hunt grinned at Jake. "You don't make my job sound too noble."

"You keep out of this, Counselor," interrupted Vince. He nodded at the thugs. "Guys, go for it."

As the two men approached Jake from different angles, he knew he was in for it. There was no way he could fight off the two men with Dante Lazlo pointing the gun straight at him.

Jake did the best he could, but five minutes later the two were breathing hard and Jake was lying on the ground, his face bloodied.

"He's tougher than he looks, Boss," one of the fighters said with a grin. "I like a guy who can give me a workout."

"Take him out somewhere and dump him."

"I'll take care of that," Devon-Hunt said. "Put him in my car."

"He'll bleed all over your Rolls." Lazlo grinned.

"He ain't your problem," Vince said to the attorney.

"I'm trying to keep you out of a lawsuit here. This wasn't the smartest thing you've ever done, Vince."

Vince gave the lawyer a hard glance and said, "Do what you want. Put him in the car, guys."

● ● ●

After Kate had taken Jeremy to school she returned home and spent the morning trying to clean up her room. She was resentful that Jake was a better housekeeper than she was, and she was trying to do something about it. As she hung up her clothes, the doorbell sounded. She opened the door to find a tall man standing there.

"Is this where Mr. Novak lives?" She heard the words, but it was the accent that struck her. Australian? British?

"Yes, Jake lives here," Kate said.

"My name is Devon-Hunt. I'm afraid I've got bad news. He's had an accident of sorts."

Kate was momentarily confused. "A motorcycle accident?"

"Not exactly."

"What happened? Where is he?" The alarm in Kate's voice surprised her.

"He's been...roughed up a bit. He may need a doctor, but I thought it best to have him cared for at home. He's currently bleeding all over my car." He pointed.

"Can he walk?" Kate asked, trying to remain calm.

"With a little help. I'll get him."

Kate watched as the man went out toward the car. Her eyes widened when she saw it. She couldn't identify the make, but she knew it was expensive. Devon-Hunt opened the door and with some difficulty began getting Jake out. She hurried toward them.

"Let me help you."

"I'm—okay," Jake croaked. He could barely open his eyes.

Kate was shocked at his face. He was covered with blood and his lips were swollen. She gently took his arm.

"Here, let me help you."

The two of them got him inside, and she ordered, "Put him here on the couch."

"I'll bleed all over it," Jake mumbled, finding it difficult to speak with his fat lip.

"Doesn't matter. I'll get the first-aid kit. Then I'll call a doctor."

"Don't want a doctor," Jake insisted.

"I don't care what you want. Mr. Devon-Hunt, would you stay with him a moment while I call a doctor? Don't let him move."

Devon-Hunt pulled out his wallet and began rifling through it. Finally he handed a card to Kate.

"Call this number. Best doctor around—makes house calls—use my name."

Kate looked at the card, then back at Devon-Hunt, and understanding dawned on her. She left the room.

Devon-Hunt turned back to Jake. "Now, old boy, just lie down here and mind your wife."

"Not—my wife."

"Sorry."

"What'd you bring me home for?" Jake's voice was slow and slurred.

"I'm going to try to talk you out of suing my client."

"Better talk me out of shooting him."

"Now, old chap, there's no point in doing that. Judgment will catch up with him one day. If not in this world, in another."

Kate came back and said, "He's on his way."

"Don't want a doctor." Jake's voice faded out and he closed his eyes. He appeared to have slipped into unconsciousness. Kate began gently wiping the blood from Jake's face.

"Who did this?"

"I'm afraid it was my client, Mr. Vincent Canelli."

"He's a criminal."

"Well, he hasn't been convicted of anything, although there are strong possibilities he may be one day. I didn't catch your name."

"I'm Mary Katherine Forrest."

"And I'm Beverly Devon-Hunt." He was an aristocratic-looking individual with fine British features. He had a narrow face with eyes as blue as cornflowers, and his hands were white and artistic-looking like a concert pianist's. "I hope he's not hurt too badly."

"Why did you bring him home?"

"They were going to dump him somewhere. I was afraid it would turn out badly."

"How can you work for a man who would do something like this?"

"You're asking me what happened to my honor? To tell the truth, I don't know. It didn't go all at once, I assure you, Mrs. Forrest. It wasn't like one day I had honor, the next day I didn't. It was like a mouse came in and stole a little of it. The next day another little mouse stole another little bit. Little by little I lost my honor and...well, here I am. All of my legal talent at the behest of someone like Vince Canelli. Tragic, isn't it?"

"Well, I'm going to call the police," Kate said.

"Uh, no, don't do that. It might, shall we say, create difficulties. There were no witnesses."

"There was you."

"I couldn't testify against my client. It would violate legal ethics."

Kate glared at the man, then said, "Well, anyway, thanks for bringing him home. I guess you can go."

"I'll wait for the doctor, if you don't mind. Just want to make sure Novak's going to be okay."

Kate nodded and bent over Jake, who was breathing heavily. She said not a word, and ten minutes later the doctor pulled up.

He asked no questions, but gave Jake a thorough examination and ruled out any serious injuries. He treated Jake's wounds, sewed up his eyebrow, and collected his fee, which Devon-Hunt paid.

Jake had regained consciousness and now he said thickly, "I want my Harley."

"I'll have someone get it," Devon-Hunt said. "I'd bring it back myself, but I don't have anyone to drive the car."

"I'll go," Kate said quickly.

"Fine. We'll be back, old chap, very soon. I'll be very careful with your bike."

● ● ●

As they walked out to the car, Kate realized it was a Rolls Royce. She'd never been this close to such a luxurious car before. She was about to get into the passenger seat, when Devon-Hunt stopped her.

"You're going to have to drive the car back while I'm riding Mr. Novak's Harley. You might as well drive her right now to get used to it."

Kate's eyes widened as she sat in the driver's seat and started the engine. She had never driven a car like the Rolls. It seemed to almost drive itself. It was big and heavy, but so smooth it felt like she was floating on air.

She drove for a few moments in silence, following Devon-Hunt's directions, then she turned to glance at the attorney.

"You may think this is a crazy question, but do you have anything to do with lions?"

Surprised, the Englishman turned to her. "Well, as a matter of fact, my family crest is a lion. Why do you ask?"

"I have a problem. My son's a suspect in a murder case."

"Yes, I know all about that. I'm very sorry, Mrs. Forrest. But if I understand it, there's only circumstantial evidence. Why do you ask about a lion?"

"It's just a dream I had last night, but it was so clear. Jeremy and I were walking along in the dream and there was this huge, dreadful monster about to kill us both, and just before he did, a beautiful, noble-looking lion came out of nowhere. He jumped on this monster and drove it away." She paused as if she were trying to rid herself of the visual. "You probably don't believe in dreams."

"More than I do in some things. What do you make of it?"

"I just believe that somehow someone is going to help us. The dream seemed to say the person would be like a lion. And then you showed up at my door—a powerful attorney. It seems like more than a coincidence." She paused. "Do you believe in God, Mr. Devon-Hunt?"

"Please, just call me Beverly. I detest my last name. That hyphen follows me everywhere I go. Yes, I believe in God. At least—I think He believes in me."

Kate spoke without thinking. "Would you help me, Beverly?"

Beverly Devon-Hunt turned to the woman and saw what he had already decided, that she was a woman with a great degree of vitality and imagination but all held under close restraint. She had clean-running physical lines, he saw, and her face was a mirror that changed often. He wasn't surprised by her query, as he frequently received similar requests. Out of habit he opened his mouth to tell her it was impossible.

Then he caught her eye and saw her determination. He held back his words and began to smile.

"My client would be extremely upset. As a matter of fact, I'm afraid he would become quite violent if I were to take on any other clients."

"I understand. Just forget that I asked."

But Beverly was intrigued. In all truth, he had been growing steadily more disillusioned with himself and with life, and the idea of defending the boy, even at the risk of upsetting Vince Canelli, appealed to him.

"Let's get the Harley back to Mr. Novak, and we'll talk about it."

Against all reason, Kate began to feel a little flutter of optimism within her.

"Thank you," she said quietly, and she remembered Emily Dickinson's poem that said, "Hope is the thing with feathers that perches in the soul." There was just such a bird now singing a soft song to her, and the hope she had almost lost was coming back.

Seventeen

As Jake lay on the couch, he was conscious of two things. Number one was the pain that seemed to come at him from all four directions plus up and down. His ribs hurt, he felt a throb in his thigh, his hands were aching, his knuckles stung where the skin was broken in myriad places, and his head felt as if it had been used for a soccer ball in a world-class match.

The other thing he was conscious of was the presence of the two cats, Cleo and Jacques the Ripper. Staring at Jacques through swollen eyes, Jake said, "Well, I can see you're happy, Jacques. Just what you wanted, to see me get popped." He stared at the cat that was watching him and cautiously awaiting his chance, no doubt, to use his claws. "If you could talk, Jacques, I guess you'd say I got what I deserved, huh?"

Jacques eyed the man. *Don't think I don't know what a mess you got yourself in, Intruder. I've got ears and my Person has been talking. All I can say is, you are one stupid creature to go up against a gang all by yourself. If you want to work somebody over, do what I do. Catch them when they're not looking, and rip them from the back. And don't give me any speeches about fighting fair, you two-legged simpleton.*

Cautiously Jake moved to find a more comfortable position, but only found one that was less comfortable. He groaned.

"Much as I hate to admit it, Jacques, you may be right. Maybe I deserved this. But remember General Patton? They called him Old Blood and Guts? He said one time, Success is how high you bounce when you hit bottom. You just watch me bounce. They won't keep me down."

Cleo came then and reared up on the couch with her two front feet. She reached out one paw and touched him timidly. He shook his head.

"I know you've fallen in love with me, Cleo, but go get someone else. I've got no room in my life for love."

Cautiously he swung his feet down to the floor, stopped, and caught his breath. His ribs felt as if someone was sticking ice picks in them. He stood up slowly and Jacques made a half-hearted pass at him. Jake tried to kick at the cat, which succeeded only in bringing fresh waves of pain throughout every nerve in his body. He glared at Jacques and muttered, "All right, Ripper. You're asking for it. When I get well, I'm going to run you through the meat grinder." His lips were swollen but dry, and he limped into the kitchen, where he found some orange juice. He filled the glass but his lips were so swollen that it was painful to drink. As he finished it, he heard the door slam and voices. Then he saw Kate and the Englishman come in.

Kate's eyes were shining. "Beverly's going to take Jeremy's case, Jake. Isn't that wonderful?"

"Beverly? Who would name an innocent baby boy Beverly?"

"My parents, old chap. Quite a common name in my country. Of course, here in the colonies you would attach it mostly to females."

"Why did you ask him for help, Mary Katherine? He's a dirtbag lawyer representing the scum of the earth. He'd hitch his mother to a dogsled for money."

"Why, that's not true," Beverly said, his eyes widening. "I've got scads of money. Mum is safe."

Kate said, "You want some more orange juice?"

"There's not any more except that junk you buy in the carton."

Kate said with disgust, "Why can't you just drink store-bought orange juice like everybody else?"

"If you have to ask, you'll never understand."

At that instant Bad Louie came fluttering in. He lit on Beverly's shoulder, and Jake had a moment's wild hope that the parrot would take a bite out of the Englishman's ear. No such luck. The colorful parrot leaned forward and squawked a vile word in Beverly's ear.

"I'm so sorry, Beverly," Kate said quickly. "He was owned by a group of very profane men. I'm trying to teach him better manners."

"I can easily get rid of him," Jake offered.

"No, it's not his fault."

Jake felt the room reeling and his face was flushed. "I think I better sit down," he muttered.

"Let me help you," Kate offered, coming forward to take his arm.

"Get your hands off me! I can walk." To prove this, Jake stumbled and would have fallen if Kate and Beverly hadn't grabbed him. They helped him to the couch and sat him down. Jake was staring distrustfully at Beverly.

"You'll pardon me if I'm a little suspicious. Last I heard you were exclusive counsel for the great Vincent Canelli. What gives?"

Beverly sat down in a wicker chair and crossed his legs. It was an eloquent gesture, but then everything he did was graceful. "I've been having second thoughts, don't you see, about my profession. I have my law degree from Oxford, but there's limited opportunity for practicing criminal law in England. We don't have nearly as much crime as you have here. I think you had more murders in Pittsburgh last year than we had in our whole country. I wanted to see what the underside of the criminal world is really like. How better to become a top-notch barrister than by representing those who really have no defense? Working for Vincent Canelli has been an excellent education but..."

"Well, you sure picked a great one to learn from," Jake said. "No shortage of criminal activity there."

"True enough. But now perhaps I should do some noble things to even the score."

Jake stared at the Englishman. The doctor had given him a narcotic for the pain, but it was wearing off. He reached over on the table, picked up the prescription bottle, and shook out one pill. He looked at it and shook out another one.

"That stuff is too strong. You don't need it," Kate said.

"Apparently you're handling my pain well, Mary Katherine. Maybe you don't need these pills, but I do." Jake took the two pills and then turned to Devon-Hunt.

"You haven't learned much if you think you can just walk off on Vincent Canelli. Quitting a job at Kentucky Fried Chicken would be pretty simple, but Canelli doesn't like his people to leave. As a matter of fact, I know of one that he put the whack on who left without permission."

"Oh, it's all right." Beverly waved his aristocratic hand in an airy gesture. "I'll turn on my charm when I resign."

"You can't put yourself in danger because of us, Beverly," Kate said anxiously.

"Let him spit in the soup if he wants to. It's his red wagon." Jake studied Beverly's fancy clothes and said, "One good thing. If you get capped, we won't have to do a thing to you except stick a lily in your hand."

Kate looked at Beverly apologetically. "That's his way of giving a compliment."

Humor sparkled in Lord Beverly's eyes, and he said, "I'll keep that in mind. I'll be in touch with you. In the meanwhile, I'll do a little poking around of my own. I'm sorry you got hurt, old chap."

Beverly turned and left without another word, and Jake stared at the door that he'd disappeared through. "He'll change his mind, Mary Katherine. Vince has persuasive ways—and he's got Dante Lazlo on his side. His majesty there will end up Vienna sausage if he tries to walk out on Canelli."

● ● ●

Jake came out of sleep feeling groggy. He had taken too many of the pain pills, and his voice was a mere croak as he said, "Come in."

Kate entered with a tray. "I made you eggs Benedict."

"You don't know how to make eggs Benedict."

"I found the recipe. Here, let me help you sit up." She put the tray down, and Jake protested.

"I can sit up myself. I'm not a child."

"Yes, you are. How do you feel?"

Jake considered the matter and then pointed to a spot on his left forearm. "You see that spot right there?"

"Yes, I see it."

"That doesn't hurt. It's the only place I don't hurt."

He waited while she put the tray into place, and he found that his appetite had returned.

After a couple of bites, he said, "I don't believe you made these eggs Benedict. I think you sent out for a chef."

"Is it good?"

"It'll do." But the way he was wolfing it down told her he liked it.

He put the jelly from a glass dish on the fresh roll and nodded, "That's good jelly."

"I got it from a woman who makes it herself. She grows her own berries."

Jake finished his breakfast, drank his coffee, and pushed the tray away.

"I've got to get up."

When he winced on his way to a standing position, Kate said, "Maybe you should soak in your Jacuzzi, Jake. That'll make you feel better."

"We'll see," Jake said. "Maybe for a few minutes."

As soon as she left, Jake hobbled to the bathroom and groaned as he bent over to get the water started. Finally he got in and eased himself down with a sigh of relief. He lay there, his head back against the white porcelain, and enjoyed the wash of the water that caressed his body. Finally he decided he'd had enough and discovered he was so weak he could hardly move.

With considerable effort, he gingerly got himself out of the tub. He dried off, put on a pair of cutoffs, a loose shirt, and then went slowly down the stairs. He was greeted, strangely enough, by Bad Louie who shrieked, "Hallelujah! Hallelujah!"

Jake stared at the bird in shock and Kate smiled.

"I'm teaching him good things. Don't cuss around him, you hear me?"

"I didn't think you could teach an old parrot new tricks."

"Anyone can change."

Jake sat down and she brought him the *Mobile Register* and fresh coffee. He read the paper in his usual order: sports page first, the comics second, and then scanned rest of the paper for odd or unusual items that he could fit into his Great American Novel.

"What's the news?" Kate asked.

Jake glanced over the paper at Kate. "What news? The news in the paper is like a soap opera. You know, I had a lady friend once who watched one of the soaps. I think it was *The Young and the Restless* or something like that. She left on a monthlong vacation, and when she came back she was anxious to get into the mode again so she turned on the program. The same people, same problems, nothing new happening. The news is like that. You miss a month, so what?"

The doorbell rang, and Kate got up from the table.

"That'll be the vet. Time for the first inspection in accordance with the will. If we don't pass, we'll be thrown out on the street."

"He'll be a crusty old codger who has bad breath," Jake complained. "You handle him." He put the paper up again and continued reading. He had no intention of getting involved with any veterinarian.

A minute later Jake peered over his paper as Kate entered with the veterinarian and said with a sly smile, "Jake, this is Dr. Enola Stern. Dr. Stern, this is my business associate Jake Novak."

Jake lowered the paper to his lap. The woman who stood before him had sleek black hair and the smoothest olive complexion he had ever seen. She had enormous blue-green eyes and was wearing a lace-trimmed tank top, a white pique jacket with rolled cuffs, and a cranberry-colored crinkled skirt. The skirt was loose, but the tank top was not, and Jake had to force himself to look her in the face instead of at the rest of her. He got to his feet painfully. "I'm certainly glad to meet you, Dr. Stern."

"Call me Enola. You seem to have had an accident."

"Well, I'm a thug by profession," Jake said, "but I seem to have met up with some thugs who were a little more proficient."

The vet was amused. She then ran her glance around the room. "I've been coming to this house for two years now. Miss Zophia was very particular about her pets. I hope you two like animals."

"Love 'em all!" Jake put in quickly. "My partner doesn't care much for animals, but I live for them!" Kate gave him a disgusted look and then turned back to Enola.

"The animals are fine. We enjoy taking care of them."

"Let me show you around," Jake volunteered. "Mary Katherine, why don't you fix some coffee and some of that cake for the doctor and for me?" He looked at the vet and said, "I spend a lot of time working with the little darlings. Ow!" At that moment Jacques had taken a swipe at Jake's passing leg.

"I see you and that enormous cat have a rather strange relationship," Enola said. "I'd better put some antiseptic on that."

Jake didn't protest vehemently, Kate noticed, as he had when she had offered to do the same thing. Enola knelt and administered first-aid to the leg and said, "You've been scratched before."

"The Ripper shows his affection for me in strange ways," Jake said as he grinned.

"The Ripper? I suppose that's a fitting name."

"His name is really Jacques," Kate interjected, "but we call him Jacques the Ripper."

Enola looked around the room again. "I don't see Bandit."

"He's usually outside," Kate said.

"I'll go have a look at him. Then I need to check out the rest of the animals as well."

As soon as she left, Kate said, "Jake, it's disgusting the way you're acting."

"Acting? Who's acting?"

"You're following that woman around with your tongue hanging out."

"Am not!"

"You are, too."

"Well, we've got to keep her happy," Jake said. "I'm winning her over with my charm."

After a few more minutes, Enola Stern returned and sat down to write her report. "According to the will," she said as she wrote, "I have to give a written report on the animals every month."

"How long have you been a vet?" Jake asked.

"Just three years."

Jake said, "You don't look like any vet I ever saw."

"And exactly how many vets have you been acquainted with, Jake?" Enola asked, amused.

Kate needed to interrupt the shameless flirting going on. "Dr. Stern, are you from this area?"

"No, I haven't been here for that long. My family comes from all over. Actually I'm half Jewish and half Sioux."

"You mean like Sioux Indians?" Jake asked, curious.

"That's right. I'm in a direct line from Crazy Horse."

"I've always admired Crazy Horse. He's the war chief who did Custer in at Little Big Horn," Jake noted. "What about your husband?"

"I don't have a husband," Enola said. She gave him a very direct look. "I have men friends. I used to call them boyfriends, but that sounds like I'm in high school." She finished the report and got up to leave. When Jake rose with her, she said, "You haven't told me what happened to you."

"It's a long story. Let's just say there was a fight."

"By the looks of your bruises, you better not get into another brawl until you heal."

"Well, I thought I might go out and eat tonight," Jake said. "Maybe you should go with me—you know, to make sure I don't do anything I shouldn't."

"Do you have Mrs. Forrest's permission?" Enola winked broadly at Jake.

"He can do anything he likes," Kate said curtly.

"I don't have a car," Jake said apologetically. "Just a Harley."

"I've got a Humvee. I'll pick you up at seven. See you then."

Jake watched her go, and when he turned he saw Kate rolling her eyes.

"That woman is a disgrace to her profession."

"I like her."

"I'm sure you do! Did you happen to notice that she was hitting on you?"

"You're just jealous. We got to keep the doc happy," he noted again. "It's a dirty job, but someone has to do it!"

Eighteen

Usually Jake was up at the crack of dawn, but Kate had been up drinking her coffee and staring out at the Gulf for a while, and neither Jeremy nor Jake had stirred. She felt gloomy and even a little angry for some reason she couldn't define.

Finally Jake came in yawning and looking sleepy.

"What do you want for breakfast?" she asked brusquely.

"Oh, oatmeal will be fine. You can't mess up oatmeal, I don't think."

Jake sat there as she fixed the oatmeal, not the instant kind that would be beneath him and not up to his standards, of course. She gave him a hooded glance.

"So how was your evening?"

Jake looked innocent. "Oh, fine. Dr. Enola and I talked about philosophy, things like that."

"Until three in the morning?"

"Time goes by, I guess, when you're talking about philosophy. And I didn't realize I'd asked you to wait up for me."

The doorbell rang and Kate went to answer it. When she opened the door and saw Chief O'Dell standing there with Deputy Oralee Prather, she felt a sudden jolt of fear.

"What is it, Chief?"

"We'd better come in, Mrs. Forrest."

Kate nodded and when they had entered, she asked, "Would you care for coffee?"

"No, thanks. We're here on official business," Chief O'Dell said. He looked somewhat uncomfortable. "I've got a search warrant here."

"A search warrant?"

"Yes, you can read it. It gives us permission to search the house and the outbuildings."

"What are you looking for?"

"Evidence," Oralee said, shrugging her shoulders. "We'll try not to be any trouble."

"Well, I suppose I have no choice," Kate said. "We were just having breakfast. I've got to get Jeremy to school."

"Maybe you should hold off for a little bit, Mrs. Forrest. This is just a formality. It won't take long." O'Dell nodded at Oralee. "You take the outbuildings. I'll start in here."

Kate went back to the kitchen and said, "They have a warrant to search the house."

"I figured that would be coming."

Kate went to make sure Jeremy was awake and getting dressed. She came back and poured herself another cup of coffee. She sat down at the table with Jake, both of them silent and aware of Chief O'Dell going through the house.

It was ten minutes later when the back door opened, and Deputy Prather came and called out, "Chief."

O'Dell appeared. "What is it, Deputy?"

"I found this in a tackle box." She held up a watch and O'Dell took it. "It looks like the one. You'll have to get Jeremy in here, I'm afraid, Mrs. Forrest."

"I'll get him. What's so special about the watch?"

"Just get the boy, if you will, please."

Kate went to Jeremy's room and called him. When he came out, she said, "The chief wants to talk to you."

"What does he want?"

"I don't know. Something about a watch."

Jeremy gave her a curious look and went to the kitchen with her.

Chief O'Dell said, "Hello, Jeremy."

"Chief."

"We found this watch in your tackle box. At least I assume it's your tackle box—it's got your name on it."

"Yes, Sir. That's my box."

"Is this your watch?"

"No, Sir. That's Derek's watch."

"What are you doing with it, Jeremy?" Deputy Prather demanded.

Jeremy turned pale. "He asked me to put it into my tackle box. He didn't want it to get wet."

"And you've left it in there all this time?"

"I forgot it."

"You forgot a Rolex? How could that be?"

The questioning went on for some time and finally O'Dell said, "I'm sorry, Mrs. Forrest, but Jeremy will have to come along with us."

Jake said immediately, "That's not evidence enough to arrest the boy."

"I've told you before, Novak. You're not a cop anymore. But just so you know, we found a witness who saw Jeremy in Derek's boat after the time he was supposed to have come home."

"That couldn't be!" Kate exclaimed. "It's not true, is it, Jeremy?"

"I'll have to warn you and the boy that anything you say can be held against you," O'Dell said. "What will happen is this. He'll have to appear in a lineup. The witness says the person driving the boat was wearing a red jacket with the hood up and it had a picture of Darth Vader, the guy in the Star Wars movie, on the back. You have a coat like that, I understand, Jeremy."

"I did. I lost it."

"We can't talk here, Chief," Oralee said quickly. "Take him downtown."

"Do I have to go, Mom?" Jeremy's voice was unsteady.

"I'll be with you all the time, Son. We'll get all this straightened out." She reached out and hugged him and felt him trembling. "That will be all right, won't it, Officer?"

"Yes, Ma'am, it sure will."

As the two prepared to leave, Jake said, "We'd better get that British lawyer on this right away."

"It sounds bad, doesn't it, Jake?" Kate asked.

"I wish he had told them about that watch earlier. Did you know about the coat?"

"No, I didn't notice it missing, but he does have such a coat. What's going to happen, Jake?"

Jake wanted to say something cheerful and positive, but he couldn't find the words. "It'll be okay," he said finally. "We know he didn't do it, so the thing to do is to prove it. You go along, and I'll get on this."

● ● ●

Vince Canelli tapped his pen rhythmically on his desk. It was the only sound in the room. He stared straight ahead, focused on a spot high on the wall. Finally he spoke, and his tone was low and ominous.

"I didn't really hear that, did I?" Vince's face was controlled. "You didn't just say you were going to quit."

"I'm afraid I have to, Vincent."

"People do not quit on Vincent Canelli. Especially you. You know too much, Limey."

"All I know about you is privileged communication. There's no way I can give evidence against you."

The argument went on for some time, but in the end Beverly simply said, "It hasn't worked out like I hoped, so let's part on good terms." And he walked out.

As soon as the lawyer left the room, Dante Lazlo said, "You want me to ace him, Vince?"

"No, I want you to convince him that he's a dead man if he crosses me."

"You mean work him over?"

"No, just make sure he knows what'll happen if he talks." He hesitated for one moment and his eyes grew into tiny slits. "And I want you to take Novak out."

● ● ●

The preliminary hearing was a formality. The district attorney wanted to hold Jeremy without bail, but Beverly Devon-Hunt was able to persuade the judge that there was no chance the boy would run. The judge set bail at one hundred thousand dollars.

As soon as the judge's gavel hit, an officer came to take Jeremy away. Kate's face was as white as paste, but Beverly was right beside her.

"He won't have to stay in jail. I was afraid the judge wouldn't permit any bail, but it's all right."

"But a hundred thousand dollars. I don't have that kind of money."

"You can get it from a bondsman. All you need is ten thousand dollars."

"Ten thousand dollars? Beverly, I don't have a *thousand* dollars—much less ten!"

"I thought I understood that your inheritance was substantial."

"Yes, but it's not in cash. It's all tied up in the house and in stocks."

Beverly thought for a moment.

"Well, you're my client now, and as I say I am embarrassingly wealthy. Never thought much about it before, but I'll transfer some funds over."

"What will happen to the money?"

"I'll get it back after the trial's over. Jeremy's not going to run away. Now, why don't you go home and I'll bring Jeremy home as soon as I make the arrangements."

"No, I want to wait here for him. Can we take him today?"

"Just have to go through the formalities and sign some papers. They don't take checks so I'll have to go get the cash from the bank. You sure you don't want to go home?"

"No, I'll wait here."

• • •

Jake was still stiff and achy, but he knew the best thing for a beat-up man was exercise. He walked eastward along the beach. To his right, the sand dunes rose up, filled with sea oats. To his left the green Gulf washed the shores and snow-white sands. Trouble had come along with him, and he kept chasing the waves out, enjoying plunging into the water.

Jake was thinking about Beverly Devon-Hunt. He couldn't understand the man. *He's like a different species, rich and got a title. What's he doing fooling around over here with a case like this? Something's just not right. Still, he did pay Jeremy's bail.*

He saw a large sand dollar in front of him and knew that Jeremy was making a collection of them. He bent over and just as he did, something seemed to tug at the back of his shirt. An instant later he heard the sound of the shot. He knew that sound and immediately glanced out and saw a speedboat with an inboard engine. The sun glinted on the barrel of a rifle. He threw himself over into a shallow depression, and slugs began to fall around him. Desperately he tried to wiggle out of range so that the shooter couldn't see him. Trouble was barking wildly. Jake yelled, "Come here, Trouble!"

Even as Trouble raced to throw himself into the ocean toward the boat, the big dog tumbled over backward with a grunt.

Jake saw the red blood stain the dog's white coat and despite the seriousness of the situation he felt a pang of grief. He had started to like the big dog, even though he would never admit it to Kate.

The rifleman continued to rake the sand, and he figured sooner or later a bullet would find its mark—then a loud *crack!*—a different kind of rifle shot—came from the sand dune to his right. He glanced up and saw someone lying prone and firing rapidly at the boat. Someone on the boat scrambled to the controls, and the boat threw itself forward with full thrust.

Jake got to his feet slowly and turned to see Deputy Oralee Prather rise up and come toward him, her face set.

"You okay, Novak?"

"Thanks to you."

"What about the dog?"

The two of them went over and found that Trouble had been hit but was still alive.

"We've got to get him to Doc Stern," Oralee said. "Did you see the guy who was shooting?"

"Didn't have to. I know who it was."

Oralee Prather stared at the big man. "Got a name for me?"

"Nah, Deputy. I guess something will probably happen to him," he said. "Let's get Trouble to the good-looking vet."

Nineteen

When Jake and Deputy Prather walked into Enola Stern's office, the reception desk was empty so they made their way back to the exam room. There they found Enola talking to a woman who was holding one of the fattest dogs Jake had ever seen. It looked like a hairy sausage stuffed until it was near exploding. The owner of the dog was built along the same lines.

"We have an emergency, Dr. Stern," Jake said.

The plump woman glared at Jake. "You'll have to wait your turn," she said, ignoring the bloody dog he was holding.

Enola was wearing a pair of stone-washed blue jeans and a plaid cotton shirt. She moved toward Jake and motioned for him to put Trouble on the stainless steel table, even as she faced the woman and said, "There's nothing wrong with your dog except you're feeding him too much rich food off the table."

"Is that all you're going to tell me?"

"You want the truth, don't you? You're going to kill that dog if you don't stop feeding him people food."

Enola and Jake got Trouble settled on the examination counter.

"I refuse to listen to this! There are other veterinarians—and some of them certainly dress more appropriately than you. Don't bother to send me a bill because I won't pay it!"

The woman stormed out, and Enola began gently pushing aside Trouble's fur so that she could see the wound. "What happened to him?"

"He was shot, Enola," Jake said.

"The bullet entrance is here. No exit. I'll have to probe for it."

"Do your best for him, Doc."

Enola was studying Trouble carefully. She moved over to a cabinet, opened one of the drawers, and came out with several instruments. "He's unconscious so it would be dangerous to give him anesthetic. Will it make you nervous to watch this?"

"It bothers me," Oralee said. "I can see people shot easier than I can see an animal hurt. I'll wait outside."

"Thanks a lot, Oralee," Jake said. "You saved my bacon."

"No extra charge. I'll have to make out a report after you get the dog cared for."

As soon as the deputy left, Enola began probing for the bullet. She moved swiftly and surely and came up with the bullet almost immediately. "Going to have to bandage that. He's lost a lot of blood."

"Do dogs get blood transfusions?"

"Sometimes, but we'll see if he needs it."

Jake was standing slightly back from the table, and he took a step closer. Reaching out, he put his hand on the big dog's head, saying nothing.

Enola watched him and then completed the bandaging. "It'll be touch and go. Pretty hard to have a pet you love in danger."

"I'm not really a dog lover."

Enola stopped dead and turned to look up at him. She was a woman with a great degree of vitality and imagination, and Jake had the feeling that she was the kind of woman who could, if necessary, shoot a man down and not go to pieces afterward. He hadn't known many women like that—although plenty of men fit the description. Jake watched the slight changes of her face, the quickening, the loosening, the small expressions coming and going. Her black hair rose back from her temples, made its mass on her head, and was caught up into a ball behind. She wasn't smiling exactly, and yet something about his statement amused her.

"What kind of a lover are you then, if not a dog lover?"

"I don't know. Maybe I'm not a lover of anything."

There was a straightforward quality about Enola Stern. She stood there watching him. "Why are you afraid to admit you love something, Jake?"

Jake looked away, unable to meet her eyes. Finally he lifted his gaze and noted that the woman had a long, composed mouth and a manner that could charm a man or chill him to the bone.

"I'm not sure about this love thing," he said finally. He looked at her defiantly adding, "I thought I knew what it was once, but now I don't know."

Enola reached out and laid her hand on his arm. "You can't live in a cave, Novak. Everyone who loves takes a chance on getting hurt. That's what it costs to love somebody."

Jake's eyes were hooded, but he sighed heavily and shook his head. "I've got to call Mary Katherine. She'll be worried."

Enola watched as Jake went to the phone, picked it up, and dialed. She was a woman who liked men—a few of them at least—and she studied Jake, noting that he was taller than average. She noted his face, observing that his lip corners had a tough, sharp set. She watched him with a closeness that could come only of a deep, personal interest. She knew he had a man's strength, and also a man's weakness. She sensed that, behind the silence, he had a temper that could flare out hard and hot as fire. She turned back to the dog, put her hand on his head, and whispered, "Come on, Boy, you can make it."

● ● ●

"I'm sure I don't make tea like they make it in England."

"This is very good, Kate," Beverly said, taking another sip as he and Kate sat in Kate's kitchen. She studied the man across from her curiously. "I've never known an Englishman before."

"You've missed a great blessing then."

"You have family in England?" she asked.

"Actually, not much of a family. My mother died some years ago. My father passed away just two years ago, and his title came to me."

"You have a title?"

"Oh, I don't pay much attention to it."

"What is it?"

"I'm the Earl of Devon."

Kate was fascinated. "And I ought to be calling you Lord Devon or something like that."

"Please don't! Those pesky things should have gone out with other useless baggage during the Middle Ages. I don't usually let people know. It's sort of a secret."

"Why would you keep it a secret?"

"It really doesn't mean much to me. My family isn't one of the better known ones. My grandfather made his living in trade, so the real peerage doesn't look too kindly on us."

The two sat talking for a few minutes, and finally Bev said, "Kate, I want to ask you something. I guess like everyone else, I wonder about you and Jake."

"You mean living in the same house?"

"A little unusual. None of my business, of course."

"Everyone assumes we're...well...intimate," Kate said tersely, "but we aren't. Sometimes we barely tolerate each other."

"You know, My Dear, he's the sort of chap that could be a little bit frightening—like a bottle of nitroglycerine. You don't want to bump it or it'll go off with a bang."

"You're exactly right about that," Kate agreed. "I've seen that in him, too. Strange how we've been thrown together, but one good thing about it, Jeremy has needed a man to look up to. Someone to teach him guy things. Jake hasn't really taken to the animals, but he spends a lot of time with Jeremy. I wish—" The phone rang and she said, "Excuse me," and walked over to pick it up.

"Hello?" She listened carefully without speaking, then said, "We'll come right over."

She put the phone down.

"I've got to go to Dr. Stern's. There's been an attempt on Jake's life, and Trouble got shot."

"Is he all right—Jake, I mean?"

"Yes, but the dog's badly injured."

"I'll take you. My car's outside."

● ● ●

As Beverly and Kate entered, they found Jake, Enola, and Oralee chatting in the outer office. Kate found it irritating that Jake could be so laid back when Trouble was so badly hurt. Her voice was curt as she asked, "Is he going to be all right?"

"He's holding his own and resting peacefully," Enola answered. Then, noticing Bev, she said, "I don't believe I've met your friend."

"Oh, I'm sorry," Kate said, breathing a sigh of relief. "This is the Earl of Devon."

"I'm glad to know you," Enola said.

"I'm happy to make your acquaintance, Doctor," Bev said.

"Bev is Vince Canelli's lawyer, Enola," Jake said.

"Past tense, old chap. Mr. Canelli and I have parted company. Now tell us about what happened. Someone shot at you?"

"Nearly got me, too," Jake said. "If Oralee Prather hadn't come along, I think he would have finished me off."

"I suppose the deputy filed a report?"

"Sure did," Oralee said. "But the shooter was in a boat. The registration numbers would help, but Jake was too busy dodging bullets to make them out."

"Was he shooting at the dog?" Enola asked curiously.

"No, they were shooting at me," Jake said.

"If I were to pick someone as a candidate," Bev nodded, "I think I'd put my money on Vincent. He's got plenty of hired men who do this sort of thing."

"Why would he want to kill Jake?" Kate asked.

"Jake threatened his brother," Bev said. "That's probably what set him off." He changed the subject by saying, "You know, I've been thinking more about the Maddux boy's murder. Money is usually tied in with homicide."

"Not this time," Kate said. "Derek was just a boy. He had no money."

"Ah, but his father has plenty. He's very rich. I'd like to see Mr. Maddux's will. And I'd like to know what kind of business dealings Vincent had with Maddux."

Kate frowned. "Earl Maddux is not very likely to offer us that information, Bev."

Jake straightened up. "There are ways of getting around that," he said. "Mary Katherine, I've got a little errand to do. You take care of Trouble and the other animals, will you?" He turned to Oralee. "I haven't got a vehicle. Wanna drive?"

Without another word the two left the room. Going to the window, Enola said, "Obviously he had something on his mind."

"Like I said," Beverly shrugged, "he's a stick of dynamite. Doesn't take much to set him off."

Enola said, "Here, sit down, Your Majesty. I've never known anyone with a title."

"He has a hyphen, too," Kate put in.

"A hyphen? What do you mean?" Enola asked.

"Well, my name is Beverly Devon-Hunt," the barrister answered.

"That must be exciting. What can you do with a hyphen?"

"Spend your life explaining it, I'm afraid."

Kate watched the two and was very conscious that once again, Enola was putting on the charm. Kate excused herself. "I'll go back and sit with Trouble while you two get acquainted."

"You do that," Enola said. "Now, Sir Beverly Devon-Hunt, tell me all about your wife."

"I don't have one. Not of my own, that is."

Enola found this to be vastly amusing. "Tell me how you escaped matrimony. It must be a fascinating story."

● ● ●

Lew Steinmetz blinked with surprise when Jake entered his locksmith shop. "Jake Novak! Man, it's good to see you." He came out from behind the counter, put out his hand, and pumped Jake's up and down enthusiastically. He was a short, pudgy man with a pair of guileless blue eyes and a moustache that was a mistake. His only redeeming physical feature was a pair of beautifully made hands—long, shapely fingers like those of a concert violinist.

"Good to see you, Lew. How's business?"

"Well, it's not bad, Jake. I'm making enough I can afford to get married."

"Well, congratulations. Who is she?"

"Her name's Laura. She's a professor at Springhill College. She teaches Latin, but I don't hold that against her."

Jake grinned suddenly. "Does she know what a devious character you are?"

"You mean that I cracked safes for a living? Yeah, I told her all that. She made sure I've reformed. I told her all about you. If you hadn't been around, I'd probably be in the slammer still. Can't believe we ended up in the same little corner of the woods."

Lew Steinmetz had been one of the best safecrackers in Chicago. He had gone to prison for it, and it had been through Jake's effort that he had passed the parole board. Jake had vouched for him and had kept Lew on the straight and narrow when he got out. The two had become friends, and there was nothing that Lew wouldn't do for Jake.

"I've come to get some help, Lew."

"Just name it." Lew Steinmetz sat there and listened while Jake talked. His eyes glowed and finally he nodded, "For you, I'll do it!"

● ● ●

Kate had invited Enola to supper, but the vet had somehow managed to bring Beverly along, and so far the two of them had done most of the talking. Now they had finished the main course and were eating a cake that Kate had bought at Wal-Mart.

"Listen, there's Jake coming in," Kate said as she heard the sound of the Harley pull up.

The three of them waited, and Jake came in looking tired. He hadn't shaved in the two days he'd been gone, but there was a satisfied look in his eyes. He passed by Jacques, who took a swipe at him. Jake said, "That's the Ripper—always reliable. You're not going to be satisfied until you get my heart's blood. I think if Dracula had a cat, he'd be just like you." He turned to Enola and asked directly, "How's Trouble?"

"He's getting along fine. He'll be coming home in a couple of days."

Jake cast a look at Jacques and asked, "What do you charge for declawing cats, Enola?"

"You're not having Jacques declawed," Kate declared.

Jake laughed, held up an envelope, and waved it in the air toward Bev. "A present for you, Counselor."

Bev took the envelope, opened it, and perused the documents inside. Surprise mirrored in his face and he continued reading as he murmured, "This is Maddux's will...nice work, Novak."

"Maddux's will!" Kate exclaimed "How did you get that?"

Jake didn't answer. He went over to the stove, cut himself a piece of the roast beef that Kate had made, and came back, sitting down.

Bev was reading the will rapidly. "Hmm. It appears we have a likely candidate for the killer of Derek."

"Who is it?" Enola asked.

"The terms of the will are simple. The bulk of the money and property go to Derek, a token amount to Arlene." A caustic smile turned up the corners of Bev's lips. "So, she is the one who would benefit from the boy's death."

"Why does that not surprise me?" Jake said.

"Here's something that may surprise you," Bev continued. "Turns out Arlene's not Derek's mother. She's Earl's second wife and Derek's stepmother."

They all looked at each other in surprise. Jake nodded.

"There you go. It all makes sense. Arlene's a viable suspect."

"I've got another candidate," Bev said. "While you were gone I did some prowling around. You never know what'll fall out of a tree until you throw a rock into it. I already knew that Vince Canelli did indeed have some business dealings with Maddux. But apparently things went sour and threats were exchanged."

Enola asked, "Do you really think Vince Canelli would kill a child just to get back at his father? Sounds truly evil."

Bev put in, "I know him well and I have to admit, killing a young boy is going a bit too far, even for him. But you just never know."

Kate was bewildered. "How could so many people have a reason to kill a fourteen-year-old boy? And how will we figure out who it was and clear Jeremy's name?"

"We'll keep poking sticks down holes," Jake said. "Sooner or later something will come out."

● ● ●

After Enola and Bev left, Jake noticed that Kate wasn't saying much. He loaded the dishes into the dishwasher and Kate went outside.

He walked out and asked, "Where's Jeremy?"

"He went on a field trip with his class. Hope's taking care of him. They went to Richmond to see the artifacts from the Civil War."

The two stood there, Jake feeling strangely uncomfortable, and there was tension in Kate. Her shoulders were slumped, and she leaned against the rail of the deck as if for support. He watched her for a moment.

"What's wrong, Mary Katherine?"

She turned to him and the moonlight threw its silver beams on her face. Jake was alarmed to see a tear rolling down her cheek.

"He's all I have, Jake." The tears multiplied, and Jake tentatively reached forward. She leaned into his chest and began to sob in earnest.

"Maybe," he said quietly, "I can help."

He held her as she wept. Fear and grief swept her as if a wind had shaken her. Finally she grew still and looked up, and her eyes caught the reflection of the moon. He knew she was vulnerable, and there was an urge in Jake to protect her. Her lips were half parted and almost without thinking he leaned forward, bent his head, and kissed her.

He was on the near edge of rashness, which was unusual for him, and was surprised at how content he felt holding her. But she pulled away from him, obviously disturbed at the emotion that his caress had created. Jake knew she had built up a wall against men, and now he'd broken through. She seemed angry all of a sudden, and she stiffened.

"I caught you at a weak moment, Mary Katherine. I'm sorry. I guess we're entitled to one mistake." He turned and walked into the house, leaving her to wrestle with her demons. But in truth, he really wasn't sorry.

Twenty

The sun was setting in the west as Jeremy sat on the deck mindlessly playing with his Game Boy. His mother had gone to Dr. Stern's to check on Trouble, and Jake was upstairs playing classical music as he worked on his novel.

Lifting his eyes, Jeremy saw a group of dolphins pass, and, as always, the beauty of the strange creatures fascinated him. There were five of them in a row, and he wondered if they were a family or just good friends.

Something soft touched his leg, and he looked down to see Cleo pushing against him, begging to be petted. He reached down and stroked her silky fur and then glanced over at Jacques, who was glaring at him from the top rail.

Jacques bowed his back and hissed slightly. His entire body language expressed disgust with Cleo.

Why don't you go catch a mouse or something? All you do is try to con our Persons into petting you or giving you something to eat. You'd do anything for tuna, wouldn't you?

That's not true, Jacques. I really like our Persons.

What's to like? They exist for the purpose of feeding us and seeing to our needs. They never have any life of their own. Look at that Person you're pushing on there. He's done nothing but mope around and pout for days.

He's got problems, I think. You need to be more understanding, Jacques.

No, I've got problems. First, I have the Intruder to contend with. Now that beautiful yellow cat, the one named Delilah, across the highway. She won't have anything to do with me. She's all caught up with that mangy alley cat that hangs around, but I'm going to cut him out tonight. Just wait. I'm going to put a whack on him.

Jeremy watched the two cats with interest. He knew there was some kind of secret language between them, and he muttered, "I'll bet if I could hear what you're thinking, Jacques, I'd be ready to take you to the vet and have you put down." He looked up and saw Hope Barclay walking along the beach, coming from the east. Jeremy tossed the Game Boy down and headed toward the surf line, carefully avoiding Jacques as he went by. Jacques made a half-hearted pass at him but missed.

As soon as he got close enough, Jeremy called out, "Hey, Miss Barclay!"

"Hey yourself, Jeremy." Hope Barclay was wearing a white blouse and a pair of light-green shorts. She was carrying her sandals in her hand. "I love to walk barefoot on the beach."

"So do I, but be careful. You can step on a sharp shell and cut your foot."

Hope smiled at the boy. "We have to take chances for the things we want," she said as she studied his face. "What's the matter, Jeremy? You look like you haven't slept in a week."

"Yeah...I wish I could get away from all the stuff going on."

Moving closer to him, Hope reached out and pushed the hair away from Jeremy's eyes. "We can't run away from things, Jeremy. Sooner or later you have to stop running and face up to the thing that troubles you."

"I know...but I'm scared. I didn't do anything wrong, but they're treating me like a criminal."

"Jeremy, somebody once said that every evening we should turn our worries over to God since He's going to be up all night anyway." She paused. "I trust Him in this. You've got to believe that this crisis isn't going to destroy you."

"But I can't help worrying."

"That's normal. But it's going to be all right. We've all had our troubles."

Jeremy looked down at the sand. "You were never a suspect in a murder case."

He waited for her to answer, and when she didn't, he looked up and noticed a strange expression on her face. "I've been in trouble, Jeremy, and it nearly destroyed me."

"What kind of trouble?"

"A kind so bad I have difficulty sleeping even now, but I survived. So will you." She seemed uncomfortable with the conversation and said, "Why don't you come for a walk with me? Two are better than one. I need your company."

"Yeah. Sure." Jeremy turned to walk beside Hope as they headed west along the beach. He heard a yowling noise and turned to see that Jacques had come down and was following them. "You go home, Jacques," he said.

"That's the strangest cat," Hope said. "Does he like anybody?"

"Nobody really except Mom. He puts up with me. He hates Jake like poison."

As they walked along the beach, Jeremy was able for a time to put his troubles aside. But as they passed the Maddux place, Jacques darted toward the boathouse. "I wish he wouldn't do that," Jeremy said. "He's always going into that boathouse. Mr. Maddux said he was going to shoot him if we didn't keep him home."

"What does he do in there?"

"I followed him once. He was always scratching the wall. He does crazy things."

A shudder ran through Hope. "I don't like this place. I can't help thinking about Derek."

"Me, too." Jeremy had a hard time framing his words. "He wasn't always nice, but we were friends—sort of. I'm sorry that he died." He kicked at a broken sand dollar, watched it fly through the air, and shook his head. "And the police think I did it."

"I know you didn't kill Derek, Jeremy. You wouldn't do a thing like that."

Jeremy gave her a sudden look of appreciation. "I'm glad you believe me anyway, Miss Barclay."

"Come on. Let's do double time and get away from here."

They walked rapidly, and as soon as they were out of sight of the Maddux house, they both felt better.

"Look," he said finally. "There's the Brice house."

"That's a terrible looking shack. Who lives there?"

"An old man and his granddaughter. Mr. Brice is his name. He's a professor of some kind."

"Oh, yes, I know about them. He's the one who homeschools his granddaughter, isn't he?"

"Yes. She's a sight! I don't know what to think about her. She's got a strange name that sounds like Rye-ann-on. It's spelled funny, but that's what she calls herself."

"That sounds like a Welsh name."

Suddenly Jeremy nodded. "There she is." He lifted his voice and said, "Hey, Rhiannon!"

The two stopped and the girl came forward to meet them.

"Hello, Jeremy," she said. She was wearing a pair of baggy shorts faded to a leprous gray and a bright-green T-shirt evidently just purchased.

"How's your granddad, Rhiannon?" Jeremy asked.

"He's having a bad day."

"Sorry to hear that. Hey, this is Miss Barclay. She's my English teacher. This is Rhiannon Brice, Miss Barclay."

"I'm glad to know you, Rhiannon," Miss Barclay said. "I'm so sorry to hear your grandfather isn't feeling well."

The girl didn't answer. There was a barrier around her, it seemed to both of them. She was watching them carefully and finally Miss Barclay said, "Maybe he needs to see a doctor—your grandfather, I mean."

"He won't go," the girl said.

Rhiannon looked at Jeremy with her head cocked to one side, and said, "I've got something to tell you."

"Me? What is it?" Jeremy asked. Rhiannon seemed uncharacteristically nice.

"It's not about you. It's about him," she pointed at Jacques who had pulled himself off to one side and was staring suspiciously at the girl.

"What about him?"

"I had a dream about him. I don't know what it all means, but someone was trying to hurt you and that cat was trying to protect you. It was all kind of fuzzy."

"Someone shot our dog, Trouble," Jeremy said.

"Well, that cat was in my dream, and I think he's going to do something strange and wonderful."

"Jacques? He never does *anything* wonderful. Strange, yes, but wonderful—no."

"I don't believe too much in dreams," Hope said.

"I do," Rhiannon said shortly. "You'd better watch Jacques, Jeremy. He's going to do something really wonderful." She turned then and stalked back toward the house. The two stood watching her.

"What a strange girl," Hope mused.

"Yeah, she's really odd, all right."

"I guess we'd better go back," Miss Barclay said. "I'm getting a sunburn."

The two trudged back, and more than once Jeremy glanced at Jacques who was chasing sandpipers. "I wonder what that dream stuff is all about?"

"Dreams don't mean much, I don't think," Miss Barclay said. "We have to depend on reality."

Jeremy watched the black cat who had a peculiar beauty in his gait as he loped along the sand.

"I guess so," he said, but he knew that he would think of Rhiannon's dream again.

● ● ●

Rita Chavez, the assistant district attorney, was a trim woman with a wealth of brown hair and deep-brown eyes. Her skin was olive, and she was loaded equally with ambition and good looks. Beverly had told Jake, "She's got a great record of convictions. She doesn't jump into things easily, but when she does, she's like a bulldog."

Rita was standing in front of her desk beside Chief O'Dell, who spoke as Beverly and Jake listened. "We've been working on this attempt on your life, Mr. Novak. Not getting very far with it. It might help if you could remember a registration number on that boat."

"I was too busy trying to dig a hole in the sand, Chief, but I can give you the name, address, and phone number of the guy who hired the shooter. To sum it all up: Vince Canelli."

"Did you see him on the boat?" Rita demanded sharply.

"All I saw was sand."

"Well, we can't arrest Canelli on a testimony like that," O'Dell protested.

"He's a pretty clever item, Canelli is, but he's dangerous," Jake said. "If you cross him, usually it means you're going to be getting a tag on your toe sooner or later." He turned and faced Rita, but Bev spoke before he could open his mouth.

"Chief O'Dell, we appreciate your efforts to identify the person responsible for the attempt on Jake's life, and we trust that investigation is in good hands." He gave Jake a pointed look, and then turned back to face O'Dell and Chavez. "However, I'm here to discuss the murder of Derek Maddux. There's really not enough evidence against Jeremy Forrest for you to charge him."

Rita Chavez had a very direct gaze, and she put her eyes on the two before her.

"The victim loved his watch," the woman began. "He would never have given it to anyone, but your client had it—and never mentioned it. That's item one. Two, your client had a fight with Derek Maddux the day before he was killed. And three, we have an eyewitness who saw your client in the boat headed out to open water."

"It was dark," Jake countered. "How could an eyewitness see anything?"

"He made a positive identification. Your client owns a very distinctive jacket, fire-engine red with Darth Vader on the back."

"Anyone could have put on that jacket," Jake said shortly.

"The Forrest boy said he 'lost' it," Rita said. "Not a very strong defense."

The argument went on for some time and finally Jake interrupted. "Miss Chavez, may I call you Rita?"

"No."

"Well, Miss Chavez, Arlene Maddux has got more of a motive and an opportunity than Jeremy Forrest does. Maddux's will says she would have gotten very little if Earl Maddux died."

"I'd be interested in knowing how you got a copy of that will."

Bev answered smoothly, "Oh, we have our methods, but it's true enough. Mr. Novak is right about that. The woman did have a motive, and she did have opportunity."

"She says she never went down to the boathouse after dark that evening. Can you prove she's lying?" Rita demanded.

"No, but that doesn't mean that she couldn't have done it," Beverly said.

"Canelli's boys could have done it, too." Jake said. "Vince's business with Earl Maddux had apparently gone sour."

"You don't know that," Rita said. "Based on what we *do* know, I'm going to recommend to the district attorney that we go to trial."

"You'll lose," Bev said grimly.

Rita smiled. "I don't lose very often."

Jake gazed at Rita and said, "You know, I think you're too good looking to be in this job. As a writer, I'd describe you as 'provocative with a saucy hint of invitation and a mouth that invites attention.'"

Rita Chavez glared at him and said, "If you put that in your book, Mr. Novak, be sure you spell my name right."

Bev stared at the two. "You're going to lose this case, Miss Chavez."

"I'll see you in court, Counselor," the woman replied as she opened the door, inviting the two men to leave.

● ● ●

Vince Canelli poured his glass full of the amber liquor and drank it down as if it were water. His face was flushed and as he glared at Dante Lazlo, anger tightened his features. His mouth drew into a white line and he said, "I didn't get where I am by leaving loose ends, Lazlo."

Lazlo shrugged his shoulders but said nothing. As he stood there, his heart seemed to be beating out of rhythm, and he knew that one day he would simply keel over dead from his ailing heart. It was like walking around with a time bomb inside his chest.

"We've got to do something about that limey lawyer." Vince's voice was tense.

"Because he's defending the Forrest kid?"

"I don't care about that. What I care about is that he knows all about our operation. All he has to do is drop a dime on us and turn us over to the feds. He'd be a powerful witness."

Lazlo shrugged. "I told you not to use him, Vince."

"Yeah, you did. So I made a mistake. But that's why pencils have erasers."

"You want me to erase the Brit?"

"I want it done so it can't be traced back to me. Not even the slightest trail, you hear?"

"You know me. I'll take care of it."

Twenty-one

Jake was sitting on the floor next to Trouble, who was lying on a blanket that Jake had placed there for him. The dog had his chin hooked over Jake's leg and his soulful eyes were staring up at him. From time to time Jake reached out to a bowl beside him, took a piece of boiled chicken that he had fixed especially for Trouble, and handed it to him. Trouble took the morsel, wolfed it down, and put his chin back on Jake's leg.

"You worthless outfit! Why am I doing this?" Jake murmured. He ran his hand over the dog's smooth hide and thought of how he had sat up with him almost all night, comforting him and periodically giving him the painkiller that Enola had prescribed. He had never imagined himself behaving this way toward an animal, but Trouble had, in effect, saved his life, so Jake convinced himself that he owed the dog something.

Cleo came padding up, stuck her nose down toward the chicken, and Jake glared at her. "You haven't been shot."

"Wow!" Cleo said and moved in even closer, her eyes fixed firmly on the chicken. Jake reached out, gave her a piece of it, and then he saw the Ripper had appeared also. Jacques was glaring at him with his *why don't I kill him?* expression, which was normal for him. Jake smiled and grabbed a large piece of the chicken and tossed it over to Jacques. "There. Maybe if I'm nice to you, you won't rip my legs up anymore—but I doubt it."

Something touched Jake's back and he jerked but then he felt tiny paws. He glanced around to see that Abigail the ferret was staring at him with her bright eyes.

"You're another troublemaker," he said. He reached out and stroked her

211

back with his forefinger. "Actually you're kind of cute. But I'd never admit that to anybody. He paused for a moment, looking at the animals all around him.

"What's *wrong* with me? I must be getting soft-hearted or something! Don't you guys tell Mary Katherine about this. Now, Abby, I suppose you want chicken, too?"

Abigail took the piece Jake handed her and scurried off.

The outside cat door swung open and Bandit came in. His eyes brightened, and he scurried over to stand, his head stretched forward, near the bowl of chicken.

Jake shook his head and smiled. "All right. Why should you be different?" He offered Bandit some morsels, and Bandit propped up on his hind legs holding the meat in his clever little hands. He nibbled at it and then went over to the water bowl and proceeded to wash it. When he had eaten it, he came back and begged for more.

"What have I done to deserve this?" Jake growled. "I'm the guy who hates animals, and now I wind up in the middle of a blasted zoo!" A faint sound caught Jake's attention. He swiveled his head and saw Kate had exited her room and was advancing toward him. She was dressed, but her hair had only a perfunctory going over and her eyes were still crinkled as if she had just awakened.

"What are you doing?" she asked. But she saw at a glance the bowl of chicken and took in the animals crowded around him. "Jake Novak, don't tell me you're—no, it couldn't be—you're taking care of the animals?"

Jake gave her an irritated glance. "I don't know what I'm doing anymore. I don't have any sense left at all since I moved into this menagerie. Get these animals off me."

Kate laughed softly. She had a pleasant laugh, melodious, and Jake had to admit he found it very attractive. He was disturbed at the thought that she had a powerful effect on him. Somehow she colored the room and put something into it, something like a faint charge of electricity. For one instant Jake admired what he saw and felt that curious combination of appreciation and dejection that a man feels when he looks upon beauty and knows it will never be for him.

Kate knelt down and put her hand on Trouble's broad head. Compassion softened her lips and she whispered, "You're going to be all right, Trouble." She looked up at Jake, and there was something in her at that instant that made her a more complex and unfathomable woman. Quick breathing disturbed her composure and color ran freshly across her cheeks.

She's thinking about the kiss I gave her, Jake thought. And he was thinking of the same thing.

"You're a fraud, Jake Novak." There was just a hint of smile behind the words.

"What are you talking about?"

"I mean you're a fraud. You're a tough guy afraid to admit you've got a soft spot right in the middle of you."

"Oh, yeah," Jake huffed, "that's what they called me in the homicide squad—Old Soft Spot."

"I'll bet they did."

"Yep, I was the guy they called in to take care of all the hard problems. They knew I'd fold up and cry every time I saw one."

Kate felt a nudge at her side and looked around. Jacques had come over and pushed his big head against her. She reached over and rubbed his head. His hoarse purr filled the room.

"He never does that to me," Jake said. "Not that I want him to."

"I think you're too much alike."

"What are you talking about? I'm nothing like that mangy cat."

"Sure you are. Both of you are big and tough and afraid to show affection."

"You ask some of the babes I've had in the past whether I was able to show affection or not!" Jake rose quickly and left the room to ascend the stairs.

Kate rubbed Jacques's head, whispering, "Why don't you be nice to Jake?"

Jacques leaned against Kate's soft form and glanced over toward Cleo. *Will you listen to this, Cleo? She's like all females. Doesn't understand us males.*

She's right, Jacques. You really are nice deep down. You just need to show it.

No, I'm not! I'm tough and I don't put up with anything from anybody.

Just wait until you get hurt or sick or lonely. You'll need somebody then.

Cleo purred and tried to climb into Kate's lap. She laughed and pushed the cat away. "You're a mooch, Cleo."

Jacques looked disgusted and took a swipe at Bandit, who had managed to take a piece of chicken out of the bowl. Bandit's eyes grew wide and he backed up quickly, dropping the morsel and uttering a small cry. He looked longingly at the chicken, but Jacques was now standing over it, nibbling at his own rate.

Jacques, you really ought to share with Bandit.

I'm not sharing with anybody.

This was Jacques's attitude, and he revealed it plainly as always, glaring around at the other animals and daring them to come into claw range.

● ● ●

Jake opened the door and grinned at Beverly, who stood waiting for him.

"Well, if it isn't the man with the hyphen."

"You're just jealous because you don't have one," Bev said. "I've got to talk to you, Jake." Beverly entered the house and looked around quickly. "Where's Kate?"

"She went to the store and took Jeremy with her. What's going down?"

"What's going down? You Americans have a peculiar way of communicating thoughts. You do horrible things to the English language! Nothing's going down, but if you would ask me what is happening, I could give you a respectable answer."

Jake grinned crookedly. "You English are the ones who have trouble with the language. All right. What's happening?"

Beverly looked keyed up. His blue eyes flashed and he moved his feet excitedly. "I just got a phone call. It was from a man who says he knows something that could help my client."

Jake shook his head, and his native skepticism appeared. "Why doesn't he just come to see you? Why the phone call business?"

"Haven't a clue, but I can't pass this up."

"What'd he want?"

"He gave me a time and a place. He said he'd meet me out on Fort Morgan Road in that wildlife reserve at three o'clock this afternoon."

"What else did he say?"

"That's all, but I must go, of course."

"So you think it's legitimate?"

"Not at all. Somebody wants to get me alone for something—I'm just not sure what it is."

"I don't like it."

Beverly nodded, his mouth drawn into a thin line. "I feel the same way, but I can't afford to ignore it."

"I'd better go with you. Let me get my cap." Jake turned and ran upstairs. He was soon back, and he had a Chicago Cubs baseball cap on his head and in his hand a huge pistol.

"What in the world is that thing? It looks like a cannon."

"It's a .357 Magnum." Jake rolled the cylinder and pointing it at the floor, looked at the cartridges that showed. "Biggest handgun made at one time. It'll knock the engine block out of a car. I think it'd even stop an elephant, if you hit him right."

"Well, we're not likely to meet any elephants in White Sands. They're rather rare in this area."

Jake fished a smaller pistol from his pocket. "Here, you take this one."

Bev looked at the gun and said, "I hate guns."

"Sometimes," Jake said, "they're man's best friend." He would have said more, but at that instant a car pulled up. Jake put the smaller gun back in his pocket and said quickly, "Here comes Kate. I don't think we ought to tell her anything about this."

"Why not?"

"The less women know, the better."

"How archaic! Jake, you're a a total misogynist."

"Yeah, and I don't like women, either," Jake said with a grin. They waited until Kate came in with Jeremy beside her. They were both holding plastic bags from Wal-Mart when she saw the Magnum in Jake's hand.

"Jake, what are you going with *that*?"

"Just going out to do some target practice."

"That's not true," Kate said knowingly.

"No, it's not," Jake admitted. "But lying is one of my more appealing attributes."

"Bev, I can't get any sense out of him," Kate said, exasperated. "Where are you two going?"

"Kate, I got a phone call. A man says he knows something that will help Jeremy. We're going out to see about it."

"I'm going with you," she said, setting her bag of groceries on the nearest chair.

"No, you aren't," Jake snapped. He glared at Beverly. "I told you not to tell her."

"He's right about one thing, Kate," Bev said. "You don't need to go. We don't know who this man is, and he might be dangerous."

"I'm going with you," she said adamantly. "I'm Jeremy's mother."

Jake groaned. "I knew it was a mistake to teach women how to count money and let them eat at the table with us!"

"You are impossible!" Kate was suddenly seething.

Just then Bad Louie came winging in. He fluttered down on her shoulder and pushed himself up and down in that strange motion of parrots. "Bless you! Bless you!"

"He's never said a nice thing like that to me," Jake said. At that instant Bad Louie muttered an obscenity, and Kate reached up and clamped his beak shut. "You hush, Bad Louie! Bad bird! Bad bird!" She composed herself and faced the two men again.

"Please let me go with you," she said.

"No, Kate. You stay here and take care of Jeremy," Bev said sympathetically.

Jeremy was staring at the gun in Jake's hand. "Jake, are you going to shoot somebody?"

"I doubt it, Slick. This is what's called insurance."

Kate's face had a stricken expression. "Why don't you get the police to go with you?"

"The guy was very particular about that," Bev said. "No cops."

"What about Jake?"

"I thought I'd better have a little company on this one."

Jake was impatient. "We're wasting time. Come on."

Kate caught Jake's arm. "Jake," she said, "be careful."

"Sure," Jake nodded. He went outside and got into Bev's Rolls Royce and waited until Bev started the engine. "Nice to have a car that no one will notice, sort of fades into the background. I may get one myself someday."

"They're a nuisance really," Bev said. "You can't go into Wal-Mart and buy a part, for one thing. They have to ship a mechanic all the way to where you are."

"Some people sure have it rough. Say, do you know where you're going?"

"I've got the instructions. It's in the wildlife preserve. He says there's a white post with the number sixteen on it. We turn right there. It's an old road that goes into the woods."

As they pulled away from the house Bev looked over his shoulder and saw Kate watching. "Nice to have a woman worry about you, isn't it, Novak?"

"She's a pest."

Bev grinned, put the Rolls into gear, and it moved silently down the driveway.

He drove down the highway, turned right on 59 and then left onto Fort Morgan Road.

After a few moments of silence, Bev cleared his throat and said, "Jake, I need to ask you something, old boy."

"Fire away, Sir Devon-Hunt."

"I wish you wouldn't call me that," Bev protested. "I want to ask you about Kate."

"What about her?"

"Well, I admire her greatly. I've been thinking about asking her out."

Jake swiveled his head and studied Beverly's profile. "I don't think she'd suit you, *old chap*. A man with a hyphen needs a woman high on the social scale."

"Well, I don't want to cut in, but it seems that the two of you do nothing but disagree with one another. You wouldn't shoot me with that cannon you're carrying if she did go out with me, would you?"

"Maybe just in the leg to slow you down."

Bev grinned but said nothing.

Five minutes later he said, "There's that road marker. But I don't see a road."

"Sure, it's there. You can barely see it. Probably an old logging road, I guess. Are you going to put this fine car in the brush like that? It looks pretty rough."

"It's only a clump of metal."

Beverly turned abruptly and the Rolls thumped and scraped along through the saplings that made a narrow margin for the road.

Finally Bev shook his head. "He said the road would play out. I guess this is it."

"Here's where we get out then. Watch yourself."

Beverly got out and looked around at the wilderness. "I don't see anybody."

Jake moved cautiously, his eyes going from point to point. "Good place for a sniper," he said. "He could be anywhere out there."

The two moved forward and were side by side advancing down what appeared to be a trail.

Suddenly Jake caught a flash of light, a reflection of the sun on metal and instantly he threw himself at Beverly. He knocked the tall Englishman down and at the same instant a sharp report of a rifle broke the silence of the woods. "Stay down!" Jake yelled. "Crawl behind the car!"

"What are you going to do?"

"Just do what I tell you!"

Jake's voice was savage, and his eyes were half shut as he scanned the foliage. As soon as he saw Beverly was safe behind the Rolls, he waited for a moment, got up halfway and then fell again. The exposure drew the fire of the shooter, and it hit the dirt directly in front of him. Instantly he got up and threw himself behind a scrub oak. Two more shots hit the tree, sending bark flying. Jake wiggled his way deeper into the brush, and as soon as he thought it was safe, he got to his feet.

He had clear, vivid, and rather terrible memories of his days in the Delta Force when he had done this sort of thing for a living. Now dodging and bumping through the undergrowth, he held the Magnum in his right hand, shoving the branches aside with his left. He made a semicircle around, intending to flank the sniper.

He reached a point where he thought he could close in and even as he did, another shot rang out and hit three feet over to his left. Jake saw a dim figure. Lifting the Magnum, he held his wrist and fired a shot. The huge weapon kicked up and sounded like a cannon going off. Throwing himself to the right, he ran a zigzag pattern.

The shooter was backing up as Jake was advancing. Jake had a pocketful of shells, and when he had emptied the Magnum, he stopped long enough to reload. He was puzzled. *Any good sniper would have gotten me before this. Something's wrong here.* He made a dash to his left, expecting to draw fire, but there was none.

"That's funny. What's the matter with him?" he wondered. He forged his way through the brush and caught a glimpse of something ahead. He brought the Magnum up but didn't fire. *He's lying in a prone position trying to get me,* he thought. Quickly he changed his direction and came at a different angle toward the shooter, but he saw that the shooter was down, lying flat on his back. Jake advanced, holding the Magnum on the motionless figure. "I couldn't have hit him." He moved forward and called out, "Don't move," and saw that the man's head turned. When he got closer, he found pretty much what he had expected.

Dante Lazlo was lying on his back with the sniper's rifle off to one side.

"Did I hit you, Lazlo?"

Lazlo turned his head, and Jake saw that his face was flushed and his lips were purple. "What's wrong?"

Lazlo didn't speak until Jake knelt beside him.

"Heart," he whispered.

Indeed, Jake saw that there was no obvious wound in Lazlo. When he laid his hand on the man's chest, he felt the wildly erratic beat.

Lazlo raised his hand and put it over his heart. "Ticker," he gasped. "Been going a long time."

Jake raised up and called, "Beverly, come on over here. This way."

He knelt back down and said, "We'll get you to a hospital, Dante."

"For what? This is it. I'm dying, Novak."

There in the stillness of the wilderness Jake Novak had a strange feeling. He had seen men die before, and this man had just tried to kill him. But there was something in the ashen face and the agonized expression that troubled him. He heard Beverly coming.

When the tall Englishman knelt down he asked, "What is it?"

"Heart attack."

"We'd better get him to a hospital."

"No time," Lazlo whispered. "I've run out of time."

A group of gulls flew overhead making their harsh cries, but none of the three paid any attention to them. Lazlo's eyes opened, and his lips twisted in pain. "You know, I've never been afraid of anything, but I'm afraid now."

Jake glanced at Bev but neither of them knew what to say. "We might make it if we can get you to a hospital."

"No, too late for that." Lazlo closed his eyes.

Jake had never felt more helpless. The man was a killer and had shown no mercy to others, but now he was just a helpless, dying man. He wished there were a chaplain around. He turned to Bev and said, "Talk to him, Bev."

Beverly stared at Jake and then looked down. "I say, it wouldn't be a bad idea for you to call upon God and tell Him you're sorry."

"No."

"Why not, old boy?"

"How can I do that when I've ignored Him all my life?"

Bev leaned forward and took Lazlo's hand. He found it cold and clammy. "Remember the story of the dying thief on the cross next to Jesus? He was a pretty bad chap himself, I suppose, but Jesus heard him."

Lazlo listened as Beverly spoke, and Jake was rather amazed at Bev knowing what to say. He hadn't thought the Englishman to be all that religious.

"I wish it hadn't ended like this for you, Lazlo," Jake said finally.

"That's because you and me are alike."

The three men were quiet then. There was a sound of the wind coming through the trees and from far off a dog was barking at something. Jake realized a hopeless wish that Dante Lazlo would call on God, but there seemed little likelihood.

"There's a man called Pascal, Lazlo," Bev said. "He was a famous mathematician and known for his religious writings. He said it's a better bet to believe in God than not. If you believe in God and there is no God, what have you lost? But if you disbelieve and there is a God, you've lost it all. So, it's a safer bet to just call on God."

"I can't do it."

"Sure you can, Dante," Beverly said, his voice soft as a summer's breeze in the trees.

Lazlo said, "Pray for me...if you know how."

Both Jake and Bev were held as if they were frozen, and finally Beverly spoke a brief prayer. Before he was finished Lazlo made a soft and articulate cry, and Jake saw a terrible stillness come over him.

The two men stood looking down at the dead man. "Do you think he made it?" Jake whispered.

"I hope so."

Twenty-two

The office of Chief Ray O'Dell had all the charm of a restroom at Burger King. There was nothing in it that wasn't absolutely essential: only a gray metal desk with nothing on the top except a pen that lay exactly in the center and a wire basket with no papers in it. The seating consisted of three mismatched chairs, and there were no pictures on the walls. Jake and Bev had come into this inner sanctum without knocking, and now the chief and Rita Chavez greeted them with less than a show of warmth.

"What do you want?" O'Dell growled.

"I thought you might need some help on this Derek Maddux case."

O'Dell's face had all the expression of an anvil. "Well, thank heaven you two have come. I've had this murder take place and it's got us all stumped. The district attorney here just said, 'There's only two men who can solve this: Jake the Take and Hyphen-Man. Send for them.'"

Despite himself Jake smiled. "That's a good act you got there, Chief. Can I call you Ray?"

"No."

"Well, Chief O'Dell, Mr. Hyphen-Man Devon-Hunt and myself have a few things we think might be helpful to your investigation."

Rita was wearing a black skirt and a pure white blouse that didn't leave much to Jake's imagination.

"Really?" she said sarcastically. "Can't wait to hear it."

"Jake and I have some new dirt on a suspect," Bev said.

"Oh, good. Just what we need," Rita said. "Who is it, Sir Beverly?"

"You could just call me Bev. I like to keep the common touch. I found

221

out Arlene Maddux has everything a murderer needs. She has motive and opportunity."

"Are you crazy?" O'Dell snapped. "She's the boy's mother."

"Stepmother, old boy." Bev nodded and his light-blue eyes gleamed. "And therein lies a tale."

"I know you're trying to get your client off," Rita said, "but you're going to have to do better than that."

"Miss Chavez, you've seen a copy of the will," Jake said.

"And I'd still like to know where you got it."

"Doesn't matter," Beverly said firmly. "You know that Earl Maddux left practically everything he had to his son and almost nothing to his wife. He left her only a flat sum. The bulk of his estate would have gone to Derek."

"Nice juicy motive, wouldn't you say?" Jake added. "But there's something else. You remember that she has said all along that she didn't see Derek on the night he was killed?"

"That's right," O'Dell agreed. "She said she didn't see him after he and the Forrest boy went fishing."

Beverly leaned in. "Well, she told me a different story. She let it slip that on that very night she went down to the boat dock after Derek got back, and she told me she had bawled him out. She said she was going to tell Earl not to let him have the boat since he couldn't follow the rules."

"She told you that?" Rita demanded.

"Yes."

"It's still just hearsay."

"Oh, no, I have it all on tape." Beverly reached into his inner shirt pocket and pulled out a cassette. "It's all here, clear as a bell."

"How did you get that?" Rita asked.

"I was checking out something on Earl for a client and overheard Arlene talking. I thought the information might come in handy, so I taped it," Bev admitted.

"This changes things a little bit, Chief." She glanced across at the two men and said, "I'll go have a talk with Arlene Maddux."

"Want me to go along and rough her up, Miss D.A.?" Jake asked.

"I think I can handle it."

"Call on me anytime. It's my function to keep the world safe for democracy."

"Also, Jake, we're trying to get a line on who took a shot at you, but it's hard to do since you weren't able to get a registration number off the boat."

"I don't need a registration number. Vince Canelli's your man," Jake said.

"You have no proof of that," Rita snapped. "As a matter of fact, I've already checked and he has a perfect alibi. He has three witnesses who will swear they were with him during the time of the shooting."

"He doesn't do his own killing. That's what he keeps Dante Lazlo for. He's your man," Beverly said.

Chief O'Dell shook his head, his face frozen in a grim expression. "And he's dead—which makes things terribly inconvenient."

"Guys, we'll take it from here, if you don't mind," Rita said, her tone obviously dismissing them. "We'll be in touch."

Jake turned to O'Dell and said, "Chief, you run a nice little department here. I've been watching you."

O'Dell leaned back, "Oh, yeah, apart from divisions based on politics, religion, and racial backgrounds, we're just one happy little family. Now, get out of here, you two!"

● ● ●

Arlene Maddux didn't respond well to direct questioning. The assistant district attorney had caught her off guard, and now Arlene's acting skills seemed to have deserted her.

"What—what did you ask me?" She kept glancing over at Earl, who sat silently by.

"I asked, Did you see Derek the night he was killed?"

"I've already told you I didn't."

"That's what you told me," Rita said, "but I have a tape here in which you tell a different story."

Arlene stared at the tape as a mouse might stare at a cobra. "Where did you get that?"

"The Forrest boy's lawyer gave it to me. You want to hear it?"

Arlene paused for a moment, then said, "Maybe—maybe I made a mistake."

"You going to change your story?" Rita asked sarcastically.

"Yes—yes, I did go down to the boathouse. I heard the boys come in and I went down and spoke to Derek. Earl told him never to stay out in the boat after dark, and I told him since he couldn't keep the rules I was going to see that he didn't get free use of the boat."

"And you forgot all about that conversation?"

"You don't understand the pressure I've been under. My stepson is dead, Miss Chavez. Do you know what it's like to have a child die?"

Earl Maddux had been taking in the conversation. Now his eyes grew as hard as agates, and he said, "You never told me you spoke to Derek that night."

"I simply forgot."

"Was the Forrest boy there when you went down to the boathouse?" Rita asked.

Arlene cast an agonizing glance at her husband then said, "No, he was already gone."

"I see. Let me ask you another question. Are you aware of the nature of your husband's will, Mrs. Maddux?"

"No."

"Stop lying, Arlene," Earl said. "I've told you what's in the will. You get a flat sum and Derek gets the rest of the estate."

"I never pay attention to things like that," Arlene said.

Maddux laughed harshly. "That's right. You have no interest at all in money and diamonds and expensive cars. You spurn all that, don't you, Arlene?"

"Please, Earl, don't talk like that!"

"You understand, Mrs. Maddux, this makes a big difference in our investigation."

"What do you mean?"

"I mean you had motive and you had opportunity."

"What opportunity?"

"According to your own story, you were the last one to see Derek alive. There was nothing to stop you from killing him, getting into the boat and taking it out, and dumping the body."

"You *can't* be serious," Arlene huffed, almost in tears. "I couldn't do a thing like that. You can't say those things to me!" It was either good acting or else she was genuinely moved by the situation. Rita Chavez kept at her for another fifteen minutes, and when she left she dialed a number on her cell phone and said, "She's a legitimate suspect, Chief. Motive and opportunity. She's got both."

● ● ●

Bev drove Jake back to the house on the beach. When he pulled the Rolls up, Jake said, "Come on in. I'll fix us something to eat."

"That sounds wonderful. I'm starved."

The two went into the house, and the first living thing they met was the Ripper. He hissed at Jake, who walked around him carefully keeping an eye on him, and then went to Beverly and rubbed up against his leg.

"I can't understand why this cat likes me and seems to hate you," Bev mused.

"I can't understand it either," Jake said. "They say you can trust a man that animals like."

"But that's not true is it, Old Chap? You're a trustworthy fellow."

"You're right—it's a crock of oatmeal. The worst killer I ever saw was loved by every dog and cat he ever met. And he killed twelve people. Come on in."

They entered the kitchen and found Kate warming up a Stouffer's lasagna.

"What did they say?" she asked, turning from the microwave.

"Throw away that mess you just put in there," Jake said. "We're having a real dinner. Sit down, Bev. I'll make us something fit to eat."

"I think we convinced that assistant district attorney that Arlene Maddux may be a legitimate suspect," Beverly said.

"That's good, isn't it? How did you do it?"

"I dazzled her with my wit and sophistication," Jake said. He jerked the lasagna out of the microwave and dumped it into the trash. "This stuff tastes like adhesive tape. I'll make a salad that will steal your heart away."

Bev summarized for Kate the entire scene they had with Chief O'Dell and Miss Chavez.

"Well, that's good, isn't it?" Kate said eagerly.

"I think it is. According to her own story, Jeremy had already left. That ought to count for something. Jeremy wasn't the last one to see Derek alive after all."

Jake fixed a salad out of fresh vegetables and added strips of chicken that he'd broiled. He set the three salads down and then brought over a bottle. "This is my special salad dressing."

"What's in it?"

"Sugar and spice and everything nice, Bev. Eat it and don't ask questions."

Beverly began to eat hungrily, and Jake was well aware of how Kate kept her eyes fixed on the attorney.

Kate finally noticed that Jake was staring at her. She turned to him and said, "What's the matter, Jake? You're being very quiet."

Jake had the last bit of salad on his fork. He stared at it and then put it down. "I can't quit thinking about Lazlo," he said.

Kate exchanged a quick glance with Beverly, and both had the same thought: *He's a very tough man, but something about that death has gotten to him.*

"It was a brutal thing. But you didn't shoot him," Kate reminded hm. "If I understand correctly, he hadn't long to live with a bad heart like that."

Jake didn't answer. He was pushing the piece of lettuce around with his fork. His face was moody, and Kate noticed that his lips had a tough, sharp set. His head was dropped forward, and the rough humor that was part of him wasn't there. The edges of his jaws were sharp against his heavily tanned skin, and she noticed once again the small bump at the bridge of his nose. When he lifted his eyes, she saw that the rash and reckless will that was usually there was gone, and there was something sad about the dark preoccupation in his face. "One minute he was there, the next minute he was gone," Jake murmured.

"Maybe he called on God," Beverly said quickly. He turned to Kate. "I did my best to explain how God loves sinners."

Kate leaned over and put her hand over Jake's. She noticed how blunt his fingers were and how strong his hands appeared. "It only takes a moment, Jake. God is merciful."

Jake dropped his head before rising abruptly and leaving the room. They heard his footsteps on the stairs.

Bev was puzzled. "That was strange," he said. "You wouldn't think a tough guy like Jake Novak would be so affected. He's seen men killed before."

Kate didn't answer. She was thinking of the expression that was on Jake's face and it created a sense of grief in her.

● ● ●

The trial was set for a week away, and Jake was grilling fish outside on the deck. Kate and Jeremy were watching. Bad Louie fluttered out, and after circling the three of them finally lit on Jake's shoulder and said a bad word.

"Bad Louie, I'm going to tape your beak shut if you don't stop using that awful language!" Kate exclaimed.

"You can't break a bird from cussing," Jake said.

"Yes, you can. People can change. So can parrots. If he hears good things, he'll say good things."

Jake flipped the fish over, staring at them clinically. Then he lifted his eyes to Jacques who was watching him steadily from the top railing of the deck. "What about the Ripper? Is there hope for him?"

"I like to think there's hope for everyone."

Jake said, "I'm glad you feel that way. You haven't known some of the hard customers I have."

Jeremy said, "Look, we've got company."

Jake turned to see a young girl walking along the beach. She was wearing a pair of oversized shorts, a faded T-shirt, and a billed cap on her head. "Who's that?" he asked.

"It's Rhiannon. I told you about her, Mom. She lives with her grandfather down on the beach."

"She's not going to be a fashion model, I take it," Jake said.

They all more or less expected the girl to continue her walk along the beach, but she turned and made straight for the house. She came up on the deck and stared at the three of them with a strange expression.

Jake took in the black, curly hair and the unusual green eyes. "Hello," he said. "My name's Jake. What's yours?"

"Her name's Rhiannon. It's Welsh," Jeremy said. "This is my mom and this is Jake Novak."

"How about having a bite to eat with us, Rhiannon?" Jake asked. "I like that name."

There was no hesitation in Rhiannon's manner. "All right," she said.

"Well, it's all ready. You get the drinks, Mary Katherine. Jeremy, you drag out an extra plate for our guest."

Jake served the fish, and when Rhiannon tasted it, she said, "This isn't as good as the fish I cook."

Kate laughed. "She's just like you, Jake!"

"Not as good, huh?" Jake was amused at her direct manner.

"No, I have a secret formula that makes it taste better."

Jake grinned, "I'd like to have it."

"I don't give it away to anybody." She turned to Jeremy and said, "I came to tell you about my dream, Jeremy."

"You mean the one about the cat?"

"Yes. I've had it three times—the same dream."

"What dream is that, Rhiannon?" Kate asked.

"I dreamed that your big cat there is going to do something that nobody would believe. He's going to save somebody's life."

"It's not very likely mine," Jake admitted. "That animal hates me."

Rhiannon turned to face Jake. She couldn't have been more than ten years old, Jake assumed, but there was something disconcerting about her stare. Her green eyes were the exact color of the sea just before a storm.

"You don't believe in dreams, do you, Mr. Novak?"

"What makes you think I don't?"

"I can see it in your eyes." Rhiannon got up. "I feel sorry for you. You don't believe in dreams or in God." Without another word she turned and walked away.

For some reason Jake was shaken by the charge of the young girl. "That's not a child. She must be a midget," he whispered under his breath.

"Jake Novak!" Kate admonished.

"She doesn't mean anything by it, Jake," Jeremy said. "She's just like that."

"Maybe she's right," Kate said. "The Bible often speaks of dreams that mean something. Like Joseph's dream that he would rule over his brothers. It came to pass just like he dreamed it."

Jake looked over at Jacques, who was eyeing him carefully. "I can't believe that cat would ever do good for anyone."

Jacques had watched the young girl, and now he arched his back and stared at Jake.

If you'd listen more, you'd know more, you dumb two-legged Intruder. The reason I don't like you is you won't listen to anybody. Well, go ahead and ignore the truth. See what it gets you.

This unspoken comment communicated itself to Jake, who stared at the huge black cat and shook his head. "I'm glad he can't talk. I'd hate to hear what he has to say."

● ● ●

When Beverly asked Kate to go out with him, she had been surprised but not too off-guard to say yes. The Englishman had a pixyish charm despite his size and she was fascinated, as many Americans were, by titled Englishmen. He called for her and took her out to Zeke's for supper. Afterward they went out to watch the charter boats come in with their loads of fish. They headed toward home early. The Rolls made only a slight whisper, and she ran her hand along the smoothness of the seat. "This is beautiful leather," she said.

"They keep a herd of cows in Spain, the Basque people do. They keep them without fences so they can't get their hides scarred."

"Is that true?"

Bev looked at her in surprise. "Of course it's true. Why would I lie about a thing like that?"

"Oh, I don't know. I just don't know much about Englishmen, I suppose. Especially lords."

"Being a lord doesn't mean too much anymore, Kate."

"I think it does," Kate said. "And I'm flattered to have been asked out by a lord. I can't imagine why you'd want to go out with me."

"I'm looking for a wife, of course."

The brash statement caught Kate off-guard. She laughed shortly and shook her head. "Bev, you must have had plenty of chances. You're rich, you have a title, and you're fairly good looking."

"Only fairly?"

"Well, perhaps a B-plus."

"Oh, yes, I've had chances, but in the line of work I've been in, most of the women are after the things I have, not me. They want to be called 'Lady.' But I don't think you're really impressed with titles, are you?"

"Not really. I may not be your wife, but I wouldn't mind having you for a friend."

"Sounds downright boring, but it's a start, I guess," Bev said with a sigh. They pulled up in front of the house, and he turned and pulled her close. "I'm about to break a promise."

"I can guess what it is." Kate's eyes were dancing.

"I promised my sainted mother that I would never kiss a girl on the first date." He pulled her closer and kissed her.

When their lips parted, Kate opened her eyes to see that Bev's eyes were sparkling with humor.

"I was just thinking about Jake," he said. "He might get jealous and beat me up."

"No, he won't."

"Are you sure?"

"There's nothing between me and Jake," Kate said.

Bev kissed her again lightly on the lips and smiled. "I say, that was terribly lackluster, wasn't it?"

"It was nice. Good night, Bev." Kate stepped out of the car and watched as the Rolls drove slowly away. "He must be crazy." She laughed aloud. "Me—Lady Katherine. Wouldn't that be a kick in the head!"

Twenty-three

The first dawn light had thrown its rays over the Gulf, turning the water from a dull gray to a pale green. Jake had been standing at the glass doors of the kitchen watching a group of dolphins as they frolicked by.

Jake's face was lined with fatigue. He had been up most of the night trying to hammer out the ending of his novel. It had been a rough writing session, and only iron discipline kept him at it. Going over to the refrigerator, he pulled out a pitcher of cranberry juice, poured a glassful, and then sat down at the kitchen island. He sipped the juice, very much aware of Cleo and Jacques, who were watching him steadfastly. He couldn't help but laugh as Cleo gave him one of her cat-smiles.

"You're the only feline I've seen who can smile," he said. Then he turned his eyes to Jacques. "You don't *ever* smile, do you? No, you don't. You've got a face like a criminal. You remind me of a psychopath I caught up with a few years ago. He'd killed six young women and had no more remorse about that than if he had jaywalked. That's what you are, Jacques, a psychocat. You've got no feelings at all."

Jacques had been watching Jake, wondering where he might most effectively sink his claws in. Now he gave a look of disgust at Cleo, who walked across the kitchen floor and began nudging Jake with her head, begging to be picked up.

You're hopeless, Cleo. That Person you're making up to is a cold, callous, biped. He doesn't care about anything or anyone except himself.

Cleo succeeded in her mission, and Jake perched her on his lap and began to scrub her head. Cleo looked at Jacques smugly.

231

He likes me—and he likes our Person, too, and the child of our Person. The trouble with you, Jacques, is that you've got poor judgment about people.

You're wrong about that. I've got his number. He's got no heart, Cleo. I'm going to give him a set of claw marks on his legs the first chance I get.

Jake watched the two cats carefully. "If I weren't convinced that you two have oatmeal for brains," he murmured, "I'd almost believe that you are communicating. But you're not smart enough for that."

"Who you talking to?" Kate asked as she entered the room.

"Myself. I'm the only one in the room."

"I think you were talking to Cleo. See how she loves you?"

"She loves the tuna I give her."

"You give Jacques tuna. Why doesn't he like you?" She went over and stroked Jacques' back, causing it to arch. "You just don't understand him."

"Yeah, and the prisons are full of people who nobody can understand."

Kate shrugged. "I wish you would be more generous to Jacques."

"I tried that once. The Ripper nailed me before I could even move. You want to see the scars?"

"What are you drinking? It looks awful."

"Cranberry juice. It's good for you."

"I can't stand the taste of it." Kate went to the refrigerator, pulled out a Coke, and popped the cap. She sipped as Jake shook his head in disgust.

"That stuff will rot your innards. Did you know when they first came out with Coke it had cocaine in it? I think it still does. People get hooked on it just like junkies."

Kate smiled at him. She had learned to take everything Jake said with a grain of salt. "How's the book coming?" she asked. "You look tired, Jake. I bet you were up all night."

"I'm going to give up writing and get a job."

"What kind of job?"

Jake put Cleo on the floor and took another long drink of the cranberry juice. "I'm thinking of becoming a gigolo on a cruise ship. It'll give old ladies a thrill."

"You couldn't do that."

"Why not?"

She knew that he was teasing but couldn't help saying, "You look more like a professional thug. The women on those boats are looking for a caring man like—"

"Like who?"

"Like Tom Hanks."

"Tom Hanks? He doesn't care about anybody."

"You couldn't do a good job of romancing women. They would never pay any attention to you."

Jake turned on his most charming grin. "You don't know what you're talking about, and it's your loss. When I give my complete smile where my eyes crinkle at the corners, women throw their hotel room keys at me."

"I'll just bet they do." Kate turned as Abigail came scurrying into the room, begging to be picked up. Kate scooped her up and said, "Good morning, Abigail," then kissed her on the cheek.

"Don't waste your kisses on that weasel."

"She's not a weasel. She's a ferret."

"Don't you know why they bred ferrets back in the old days? They put them in rat holes so they would run the rats out so the dogs could kill them."

"Abigail wouldn't do that, would you, Sweetheart?" She caressed Abigail and at that moment Trouble ambled in. He took one look at Jake and made a valiant attempt to crawl into his lap, but Jake shoved him away.

Kate laughed. "Admit it! You've fallen for the animals, Jake. You pretend you don't like them, but you do."

Jake tried again to shove Trouble away, but the dog insisted on coming back, whining and pawing at Jake. "I'd as soon fall for a gila monster as one of these pests."

The two sat at the island arguing, but there was a camaraderie in it that struck Kate very strongly. *We're like a married couple!* The thought had entered her head so quickly and it troubled her. She fell silent for a moment as her thoughts drifted back to the situation with Jeremy. She breathed a heavy sigh.

Jake looked up. Kate had been smiling and happy, and now there was a glum look on her face.

"You still worried about the kid?" he asked.

"Of course."

"I thought you and God had made some kind of arrangement."

"I prayed for him."

"Well, if you prayed for him, you believe he'll be all right. That's what you Christians believe, isn't it?"

Kate shifted the Coke, turned the can around in her hands, and began tracing a figure on the top of the granite.

"I prayed for Jeremy, but I guess all Christians have doubts when they're in trouble." She looked up and asked abruptly, "Aren't you afraid of anything, Jake?"

"Snakes."

"Besides that. What about dying?"

"I try to avoid it."

Kate was studying Jake's face. He had a slight cleft in his chin and his mouth was wide. His lips seemed drawn together under the guard of his will, and as he sat there his eyes were fixed on some distant point. She knew he was thinking hard. She had become familiar with his face in the brief time she had known him, and now she was aware that there was a stirring of feelings within her. "Do you ever think about what happens after you die, about judgment from God?"

Jake lifted his eyes and there was a shadow on his face. "I heard a story once about W.C. Fields, the old comedian. He was an alcoholic and led a godless life. One day one of his friends found him reading the Bible. 'What are you reading the Bible for, W.C.?' the friend asked. Fields looked up and said, 'I'm looking for a loophole.'"

Jake shook his head. "I don't kid myself about things like that. There are no loopholes, I know that. A man's got to be responsible for what he's done."

The two fell silent, and Jake reached down and stroked Trouble's scarred head. Kate petted the silky fur of Abigail and finally said haltingly, "I wish you were ready to meet God."

Jake was intrigued by this. "Women have wanted a lot of things from me, Mary Katherine, but that's never been one of them."

He studied her and noted that there was a richness, a completeness that he had not found in any of the other women he had known. He knew that even the toughest of men had a picture of a woman secretly in their hearts, fashioned out of their deep desires. He had not formed such a picture in his own spirit because of his cynicism—he knew the picture rarely materialized. At that moment there were things he wanted to say to her that he had never said to any woman, but a series of catastrophes with other women rose up like specters so he let the moment go by.

"Is that the only part of me you're interested in, Mary Katherine?"

"I—I don't want anything bad to happen to you, Jake."

Jake had no answer for this simple reply. She had spoken out of a sincerity that he had already discovered ran clear to her heart and to the bone. No reply came to him, and he was was saved from the moment by the doorbell.

Instantly Kate, who was as flustered as Jake, said quickly, "That's Hope. She said she'd be coming over. We're going to make some plans for the youth group."

"I'll fix breakfast," Jake said, moving toward the refrigerator.

Kate went to the door and greeted Hope, who smiled at her winsomely. There was a bond between the two women that had been formed by their work with the youth. "Come on in, Hope. Jake's going to fix breakfast."

"Wow, it must be nice to have a live-in cook."

For an instant Kate thought there was a hidden meaning in Hope's words, but there was nothing in Hope's eyes or her expression to indicate such.

"It's a good thing one of us can cook. Jeremy and I would probably starve to death if it weren't for Jake. Come on in. We'll have some coffee and talk about the conference in New Orleans. I think we can raise the money to take at least a hundred young people over there."

The two women went into the kitchen, and Hope spoke cheerfully. "Hello, Jake."

"Hello, Hope. You hungry?"

"I'm starved. It's a good thing you're not my cook. I'd be as fat as a hippo."

Jake smiled at her and then turned to the food preparations.

The two women sat down with their steaming mugs and began filling out a notebook and making plans. They were both watching Jake from time to time, who was moving around efficiently. He was, Kate thought, the most effective man she had ever seen in a kitchen.

"What are you making now, Jake?" Kate asked.

"Hot cross buns."

"I've heard of those but never had any," Hope commented.

Jake grinned crookedly at her. "You weren't raised right."

The women watched as he threw in flour, shortening, and eggs. He added sugar and spices. He dropped in cinnamon, ginger, nutmeg, and cloves, and then mixed in yeast. The mass rose until it doubled in bulk. He shaped the dough into round flat buns and brushed them with egg whites. He then cut a cross on the bun with scissors. Opening both of the twin ovens, he put them inside and set the oven for four hundred and fifty degrees.

"How did you learn to cook, Jake?" Hope asked.

"I was raised with my two brothers. My mother died early, so it was just us four men—us boys and my dad. We took turns cooking. I learned to cook in self-defense, I guess."

He resumed moving rapidly around the room and appeared to be throwing everything but the kitchen sink into a large skillet. Fifteen minutes later Jake said, "Time to eat. Go call Jeremy."

Kate moved quickly to Jeremy's room and called him. He came out rubbing his head. Kate said, "Come on, Buddy, it's time for a hot breakfast."

Jeremy plunked himself down in one of the tall chairs as Jake was taking a pan out of the oven. "What's that, Jake?"

"Hot cross buns."

"Why do they call 'em that?"

"Because they're hot, and they've got a cross on 'em. You see? You ought to be able to figure out things like that, smart as you are."

Jeremy looked up and out the sliding patio doors. "There comes Rhiannon," he said.

Jake turned and peered out the door. "That is one strange girl."

"I like her," Jeremy said. "She's a little bit strange, but she's all right. Her grandfather's smart."

"It looks like she's coming to visit," Kate said. She went over to the door, slid it open, and said, "Good morning, Rhiannon. How are you today?"

Rhiannon didn't answer. "I've come to see Jeremy."

"Well, come on in. We're just about to have breakfast. Would you like to join us?"

"Yes."

Jake laughed. "She's probably the only female in North America who can answer in one syllable. She's strictly a yes/no girl, aren't you, Rhiannon?"

"No." Rhiannon stared at him with her brilliant green eyes. "Sometimes I talk a lot."

"Foiled again. Well, sit down. We're going to eat, but Mary Katherine's got to pray over it first. We never eat a bite of unsanctified food around here."

Rhiannon plopped herself down on one of the tall seats, and Kate put a plate in front of her. She bowed her head, said a quick blessing, and then Jake began dishing out the contents of the huge skillet. When he had filled all five of their plates, he passed the hot cross buns around and said, "Plunge in."

"What is this, Jake?" Hope said.

"It's a secret. See how you like it."

They all began eating. Kate, after the first bite, said, "Oh, this is delicious!"

"It is good," Hope agreed. "I hope you made plenty."

"If not, I can make some more. How do you like it, Slick?"

"It's good, Jake. What is it?"

"My secret formula for eggs. What about you, Rhiannon?"

Rhiannon was eating like a starved wolf. She was shoving the egg dish into her mouth as quickly as she could get it there. Jake sat down and seemed to be secretly amused. He waited until they were all more than half through, then he said, "Would you all like to know what it is?"

"Well, I know it's eggs. What else is it?"

"It's calf brains and eggs," Jake said, his expression bland.

Four sets of eyes turned on Jake, and Jeremy gasped. "You don't mean *real* calf brains, do you?" he asked.

"Well, they're not artificial calf brains, Slick. All you do is take the membrane off, put some bacon drippings in the skillet, add water to cover it, and then you scramble the eggs in the brain, throw in some salt and pepper and some more secret ingredients. My favorite way to eat eggs." Jake put a huge amount on his fork and put it into his mouth. He spoke around it, "You can't get better than calf brains and eggs."

Jake saw that Hope, Kate, and Jeremy were looking somewhat stunned, but Rhiannon had finished hers. "I want some more," she said. "It's good."

"Here you go, Sweetheart." Jake dished it up.

He saw that the others were reluctant to go on, and he said, "What's the matter with you people? This is my specialty."

"I—I don't think I can eat brains," Hope said.

Jake grinned at the teacher. "Well, in France they eat snails. You probably eat liver. That's the inward part of a cow. What's the difference between a liver and the brain?"

Suddenly Hope laughed. "None, I guess. It's all in the mind. Pun intended."

They laughed and worked on the breakfast until it was gone. All the while, Jeremy had been watching Rhiannon. "You're going to pop, Rhiannon. I've never seen a girl eat so much."

Rhiannon was drinking from a mug of milk that Jake had put out for her. She had a white mustache and didn't bother to wipe it off. "I came to tell you about my dream," she announced to Jeremy.

"You mean the one about Jacques the Ripper?"

"I think you ought to give him a better name. That's not too nice."

"He is what he is," Jake said. "You had the dream again?"

Rhiannon turned to face Jake. "Yes, but it was more clear this time. Jacques is going to save Jeremy from going to jail somehow."

"I don't see how that could be." Hope frowned. "How could a cat help anybody?"

"Cats are smarter than people in some ways," Rhiannon said. "As a matter of fact, they're superior in many ways."

Jacques had been lurking over in the apex of the corner where the two walls met, eyeing Jake.

That's a smart Person, Cleo. Not many people have sense enough to know that cats are superior. He wheeled and loped out of the room, intent on one of the strange missions that he threw himself into from time to time.

Jake watch Jacques leave, but he was fascinated by Rhiannon's statement. "I don't like cats myself, but why do you think they're smarter than we are?"

Rhiannon stared at Jake. "They can hear sounds two octaves higher than humans can. Of course, mice can hear sounds nearly twice as high as cats. But you take porpoises; they can hear sounds almost three times higher than cats and seven times higher than human beings."

"How do you know all this stuff, Rhiannon?" Kate asked.

"I'm reading through the *Encyclopedia Britannica.* I'm still only on the J volume so I don't know much after that."

"Well, I'm inclined to believe you about the cats," Jake said. "Where is that cat anyway?"

Rhiannon pointed over to the west. "He went toward that boathouse where the boy was killed."

"I'd better go bring him home," Kate said with alarm. "Earl Maddux said he'd shoot him if we didn't keep him home."

"I'd better go along then," Jake said. "I don't trust that guy."

"Well, let's *all* go then," said Hope.

They all left the house and walked along the shore until they approached the boathouse. "Look, there's Jacques. He's going into the boathouse," Jeremy said. "I'll go get him."

"Wait a minute. We can't go in there," Hope said nervously. "That's private property."

Kate considered this, and then said, "We'll just go in and get him and then we'll leave."

"I wish you wouldn't," Hope said. "He'll come home sooner or later."

"What are you afraid of, Hope?" Kate asked. "Mr. Maddux isn't going to shoot us...I don't think."

Jake glanced at Hope and saw that she was pale. "Better let *me* go get him," he said.

"No, he'll claw you to bits," Kate said. She turned and walked with Jeremy toward the boathouse. Rhiannon marched along beside them.

"Come on, Hope," Jake said. "It may take all of us to round him up."

"I—I don't want to go in there."

Jake turned and looked at Hope. "What's the matter?" he asked quietly.

"That's—that's where that boy was killed. It gives me the willies."

"You wait here then," he said.

"No, I'll go with you."

Jake glanced at her strangely and shrugged. "It won't take but a minute." The two entered the boathouse and found Kate, Jeremy, and Rhiannon watching Jacques, who was clawing at the wall. The wall only went up three feet and was made of treated lumber that would not rot. There was a space between the outer walls and the inner wall, and Jacques was clawing furiously at it.

"What's the matter with that cat?" Jake exclaimed.

"It almost looks like he's trying to get something in that wall. When I came in," Kate said, "he was up on the top trying to reach down into it."

Jake approached warily. "All right, Jacques," he said, "don't slash my jugular. What's bothering you?"

Kate turned and watched as Jake knelt down and began prying at a board.

"Loose board here," Jake said. "Must be something in there. Maybe a rat he hears." He pulled at the board and it popped off. "The nails had hollowed out a hole," he muttered. "Hey—there's something here." He reached inside and pulled something out. It was dark in the boathouse compared to the brilliance of the morning sunlight.

"What is it, Jake?" Kate asked.

"Some kind of cloth," Jake said. He stood up and spread it out.

Kate moved closer, "Why, it's a blouse, a woman's blouse."

"It's got blood on it. Look," Jake said.

Suddenly Kate stood stock still. She could not move for a minute and thoughts raced through her head. She narrowed her eyes, stepped forward, and took the blouse away from Jake. She moved to where the sunlight from the doorway would fall on it, and then slowly she turned and faced Hope whose face was now pasty white. Her lips were trembling and so were her hands. She held them clenched tightly together.

"Hope," Kate whispered. "This is your blouse."

Instantly Jake's eyes flew to Hope. She said nothing, but Kate added quickly, "*You* killed Derek, didn't you? You were wearing this blouse the day he was killed. You were at our house, and I saw you wearing it."

Hope whirled and started to run but Jake was too quick. He caught her by the arm and turned her around. "Why did you do it, Hope?" he asked and looked into her eyes.

"He—it was an accident," she cried. Tears began running down her face. "I didn't mean to do it."

"What kind of an accident?" Kate asked.

"He'd been blackmailing me for a long time. He was always demanding more from me."

"Derek? Blackmailing you about what? What have you done?" Kate questioned. She glanced over and saw that Jeremy's face was pale and that Rhiannon's eyes were fixed on Hope with a stern fascination.

"He found out about my past."

"Your past? What are you talking about?"

Hope looked at each of them in turn. Fear was in her eyes. Then she said slowly, "I got involved at the school where I worked before—with a senior, a student. It was a crime. I was arrested and put in jail. I served six months. When I got out I changed my name, moved here, and I got this job."

"How did Derek find out about your past?" Jake asked.

"There was a story in a magazine about the scandal, and my picture was in it. I don't know why Derek was reading an old magazine, but somehow he saw it. He showed it to me and told me I'd have to do what he said or he'd expose me. I—I couldn't lose this job!"

"But why, Hope?" Kate wondered. "Derek had plenty of money, and you don't make all that much as a teacher."

"He didn't want money." Hope shook her head in despair. "He wanted good grades in English—and he made me do his schoolwork for him. I wrote term papers, things like that. Sometimes I didn't have time to do the work, and he forced me to change his grades in the records." She began to weep, and then cried, "He was a horrible monster! A beast!"

"What did you do to Derek?" Jeremy spoke up suddenly. He took a step closer and anger was written on his face. "What did you do to him?" he cried.

"Be quiet, Jeremy," Kate said. But she waited for the woman to speak.

"Eventually he wanted more than just good grades. He called me and told me to meet him here. He said if I didn't come, he'd tell what he knew. I came here that night, and he'd been drinking. He started kissing me and pulling at my clothes. I fought him off, but he said if I didn't let him have his way, he'd go to the school board. We were up on the dock and the boat was pulled up here just where you two had left it." She looked at Jeremy and then couldn't face him. "He laughed at me and said he'd tell. He was so cruel. I *begged* him not to tell. When he laughed at me I hit at him with both my fists. Hit him in his chest. He fell off the dock and into the boat. His head hit the side of the boat. I got down and I saw that he was unconscious. I tried to bring him around. I tried CPR and everything. But he was gone."

"Why didn't you call the police?"

"They'd find out about my record and wouldn't believe me. They wouldn't believe it was an accident."

"Why did you put your blouse in that wall?" Kate asked.

"I got blood on it when I went down to help Derek. I pulled him up and held him—and the blood got all over my blouse. I panicked and stuffed it in that wall."

"I think I can guess what you did," Jake said. "You put on that red coat that belonged to Jeremy with Darth Vader on it and took Derek out to sea and put him overboard."

"I'm sorry, Jeremy," Hope said, tears running down her cheeks. "I never thought they'd blame you. I didn't know you'd been with him. I thought they'd think he fell out of the boat and drowned."

"How did you get to shore?" Jake asked. "The boat was found a mile out."

"I was always a good swimmer." Hope's voice now was completely quiet, and she said, "I didn't *mean* to kill him. I swam to shore and I walked to my car and went home. It was an accident." She turned to Jeremy and said, "I'm so sorry. I'm sorry for all you've been through. I wanted to come forward, but I was so scared."

Jake's face was hard. "You made a mistake not calling the police. And then not confessing once you knew Jeremy was a suspect."

Hope's face twisted with agony and grief and disappointment. "I know. I've made so many mistakes."

"Well, this one was a lulu," Jake said. "You'll end up in jail for murder."

Hope wept helplessly. "I wanted to have a good life. Now I'll never have it. Nobody will ever trust me again."

Kate went to her. A blinding rage had touched her spirit but only for a moment. She thought of how this woman she trusted had almost allowed her son to go to trial for murder. He could have been sentenced to a reform school—or worse. Hope had done this, but one look at the woman's pitiful expression and Kate knew she couldn't maintain that anger. She put her arms around her and said, "Don't cry."

"I can't help it, Kate. I'm so sorry. Jeremy," she said, "I'm sorry."

Jeremy stared at her but was silent.

"What will happen to me?" Hope asked.

Jake could see Kate's face as she held the woman in her embrace. Her lips were broad and maternal, and he heard her whisper, "God is still in control. He hasn't forgotten you and I won't, either."

Twenty-four

As Jeremy approached the Brice house, he found Rhiannon and her grandfather sitting outside in their usual positions. The umbrella over the table was large but had a large rip in it that allowed the bright rays of the sun to slant down over the face of the old man. The wind was blowing softly, and the sea oats that surrounded the house did a sprightly dance looking almost like ballet dancers—at least the way Jeremy thought ballet dancers might look.

"Well, it's you, Jeremy. Come and sit down. Here, let me pour you a glass of juice." The grandfather picked up a pitcher, poured a glass of thick fluid into the extra glass, and said, "Tomato juice. It's not my favorite, but it's cheap."

"I like tomato juice," Jeremy said.

"Fine. We ought to get all the enjoyment we can out of every moment."

Rhiannon studied Jeremy and her eyes went to Jacques, who had accompanied Jeremy as usual. "What's happened to Miss Barclay?"

"Well, she's going to have to go to jail—for a while anyway," Jeremy said. "That Englishman, the one who was representing me, he took her case on and I guess he got her off with a fairly light sentence."

"Does that disturb you?" Mr. Brice said.

"No, Sir. Why would it?"

"Well, she was responsible for the death of your friend."

Jeremy took a sip of the tomato juice. He really despised the stuff but he couldn't admit that to Mr. Brice. "I'm sorry he's dead, but he wasn't really a good friend of mine. She didn't do it on purpose. I hate to say it, but Derek was doing some pretty awful stuff to her. I liked Miss Barclay."

243

Morgan stroked his gaunt cheeks. The disease had sapped him, but he was still a handsome man. "I know she was kind to you Jeremy. But she did a wrong thing and will have to bear some accountability for it. That's the way it is with all of us. We have good and we have bad in us. You just remember the good that she did for you, and let God take care of the rest."

"I knew it would happen," Rhiannon said. "Remember, it was in my dream."

"I'm still not sure about dreams."

"That's because you don't know enough."

Morgan laughed. "She's smart, Jeremy, but she hasn't learned much about humility."

Rhiannon put the book down and leaned forward, her face intent. "I've been thinking that I'm going to marry Beverly Devon-Hunt."

Jeremy stared at her as if she had announced that she was going to jump over the house. "He's too old for you, he finally got out."

"He's thirty and I'm ten. Lots of girls get married when they're seventeen. He'd only be thirty-seven."

Jeremy laughed. "But when you're forty, he'll be sixty."

"That'll be all right. I'll be young enough to take care of him when he gets old."

Morgan slapped his leg and laughed. "Rhiannon wants to plan her life out in fine detail."

Jeremy said, "Well, I don't. I don't want to know what's going to happen next."

"I think that's wise, young man. Now, I think I'd like to teach you two something that will be useful to you. What will it be?"

Before Jeremy could say a word Rhiannon piped up. "Teach us how to get whatever we want."

Morgan's face revealed a flash of humor. "What about if I teach you how to be content with whatever you have or whatever you become?"

Jeremy answered before Rhiannon could speak. "I'd like to know that, Mr. Brice."

"All right. We'll start with a statement from a man who knew more than most. He said, 'I have learned, in whatsoever state I am, therewith to be content.'"

"I bet whoever said that was rich and famous," Rhiannon said as she nodded wisely.

"No, Rhiannon, as a matter of fact, he was in a cold, dank dungeon with no light and bad food. And he didn't know from day to day if he would be alive. He could be taken out and executed at any moment."

"Who was he, Mr. Brice?" Jeremy asked.

"Oh, I expect you've heard about him. His name was Paul. He was an apostle. He wrote a large portion of the New Testament." The old man spoke easily for a time. There was something about his air and his spirit that held them quiet, and they hung onto his words. Overhead a flight of pelicans in V formation flew lazily by, but neither Rhiannon nor Jeremy looked up. The old man continued to speak, and the two youngsters listened, their eyes fixed on him.

● ● ●

Vince Canelli was glaring at Beverly. Then his eyes went to Jake Novak, who had joined the barrister but was saying nothing. "What do you two want?" Canelli asked.

Beverly grinned and said, "Just a word of advice to a former employer."

"I don't want to hear anything you've got to say."

"Oh, I insist, Vincent," Beverly said. "I want you to know that I will never reveal anything that I have learned about your activities. As you're aware, I know enough to put you in jail for a long time, but it is all privileged communication."

"You just remember that," Canelli growled, a threatening note in his voice.

"What I have done," Bev continued cheerfully, "is written it all down with very careful documentation. I placed it in the hands of a high-ranking government official. Now, he is forbidden to read what I have left—as long as I'm alive."

Canelli's face changed.

"As long as I'm alive," Bev said, "you'll be fine. I think it's to your advantage to see that I live to be a very old man, Vince."

Canelli couldn't speak. He had put enough people in hard positions to realize that he was caught in a trap. He turned to face Jake and said, "What about *you,* Novak?"

Jake shrugged. "I'm just a simple man, Vince. If anyone tries to hurt me, or anyone I care for, you'll wake up one night and I'll be standing over you. And that will be the last sight you will ever see on this green earth."

Canelli had known many hard men. He knew some only appeared to be tough, but Jake was not one of these. He knew enough about Jake Novak to realize he was hearing the absolute, unvarnished truth. "Get out of here, you two! I don't want nothing to do with either one of you."

Jake smiled. "Fine. The feeling is mutual. Have a good day, Vince."

The two men left, and as soon as they were outside, Bev said, "Do you think he'll let us alone?"

"He's a piece of garbage," Jake said, "but he's not stupid. He knows that what you've written could put him in a cell for a long, long time and he doesn't want that."

The two men got into the Rolls, and when Jake shut the door on his side, he said, "I don't guess there's anything to keep you here now that you're no longer working for Canelli."

"Oh, I plan on staying for some time."

"I hope it's not because of Mary Katherine."

Beverly started the engine of the Rolls. Bev listened to the engine and said, "Do you know when you're going sixty miles an hour in this car, the loudest sound is the ticking of the clock?"

"Never mind the clock. I want you to understand *I'm* responsible for Mary Katherine."

"You sound like her father, Jake." Bev twisted his head to stare at his companion.

"I want to know what your intentions are."

"Are you asking if my intentions are honorable?"

"That's what I'm asking."

"Yes, they are. What about *yours,* Novak?"

Jake glared at the Englishman and then laughed. "I'll keep an eye on you, Sir Beverly. You Englishmen are not to be trusted."

● ● ●

Jake was watching the sheets of paper flow out of the printer. When the last stack appeared, he took the sheets, tapped the edges, and put them on top of a thick manuscript. He stared at the stack of paper, thinking of the many hours, days, weeks, and months that had gone into creating the five hundred pages that lay there.

A slight knock caught his attention, and he said, "Abandon hope all you who enter here."

Kate walked in and stood beside him. She was wearing a blue skirt with a white blouse and looked neat as she always did. It never ceased to amaze Jake how Mary Katherine Forrest could look so neat in her person yet her room always looked as though a bomb had gone off in it.

"I didn't want to bother you while you were working, but I thought you might be hungry."

"No, I'm not hungry."

Kate looked at him in surprise. "What's the matter?"

"Nothing."

"Is the book going any better?"

"It's finished."

"Why, Jake, that's wonderful!" Kate exclaimed. "Why didn't you tell me?"

"Because it's a lousy book." He picked up the manuscript and glared at it as if it were a piece of trash. "It's a shoddy piece of work. I must have been crazy to think I could write."

"Jake, you're tired. You've been under a strain. It probably needs a little work."

"It's just no good, Mary Katherine."

"Let me read it. I'm no critic, but I'd like to see what you've done."

"Go ahead." He shrugged and pushed the manuscript toward her. "When you're finished you can dump it into the trash."

"I won't do that." She held the manuscript to her breast and tried to say something that would cheer him up. His mood disturbed her. "Life will be easier now. It's been hard. You know, Jake, I haven't thanked you yet for standing by Jeremy—and me, of course. It if weren't for you and Bev, I don't know what we would have done."

"The limey. Has he asked you out again?"

"Why no, he hasn't."

"Good. I told him it wouldn't be a good idea."

Kate blinked with surprise. "Why did you tell him that?"

"You don't need him. You wouldn't be interested in a guy like that anyway."

"I suppose not." Kate's eyes sparkled with a flash of temper. "All he has going for him is money, charm, a title, fine manners, an education, a great job, and good looks."

"He's not for you."

Anger rushed through Kate's voice. "I am fully capable of making that decision for myself, Jake Novak! You are so insufferable!" She whirled and stormed out of the room.

Jake went downstairs and saw his manuscript on the island. He glanced up and saw that Kate was standing outside on the deck. He moved through the kitchen and stepped over beside her. Her back was as stiff as a soldier's, and when she turned her head she gave him a look that would curdle milk.

Jake stood there for a long time, waiting for her to speak, but when she said nothing, he cleared his throat. "You know, when I was growing up I wanted to be an astronomer."

Kate didn't turn. "Why didn't you?" she said frostily.

"Somebody told me that you're not looking at the actual stars when you see those sparkling things up there."

"What do you mean?"

"Well, that's just the light that was generated eons ago. You see that bright star right there?" He moved closer to her and, reaching forward, turned her slightly. "Right over there."

"Yes, I see it."

"Well, that star may have burned out many, many years ago. I didn't want to study something that didn't exist. I wanted to study something real."

The pungent odors of the beach wafted to them on the breeze, and Jake tried to think of some way to express what he was feeling. "People are like that, Mary Katherine, like the stars. You know, I look at a woman and I see the outside, but that's not real sometimes."

Kate turned to face him. "You must have been badly hurt by someone."

"It was a long time ago."

"You haven't forgotten her. I can still hear the echo of her walking around in your heart."

"No, I guess I haven't," Jake admitted. "Look, I like Bev, and he's got glitter and you've been alone a long time. It'd be easy for you to mistake that glamor of his for the real thing."

"What *is* the real thing, Jake?"

"I can't name it, but I've seen it a few times. When a man and a woman find it together, Mary Katherine, they've got everything."

Kate was quiet. The surf sounded like a symphony. It came in regular beats, and they stood there close, listening to it.

"I thought I was looking out for you, Mary Katherine. That's all I wanted to do." He turned her around and pulled her forward. He bent his head, and his lips touched hers. He felt her response, but at that moment he let out a shrill yelp and jumped away.

They both turned and saw Jacques the Ripper, who had nailed Jake.

"You can't be mad at Jacques," Kate said. "He was just trying to protect me. He doesn't think you're the right person for me just like you don't think Bev is the right person for me. I'm overprotected, I think."

Jake was looking down at his ripped pants. "Well, he ruined the pants but he didn't get my leg." He straightened up and said, "Mary Katherine, I'm telling you these things because I'm thinking of leaving."

Suddenly Kate was very still. "Leaving for where?"

"Back to my old job in Chicago."

"You can't do that, Jake. You want to be a writer."

"I don't think I've got it in me." Jake's face was drawn, and he added, "I finished this book, but I'm not sure I can ever write another one. It's a lot harder than I thought it'd be. It would be a lot easier going back to my old life."

There was such gloom and despair in the big man's face and voice that Mary Katherine reached up and put her hand on his cheek. "No, you can't go," she whispered. "I need to keep you around."

"What for?"

"To fight off all the rich, talented Englishmen who are falling in love with me."

For a moment the two stood there. She saw the wish to kiss her in his face and in his expression. "I'm hungry. You make me an omelet, and I'll start reading your book. And no more of this silly tale about leaving." She reached up and pulled him gently toward her. She kissed him.

When they parted, Jake said, "On second thought, I think I'll stay."

They went inside and Jacques watched the two, swishing his tail angrily.

Let the Intruder go, you silly Person. You've got me and Cleo. What do you want him hanging around for?

Cleo moved over and sat beside Jacques the Ripper. She leaned against him and whispered, *It's a female thing, Jacques. You wouldn't understand!*